Night Shadows

NIGHT SHADOWS

TWENTIETH-CENTURY
STORIES OF THE
UNCANNY

EDITED AND INTRODUCED BY
JOAN KESSLER

DAVID R. GODINE
PUBLISHER · BOSTON

First published in 2001 by
David R. Godine · Publisher
Post Office Box 450
Jaffrey, New Hampshire 03452
www.godine.com

Library of Congress Cataloging-in-Publication Data

Night shadows : twentieth-century stories of the uncanny /
edited and introduced by Joan Kessler.—1st ed.
p.   cm.
ISBN 1–56792–180–9 (softcover : alk. paper)
1. Horror tales, American. 2. Horror tales, English.
3. Supernatural—Fiction. I. Kessler, Joan.
PS648.H6 N498 2001
813'.0873808—dc21   2001040668

First Edition 2001
Printed in Canada

For my mother and father
and
For Howard

Contents

Hopper's "Night Shadows"

It is the quintessential late-night corner
enfolding the quintessential darkened shop:
the corner drugstore closed for the night
but bathed in the harsh light
of an electric street lamp
positioned out of sight.
The cornering street is all but empty,
a clean, well-lit, deserted space
viewed vertiginously from an adjacent height.
The unseen single source of light
thrusts the fingering shadow of an unseen pole
athwart the crooking elbow of the street
to strike the hooded face of the pharmacy—
where mingling with more amorphous,
more contorted shadow shapes
it undergoes an eerie metamorphosis,
growing like a genie to suggest
a gigantic second-story man
darkly bent against the bolted building.
All this from the position of one unseen
who peers from an upper window
at whomever it is who passes just below,
striding alone down the empty street
as though he had sufficient reason
to still be on the go
at dead of night among the shadows,
himself followed by yet another, his own.

CSK

Introduction

THE THIRTY-SOMETHING HEROINE of Shirley Jackson's "The Demon Lover" awakens in her small New York City apartment on the morning of her wedding day, makes herself coffee, puts clean sheets and pillowcases on the bed, agonizes about which dress to wear, and watches impatiently as the clock ticks past the hour at which her fiancé had promised to meet her. Although she does not yet admit it to herself, she is standing at the top of that perilous slope which leads from ordinary anxiety to the dread of nightmare. In Elizabeth Bowen's story of the same title, the main character is haunted not by a mysterious absence but by an uncanny presence: returning on an errand to her shut-up house in wartime London, she finds on the hall table a letter from the cold and enigmatic man to whom she had been briefly engaged during the first World War, before he was declared missing and presumed dead. She will soon find herself stalked by someone who seems to have anticipated every one of her movements, including her attempts at escape.

The protagonist of Joyce Carol Oates's story, "The Doll," is driving along a tree-shaded avenue in the small town where she will be attending an academic conference, when she suddenly sees it: the antique dolls' house of her childhood, which now

JOAN KESSLER

looms before her, large as life, with its cupola, steep gabled roof and dark shutters. She parks her car and walks slowly up to the veranda steps, feeling vulnerable and disoriented, as if she had "stepped into another world." Before she can ring the doorbell, she is seized by a panic attack and retreats, seeking refuge from her unease in the familiar conference activities. But like a sleeper sliding into an unpleasant dream, she will find no escape until she has returned to the house to confront there whatever it is that darkly and perversely compels her.

In other stories in this collection, a bachelor professor staying at a peaceful seaside resort advances unsuspectingly toward a confrontation with something monstrous in the sheets of the spare bed in his room; a newly married woman is torn by suspicion that her husband's deceased first wife is seeking to come between them; a famous novelist receives a series of ominous postcards, postmarked from towns ever nearer his home; a poet on the lecture circuit is faced with disturbing signs that a mysterious stranger is all too successfully impersonating her.

These short masterpieces of British and American uncanny fiction do not feature the traditional phantoms who haunt country houses or loom up in deserted marshland or shadowy churchyard. Rather, their settings are the familiar scenes of modern, everyday life, and their characters are ordinary, twentieth-century people. As one might expect, these stories are more disquieting, their horrors sharper-edged, for their down-to-earth realism and verisimilitude. What their protagonists have in common, regardless of age, profession, or social status, is that at a certain point in their lives, by imperceptible degrees or with disarming suddenness, reality turns strange, the unthinkable becomes actual, and uncertainty and fear become their constant companions.

The men and women in these stories are surely haunted, but is the threat from without or from within? Like all of us, they are prey to anxieties, fears, and desires that for the most part they are able to keep within reasonable bounds — until something provokes a crisis. The uncanny "Other" which closes in on them,

XII

or lures them mysteriously into encounters that they dread, is in one sense a suppressed or buried part of themselves from which they can no longer hide. This may be what the writer Robert Aickman had in mind when he observed, on the subject of ghosts, "We are glad to meet them when we are glad to meet ourselves, but that is to be one man (or woman) marked out of ten thousand."[1] Many stories of the uncanny are keen studies of compulsion: the supernatural is a fitting embodiment for a force so powerful that it can subjugate our judgment and our will, leading us inescapably toward our own destruction. Obsession, a related theme in these tales, reveals itself to be perilously contagious, often ensnaring those who struggle to free someone they love from its dire clutches.

The energies and tensions of family relationships provide fertile ground for the uncanny, as repressed hostility, jealousy, guilt, fear, and paranoia take on a life of their own. One thinks of Wharton's and Graves's tormented and tormenting husbands and wives, Aickman's intimation of unplumbed depths in an idealized mother-daughter relationship, and Campbell's dysfunctional family drama unsettlingly played out between mother, father, and son. Both Campbell and Bradbury are chillingly effective in transporting the reader back to a half-forgotten world of childhood terrors. Seen through adult eyes, these youthful fears might appear extravagant or irrational, but the stories weave a powerful spell, convincing us that the child protagonists are not just imagining the obscure horrors that threaten them. In several of the other stories, notably those by Capote, Aickman, and Oates, the experience of the uncanny is intimately related to a regression or reversion to childhood — not merely to a state of childlike helplessness and vulnerability, but to something mysteriously primal and instinctual.

More than eighty years ago, Sigmund Freud published an essay, "Das Unheimliche" ("The Uncanny"), in which he postulated that the sensation of the uncanny derives from the reactivation of something old and familiar in the mind, which has become strange only through a long process of suppression and concealment. When we experience an "uncanny" effect, Freud suggests, we are calling up vestiges of a very early stage of mental development, with all the fantasies, fears, aggressivities, as well as superstitious "animistic" beliefs, that we thought we had surmounted as fully rational adults. The writer V. S. Pritchett expressed a similar insight when he described the ghosts of the earlier writer, Le Fanu, as "blobs of the unconscious that have floated up to the surface of the mind."[2]

The pre-rational world of the child has its counterpart in the extravagant realm of dream, which is not bound by the laws of nature or reason but possesses its own bizarre, supra-natural logic. Dreams give free reign to the imagination, but also to the dark imperatives of the most instinctual regions of the psyche. All truly "uncanny" tales incorporate at least to some degree the atmosphere and texture of dream, with its richly allusive patterns of image and incident, its queer shifts and turns, its stratagems, tensions, and premonitions. In this familiar yet strangely altered landscape, anything, even the worst, may happen.

The supernatural has always been with us; tales of ghosts, demons, and vampires were some of the earliest products of the human imagination. Yet before the eighteenth-century Enlightenment, there was strictly speaking no such thing as the "uncanny" tale, which depends for its effect on the tension between the reader's faith in common sense rationality and the more primitive substratum of feeling that exists, as Edith Wharton observed, "in the warm darkness of the pre-natal fluid far below our conscious reason."[3] Writers working in this new genre would increasingly employ the techniques of realism and verisimilitude in order to engender in their readers a shuddering hesitation as to whether (as Freud phrased it) things that "[were] regarded as incredible [were] not, after all, possible."[4]

As the literature of the supernatural grew more sophisticated in the course of the nineteenth century, it was no longer simply the hesitation between a natural or supernatural explanation which would provide the thrill of this kind of fiction. The possibility that denizens of an unearthly realm could interfere with the natural order of things was less interesting in itself than the possibility that the dualistic dichotomy between "spiritual" and "material" was itself nonexistent. The modern "ghost" or phantasm is a complex, multi-faceted phenomenon — not an autonomous spiritual essence but an ominous and threatening aspect of the world we all inhabit, part of the perplexing tangle of motivation and impulse which we call "ourselves." It has been said of Henry James, author of *The Turn of the Screw*, that for him "the human mind is . . . by definition a haunted mind."⁵ This applies equally well to his successors in the art of supernatural fiction.

The literary uncanny, especially in our own agitated century, may appear on the surface to be an escapist mode of fiction, since it privileges fantasy, inwardness, and private demons over the banalities and commonplaces of society and mass culture. Yet it may in fact be just the opposite of escapist, forcing us to confront realities that in the mechanized bustle of our contemporary age we are increasingly successful in avoiding. One of these is the disquieting awareness that the seeming stability of our everyday lives could at any moment give way, and our familiar world crack open to reveal a yawning abyss. It was this recognition, carried to a terrifying extreme, that came suddenly and without warning to Henry James's brother, the psychologist William James, when after a waking vision he was left "with a horrible dread at the pit of my stomach, and with a sense of the insecurity of life that I never knew before . . . [or] since."⁶

The stories gathered here, whether by Robert Aickman or Hortense Calisher, Elizabeth Bowen or Alison Lurie, Shirley Jackson or Ramsey Campbell, give us a glimmer — often much more than a glimmer — of just how vulnerable we really are, how thin the surface is upon which we daily and hourly tread. All our reassuring habits and certainties begin to pale before two enduring enigmas — the mystery within ourselves and, beyond that, the

JOAN KESSLER

ultimate mystery of death. Both of these threaten or call into question our rational being, our personality and ego-self as we know it;
both are so unsettling that we rarely look them in the face, except
in the nocturnal landscapes of dream and nightmare. As the characters of many of these stories come to learn, there is something
"not us" that inhabits us, a dark, nameless Other that makes us a
stranger to ourselves. To momentarily encounter this most foreign, least humanized region of the self, this ominous, impersonal
force larger than any individual consciousness (and which may
bear some resemblance to that mysterious realm of the not-human
which we all must ultimately enter) is indeed to confront the
uncanny. Readers of these compelling works of short fiction are
more fortunate than many of the protagonists: we can emerge
once more into the commonplace light of day, resume again our
familiar routines, after being granted an unforgettable glimpse
into a realm of shadows.

Night Shadows

M. R. JAMES

"Oh, Whistle, and I'll Come to You, My Lad"

M.R. James, familiar to many today as a twentieth-century master of the ghost story, was better known to his contemporaries as a distinguished scholar of medieval manuscripts. He composed his now famous tales for his own pleasure and that of his friends and colleagues at Cambridge, to whom he read a story aloud each Christmas Eve. James's successors in the art of the uncanny tale owe much to his stylistic polish and restraint, and to his ability to orchestrate a crescendo of tension that builds to an arresting climax. James wrote of his technique, "Let us see [the characters] going about their ordinary business, undisturbed by forebodings . . .; and into this calm environment let the ominous thing put out its head, unobtrusively at first, and then more insistently, until it holds the stage."[7]

Many of M.R. James's protagonists are scholars or antiquarians who, through their imprudent curiosity, inadvertently summon up a darkly malevolent presence. In "Oh, Whistle, and I'll Come to You, My Lad" (1904), it is not an ordinary ghost that inhabits the sheets of the spare bed in Professor Parkins's hotel room, but rather a blind, groping entity that suggests something of the random, impersonal force of nature and the instinctual drives. The levels of suggestiveness in this story only add to its power for a modern audience, yet for its author, the true mark of its success was its ability to elicit from the reader the pleasurable chills and shudders of fear.

3

"I SUPPOSE you will be getting away pretty soon, now Fall term is over, Professor," said a person not in the story to the Professor of Ontography, soon after they had sat down next to each other at a feast in the hospitable hall of St. James's College.

The Professor was young, neat, and precise in speech.

"Yes," he said; "my friends have been making me take up golf this term, and I mean to go to the East Coast — in point of fact to Burnstow — (I dare say you know it) for a week or ten days, to improve my game. I hope to get off to-morrow."

"Oh, Parkins," said his neighbour on the other side, "if you are going to Burnstow, I wish you would look at the site of the Templars' preceptory, and let me know if you think it would be any good to have a dig there in the summer."

It was, as you might suppose, a person of antiquarian pursuits who said this, but, since he merely appears in this prologue, there is no need to give his entitlements.

"Certainly," said Parkins, the Professor: "if you will describe to me whereabouts the site is, I will do my best to give you an idea of the lie of the land when I get back; or I could write to you about it, if you would tell me where you are likely to be."

"Don't trouble to do that, thanks. It's only that I'm thinking of taking my family in that direction in the Long, and it occurred to me that, as very few of the English preceptories have ever been properly planned, I might have an opportunity of doing something useful on off-days."

The Professor rather sniffed at the idea that planning out a pre-ceptory could be described as useful. His neighbour continued:

"The site — I doubt if there is anything showing above ground — must be down quite close to the beach now. The sea has encroached tremendously, as you know, all along that bit of coast. I should think, from the map, that it must be about three-quarters of a mile from the Globe Inn, at the north end of the town. Where are you going to stay?"

"Well, *at* the Globe Inn, as a matter of fact," said Parkins; "I have engaged a room there. I couldn't get in anywhere else; most of the lodging-houses are shut up in winter, it seems; and, as it is, they tell me that the only room of any size I can have is really a double-bedded one, and that they haven't a corner in which to store the other bed, and so on. But I must have a fairly large room, for I am taking some books down, and mean to do a bit of work; and though I don't quite fancy having an empty bed — not to speak of two — in what I may call for the time being my study, I suppose I can manage to rough it for the short time I shall be there."

"Do you call having an extra bed in your room roughing it, Parkins?" said a bluff person opposite. "Look here, I shall come down and occupy it for a bit; it'll be company for you."

The Professor quivered, but managed to laugh in a courteous manner.

"By all means, Rogers; there's nothing I should like better. But I'm afraid you would find it rather dull; you don't play golf, do you?"

"No, thank Heaven!" said rude Mr. Rogers.

"Well, you see, when I'm not writing I shall most likely be out on the links, and that, as I say, would be rather dull for you, I'm afraid."

"Oh, I don't know! There's certain to be somebody I know in the place; but, of course, if you don't want me, speak the word, Parkins; I shan't be offended. Truth, as you always tell us, is never offensive."

Parkins was, indeed, scrupulously polite and strictly truthful. It is to be feared that Mr. Rogers sometimes practiced upon his knowledge of these characteristics. In Parkins's breast there was a conflict now raging, which for a moment or two did not allow him to answer. That interval being over, he said:

"Well, if you want the exact truth, Rogers, I was considering whether the room I speak of would really be large enough to accommodate us both comfortably; and also whether (mind, I shouldn't have said this if you hadn't pressed me) you would not constitute something in the nature of a hindrance to my work."

Rogers laughed loudly.

"Well done, Parkins!" he said. "It's all right. I promise not to interrupt your work; don't you disturb yourself about that. No, I won't come if you don't want me; but I thought I should do so nicely to keep the ghosts off." Here he might have been seen to wink and to nudge his next neighbour. Parkins might also have been seen to become pink. "I beg pardon, Parkins," Rogers continued; "I oughtn't to have said that. I forgot you didn't like levity on these topics."

"Well," Parkins said, "as you have mentioned the matter, I freely own that I do *not* like careless talk about what you call ghosts. A man in my position," he went on, raising his voice a little, "cannot, I find, be too careful about appearing to sanction the current beliefs on such subjects. As you know, Rogers, or as you ought to know; for I think I have never concealed my views —"

"No, you certainly have not, old man," put in Rogers *sotto voce*.

"— I hold that any semblance, any appearance of concession to the view that such things might exist is equivalent to a renunciation of all that I hold most sacred. But I'm afraid I have not succeeded in securing your attention."

"Your *undivided* attention, was what Dr. Blimber actually *said*,"★ Rogers interrupted, with every appearance of an earnest desire for accuracy. "But I beg your pardon, Parkins: I'm stopping you."

"No, not at all," said Parkins. "I don't remember Blimber; perhaps he was before my time. But I needn't go on. I'm sure you know what I mean."

"Yes, yes," said Rogers, rather hastily — "just so. We'll go into it fully at Burnstow, or somewhere."

In repeating the above dialogue I have tried to give the impression which it made on me, that Parkins was something of an old woman — rather hen-like, perhaps, in his little ways;

★ Mr. Rogers was wrong, vide *Dombey and Son*, chapter xii.

totally destitute, alas! of the sense of humour, but at the same time dauntless and sincere in his convictions, and a man deserving of the greatest respect. Whether or not the reader has gathered so much, that was the character which Parkins had.

On the following day Parkins did, as he had hoped, succeed in getting away from his college, and in arriving at Burnstow. He was made welcome at the Globe Inn, was safely installed in the large double-bedded room of which we have heard, and was able before retiring to rest to arrange his materials for work in applepie order upon a commodious table which occupied the outer end of the room, and was surrounded on three sides by windows looking out seaward; that is to say, the central window looked straight out to sea, and those on the left and right commanded prospects along the shore to the north and south respectively. On the south you saw the village of Burnstow. On the north no houses were to be seen, but only the beach and the low cliff backing it. Immediately in front was a strip — not considerable — of rough grass, dotted with old anchors, capstans, and so forth; then a broad path; then the beach. Whatever may have been the original distance between the Globe Inn and the sea, not more than sixty yards now separated them.

The rest of the population of the inn was, of course, a golfing one, and included few elements that call for a special description. The most conspicuous figure was, perhaps, that of an *ancien militaire*, secretary of a London club, and possessed of a voice of incredible strength, and of views of a pronouncedly Protestant type. These were apt to find utterance after his attendance upon the ministrations of the Vicar, an estimable man with inclinations towards a picturesque ritual, which he gallantly kept down as far as he could out of deference to East Anglian tradition.

Professor Parkins, one of whose principal characteristics was pluck, spent the greater part of the day following his arrival at Burnstow in what he had called improving his game, in company with this Colonel Wilson: and during the afternoon — whether

the process of improvement were to blame or not, I am not sure
— the Colonel's demeanour assumed a colouring so lurid that
even Parkins jibbed at the thought of walking home with him
from the links. He determined, after a short and furtive look at
that bristling moustache and those incarnadined features, that it
would be wiser to allow the influences of tea and tobacco to do
what they could with the Colonel before the dinner-hour should
render a meeting inevitable.

"I might walk home to-night along the beach," he reflected —
"yes, and take a look — there will be light enough for that — at
the ruins of which Disney was talking. I don't exactly know
where they are, by the way; but I expect I can hardly help stumbling on them."

This he accomplished, I may say, in the most literal sense, for
in picking his way from the links to the shingle beach his foot
caught, partly in a gorse-root and partly in a biggish stone, and
over he went. When he got up and surveyed his surroundings, he
found himself in a patch of somewhat broken ground covered
with small depressions and mounds. These latter, when he came
to examine them, proved to be simply masses of flints embedded
in mortar and grown over with turf. He must, he quite rightly
concluded, be on the site of the preceptory he had promised
to look at. It seemed not unlikely to reward the spade of the
explorer; enough of the foundations was probably left at no great
depth to throw a good deal of light on the general plan. He
remembered vaguely that the Templars, to whom this site had
belonged, were in the habit of building round churches, and he
thought a particular series of the humps or mounds near him did
appear to be arranged in something of a circular form. Few people
can resist the temptation to try a little amateur research in a
department quite outside their own, if only for the satisfaction of
showing how successful they would have been had they only
taken it up seriously. Our Professor, however, if he felt something
of this mean desire, was also truly anxious to oblige Mr. Disney. So
he paced with care the circular area he had noticed, and wrote

down its rough dimensions in his pocket-book. Then he proceeded to examine an oblong eminence which lay east of the centre of the circle, and seemed to his thinking likely to be the base of
a platform or altar. At one end of it, the northern, a patch of the
turf was gone — removed by some boy or other creature *ferae nat-*
urae. It might, he thought, be as well to probe the soil here for evidences of masonry, and he took out his knife and began scraping
away the earth. And now followed another little discovery: a por-
tion of soil fell inward as he scraped, and disclosed a small cavity.
He lighted one match after another to help him to see of what
nature the hole was, but the wind was too strong for them all. By
tapping and scratching the sides with his knife, however, he was
able to make out that it must be an artificial hole in masonry. It
was rectangular, and the sides, top, and bottom, if not actually
plastered, were smooth and regular. Of course it was empty. No!
As he withdrew the knife he heard a metallic clink, and when he
introduced his hand it met with a cylindrical object lying on the
floor of the hole. Naturally enough, he picked it up, and when he
brought it into the light, now fast fading, he could see that it, too,
was of man's making — a metal tube about four inches long, and
evidently of some considerable age.

By the time Parkins had made sure that there was nothing
else in this odd receptacle, it was too late and too dark for him to
think of undertaking any further search. What he had done had
proved so unexpectedly interesting that he determined to sacrifice a little more of the daylight on the morrow to archaeology.
The object which he now had safe in his pocket was bound to be
of some slight value at least, he felt sure.

Bleak and solemn was the view on which he took a last look
before starting homeward. A faint yellow light in the west showed
the links, on which a few figures moving towards the club-house
were still visible, the squat martello tower, the lights of Aldsey
village, the pale ribbon of sands intersected at intervals by black
wooden groynes, the dim and murmuring sea. The wind was bitter from the north, but was at his back when he set out for the

Globe. He quickly rattled and clashed through the shingle and gained the sand, upon which, but for the groynes which had to be got over every few yards, the going was both good and quiet. One last look behind, to measure the distance he had made since leaving the ruined Templars' church, showed him a prospect of company on his walk, in the shape of a rather indistinct personage, who seemed to be making great efforts to catch up with him, but made little, if any, progress. I mean that there was an appearance of running about his movements, but that the distance between him and Parkins did not seem materially to lessen. So, at least, Parkins thought, and decided that he almost certainly did not know him, and that it would be absurd to wait until he came up. For all that, company, he began to think, would really be very welcome on that lonely shore, if only you could choose your companion. In his unenlightened days he had read of meetings in such places which even now would hardly bear thinking of. He went on thinking of them, however, until he reached home, and particularly of one which catches most people's fancy at some time of their childhood. "Now I saw in my dream that Christian had gone but a very little way when he saw a foul fiend coming over the field to meet him." "What should I do now," he thought, "if I looked back and caught sight of a black figure sharply defined against the yellow sky, and saw that it had horns and wings? I wonder whether I should stand or run for it. Luckily, the gentleman behind is not of that kind, and he seems to be about as far off now as when I saw him first. Well, at this rate he won't get his dinner as soon as I shall; and, dear me! it's within a quarter of an hour of the time now. I must run!"

Parkins had, in fact, very little time for dressing. When he met the Colonel at dinner, Peace — or as much of her as that gentleman could manage — reigned once more in the military bosom; nor was she put to flight in the hours of bridge that followed dinner, for Parkins was a more than respectable player. When, therefore, he retired towards twelve o'clock, he felt that he had spent his evening in quite a satisfactory way, and that, even for so long as a fortnight or three weeks, life at the Globe would be supportable under similar conditions — "especially," thought he, "if I go on improving my game."

As he went along the passages he met the boots of the Globe, who stopped and said:

"Beg your pardon, sir, but as I was a-brushing your coat just now there was somethink fell out of the pocket. I put it on your chest of drawers, sir, in your room, sir — a piece of a pipe or somethink of that, sir. Thank you, sir. You'll find it on your chest of drawers, sir — yes, sir. Good night, sir."

The speech served to remind Parkins of his little discovery of that afternoon. It was with some considerable curiosity that he turned it over by the light of his candles. It was of bronze, he now saw, and was shaped very much after the manner of the modern dog-whistle; in fact it was — yes, certainly it was — actually no more nor less than a whistle. He put it to his lips, but it was quite full of a fine, caked-up sand or earth, which would not yield to knocking, but must be loosened with a knife. Tidy as ever in his habits, Parkins cleared out the earth on to a piece of paper, and took the latter to the window to empty it out. The night was clear and bright, as he saw when he had opened the casement, and he stopped for an instant to look at the sea and note a belated wanderer stationed on the shore in front of the inn. Then he shut the window, a little surprised at the late hours people kept at Burnstow, and took his whistle to the light again. Why, surely there were marks on it, and not merely marks, but letters! A very little rubbing rendered the deeply-cut inscription quite legible, but the Professor had to confess, after some earnest thought, that the meaning of it was as obscure to him as the writing on the wall to Belshazzar. There were legends both on the front and on the back of the whistle. The one read thus:

$$\begin{array}{ccc} & \text{F L A} & \\ \text{F}\cup\text{R} & & \text{B I S} \\ & \text{F L E} & \end{array}$$

The other:

QUIS EST ISTE QUI VENIT

"I ought to be able to make it out," he thought; "but I suppose I am a little rusty in my Latin. When I come to think of it, I don't believe I even know the word for a whistle. The long one does seem simple enough. It ought to mean, 'Who is this who is coming?' Well, the best way to find out is evidently to whistle for him."

He blew tentatively and stopped suddenly, startled and yet pleased at the note he had elicited. It had a quality of infinite distance in it, and, soft as it was, he somehow felt it must be audible for miles round. It was a sound, too, that seemed to have the power (which many scents possess) of forming pictures in the brain. He saw quite clearly for a moment a vision of a wide, dark expanse at night, with a fresh wind blowing, and in the midst a lonely figure — how employed, he could not tell. Perhaps he would have seen more had not the picture been broken by the sudden surge of a gust of wind against his casement, so sudden that it made him look up, just in time to see the white glint of a sea-bird's wing somewhere outside the dark panes.

The sound of the whistle had so fascinated him that he could not help trying it once more, this time more boldly. The note was little, if at all, louder than before, and repetition broke the illusion — no picture followed, as he had half hoped it might. "But what is this? Goodness! what force the wind can get up in a few minutes! What a tremendous gust! There! I knew that window-fastening was no use! Ah! I thought so — both candles out. It's enough to tear the room to pieces."

The first thing was to get the window shut. While you might count twenty, Parkins was struggling with the small casement, and felt almost as if he were pushing back a sturdy burglar, so strong was the pressure. It slackened all at once, and the window banged to and latched itself. Now to relight the candles and see what damage, if any, had been done. No, nothing seemed amiss; no glass even was broken in the casement. But the noise had evidently roused at least one member of the household: the Colonel was to be heard stumping in his stockinged feet on the floor above, and growling.

Quickly as it had risen, the wind did not fall at once. On it went, moaning and rushing past the house, at times rising to a cry so desolate that, as Parkins disinterestedly said, it might have made fanciful people feel quite uncomfortable; even the unimaginative, he thought after a quarter of an hour, might be happier without it.

Whether it was the wind, or the excitement of golf, or of the researches in the preceptory that kept Parkins awake, he was not sure. Awake he remained, in any case, long enough to fancy (as I am afraid I often do myself under such conditions) that he was the victim of all manner of fatal disorders: he would lie counting the beats of his heart, convinced that it was going to stop work every moment, and would entertain grave suspicions of his lungs, brain, liver, etc. — suspicions which he was sure would be dispelled by the return of daylight, but which until then refused to be put aside. He found a little vicarious comfort in the idea that someone else was in the same boat. A near neighbour (in the darkness it was not easy to tell his direction) was tossing and rustling in his bed, too.

The next stage was that Parkins shut his eyes and determined to give sleep every chance. Here again over-excitement asserted itself in another form — that of making pictures. *Experto crede*, pictures do come to the closed eyes of one trying to sleep, and are often so little to his taste that he must open his eyes and disperse them.

Parkins's experience on this occasion was a very distressing one. He found that the picture which presented itself to him was continuous. When he opened his eyes, of course, it went; but when he shut them once more it framed itself afresh, and acted itself out again, neither quicker nor slower than before. What he saw was this:

A long stretch of shore — shingle edged by sand, and intersected at short intervals with black groynes running down to the water — a scene, in fact, so like that of his afternoon's walk that, in the absence of any landmark, it could not be distinguished therefrom. The light was obscure, conveying an impression of gathering storm, late winter evening, and slight cold rain. On this bleak stage at first no actor was visible. Then, in the distance, a bobbing black object appeared; a moment more, and it was a man running, jumping, clambering over the groynes, and every few seconds looking eagerly back. The nearer he came the more obvious it was that he was not only anxious, but even terribly frightened, though his face was not to be distinguished. He was, moreover, almost at the end of his strength. On he came; each successive obstacle seemed to cause him more difficulty than the last. "Will he get over this next one?" thought Parkins; "it seems a little higher than the others." Yes; half climbing, half throwing himself, he did get over, and fell all in a heap on the other side (the side nearest to the spectator). There, as if really unable to get up again, he remained crouching under the groyne, looking up in an attitude of painful anxiety.

So far no cause whatever for the fear of the runner had been shown; but now there began to be seen, far up the shore, a little flicker of something light-coloured moving to and fro with great swiftness and irregularity. Rapidly growing larger, it, too, declared itself as a figure in pale, fluttering draperies, ill-defined. There was something about its motion which made Parkins very unwilling to see it at close quarters. It would stop, raise arms, bow itself toward the sand, then run stooping across the beach to the water-edge and back again; and then, rising upright, once more continue its course forward at a speed that was startling and terrifying. The moment came when the pursuer was hovering about from left to right only a few yards beyond the groyne where the runner lay in hiding. After two or three ineffectual castings hither and thither it came to a stop, stood upright, with arms raised high, and then darted straight forward towards the groyne.

It was at this point that Parkins always failed in his resolution to keep his eyes shut. With many misgivings as to incipient failure

14

of eyesight, overworked brain, excessive smoking, and so on, he finally resigned himself to light his candle, get out a book, and pass the night waking, rather than be tormented by this persistent panorama, which he saw clearly enough could only be a morbid reflection of his walk and his thoughts on that very day.

The scraping of match on box and the glare of light must have startled some creatures of the night — rats or what not — which he heard scurry across the floor from the side of his bed with much rustling. Dear, dear! the match is out! Fool that it is! But the second one burnt better, and a candle and book were duly procured, over which Parkins pored till sleep of a wholesome kind came upon him, and that in no long space. For about the first time in his orderly and prudent life he forgot to blow out the candle, and when he was called next morning at eight there was still a flicker in the socket and a sad mess of guttered grease on the top of the little table.

After breakfast he was in his room, putting the finishing touches to his golfing costume — fortune had again allotted the Colonel to him for a partner — when one of the maids came in.

"Oh, if you please," she said, "would you like any extra blankets on your bed, sir?"

"Ah! thank you," said Parkins, "Yes, I think I should like one. It seems likely to turn rather colder."

In a very short time the maid was back with the blanket.

"Which bed should I put it on, sir?" she asked.

"What? Why, that one — the one I slept in last night," he said, pointing to it.

"Oh yes! I beg your pardon, sir, but you seemed to have tried both of 'em; leastways, we had to make 'em both up this morning."

"Really? How very absurd!" said Parkins. "I certainly never touched the other, except to lay some things on it. Did it actually seem to have been slept in?"

"Oh yes, sir!" said the maid. "Why, all the things was crumpled and throwed about all ways, if you'll excuse me, sir — quite as if anyone 'adn't passed but a very poor night, sir."

"Dear me," said Parkins. "Well, I may have disordered it more than I thought when I unpacked my things. I'm very sorry to have given you the extra trouble, I'm sure. I expect a friend of mine soon, by the way — a gentleman from Cambridge — to come and occupy it for a night or two. That will be all right, I suppose, won't it?"

"Oh yes, to be sure, sir. Thank you, sir. It's no trouble, I'm sure," said the maid, and departed to giggle with her colleagues.

Parkins set forth, with a stern determination to improve his game.

I am glad to be able to report that he succeeded so far in this enterprise that the Colonel, who had been rather repining at the prospect of a second day's play in his company, became quite chatty as the morning advanced; and his voice boomed out over the flats, as certain also of our own minor poets have said, "like some great bourdon in a minster tower."

"Extraordinary wind, that, we had last night," he said. "In my old home we should have said someone had been whistling for it."

"Should you, indeed!" said Parkins. "Is there a superstition of that kind still current in your part of the country?"

"I don't know about superstition," said the Colonel. "They believe in it all over Denmark and Norway, as well as on the Yorkshire coast; and my experience is, mind you, that there's generally something at the bottom of what these country-folk hold to, and have held to for generations. But it's your drive" (or whatever it might have been: the golfing reader will have to imagine appropriate digressions at the proper intervals).

When conversation was resumed, Parkins said, with a slight hesitancy:

"Apropos of what you were saying just now, Colonel, I think I ought to tell you that my own views on such subjects are very strong. I am, in fact, a convinced disbeliever in what is called the 'supernatural.'"

"What!" said the Colonel, "do you mean to tell me you don't believe in second-sight, or ghosts, or anything of that kind?"

"In nothing whatever of that kind," returned Parkins firmly.

"Well," said the Colonel, "but it appears to me at that rate, sir, that you must be little better than a Sadducee."

Parkins was on the point of answering that, in his opinion, the Sadducees were the most sensible persons he had ever read of in the Old Testament; but, feeling some doubt as to whether much mention of them was to be found in that work, he preferred to laugh the accusation off.

"Perhaps I am," he said; "but — Here, give me my cleek, boy! — Excuse me one moment, Colonel." A short interval. "Now, as to whistling for the wind, let me give you my theory about it. The laws which govern winds are really not at all perfectly known — to fisher-folk and such, of course, not known at all. A man or woman of eccentric habits, perhaps, or a stranger, is seen repeatedly on the beach at some unusual hour, and is heard whistling. Soon afterwards a violent wind rises; a man who could read the sky perfectly or who possessed a barometer could have foretold that it would. The simple people of a fishing-village have no barometers, and only a few rough rules for prophesying weather. What more natural than that the eccentric personage I postulated should be regarded as having raised the wind, or that he or she should clutch eagerly at the reputation of being able to do so? Now, take last night's wind: as it happens, I myself was whistling. I blew a whistle twice, and the wind seemed to come absolutely in answer to my call. If anyone had seen me —"

The audience had been a little restive under this harangue, and Parkins had, I fear, fallen somewhat into the tone of a lecturer; but at the last sentence the Colonel stopped.

"Whistling, were you?" he said. "And what sort of whistle did you use? Play this stroke first." Interval.

"About that whistle you were asking, Colonel. It's rather a curious one. I have it in my — No; I see I've left it in my room. As a matter of fact, I found it yesterday."

And then Parkins narrated the manner of his discovery of the whistle, upon hearing which the Colonel grunted, and opined that, in Parkins's place, he should himself be careful about using a thing that had belonged to a set of Papists, of whom, speaking generally, it might be affirmed that you never knew what they might not have been up to. From this topic he diverged to the enormities of the Vicar, who had given notice on the previous Sunday that Friday would be the Feast of St. Thomas the Apostle, and that there would be service at eleven o'clock in the church. This and other similar proceedings constituted in the Colonel's view a strong presumption that the Vicar was a concealed Papist, if not a Jesuit; and Parkins, who could not very readily follow the Colonel in this region, did not disagree with him. In fact, they got on so well together in the morning that there was no talk on either side of their separating after lunch.

Both continued to play well during the afternoon, or, at least, well enough to make them forget everything else until the light began to fail them. Not until then did Parkins remember that he had meant to do some more investigating at the preceptory; but it was of no great importance, he reflected. One day was as good as another; he might as well go home with the Colonel.

As they turned the corner of the house, the Colonel was almost knocked down by a boy who rushed into him at the very top of his speed, and then, instead of running away, remained hanging on to him and panting. The first words of the warrior were naturally those of reproof and objurgation, but he very quickly discerned that the boy was almost speechless with fright. Inquiries were useless at first. When the boy got his breath he began to howl, and still clung to the Colonel's legs. He was at last detached, but continued to howl.

"What in the world *is* the matter with you? What have you been up to? What have you seen?" said the two men.

"Ow, I seen it wive at me out of the winder," wailed the boy, "and I don't like it."

"What window?" said the irritated Colonel. "Come, pull yourself together, my boy."

"The front winder it was, at the 'otel," said the boy.

At this point Parkins was in favour of sending the boy home, but the Colonel refused; he wanted to get to the bottom of it, he said; it was most dangerous to give a boy such a fright as this one had had, and if it turned out that people had been playing jokes, they should suffer for it in some way. And by a series of questions he made out this story: The boy had been playing about on the grass in front of the Globe with some others; then they had gone home to their teas, and he was just going, when he happened to look up at the front winder and see it a-wiving at him. *It* seemed to be a figure of some sort, in white as far as he knew — couldn't see its face; but it wived at him, and it warn't a right thing — not to say not a right person. Was there a light in the room? No, he didn't think to look if there was a light. Which was the window? Was it the top one or the second one? The seckind one it was — the big winder what got two little uns at the sides.

"Very well, my boy," said the Colonel, after a few more questions. "You run away home now. I expect it was some person trying to give you a start. Another time, like a brave English boy, you just throw a stone — well, no, not that exactly, but you go and speak to the waiter, or to Mr. Simpson, the landlord, and — yes — and say that I advised you to do so."

The boy's face expressed some of the doubt he felt as to the likelihood of Mr. Simpson's lending a favourable ear to his complaint, but the Colonel did not appear to perceive this, and went on:

"And here's a sixpence — no, I see it's a shilling — and you be off home, and don't think any more about it."

The youth hurried off with agitated thanks, and the Colonel and Parkins went round to the front of the Globe and reconnoitred. There was only one window answering to the description they had been hearing.

"Well, that's curious," said Parkins; "it's evidently my window the lad was talking about. Will you come up for a moment, Colonel Wilson? We ought to be able to see if anyone has been taking liberties in my room."

They were soon in the passage, and Parkins made as if to open the door. Then he stopped and felt in his pockets.

"This is more serious than I thought," was his next remark.

"I remember now that before I started this morning I locked the door. It is locked now, and, what is more, here is the key." And he held it up. "Now," he went on, "if the servants are in the habit of going into one's room during the day when one is away, I can only say that — well, that I don't approve of it at all." Conscious of a somewhat weak climax, he busied himself in opening the door (which was indeed locked) and in lighting candles. "No," he said, "nothing seems disturbed."

"Except your bed," put in the Colonel.

"Excuse me, that isn't my bed," said Parkins. "I don't use that one. But it does look as if someone had been playing tricks with it."

It certainly did: the clothes were bundled up and twisted together in a most tortuous confusion. Parkins pondered.

"That must be it," he said at last: "I disordered the clothes last night in unpacking, and they haven't made it since. Perhaps they came in to make it, and that boy saw them through the window; and then they were called away and locked the door after them. Yes, I think that must be it."

"Well, ring and ask," said the Colonel, and this appealed to Parkins as practical.

The maid appeared, and, to make a long story short, deposed that she had made the bed in the morning when the gentleman was in the room, and hadn't been there since. No, she hadn't no other key. Mr. Simpson he kep' the keys; he'd be able to tell the gentleman if anyone had been up.

This was a puzzle. Investigation showed that nothing of value had been taken, and Parkins remembered the disposition of the small objects on tables and so forth well enough to be pretty sure that no pranks had been played with them. Mr. and Mrs. Simpson furthermore agreed that neither of them had given the duplicate key of the room to any person whatever during the day. Nor could Parkins, fair-minded man as he was, detect anything in the demeanour of master, mistress, or maid that indicated guilt. He was much more inclined to think that the boy had been imposing on the Colonel.

The latter was unwontedly silent and pensive at dinner and throughout the evening. When he bade good night to Parkins, he murmured in a gruff undertone:

"You know where I am if you want me during the night."

"Why, yes, thank you, Colonel Wilson, I think I do; but there isn't much prospect of my disturbing you, I hope. By the way," he added, "did I show you that old whistle I spoke of? I think not. Well, here it is."

The Colonel turned it over gingerly in the light of the candle.

"Can you make anything of the inscription?" asked Parkins, as he took it back.

"No, not in this light. What do you mean to do with it?"

"Oh, well, when I get back to Cambridge I shall submit it to some of the archaeologists there, and see what they think of it; and very likely, if they consider it worth having, I may present it to one of the museums."

" 'M!" said the Colonel. "Well, you may be right. All I know is that, if it were mine, I should chuck it straight into the sea. It's no use talking, I'm well aware, but I expect that with you it's a case of live and learn. I hope so, I'm sure, and I wish you a good night."

He turned away, leaving Parkins in act to speak at the bottom of the stair, and soon each was in his own bedroom.

By some unfortunate accident, there were neither blinds nor curtains to the windows of the Professor's room. The previous night he had thought little of this, but to-night there seemed every prospect of a bright moon rising to shine directly on his bed, and probably wake him later on. When he noticed this he was a good deal annoyed, but, with an ingenuity which I can only envy, he succeeded in rigging up, with the help of a railway-rug, some safety-pins, and a stick and umbrella, a screen which, if it only held together, would completely keep the moonlight off his bed. And shortly afterwards he was comfortably in that bed. When he had read a somewhat solid work long enough to produce a decided wish for sleep, he cast a drowsy glance round the room, blew out the candle, and fell back upon the pillow.

He must have slept soundly for an hour or more, when a sudden clatter shook him up in a most unwelcome manner. In a moment he realized what had happened: his carefully-constructed screen had given way, and a very bright frosty moon was shining directly on his face. This was highly annoying. Could he possibly get up and reconstruct the screen? Or could he manage to sleep if he did not?

For some minutes he lay and pondered over the possibilities; then he turned over sharply, and with all his eyes open lay breathlessly listening. There had been a movement, he was sure, in the empty bed on the opposite side of the room. To-morrow he would have it moved, for there must be rats or something playing about in it. It was quiet now. No! the commotion began again. There was a rustling and shaking: surely more than any rat could cause.

I can figure to myself something of the Professor's bewilderment and horror, for I have in a dream thirty years back seen the same thing happen; but the reader will hardly, perhaps, imagine how dreadful it was to him to see a figure suddenly sit up in what he had known was an empty bed. He was out of his own bed in one bound, and made a dash towards the window, where lay his only weapon, the stick with which he had propped his screen. This was, as it turned out, the worst thing he could have done, because the personage in the empty bed, with a sudden smooth motion, slipped from the bed and took up a position, with outspread arms, between the two beds, and in front of the door. Parkins watched it in a horrid perplexity. Somehow, the idea of getting past it and escaping through the door was intolerable to him; he could not have borne — he didn't know why — to touch it; and as for its touching him, he would sooner dash himself through the window than have that happen. It stood for the moment in a band of dark shadow, and he had not seen what its face was like. Now it began to move, in a stooping posture, and all at once the spectator realized, with some horror and some relief, that it must be blind, for it seemed to feel about it with its muffled arms in a groping and random fashion. Turning half away from him, it became suddenly conscious of the bed he had just left, and darted towards it, and bent and felt over the pillows in a way which made Parkins shudder as he had never in his life thought it possible. In a very few moments it seemed to know that the bed was empty, and then, moving forward into the area of light and facing the window, it showed for the first time what manner of thing it was.

Parkins, who very much dislikes being questioned about it, did once describe something of it in my hearing, and I gathered that what he chiefly remembers about it is a horrible, an intensely horrible, face *of crumpled linen*. What expression he read upon it he could not or would not tell, but that the fear of it went nigh to maddening him is certain.

But he was not at leisure to watch it for long. With formidable quickness it moved into the middle of the room, and, as it groped and waved, one corner of its draperies swept across Parkins's face. He could not — though he knew how perilous a sound was — he could not keep back a cry of disgust, and this gave the searcher an instant clue. It leapt towards him upon the instant, and the next moment he was half-way through the window backwards, uttering cry upon cry at the utmost pitch of his voice, and the linen face was thrust close into his own. At this, almost the last possible second, deliverance came, as you will have guessed: the Colonel burst the door open, and was just in time to see the dreadful group at the window. When he reached the figures only one was left. Parkins sank forward into the room in a faint, and before him on the floor lay a tumbled heap of bed-clothes.

Colonel Wilson asked no questions, but busied himself in keeping everyone else out of the room and in getting Parkins back to his bed; and himself, wrapped in a rug, occupied the other bed for the rest of the night. Early on the next day Rogers arrived, more welcome than he would have been a day before, and the three of them held a very long consultation in the Professor's room. At the end of it the Colonel left the hotel door carrying a small object between his finger and thumb, which he cast as far into the sea as a very brawny arm could send it. Later on the smoke of a burning ascended from the back premises of the Globe.

Exactly what explanation was patched up for the staff and visitors at the hotel I must confess I do not recollect. The Professor was somehow cleared of the ready suspicion of delirium tremens, and the hotel of the reputation of a troubled house.

There is not much question as to what would have happened to Parkins if the Colonel had not intervened when he did. He would either have fallen out of the window or else lost his wits. But it is not so evident what more the creature that came in answer to the whistle could have done than frighten. There seemed to be absolutely nothing material about it save the bedclothes of which it had made itself a body. The Colonel, who remembered a not very dissimilar occurrence in India, was of the opinion that if Parkins had closed with it it could really have done very little, and that its one power was that of frightening. The whole thing, he said, served to confirm his opinion of the Church of Rome.

There is really nothing more to tell, but, as you may imagine, the Professor's views on certain points are less clear cut than they used to be. His nerves, too, have suffered: he cannot even now see a surplice hanging on a door quite unmoved, and the spectacle of a scarecrow in a field late on a winter afternoon has cost him more than one sleepless night.

The Shout

Robert Graves, best known for his poetry, historical fiction (I, Claudius), and mythological theory (The White Goddess), deserves also to be remembered for his one masterpiece of short fiction. In "The Shout" (1929), a strikingly original tale of the divided self and the struggles-to-the-death in love and marriage, the supernatural is inextricably interwoven with the realms of dream and madness.

The seductive stranger who enters the lives of a seemingly happily married couple has an uncanny power to release, by his very presence, untapped springs of jealousy, hatred, fear, and self-doubt. The husband's rival is in some sense, perhaps, his dark, murderous alter ego, who has erupted upon the scene with the force of the return of the repressed.

It is telling that the savage, deafening force of Crossley's shout mimics the thunderous energies of battle: Graves suffered severe emotional trauma for years after being wounded by a shell in 1916. His war experience left him with a guilt-haunted vision of the murderer that each man carries within himself. Whatever the autobiographical roots of "The Shout" (one might also note Graves's own turbulent domestic triangle in the years prior to the story's composition), it certainly casts a powerful spell. We are left with an unforgettable portrait of psychological doubleness, and the alternately life-giving and destructive faces of human love.

When we arrived with our bags at the Asylum cricket ground, the chief medical officer, whom I had met at the house where I was staying, came up to shake hands. I told him that I was only scoring for the Lampton team today (I had broken a finger the week before, keeping wicket on a bumpy pitch). He said: "Oh, then you'll have an interesting companion."

"The other scoresman?" I asked.

"Crossley is the most intelligent man in the asylum," answered the doctor, "a wide reader, a first-class chess-player, and so on. He seems to have travelled all over the world. He's been sent here for delusions. His most serious delusion is that he's a murderer, and his story is that he killed two men and a woman at Sydney, Australia. The other delusion, which is more humorous, is that his soul is split in pieces — whatever that means. He edits our monthly magazine, he stage manages our Christmas theatricals, and he gave a most original conjuring performance the other day. You'll like him."

He introduced me. Crossley, a big man of forty or fifty, had a queer, not unpleasant, face. But I felt a little uncomfortable, sitting next to him in the scoring box, his black-whiskered hands so close to mine. I had no fear of physical violence, only the sense of being in the presence of a man of unusual force, even perhaps, it somehow came to me, of occult powers.

It was hot in the scoring box in spite of the wide window. "Thunderstorm weather," said Crossley, who spoke in what country people call a "college voice," though I could not identify the college. "Thunderstorm weather makes us patients behave even more irregularly than usual."

I asked whether any patients were playing.

"Two of them, this first wicket partnership. The tall one, B. C. Brown, played for Hants three years ago, and the other is a good club player. Pat Slingsby usually turns out for us too — the Australian fast bowler, you know — but we are dropping him today. In weather like this he is apt to bowl at the batsman's head. He is not insane in the usual sense, merely magnificently ill-tempered. The doctors can do nothing with him. He wants shooting, really." Crossley began talking about the doctor. "A goodhearted fellow and, for a mental-hospital physician, technically well advanced. He actually studies morbid psychology and is fairly well-read, up to about the day before yesterday. I have a good deal of fun with him. He reads neither German nor French, so I keep a stage or two ahead in psychological fashions; he has to wait for the English translations. I invent significant dreams for him to interpret; I find he likes me to put in snakes and apple pies, so I usually do. He is convinced that my mental trouble is due to the good old 'antipaternal fixation' — I wish it were as simple as that."

Then Crossley asked me whether I could score and listen to a story at the same time. I said that I could. It was slow cricket.

"My story is true," he said, "every word of it. Or, when I say that my story is 'true,' I mean at least that I am telling it in a new way. It is always the same story, but I sometimes vary the climax and even recast the characters. Variation keeps it fresh and therefore true. If I were always to use the same formula, it would soon drag and become false. I am interested in keeping it alive, and it is a true story, every word of it. I know the people in it personally. They are Lampton people."

We decided that I should keep score of the runs and extras and that he should keep the bowling analysis, and at the fall of every wicket we should copy from each other. This made story-telling possible.

Richard awoke one morning saying to Rachel: "But what an unusual dream."

"Tell me, my dear," she said, "and hurry, because I want to tell you mine."

"I was having a conversation," he said, "with a person (or persons, because he changed his appearance so often) of great intelligence, and I can clearly remember the argument. Yet this is the first time I have ever been able to remember any argument that came to me in sleep. Usually my dreams are so different from waking that I can only describe them if I say: 'It is as though I were living and thinking as a tree, or a bell, or middle C, or a five-pound note; as though I had never been human.' Life there is sometimes rich for me and sometimes poor, but I repeat, in every case so different, that if I were to say: 'I had a conversation,' or 'I was in love,' or 'I heard music,' or 'I was angry,' it would be as far from the fact as if I tried to explain a problem of philosophy, as Rabelais's Panurge did to Thaumast, merely by grimacing with my eyes and lips."

"It is much the same with me," she said. "I think that when I am asleep I become, perhaps, a stone with all the natural appetites and convictions of a stone. 'Senseless as a stone' is a proverb, but there may be more sense in a stone, more sensibility, more sensitivity, more sentiment, more sensibleness, than in many men and women. And no less sensuality," she added thoughtfully.

It was Sunday morning, so that they could lie in bed, their arms about each other, without troubling about the time; and they were childless, so breakfast could wait. He told her that in his dream he was walking in the sand hills with this person or persons, who said to him: "These sand hills are a part neither of the sea before us nor of the grass links behind us, and are not related to the mountains beyond the links. They are of themselves. A man walking on the sand hills soon knows this by the tang in the air, and if he were to refrain from eating and drinking, from sleeping and speaking, from thinking and desiring, he could continue among them for ever without change. There is no life and no death in the sand hills. Anything might happen in the sand hills."

Rachel said that this was nonsense, and asked: "But what was the argument? Hurry up!"

He said it was about the whereabouts of the soul, but that now she had put it out of his head by hurrying him. All that he remembered was that the man was first a Japanese, then an Italian, and finally a kangaroo.

In return she eagerly told her dream, gabbling over the words.

"I was walking in the sand hills; there were rabbits there, too; how does that tally with what he said of life and death? I saw the man and you walking arm in arm towards me, and I ran from you both and I noticed that he had a black silk handkerchief; he ran after me and my shoe buckle came off and I could not wait to pick it up. I left it lying, and he stooped and put it into his pocket."

"How do you know that it was the same man?" he asked.

"Because," she said, laughing, "he had a black face and wore a blue coat like that picture of Captain Cook. And because it was in the sand hills."

He said, kissing her neck: "We not only live together and talk together and sleep together, but it seems we now even dream together."

So they laughed.

Then he got up and brought her breakfast.

At about half past eleven, she said: "Go out now for a walk, my dear, and bring home something for me to think about: and be back in time for dinner at one o'clock."

It was a hot morning in the middle of May, and he went out through the wood and struck the coast road, which after half a mile led into Lampton.

("Do you know Lampton well?" asked Crossley. "No," I said, "I am only here for the holidays, staying with friends.")

He went a hundred yards along the coast road, but then turned off and went across the links: thinking of Rachel and watching the blue butterflies and looking at the heath roses and thyme, and thinking of her again, and how strange it was that they could be so near to each other; and then taking a pinch of gorse flower and smelling it, and considering the smell and thinking, "If she should die, what would become of me?" and taking a slate from the low wall and skimming it across the pond and thinking, "I am a clumsy fellow to be her husband;" and walking towards the sand hills, and then edging away again, perhaps half in fear of meeting the person of their dream, and at last making a half circle towards the old church beyond Lampton, at the foot of the mountain.

The morning service was over and the people were out by the

cromlechs behind the church, walking in twos and threes, as the custom was, on the smooth turf. The squire was talking in a loud voice about King Charles, the Martyr: "A great man, a very great man, but betrayed by those he loved best," and the doctor was arguing about organ music with the rector. There was a group of children playing ball. "Throw it here, Elsie! No, to me, Elsie, Elsie, Elsie!" Then the rector appeared and pocketed the ball and said that it was Sunday; they should have remembered. When he was gone they made faces after him.

Presently a stranger came up and asked permission to sit down beside Richard; they began to talk. The stranger had been to the church service and wished to discuss the sermon. The text had been the immortality of the soul: the last of a series of sermons that had begun at Easter. He said that he could not grant the preacher's premise that *the soul is continually resident in the body*. Why should this be so? What duty did the soul perform in the daily routine task of the body? The soul was neither the brain, nor the lungs, nor the stomach, nor the heart, nor the mind, nor the imagination. Surely it was a thing apart? Was it not indeed less likely to be resident in the body than outside the body? He had no proof one way or the other, but he would say: Birth and death are so odd a mystery that the principle of life may well lie outside the body which is the visible evidence of living. "We cannot," he said, "even tell to a nicety what are the moments of birth and death. Why, in Japan, where I have travelled, they reckon a man to be already one year old when he is born; and lately in Italy a dead man — but come and walk on the sand hills and let me tell you my conclusions. I find it easier to talk when I am walking."

Richard was frightened to hear this, and to see the man wipe his forehead with a black silk handkerchief. He stuttered out something. At this moment the children, who had crept up behind the cromlech, suddenly, at an agreed signal, shouted loud in the ears of the two men; and stood laughing. The stranger was startled into anger; he opened his mouth as if he were about to curse them, and bared his teeth to the gums. Three of the children screamed and ran off. But the one whom they called Elsie fell down in her fright and lay sobbing. The doctor, who was near, tried to comfort her. "He has a face like a devil," they heard the child say.

The stranger smiled good-naturedly: "And a devil I was not so very long ago. That was in Northern Australia, where I lived with the black fellows for twenty years. 'Devil' is the nearest English word for the position that they gave me in their tribe; and they also gave me an eighteenth-century British naval uniform to wear as my ceremonial dress. Come and walk with me in the sand hills and let me tell you the whole story. I have a passion for walking in the sand hills: that is why I came to this town . . . My name is Charles."

Richard said: "Thank you, but I must hurry home to my dinner."

"Nonsense," said Charles, "dinner can wait. Or, if you wish, I can come to dinner with you. By the way, I have had nothing to eat since Friday. I am without money."

Richard felt uneasy. He was afraid of Charles, and did not wish to bring him home to dinner because of the dream and the sand hills and the handkerchief: yet on the other hand the man was intelligent and quiet and decently dressed and had eaten nothing since Friday; if Rachel knew that he had refused him a meal, she would renew her taunts. When Rachel was out of sorts, her favourite complaint was that he was overcareful about money; though when she was at peace with him, she owned that he was the most generous man she knew, and that she did not mean what she said; when she was angry with him again, out came the taunt of stinginess: "Tenpence-halfpenny," she would say, "tenpence-halfpenny and threepence of that in stamps;" his ears would burn and he would want to hit her. So he said now: "By all means come along to dinner, but that little girl is still sobbing for fear of you. You ought to do something about it."

Charles beckoned her to him and said a single soft word; it was an Australian magic word, he afterwards told Richard, meaning *Milk*: immediately Elsie was comforted and came to sit on Charles' knee and played with the buttons of his waistcoat for a while until Charles sent her away.

"You have strange powers, Mr. Charles," Richard said.

Charles answered: "I am fond of children, but the shout startled me; I am pleased that I did not do what, for a moment, I was tempted to do."

"What was that?" asked Richard.

"I might have shouted myself," said Charles.

"Why," said Richard, "they would have liked that better. It would have been a great game for them. They probably expected it of you."

"If I had shouted," said Charles, "my shout would have either killed them outright or sent them mad. Probably it would have killed them, for they were standing close."

Richard smiled a little foolishly. He did not know whether or not he was expected to laugh, for Charles spoke so gravely and carefully. So he said: "Indeed, what sort of shout would that be? Let me hear you shout."

"It is not only children who would be hurt by my shout," Charles said. "Men can be sent raving mad by it; the strongest, even, would be flung to the ground. It is a magic shout that I learned from the chief devil of the Northern Territory. I took eighteen years to perfect it, and yet I have used it, in all, no more than five times."

Richard was so confused in his mind with the dream and the handkerchief and the word spoken to Elsie that he did not know what to say, so he muttered: "I'll give you fifty pounds now to clear the cromlechs with a shout."

"I see that you do not believe me," Charles said. "Perhaps you have never before heard of the terror shout?"

Richard considered and said: "Well, I have read of the hero shout which the ancient Irish warriors used, that would drive armies backwards; and did not Hector, the Trojan, have a terrible shout? And there were sudden shouts in the woods of Greece.

They were ascribed to the god Pan and would infect men with a madness of fear; from this legend indeed the word "panic" has come into the English language. And I remember another shout in the *Mabinogion*, in the story of Lludd and Llevelys. It was a shriek that was heard on every May Eve and went through all hearts and so scared them that the men lost their hue and their strength and the women their children, and the youths and maidens their senses, and the animals and trees, the earth and the waters were left barren. But it was caused by a dragon."

"It must have been a British magician of the dragon clan," said Charles. "I belonged to the Kangaroos. Yes, that tallies. The effect is not exactly given, but near enough."

They reached the house at one o'clock, and Rachel was at the door, the dinner ready. "Rachel," said Richard, "here is Mr. Charles to dinner; Mr. Charles is a great traveller."

Rachel passed her hand over her eyes as if to dispel a cloud, but it may have been the sudden sunlight. Charles took her hand and kissed it, which surprised her. Rachel was graceful, small, with eyes unusually blue for the blackness of her hair, delicate in her movements, and with a voice rather low-pitched; she had a freakish sense of humour.

("You would like Rachel," said Crossley, "she visits me here sometimes.")

Of Charles it would be difficult to say one thing or another: he was of middle age, and tall; his hair grey; his face never still for a moment; his eyes large and bright, sometimes yellow, sometimes brown, sometimes grey; his voice changed its tone and accent with the subject; his hands were brown and hairy at the back, his nails well cared for. Of Richard it is enough to say that he was a musician, not a strong man but a lucky one. Luck was his strength.

After dinner Charles and Richard washed the dishes together, and Richard suddenly asked Charles if he would let him hear the shout: for he thought that he could not have peace of mind until he had heard it. So horrible a thing was, surely, worse to think about than to hear: for now he believed in the shout.

Charles stopped washing up; mop in hand. "As you wish," said he, "but I have warned you what a shout it is. And if I shout it must be in a lonely place where nobody else can hear; and I shall not shout in the second degree, the degree which kills certainly, but in the first, which terrifies only, and when you want me to stop put your hands to your ears."

"Agreed," said Richard.

"I have never yet shouted to satisfy an idle curiosity," said Charles, "but only when in danger of my life from enemies, black or white, and once when I was alone in the desert without food or drink. Then I was forced to shout, for food."

Richard thought: "Well, at least I am a lucky man, and my luck will be good enough even for this."

"I am not afraid," he told Charles.

"We will walk out on the sand hills tomorrow early," Charles said, "when nobody is stirring; and I will shout. You say you are not afraid."

But Richard was very much afraid, and what made his fear worse was that somehow he could not talk to Rachel and tell her of it: he knew that if he told her she would either forbid him to go or she would come with him. If she forbade him to go, the fear of the shout and the sense of cowardice would hang over him ever afterwards; but if she came with him, either the shout would be nothing and she would have a new taunt for his credulity and Charles would laugh with her, or if it were something, she might well be driven mad. So he said nothing.

Charles was invited to sleep at the cottage for the night, and they stayed up late talking.

Rachel told Richard when they were in bed that she liked Charles and that he certainly was a man who had seen many things, though a fool and a big baby. Then Rachel talked a great deal of nonsense, for she had had two glasses of wine, which she seldom drank, and she said: "Oh, my dearest, I forgot to tell you. When I put on my buckled shoes this morning while you were away I found a buckle missing. I must have noticed that it was

34

lost before I went to sleep last night and yet not fixed the loss firmly in my mind, so that it came out as a discovery in my dream; but I have a feeling, in fact I am certain, that Mr. Charles has that buckle in his pocket; and I am sure that he is the man whom we met in our dream. But I don't care, not I."

Richard grew more and more afraid, and he dared not tell of the black silk handkerchief, or of Charles' invitations to him to walk in the sand hills. And what was worse, Charles had used only a white handkerchief while he was in the house, so that he could not be sure whether he had seen it after all. Turning his head away, he said lamely: "Well, Charles knows a lot of things. I am going for a walk with him early tomorrow if you don't mind; an early walk is what I need."

"Oh, I'll come too," she said.

Richard could not think how to refuse her; he knew that he had made a mistake in telling her of the walk. But he said: "Charles will be very glad. At six o'clock then."

At six o'clock he got up, but Rachel after the wine was too sleepy to come with them. She kissed him goodbye and off he went with Charles.

Richard had had a bad night. In his dreams nothing was in human terms, but confused and fearful, and he had felt himself more distant from Rachel than he had ever felt since their marriage, and the fear of the shout was gnawing at him. He was also hungry and cold. There was a stiff wind blowing towards the sea from the mountains and a few splashes of rain. Charles spoke hardly a word, but chewed a stalk of grass and walked fast.

Richard felt giddy, and said to Charles: "Wait a moment, I have a stitch in my side." So they stopped, and Richard asked, gasping: "What sort of shout is it? Is it loud, or shrill? How is it produced? How can it madden a man?"

Charles was silent, so Richard went on with a foolish smile: "Sound, though, is a curious thing. I remember once, when I was at Cambridge, that a King's College man had his turn of reading the evening lesson. He had not spoken ten words before there was a groaning and ringing and creaking, and pieces of wood and dust fell from the roof; for his voice was exactly attuned to that of the building, so that he had to stop, else the roof might have fallen; as you can break a wine glass by playing its note on a violin."

Charles consented to answer: "My shout is not a matter of tone or vibration but something not to be explained. It is a shout of pure evil, and there is no fixed place for it on the scale. It may take any note. It is pure terror, and if it were not for a certain intention of mine, which I need not tell you, I would refuse to shout for you."

Richard had a great gift of fear, and this new account of the shout disturbed him more and more; he wished himself at home in bed, and Charles two continents away. But he was fascinated. They were crossing the links now and going through the bent grass that pricked through his stockings and soaked them.

Now they were on the bare sand hills. From the highest of them Charles looked about him; he could see the beach stretched out for two miles and more. There was no one in sight. Then Richard saw Charles take something out of his pocket and begin carelessly to juggle with it as he stood, tossing it from finger tip to finger tip and spinning it up with finger and thumb to catch it on the back of his hand. It was Rachel's buckle.

Richard's breath came in gasps, his heart beat violently and he nearly vomited. He was shivering with cold, and yet sweating. Soon they came to an open place among the sand hills near the sea. There was a raised bank with sea holly growing on it and a little sickly grass; stones were strewn all around, brought there, it seemed, by the sea years before. Though the place lay behind the first rampart of sand hills, there was a gap in the line through which a high tide might have broken, and the winds that continually swept through the gap kept them uncovered of sand. Richard had his hands in his trouser pockets for warmth and was nervously twisting a soft piece of wax around his right forefinger — a candle end that was in his pocket from the night before when he had gone downstairs to lock the door.

"Are you ready?" asked Charles.

Richard nodded.

A gull dipped over the crest of the sand hills and rose again screaming when it saw them. "Stand by the sea holly," said Richard, with a dry mouth, "and I'll be here among the stones, not too near. When I raise my hand, shout! When I put my fingers to my ears, stop at once."

So Charles walked twenty steps towards the holly. Richard saw his broad back and black silk handkerchief sticking from his pocket. He remembered the dream, and the shoe buckle and Elsie's fear. His resolution broke: he hurriedly pulled the piece of wax in two, and sealed his ears. Charles did not see him.

He turned, and Richard gave the signal with his hand.

Charles leaned forward oddly, his chin thrust out, his teeth bared, and never before had Richard seen such a look of fear on a man's face. He had not been prepared for that. Charles' face, that was usually soft and changing, uncertain as a cloud, now hardened to a rough stone mask, dead white at first, and then flushing outwards from the cheek bones red and redder, and at last as black as if he were about to choke. His mouth then slowly opened to the full, and Richard fell on his face, his hands to his ears, in a faint.

When he came to himself he was lying alone among the stones. He sat up, wondering numbly whether he had been there long. He felt very weak and sick, with a chill on his heart that was worse than the chill of his body. He could not think. He put his hand down to lift himself up and it rested on a stone, a larger one than most of the others. He picked it up and felt its surface, absently. His mind wandered. He began to think about shoemaking, a trade of which he had known nothing, but now every trick was familiar to him. "I must be a shoemaker," he said aloud.

Then he corrected himself: "No, I am a musician. Am I going mad?" He threw the stone from him; it struck against another and bounced off.

He asked himself: "Now why did I say that I was a shoe-

37

maker? It seemed a moment ago that I knew all there was to be known about shoemaking and now I know nothing at all about it. I must get home to Rachel. Why did I ever come out?"

Then he saw Charles on a sand hill a hundred yards away, gazing out to sea. He remembered his fear and made sure that the wax was in his ears: he stumbled to his feet. He saw a flurry on the sand and there was a rabbit lying on its side, twitching in a convulsion. As Richard moved towards it, the flurry ended: the rabbit was dead. Richard crept behind a sand hill out of Charles' sight and then struck homeward, running awkwardly in the soft sand. He had not gone twenty paces before he came upon the gull. It was standing stupidly on the sand and did not rise at his approach, but fell over dead.

How Richard reached home he did not know, but there he was opening the back door and crawling upstairs on his hands and knees. He unsealed his ears.

Rachel was sitting up in bed, pale and trembling. "Thank God you're back," she said; "I have had a nightmare, the worst of all my life. It was frightful. I was in my dream, in the deepest dream of all, like the one of which I told you. I was like a stone, and I was aware of you near me; you were you, quite plain, though I was a stone, and you were in great fear and I could do nothing to help you, and you were waiting for something and the terrible thing did not happen to you, but it happened to me. I can't tell you what it was, but it was as though all my nerves cried out in pain at once, and I was pierced through and through with a beam of some intense evil light and twisted inside out. I woke up and my heart was beating so fast that I had to gasp for breath. Do you think I had a heart attack and my heart missed a beat? They say it feels like that. Where have you been, dearest? Where is Mr. Charles?"

Richard sat on the bed and held her hand. "I have had a bad experience too," he said. "I was out with Charles by the sea and as he went ahead to climb on the highest sand hill I felt very faint and fell down among a patch of stones, and when I came to myself

I was in a desperate sweat of fear and had to hurry home. So I came back running alone. It happened perhaps half an hour ago," he said.

He did not tell her more. He asked, could he come back to bed and would she get breakfast? That was a thing she had not done all the years they were married.

"I am as ill as you," said she. It was understood between them always that when Rachel was ill, Richard must be well.

"You are not," said he, and fainted again.

She helped him to bed ungraciously and dressed herself and went slowly downstairs. A smell of coffee and bacon rose to meet her and there was Charles, who had lit the fire, putting two breakfasts on a tray. She was so relieved at not having to get breakfast and so confused by her experience that she thanked him and called him a darling, and he kissed her hand gravely and pressed it. He had made the breakfast exactly to her liking: the coffee was strong and the eggs fried on both sides.

Rachel fell in love with Charles. She had often fallen in love with men before and since her marriage, but it was her habit to tell Richard when this happened, as he agreed to tell her when it happened to him: so that the suffocation of passion was given a vent and there was no jealousy, for she used to say (and he had the liberty of saying): "Yes, I am *in love* with so-and-so, but I only *love* you."

That was as far as it had ever gone. But this was different. Somehow, she did not know why, she could not own to being in love with Charles: for she no longer loved Richard. She hated him for being ill, and said that he was lazy, and a sham. So about noon he got up, but went groaning around the bedroom until she sent him back to bed to groan.

Charles helped her with the housework, doing all the cooking, but he did not go up to see Richard, since he had not been asked to do so. Rachel was ashamed, and apologized to Charles for Richard's rudeness in running away from him. But Charles said mildly that he took it as no insult; he had felt queer himself that morning; it was as though something evil was astir in the air as they reached the sand hills. She told him that she too had had the same queer feeling.

Later she found all Lampton talking of it. The doctor maintained that it was an earth tremor, but the country people said that it had been the Devil passing by. He had come to fetch the black soul of Solomon Jones, the gamekeeper, found dead that morning in his cottage by the sand hills.

When Richard could go downstairs and walk about a little without groaning, Rachel sent him to the cobbler's to get a new buckle for her shoe. She came with him to the bottom of the garden. The path ran beside a steep bank. Richard looked ill and groaned slightly as he walked, so Rachel, half in anger, half in fun, pushed him down the bank, where he fell sprawling among the nettles and old iron. Then she ran back into the house laughing loudly.

Richard sighed, tried to share the joke against himself with Rachel — but she had gone — heaved himself up, picked the shoes from among the nettles, and after awhile walked slowly up the bank, out of the gate, and down the lane in the unaccustomed glare of the sun.

When he reached the cobbler's he sat down heavily. The cobbler was glad to talk to him. "You are looking bad," said the cobbler.

Richard said: "Yes, on Monday morning I had a bit of a turn; I am only now recovering from it."

"Good God," burst out the cobbler, "if you had a bit of a turn, what did I not have? It was as if someone handled me raw, without my skin. It was as if someone seized my very soul and juggled with it, as you might juggle with a stone, and hurled me away. I shall never forget last Monday morning."

A strange notion came to Richard that it was the cobbler's soul which he had handled in the form of a stone. "It may be," he thought, "that the souls of every man and woman and child in Lampton are lying there." But he said nothing about this, asked for a buckle, and went home.

Rachel was ready with a kiss and a joke; he might have kept silent, for his silence always made Rachel ashamed. "But," he thought, "why make her ashamed? From shame she goes to self-justification and picks a quarrel over something else and it's ten times worse. I'll be cheerful and accept the joke."

He was unhappy. And Charles was established in the house: gentle-voiced, hard-working, and continually taking Richard's part against Rachel's scoffing. This was galling, because Rachel did not resent it.

("The next part of the story," said Crossley, "is the comic relief, an account of how Richard went again to the sand hills, to the heap of stones, and identified the souls of the doctor and rector — the doctor's because it was shaped like a whiskey bottle and the rector's because it was as black as original sin — and how he proved to himself that the notion was not fanciful. But I will skip that and come to the point where Rachel two days later suddenly became affectionate and loved Richard, she said, more than ever before.")

The reason was that Charles had gone away, nobody knows where, and had relaxed the buckle magic for the time, because he was confident that he could renew it on his return. So in a day or two Richard was well again and everything was as it had been, until one afternoon the door opened, and there stood Charles.

He entered without a word of greeting and hung his hat upon a peg. He sat down by the fire and asked: "When is supper ready?"

Richard looked at Rachel, his eyebrows raised, but Rachel seemed fascinated by the man.

She answered: "Eight o'clock," in her low voice, and stooping down, drew off Charles' muddy boots and found him a pair of Richard's slippers.

Charles said: "Good. It is now seven o'clock. In another hour, supper. At nine o'clock the boy will bring the evening paper. At ten o'clock, Rachel, you and I sleep together."

Richard thought that Charles must have gone suddenly mad. But Rachel answered quietly: "Why, of course, my dear." Then

41

she turned viciously to Richard: "And you run away, little man!" she said, and slapped his cheek with all her strength.

Richard stood puzzled, nursing his cheek. Since he could not believe that Rachel and Charles had both gone mad together, he must be mad himself. At all events, Rachel knew her mind, and they had a secret compact that if either of them ever wished to break the marriage promise, the other should not stand in the way. They had made this compact because they wished to feel themselves bound by love rather than by ceremony. So he said as calmly as he could: "Very well, Rachel. I shall leave you two together."

Charles flung a boot at him, saying: "If you put your nose inside the door between now and breakfast time, I'll shout the ears off your head."

Richard went out this time not afraid, but cold inside and quite clearheaded. He went through the gate, down the lane, and across the links. It wanted three hours yet until sunset. He joked with the boys playing stump cricket on the school field. He skimmed stones. He thought of Rachel and tears started to his eyes. Then he sang to comfort himself. "Oh, I'm certainly mad," he said, "and what in the world has happened to my luck?"

At last he came to the stones. "Now," he said, "I shall find my soul in this heap and I shall crack it into a hundred pieces with this hammer" — he had picked up the hammer in the coal shed as he came out.

Then he began looking for his soul. Now, one may recognize the soul of another man or woman, but one can never recognize one's own. Richard could not find his. But by chance he came upon Rachel's soul and recognized it (a slim green stone with glints of quartz in it) because she was estranged from him at the time. Against it lay another stone, an ugly misshapen flint of a mottled brown. He swore: "I'll destroy this. It must be the soul of Charles."

He kissed the soul of Rachel; it was like kissing her lips. Then he took the soul of Charles and poised his hammer. "I'll knock you into fifty fragments!"

He paused. Richard had scruples. He knew that Rachel loved

Charles better than himself, and he was bound to respect the compact. A third stone (his own, it must be) was lying the other side of Charles' stone; it was of smooth grey granite, about the size of a cricket ball. He said to himself: "I will break my own soul in pieces and that will be the end of me." The world grew black, his eyes ceased to focus, and he all but fainted. But he recovered himself, and with a great cry brought down the coal hammer crack, and crack again, on the grey stone.

It split in four pieces, exuding a smell like gunpowder: and when Richard found that he was still alive and whole, he began to laugh and laugh. Oh, he was mad, quite mad! He flung the hammer away, lay down exhausted, and fell asleep.

He awoke as the sun was just setting. He went home in confusion, thinking: "This is a very bad dream and Rachel will help me out of it."

When he came to the edge of the town he found a group of men talking excitedly under a lamppost. One said: "About eight o'clock it happened, didn't it?" The other said: "Yes." A third said: "Ay, mad as a hatter. 'Touch me,' he says, 'and I'll shout. I'll shout you into a fit, the whole blasted police force of you. I'll shout you mad.' And the inspector says: 'Now, Crossley, put your hands up, we've got you cornered at last.' 'One last chance,' says he. 'Go and leave me or I'll shout you stiff and dead.'"

Richard had stopped to listen. "And what happened to Crossley then?" he said. "And what did the woman say?"

"'For Christ's sake,' she said to the inspector, 'go away or he'll kill you.'"

"And did he shout?"

"He didn't shout. He screwed up his face for a moment and drew in his breath. A'mighty, I've never seen such a ghastly looking face in my life. I had to take three or four brandies afterwards. And the inspector he drops the revolver and it goes off; but nobody hit. Then suddenly a change comes over this man Crossley. He claps his hands to his side and again to his heart, and his face goes smooth and dead again. Then he begins to laugh and dance and cut capers. And the woman stares and can't believe her

43

eyes and the police lead him off. If he was mad before, he was just harmless dotty now; and they had no trouble with him. He's been taken off in the ambulance to the Royal West County Asylum."

So Richard went home to Rachel and told her everything and she told him everything, though there was not much to tell. She had not fallen in love with Charles, she said; she was only teasing Richard and she had never said anything or heard Charles say anything in the least like what he told her; it was part of his dream. She loved him always and only him, for all his faults; which she went through — his stinginess, his talkativeness, his untidiness. Charles and she had eaten a quiet supper, and she did think it had been bad of Richard to rush off without a word of explanation and stay away for three hours like that. Charles might have murdered her. He did start pulling her about a bit, in fun, wanting her to dance with him, and then the knock came on the door, and the inspector shouted: "Walter Charles Crossley, in the name of the King, I arrest you for the murder of George Grant, Harry Grant, and Ada Coleman at Sydney, Australia." Then Charles had gone absolutely mad. He had pulled out a shoe buckle and said to it: "Hold her for me." And then he had told the police to go away or he'd shout them dead. After that he made a dreadful face at them and went to pieces altogether. "He was rather a nice man; I liked his face so much and feel so sorry for him."

"Did you like that story?" asked Crossley.

"Yes," said I, busy scoring, "a Milesian tale of the best. Lucius Apuleius, I congratulate you."

Crossley turned to me with a troubled face and hands clenched trembling. "Every word of it is true," he said. "Crossley's soul was cracked in four pieces and I'm a madman. Oh, I don't blame Richard and Rachel. They are a pleasant, loving pair of fools and I've never wished them harm; they often visit me here. In any case, now that my soul lies broken in pieces, my powers are gone. Only one thing remains to me," he said, "and that is the shout."

I had been so busy scoring and listening to the story at the same time that I had not noticed the immense bank of black cloud that swam up until it spread across the sun and darkened the whole sky. Warm drops of rain fell: a flash of lightning dazzled us and with it came a smashing clap of thunder.

In a moment all was confusion. Down came a drenching rain, the cricketers dashed for cover, the lunatics began to scream, bellow, and fight. One tall young man, the same B. C. Brown who had once played for Hants, pulled all his clothes off and ran about stark naked. Outside the scoring box an old man with a beard began to pray to the thunder: "Bah! Bah! Bah!"

Crossley's eyes twitched proudly. "Yes," said he, pointing to the sky, "that's the sort of shout it is; that's the effect it has; but I can do better than that." Then his face fell suddenly and became childishly unhappy and anxious. "Oh dear God," he said, "he'll shout at me again, Crossley will. He'll freeze my marrow."

The rain was rattling on the tin roof so that I could hardly hear him. Another flash, another clap of thunder even louder than the first. "But that's only the second degree," he shouted in my ear; "it's the first that kills."

"Oh," he said. "Don't you understand?" He smiled foolishly. "I'm Richard now, and Crossley will kill me."

The naked man was running about brandishing a cricket stump in either hand and screaming: an ugly sight. "Bah! Bah! Bah!" prayed the old man, the rain spouting down his back from his uptilted hat.

"Nonsense," said I, "be a man, remember you're Crossley. You're a match for a dozen Richards. You played a game and lost, because Richard had the luck; but you still have the shout."

I was feeling rather mad myself. Then the Asylum doctor rushed into the scoring box, his flannels streaming wet, still wearing pads and batting gloves, his glasses gone; he had heard our voices raised, and tore Crossley's hands from mine. "To your dormitory at once, Crossley!" he ordered.

"I'll not go," said Crossley, proud again, "you miserable Snake and Apple Pie Man!"

The doctor seized him by his coat and tried to hustle him out.

Crossley flung him off, his eyes blazing with madness. "Get out," he said, "and leave me alone here or I'll shout. Do you hear? I'll shout. I'll kill the whole damn lot of you. I'll shout the Asylum down. I'll wither the grass. I'll shout." His face was distorted in terror. A red spot appeared on either cheek bone and spread over his face.

I put my fingers to my ears and ran out of the scoring box. I had run perhaps twenty yards, when an indescribable pang of fire spun me about and left me dazed and numbed. I escaped death somehow; I suppose that I am lucky, like the Richard of the story. But the lightning struck Crossley and the doctor dead.

Crossley's body was found rigid, the doctor's was crouched in a corner, his hands to his ears. Nobody could understand this because death had been instantaneous, and the doctor was not a man to stop his ears against thunder.

It makes a rather unsatisfactory end to the story to say that Rachel and Richard were the friends with whom I was staying — Crossley had described them most accurately — but that when I told them that a man called Charles Crossley had been struck at the same time as their friend the doctor, they seemed to take Crossley's death casually by comparison with his. Richard looked blank; Rachel said: "Crossley? I think that was the man who called himself the Australian Illusionist and gave that wonderful conjuring show the other day. He had practically no apparatus but a black silk handkerchief. I liked his face so much. Oh, and Richard didn't like it at all."

"No, I couldn't stand the way he looked at you all the time," Richard said.

EDITH WHARTON

Pomegranate Seed

Edith Wharton's interest in the uncanny dates from her childhood. During a long convalescence from typhoid fever at age eight, she was introduced to ghostly fiction which had the effect of catapulting her into (as she later phrased it) "a state of chronic fear."[8] In her own career as an author, she penned about a dozen tales of the supernatural, including "Pomegranate Seed" (1931), written when she was at the pinnacle of her craft and imaginative power.

"Pomegranate Seed" fits Wharton's own definition of the successful short story as "a shaft driven straight into the heart of human experience."[9] The supernatural elements in the narrative not only make for a chilling drama but are used effectively to explore psychological themes — in particular, problems within relationships and marriage. The dire predicament of husband and wife, confronted by an uncanny interloper, is on an emotional level absolutely authentic. It is not so much the emergence of a "ghost from the past" that is so perilous for their marriage, but the ways in which both partners attempt to deal with it. The heroine, torn by dread and suspicion, unable to allow her husband the freedom he needs in order to work through his crisis, succeeds only in bringing to pass her worst fears.

Wharton's title recalls the Greek myth in which Persephone, kidnapped by Pluto, is forced to remain in the Underworld through a part *of each year because she has eaten a seed of the pomegranate (considered the food of the dead). At a level deeper than plot, deeper even than human psychology, this story conveys the tragic opposition between life, with its roaring bustle, and a silent and mysterious realm whose pull is stronger, at times, than vitality and anxious love.*

CHARLOTTE ASHBY paused on her doorstep. Dark had descended on the brilliancy of the March afternoon, and the grinding rasping street life of the city was at its highest. She turned her back on it, standing for a moment in the old-fashioned, marble-flagged vestibule before she inserted her key in the lock. The sash curtains drawn across the panes of the inner door softened the light within to a warm blur through which no details showed. It was the hour when, in the first months of her marriage to Kenneth Ashby, she had most liked to return to that quiet house in a street long since deserted by business and fashion. The contrast between the soulless roar of New York, its devouring blaze of lights, the oppression of its congested traffic, congested houses, lives, minds and this veiled sanctuary she called home, always stirred her profoundly. In the very heart of the hurricane she had found her tiny islet — or thought she had. And now, in the last months, everything was changed, and she always wavered on the doorstep and had to force herself to enter.

While she stood there she called up the scene within: the hall hung with old prints, the ladderlike stairs, and on the left her husband's long shabby library, full of books and pipes and worn armchairs inviting to meditation. How she had loved that room! Then, upstairs, her own drawing-room, in which, since the death of Kenneth's first wife, neither furniture nor hangings had been changed, because there had never been money enough, but which Charlotte had made her own by moving furniture about and adding more books, another lamp, a table for the new reviews. Even on the occasion of her only visit to the first Mrs. Ashby — a distant, self-centered woman, whom she had known very slightly

48

— she had looked about her with an innocent envy, feeling it to be exactly the drawing-room she would have liked for herself; and now for more than a year it had been hers to deal with as she chose — the room to which she hastened back at dusk on winter days, where she sat reading by the fire, or answering notes at the pleasant roomy desk, or going over her stepchildren's copybooks, till she heard her husband's step.

Sometimes friends dropped in; sometimes — oftener — she was alone; and she liked that best, since it was another way of being with Kenneth, thinking over what he had said when they parted in the morning, imagining what he would say when he sprang up the stairs, found her by herself and caught her to him.

Now, instead of this, she thought of one thing only — the letter she might or might not find on the hall table. Until she had made sure whether or not it was there, her mind had no room for anything else. The letter was always the same — a square grayish envelope with "Kenneth Ashby, Esquire," written on it in bold but faint characters. From the first it had struck Charlotte as peculiar that anyone who wrote such a firm hand should trace the letters so lightly; the address was always written as though there were not enough ink in the pen, or the writer's wrist were too weak to bear upon it. Another curious thing was that, in spite of its masculine curves, the writing was so visibly feminine. Some hands are sexless, some masculine, at first glance; the writing on the gray envelope, for all its strength and assurance, was without doubt a woman's. The envelope never bore anything but the recipient's name; no stamp, no address. The letter was presumably delivered by hand — but by whose? No doubt it was slipped into the letter box, whence the parlor-maid, when she closed the shutters and lit the lights, probably extracted it. At any rate, it was always in the evening, after dark, that Charlotte saw it lying there. She thought of the letter in the singular, as "it," because, though there had been several since her marriage — seven, to be exact — they were so alike in appearance that they had become merged in one another in her mind, become one letter, become "it."

49

The first had come the day after their return from their honeymoon — a journey prolonged to the West Indies, from which they had returned to New York after an absence of more than two months. Reentering the house with her husband, late on that first evening — they had dined at his mother's — she had seen, alone on the hall table, the gray envelope. Her eye fell on it before Kenneth's, and her first thought was: "Why, I've seen that writing before;" but where she could not recall. The memory was just definite enough for her to identify the script whenever it looked up at her faintly from the same pale envelope; but on that first day she would have thought no more of the letter if, when her husband's glance lit on it, she had not chanced to be looking at him. It all happened in a flash — his seeing the letter, putting out his hand for it, raising it to his shortsighted eyes to decipher the faint writing, and then abruptly withdrawing the arm he had slipped through Charlotte's, and moving away to the hanging light, his back turned to her. She had waited — waited for a sound, an exclamation; waited for him to open the letter; but he had slipped it into his pocket without a word and followed her into the library. And there they had sat down by the fire and lit their cigarettes, and he had remained silent, his head thrown back broodingly against the armchair, his eyes fixed on the hearth, and presently had passed his hand over his forehead and said: "Wasn't it unusually hot at my mother's tonight? I've got a splitting head. Mind if I take myself off to bed?"

That was the first time. Since then Charlotte had never been present when he had received the letter. It usually came before he got home from his office, and she had to go upstairs and leave it lying there. But even if she had not seen it, she would have known it had come by the change in his face when he joined her — which, on those evenings, he seldom did before they met for dinner. Evidently, whatever the letter contained, he wanted to be by himself to deal with it; and when he reappeared he looked years older, looked emptied of life and courage, and hardly conscious of her presence. Sometimes he was silent for the rest of the evening; and if he spoke, it was usually to hint some criticism of her household arrangements, suggest some change in the domestic administration, to ask, a little nervously, if she didn't think Joyce's nursery governess was rather young and flighty, or if she herself always saw to it that Peter — whose throat was delicate — was properly wrapped up when he went to school. At such times Charlotte would remember the friendly warnings she had received when she became engaged to Kenneth Ashby: "Marrying a heartbroken widower! Isn't that rather risky? You know Elsie Ashby absolutely dominated him;" and how she had jokingly replied: "He may be glad of a little liberty for a change." And in this respect she had been right. She had needed no one to tell her, during the first months, that her husband was perfectly happy with her. When they came back from their protracted honeymoon the same friends said: "What have you done to Kenneth? He looks twenty years younger;" and this time she answered with careless joy: "I suppose I've got him out of his groove."

But what she noticed after the gray letters began to come was not so much his nervous tentative faultfinding — which always seemed to be uttered against his will — as the look in his eyes when he joined her after receiving one of the letters. The look was not unloving, not even indifferent; it was the look of a man who had been so far away from ordinary events that when he returns to familiar things they seem strange. She minded that more than the faultfinding.

Though she had been sure from the first that the handwriting on the gray envelope was a woman's, it was long before she associated the mysterious letters with any sentimental secret. She was too sure of her husband's love, too confident of filling his life, for such an idea to occur to her. It seemed far more likely that the letters — which certainly did not appear to cause him any sentimental pleasure — were addressed to the busy lawyer than to the private person. Probably they were from some tiresome client — women, he had often told her, were nearly always tiresome as clients — who did not want her letters opened by his secretary and therefore had them carried to his house. Yes; but in that case the unknown female must be unusually troublesome, judging from the effect her letters produced. Then again, though his professional discretion was exemplary, it was odd that he had never uttered an impatient comment, never remarked to Charlotte, in a moment of expansion, that there was a nuisance of a woman who kept badgering him about a case that had gone against her. He had made more than one semiconfidence of the kind — of course without giving names or details; but concerning this mysterious correspondent his lips were sealed.

There was another possibility: what is euphemistically called an "old entanglement." Charlotte Ashby was a sophisticated woman. She had few illusions about the intricacies of the human heart; she knew that there were often old entanglements. But when she had married Kenneth Ashby, her friends, instead of hinting at such a possibility, had said: "You've got your work cut out for you. Marrying a Don Juan is a sinecure to it. Kenneth's never looked at another woman since he first saw Elsie Corder. During all the years of their marriage he was more like an unhappy lover than a comfortably contented husband. He'll never let you move an armchair or change the place of a lamp; and whatever you venture to do, he'll mentally compare with what Elsie would have done in your place."

Except for an occasional nervous mistrust as to her ability to manage the children — a mistrust gradually dispelled by her good humor and the children's obvious fondness for her — none of these forebodings had come true. The desolate widower, of whom his nearest friends said that only his absorbing professional interests had kept him from suicide after his first wife's death, had fallen in love, two years later, with Charlotte Gorse, and after an impetuous wooing had married her and carried her off on a tropical honeymoon. And ever since he had been as tender and loverlike as during those first radiant weeks. Before asking her to marry him he had spoken to her frankly of his great love for his first wife and his despair after her sudden death; but even then he had assumed no stricken attitude, or implied that life offered no possibility of renewal. He had been perfectly simple and natural, and had confessed to Charlotte that from the beginning he had hoped the future held new gifts for him. And when, after their marriage, they returned to the house where his twelve years with his first wife had been spent, he had told Charlotte at once that he was sorry he couldn't afford to do the place over for her, but that he knew every woman had her own views about furniture and all sorts of household arrangements a man would never notice, and had begged her to make any changes she saw fit without bothering to consult him. As a result, she made as few as possible; but his way of beginning their new life in the old setting was so frank and unembarrassed that it put her immediately at her ease, and she was almost sorry to find that the portrait of Elsie Ashby, which used to hang over the desk in his library, had been transferred in their absence to the children's nursery. Knowing herself to be the indirect cause of this banishment, she spoke of it to her husband; but he answered: "Oh, I thought they ought to grow up with her looking down on them." The answer moved Charlotte, and satisfied her; and as time went by she had to confess that she felt more at home in her house, more at ease and in confidence with her husband, since that long coldly beautiful face on the library wall no longer followed her with guarded eyes. It was as if Kenneth's love had penetrated to the secret she hardly acknowledged to her own heart — her passionate need to feel herself the sovereign even of his past.

With all this stored-up happiness to sustain her, it was curious that she had lately found herself yielding to a nervous apprehension. But there the apprehension was; and on this particular afternoon — perhaps because she was more tired than usual, or because of the trouble of finding a new cook, or for some other ridiculously trivial reason, moral or physical — she found herself unable to react against the feeling. Latchkey in hand, she looked back down the silent street to the whirl and illumination of the great thoroughfare beyond, and up at the sky already aflare with the city's nocturnal life. "Outside there," she thought, "skyscrapers, advertisements, telephones, wireless, aeroplanes, movies, motors, and all the rest of the twentieth century; and on the other side of the door something I can't explain, can't relate to them. Something as old as the world, as mysterious as life ... Nonsense! What am I worrying about? There hasn't been a letter for three months now — not since the day we came back from the country after Christmas... Queer that they always seem to come after our holidays! ...Why should I imagine there's going to be one tonight!"

No reason why, but that was the worst of it — one of the worsts! — that there were days when she would stand there cold and shivering with the premonition of something inexplicable, intolerable, to be faced on the other side of the curtained panes; and when she opened the door and went in, there would be nothing; and on other days when she felt the same premonitory chill, it was justified by the sight of the gray envelope. So that ever since the last had come she had taken to feeling cold and premonitory every evening, because she never opened the door without thinking the letter might be there.

Well, she'd had enough of it; that was certain. She couldn't go on like that. If her husband turned white and had a headache on the days when the letter came, he seemed to recover afterward; but she couldn't. With her the strain had become chronic, and the reason was not far to seek. Her husband knew from whom the letter came and what was in it; he was prepared beforehand for whatever he had to deal with, and master of the situation, however bad; whereas she was shut out in the dark with her conjectures.

"I can't stand it! I can't stand it another day!" she exclaimed aloud, as she put her key in the lock. She turned the key and went in; and there, on the table, lay the letter.

II

She was almost glad of the sight. It seemed to justify everything, to put a seal of definiteness on the whole blurred business. A letter for her husband; a letter from a woman — no doubt another vulgar case of "old entanglement." What a fool she had been ever to doubt it, to rack her brains for less obvious explanations! She took up the envelope with a steady contemptuous hand, looked closely at the faint letters, held it against the light and just discerned the outline of the folded sheet within. She knew that now she would have no peace till she found out what was written on that sheet.

Her husband had not come in; he seldom got back from his office before half-past six or seven, and it was not yet six. She would have time to take the letter up to the drawing-room, hold it over the tea-kettle which at that hour always simmered by the fire in expectation of her return, solve the mystery and replace the letter where she had found it. No one would be the wiser, and her gnawing uncertainty would be over. The alternative, of course, was to question her husband; but to do that seemed even more difficult. She weighed the letter between thumb and finger, looked at it again under the light, started up the stairs with the envelope — and came down again and laid it on the table.

"No, I evidently can't," she said, disappointed.

What should she do, then? She couldn't go up alone to that warm welcoming room, pour out her tea, look over her correspondence, glance at a book or review — not with that letter lying below and the knowledge that in a little while her husband would come in, open it and turn into the library alone, as he always did on the days when the gray envelope came.

Suddenly she decided. She would wait in the library and see for herself; see what happened between him and the letter when they thought themselves unobserved. She wondered the idea had never occurred to her before. By leaving the door ajar, and sitting in the corner behind it, she could watch him unseen... Well, then, she would watch him! She drew a chair into the corner, sat down, her eyes on the crack, and waited.

As far as she could remember, it was the first time she had ever tried to surprise another person's secret, but she was conscious of no compunction. She simply felt as if she were fighting her way through a stifling fog that she must at all costs get out of.

At length she heard Kenneth's latchkey and jumped up. The impulse to rush out and meet him had nearly made her forget why she was there; but she remembered in time and sat down again. From her post she covered the whole range of his movements — saw him enter the hall, draw the key from the door and take off his hat and overcoat. Then he turned to throw his gloves on the hall table, and at that moment he saw the envelope. The light was full on his face, and what Charlotte first noted there was a look of surprise. Evidently he had not expected the letter — had not thought of the possibility of its being there that day. But though he had not expected it, now that he saw it he knew well enough what it contained. He did not open it immediately, but stood motionless, the color slowly ebbing from his face. Apparently he could not make up his mind to touch it; but at length he put out his hand, opened the envelope, and moved with it to the light. In doing so he turned his back on Charlotte, and she saw only his bent head and slightly stooping shoulders. Apparently all the writing was on one page, for he did not turn the sheet but continued to stare at it for so long that he must have reread it a dozen times — or so it seemed to the woman breathlessly watching him. At length she saw him move; he raised the letter still closer to his eyes, as though he had not fully deciphered it. Then he lowered his head, and she saw his lips touch the sheet.

"Kenneth!" she exclaimed, and went out into the hall.

The letter clutched in his hand, her husband turned and looked at her. "Where were you?" he said, in a low bewildered voice, like a man waked out of his sleep.

"In the library, waiting for you." She tried to steady her voice: "What's the matter! What's in that letter? You look ghastly."

Her agitation seemed to calm him, and he instantly put the envelope into his pocket with a slight laugh. "Ghastly? I'm sorry. I've had a hard day in the office — one or two complicated cases. I look dog-tired, I suppose."

"You didn't look tired when you came in. It was only when you opened that letter — "

He had followed her into the library, and they stood gazing at each other. Charlotte noticed how quickly he had regained his self-control; his profession had trained him to rapid mastery of face and voice. She saw at once that she would be at a disadvantage in any attempt to surprise his secret, but at the same moment she lost all desire to maneuver, to trick him into betraying anything he wanted to conceal. Her wish was still to penetrate the mystery, but only that she might help him to bear the burden it implied. "Even if it *is* another woman," she thought.

"Kenneth," she said, her heart beating excitedly, "I waited here on purpose to see you come in. I wanted to watch you while you opened that letter."

His face, which had paled, turned to dark red; then it paled again. "That letter? Why especially that letter?"

"Because I've noticed that whenever one of those letters comes it seems to have such a strange effect on you."

A line of anger she had never seen before came out between his eyes, and she said to herself: "The upper part of his face is too narrow; this is the first time I ever noticed it."

She heard him continue, in the cool and faintly ironic tone of the prosecuting lawyer making a point: "Ah, so you're in the habit of watching people open their letters when they don't know you're there?"

"Not in the habit. I never did such a thing before. But I had to find out what she writes to you, at regular intervals, in those gray envelopes."

He weighed this for a moment; then: "The intervals have not been regular," he said.

"Oh, I dare say you've kept a better account of the dates than I have," she retorted, her magnanimity vanishing at his tone. "All I know is that every time that woman writes to you — "

"Why do you assume it's a woman?"

"It's a woman's writing. Do you deny it?"

He smiled. "No, I don't deny it. I asked only because the writing is generally supposed to look more like a man's."

Charlotte passed this over impatiently. "And this woman — what does she write to you about?"

Again he seemed to consider a moment. "About business."

"Legal business?"

"In a way, yes. Business in general."

"You look after her affairs for her?"

"Yes."

"You've looked after them for a long time?"

"Yes. A very long time."

"Kenneth, dearest, won't you tell me who she is?"

"No. I can't." He paused, and brought out, as if with a certain hesitation: "Professional secrecy."

The blood rushed from Charlotte's heart to her temples. "Don't say that — don't!"

"Why not?"

"Because I saw you kiss the letter."

The effect of the words was so disconcerting that she instantly repented having spoken them. Her husband, who had submitted to her cross-questioning with a sort of contemptuous composure, as though he were humoring an unreasonable child, turned on her a face of terror and distress. For a minute he seemed unable to speak; then, collecting himself, with an effort, he stammered out: "The writing is very faint; you must have seen me holding the letter close to my eyes to try to decipher it."

"No; I saw you kissing it." He was silent. "Didn't I see you kissing it?"

He sank back into indifference. "Perhaps."

"Kenneth! You stand there and say that — to me?"

"What possible difference can it make to you? The letter is on business, as I told you. Do you suppose I'd lie about it? The writer is a very old friend whom I haven't seen for a long time."

"Men don't kiss business letters, even from women who are very old friends, unless they have been their lovers, and still regret them."

He shrugged his shoulders slightly and turned away, as if he considered the discussion at an end and were faintly disgusted at the turn it had taken.

"Kenneth!" Charlotte moved toward him and caught hold of his arm.

He paused with a look of weariness and laid his hand over hers. "Won't you believe me?" he asked gently.

"How can I? I've watched these letters come to you — for months now they've been coming. Ever since we came back from the West Indies — one of them greeted me the very day we arrived. And after each one of them I see their mysterious effect on you, I see you disturbed, unhappy, as if someone were trying to estrange you from me."

"No, dear; not that. Never!"

She drew back and looked at him with passionate entreaty. "Well, then, prove it to me, darling. It's so easy!"

He forced a smile. "It's not easy to prove anything to a woman who's once taken an idea into her head."

"You've only got to show me the letter."

His hand slipped from hers and he drew back and shook his head.

"You won't?"

"I can't."

"Then the woman who wrote it is your mistress."

"No, dear. No."

"Not now, perhaps. I suppose she's trying to get you back, and you're struggling, out of pity for me. My poor Kenneth."

"I swear to you she never was my mistress."

Charlotte felt the tears rushing to her eyes. "Ah, that's worse, then — that's hopeless! The prudent ones are the kind that keep their hold on a man. We all know that." She lifted her hands and hid her face in them.

Her husband remained silent; he offered neither consolation nor denial, and at length, wiping away her tears, she raised her eyes almost timidly to his.

"Kenneth, think! We've been married such a short time. Imagine what you're making me suffer. You say you can't show me this letter. You refuse even to explain it."

"I've told you the letter is on business. I will swear to that too."

"A man will swear to anything to screen a woman. If you want me to believe you, at least tell me her name. If you'll do that, I promise you I won't ask to see the letter."

There was a long interval of suspense, during which she felt her heart beating against her ribs in quick admonitory knocks, as if warning her of the danger she was incurring.

"I can't," he said at length.

"Not even her name?"

"No."

"You can't tell me anything more?"

"No."

Again a pause; this time they seemed both to have reached the end of their arguments and to be helplessly facing each other across a baffling waste of incomprehension.

Charlotte stood breathing rapidly, her hands against her breast. She felt as if she had run a hard race and missed the goal. She had meant to move her husband and had succeeded only in irritating him; and this error of reckoning seemed to change him into a stranger, a mysterious incomprehensible being whom no argument or entreaty of hers could reach. The curious thing was that she was aware in him of no hostility or even impatience, but only of a remoteness, an inaccessibility, far more difficult to overcome. She felt herself excluded, ignored, blotted out of his life. But after a moment or two, looking at him more calmly, she saw that he was suffering as much as she was. His distant guarded face was drawn with pain; the coming of the gray envelope, though it always cast a shadow, had never marked him as deeply as this discussion with his wife.

Charlotte took heart; perhaps, after all, she had not spent her last shaft. She drew nearer and once more laid her hand on his arm. "Poor Kenneth! If you knew how sorry I am for you —"

She thought he winced slightly at this expression of sympathy, but he took her hand and pressed it.

"I can think of nothing worse than to be incapable of loving

60

long," she continued; "to feel the beauty of a great love and to be too unstable to bear its burden."

He turned on her a look of wistful reproach. "Oh, don't say that of me. Unstable!"

She felt herself at last on the right tack, and her voice trembled with excitement as she went on: "Then what about me and this other woman? Haven't you already forgotten Elsie twice within a year?"

She seldom pronounced his first wife's name; it did not come naturally to her tongue. She flung it out now as if she were flinging some dangerous explosive into the open space between them, and drew back a step, waiting to hear the mine go off.

Her husband did not move; his expression grew sadder, but showed no resentment. "I have never forgotten Elsie," he said.

Charlotte could not repress a faint laugh. "Then, you poor dear, between the three of us — "

"There are not — " he began; and then broke off and put his hand to his forehead.

"Not what?"

"I'm sorry; I don't believe I know what I'm saying. I've got a blinding headache." He looked wan and furrowed enough for the statement to be true, but she was exasperated by his evasion.

"Ah, yes; the gray-envelope headache!"

She saw the surprise in his eyes. "I'd forgotten how closely I've been watched," he said coldly. "If you'll excuse me, I think I'll go up and try an hour in the dark, to see if I can get rid of this neuralgia."

She wavered; then she said, with desperate resolution: "I'm sorry your head aches. But before you go I want to say that sooner or later this question must be settled between us. Someone is trying to separate us, and I don't care what it costs me to find out who it is." She looked him steadily in the eyes. "If it costs me your love, I don't care! If I can't have your confidence I don't want anything from you."

He still looked at her wistfully. "Give me time."

"Time for what? It's only a word to say."

"Time to show you that you haven't lost my love or my confidence."

"Well, I'm waiting."

He turned toward the door, and then glanced back hesitatingly. "Oh, do wait, my love," he said, and went out of the room.

She heard his tired step on the stairs and the closing of his bedroom door above. Then she dropped into a chair and buried her face in her folded arms. Her first movement was one of compunction; she seemed to herself to have been hard, unhuman, unimaginative. "Think of telling him that I didn't care if my insistence cost me his love! The lying rubbish!" She started up to follow him and unsay the meaningless words. But she was checked by a reflection. He had had his way, after all; he had eluded all attacks on his secret, and now he was shut up alone in his room, reading that other woman's letter.

III

She was still reflecting on this when the surprised parlor-maid came in and found her. No, Charlotte said, she wasn't going to dress for dinner; Mr. Ashby didn't want to dine. He was very tired and had gone up to his room to rest; later she would have something brought on a tray to the drawing-room. She mounted the stairs to her bedroom. Her dinner dress was lying on the bed, and at the sight the quiet routine of her daily life took hold of her and she began to feel as if the strange talk she had just had with her husband must have taken place in another world, between two beings who were not Charlotte Gorse and Kenneth Ashby, but phantoms projected by her fevered imagination. She recalled the year since her marriage — her husband's constant devotion; his persistent, almost too insistent tenderness; the feeling he had given her at times of being too eagerly dependent on her, too searchingly close to her, as if there were not air enough between her soul and his. It seemed preposterous, as she recalled all this, that a few moments ago she should have been accusing him of an intrigue with another woman! But, then, what —

Again she was moved by the impulse to go up to him, beg his pardon and try to laugh away the misunderstanding. But she was restrained by the fear of forcing herself upon his privacy. He was troubled and unhappy, oppressed by some grief or fear; and he had shown her that he wanted to fight out his battle alone. It would be wiser, as well as more generous, to respect his wish. Only, how strange, how unbearable, to be there, in the next room to his, and feel herself at the other end of the world! In her nervous agitation she almost regretted not having had the courage to open the letter and put it back on the hall table before he came in. At least she would have known what his secret was, and the bogy might have been laid. For she was beginning now to think of the mystery as something conscious, malevolent: a secret persecution before which he quailed, yet from which he could not free himself. Once or twice in his evasive eyes she thought she had detected a desire for help, an impulse of confession, instantly restrained and suppressed. It was as if he felt she could have helped him if she had known, and yet had been unable to tell her!

There flashed through her mind the idea of going to his mother. She was very fond of old Mrs. Ashby, a firm-fleshed clear-eyed old lady, with an astringent bluntness of speech which responded to the forthright and simple in Charlotte's own nature. There had been a tacit bond between them ever since the day when Mrs. Ashby senior, coming to lunch for the first time with her new daughter-in-law, had been received by Charlotte downstairs in the library, and glancing up at the empty wall above her son's desk, had remarked laconically: "Elsie gone, eh?" adding, at Charlotte's murmured explanation: "Nonsense. Don't have her back. Two's company." Charlotte, at this reading of her thoughts, could hardly refrain from exchanging a smile of complicity with her mother-in-law; and it seemed to her now that Mrs. Ashby's almost uncanny directness might pierce to the core of this new mystery. But here again she hesitated, for the idea almost suggested a

betrayal. What right had she to call in anyone, even so close a rela-
tion, to surprise a secret which her husband was trying to keep
from her? "Perhaps, by and by, he'll talk to his mother of his own
accord," she thought, and then ended: "But what does it matter?
He and I must settle it between us."

She was still brooding over the problem when there was a
knock on the door and her husband came in. He was dressed for
dinner and seemed surprised to see her sitting there, with her
evening dress lying unheeded on the bed.

"Aren't you coming down?"

"I thought you were not well and had gone to bed," she
faltered.

He forced a smile. "I'm not particularly well, but we'd better
go down." His face, though still drawn, looked calmer than when
he had fled upstairs an hour earlier.

"There it is; he knows what's in the letter and has fought his
battle out again, whatever it is," she reflected, "while I'm still in
darkness." She rang and gave a hurried order that dinner should
be served as soon as possible — just a short meal, whatever
could be got ready quickly, as both she and Mr. Ashby were
rather tired and not very hungry.

Dinner was announced, and they sat down to it. At first neither seemed able to find a word to say; then Ashby began to
make conversation with an assumption of ease that was more
oppressive than his silence. "How tired he is! How terribly overtired!" Charlotte said to herself, pursuing her own thoughts
while he rambled on about municipal politics, aviation, an exhibi-
tion of modern French painting, the health of an old aunt and the
installing of the automatic telephone. "Good heavens, how tired
he is!"

When they dined alone they usually went into the library
after dinner, and Charlotte curled herself up on the divan with
her knitting while he settled down in his armchair under the
lamp and lit a pipe. But this evening, by tacit agreement, they
avoided the room in which their strange talk had taken place,
and went up to Charlotte's drawing-room.

They sat down near the fire, and Charlotte said: "Your pipe?" after he had put down his hardly tasted coffee.

He shook his head. "No, not tonight."

"You must go to bed early; you look terribly tired. I'm sure they overwork you at the office."

"I suppose we all overwork at times."

She rose and stood before him with sudden resolution. "Well, I'm not going to have you use up your strength slaving in that way. It's absurd. I can see you're ill." She bent over him and laid her hand on his forehead. "My poor old Kenneth. Prepare to be taken away soon on a long holiday."

He looked up at her, startled. "A holiday?"

"Certainly. Didn't you know I was going to carry you off at Easter? We're going to start in a fortnight on a month's voyage to somewhere or other. On any one of the big cruising steamers." She paused and bent closer, touching his forehead with her lips. "I'm tired, too, Kenneth."

He seemed to pay no heed to her last words, but sat, his hands on his knees, his head drawn back a little from her caress, and looked up at her with a stare of apprehension. "Again? My dear, we can't; I can't possibly go away."

"I don't know why you say 'again,' Kenneth; we haven't taken a real holiday this year."

"At Christmas we spent a week with the children in the country."

"Yes, but this time I mean away from the children, from servants, from the house. From everything that's familiar and fatiguing. Your mother will love to have Joyce and Peter with her."

He frowned and slowly shook his head. "No, dear; I can't leave them with my mother."

"Why, Kenneth, how absurd! She adores them. You didn't hesitate to leave them with her for over two months when we went to the West Indies."

He drew a deep breath and stood up uneasily. "That was different."

65

"Different? Why?"

"I mean, at that time I didn't realize — " He broke off as if to choose his words and then went on: "My mother adores the children, as you say. But she isn't always very judicious. Grandmothers always spoil children. And sometimes she talks before them without thinking." He turned to his wife with an almost pitiful gesture of entreaty. "Don't ask me to, dear."

Charlotte mused. It was true that the elder Mrs. Ashby had a fearless tongue, but she was the last woman in the world to say or hint anything before her grandchildren at which the most scrupulous parent could take offense. Charlotte looked at her husband in perplexity.

"I don't understand."

He continued to turn on her the same troubled and entreating gaze. "Don't try to," he muttered.

"Not try to?"

"Not now — not yet." He put up his hands and pressed them against his temples. "Can't you see that there's no use in insisting? I can't go away, no matter how much I might want to."

Charlotte still scrutinized him gravely. "The question is, *do* you want to?"

He returned her gaze for a moment; then his lips began to tremble, and he said, hardly above his breath: "I want — anything you want."

"And yet — "

"Don't ask me. I can't leave — I can't!"

"You mean that you can't go away out of reach of those letters!"

Her husband had been standing before her in an uneasy half-hesitating attitude; now he turned abruptly away and walked once or twice up and down the length of the room, his head bent, his eyes fixed on the carpet.

Charlotte felt her resentfulness rising with her fears. "It's that," she persisted. "Why not admit it? You can't live without them."

He continued his troubled pacing of the room; then he

stopped short, dropped into a chair and covered his face with his hands. From the shaking of his shoulders, Charlotte saw that he was weeping. She had never seen a man cry, except her father after her mother's death, when she was a little girl; and she remembered still how the sight had frightened her. She was frightened now; she felt that her husband was being dragged away from her into some mysterious bondage, and that she must use up her last atom of strength in the struggle for his freedom, and for hers.

"Kenneth — Kenneth!" she pleaded, kneeling down beside him. "Won't you listen to me? Won't you try to see what I'm suffering? I'm not unreasonable, darling; really not. I don't suppose I should ever have noticed the letters if it hadn't been for their effect on you. It's not my way to pry into other people's affairs; and even if the effect had been different — yes, yes; listen to me — if I'd seen that the letters made you happy, that you were watching eagerly for them, counting the days between their coming, that you wanted them, that they gave you something I haven't known how to give — why, Kenneth, I don't say I shouldn't have suffered from that, too; but it would have been in a different way, and I should have had the courage to hide what I felt, and the hope that someday you'd come to feel about me as you did about the writer of the letters. But what I can't bear is to see how you dread them, how they make you suffer, and yet how you can't live without them and won't go away lest you should miss one during your absence. Or perhaps," she added, her voice breaking into a cry of accusation — "perhaps it's because she's actually forbidden you to leave. Kenneth, you must answer me! Is that the reason? Is it because she's forbidden you that you won't go away with me?"

She continued to kneel at his side, and raising her hands, she drew his gently down. She was ashamed of her persistence, ashamed of uncovering that baffled disordered face, yet resolved that no such scruples should arrest her. His eyes were lowered, the muscles of his face quivered; she was making him suffer even more than she suffered herself. Yet this no longer restrained her.

"Kenneth, is it that? She won't let us go away together?"

Still he did not speak or turn his eyes to her; and a sense of defeat swept over her. After all, she thought, the struggle was a losing one. "You needn't answer. I see I'm right," she said.

Suddenly, as she rose, he turned and drew her down again. His hands caught hers and pressed them so tightly that she felt her rings cutting into her flesh. There was something frightened, convulsive in his hold; it was the clutch of a man who felt himself slipping over a precipice. He was staring up at her now as if salvation lay in the face she bent above him. "Of course we'll go away together. We'll go wherever you want," he said in a low confused voice; and putting his arm about her, he drew her close and pressed his lips on hers.

IV

Charlotte had said to herself: "I shall sleep tonight," but instead she sat before her fire into the small hours, listening for any sound that came from her husband's room. But he, at any rate, seemed to be resting after the tumult of the evening. Once or twice she stole to the door and in the faint light that came in from the street through his open window she saw him stretched out in heavy sleep — the sleep of weakness and exhaustion. "He's ill," she thought — "he's undoubtedly ill. And it's not overwork; it's this mysterious persecution."

She drew a breath of relief. She had fought through the weary fight and the victory was hers — at least for the moment. If only they could have started at once — started for anywhere! She knew it would be useless to ask him to leave before the holidays; and meanwhile the secret influence — as to which she was still so completely in the dark — would continue to work against her, and she would have to renew the struggle day after day till they started on their journey. But after that everything would be different. If once she could get her husband away under other skies, and all to herself, she never doubted her power to release him from the evil spell he was under. Lulled to quiet by the thought, she too slept at last.

When she woke, it was long past her usual hour, and she sat up in bed surprised and vexed at having overslept herself. She always liked to be down to share her husband's breakfast by the library fire; but a glance at the clock made it clear that he must have started long since for his office. To make sure, she jumped out of bed and went into his room, but it was empty. No doubt he had looked in on her before leaving, seen that she still slept, and gone downstairs without disturbing her; and their relations were sufficiently loverlike for her to regret having missed their morning hour.

She rang and asked if Mr. Ashby had already gone. Yes, nearly an hour ago, the maid said. He had given orders that Mrs. Ashby should not be waked and that the children should not come to her till she sent for them... Yes, he had gone up to the nursery himself to give the order. All this sounded usual enough; and Charlotte hardly knew why she asked: "And did Mr. Ashby leave no other message?"

Yes, the maid said, he did; she was so sorry she'd forgotten. He'd told her, just as he was leaving, to say to Mrs. Ashby that he was going to see about their passages, and would she please be ready to sail tomorrow?

Charlotte echoed the woman's "Tomorrow," and sat staring at her incredulously. "Tomorrow — you're sure he said to sail tomorrow?"

"Oh, ever so sure, ma'am. I don't know how I could have forgotten to mention it."

"Well, it doesn't matter. Draw my bath, please." Charlotte sprang up, dashed through her dressing, and caught herself singing at her image in the glass as she sat brushing her hair. It made her feel young again to have scored such a victory. The other woman vanished to a speck on the horizon, as this one, who ruled the foreground, smiled back at the reflection of her lips and eyes. He loved her, then — he loved her as passionately as ever.

He had divined what she had suffered, had understood that their happiness depended on their getting away at once, and finding each other again after yesterday's desperate groping in the fog. The nature of the influence that had come between them did not much matter to Charlotte now; she had faced the phantom and dispelled it. "Courage — that's the secret! If only people who are in love weren't always so afraid of risking their happiness by looking it in the eyes." As she brushed back her light abundant hair it waved electrically above her head, like the palms of victory. Ah, well, some women knew how to manage men, and some didn't — and only the fair — she gaily paraphrased — deserve the brave! Certainly she was looking very pretty.

The morning danced along like a cockleshell on a bright sea — such a sea as they would soon be speeding over. She ordered a particularly good dinner, saw the children off to their classes, had her trunks brought down, consulted with the maid about getting out summer clothes — for of course they would be heading for heat and sunshine — and wondered if she oughtn't to take Kenneth's flannel suits out of camphor. "But how absurd," she reflected, "that I don't yet know where we're going!" She looked at the clock, saw that it was close on noon, and decided to call him up at his office. There was a slight delay; then she heard his secretary's voice saying that Mr. Ashby had looked in for a moment early, and left again almost immediately. . . Oh, very well; Charlotte would ring up later. How soon was he likely to be back? The secretary answered that she couldn't tell; all they knew in the office was that when he left he had said he was in a hurry because he had to go out of town.

Out of town! Charlotte hung up the receiver and sat blankly gazing into new darkness. Why had he gone out of town? And where had he gone? And of all days, why should he have chosen the eve of their suddenly planned departure? She felt a faint shiver of apprehension. Of course he had gone to see that woman — no doubt to get her permission to leave. He was as completely in bondage as that; and Charlotte had been fatuous enough to see the palms of victory on her forehead. She burst into a laugh and, walking across the room, sat down again before her mirror. What a different face she saw! The smile on her pale lips seemed to mock the rosy vision of the other Charlotte. But gradually her color crept back. After all, she had a right to claim the victory, since her husband was doing what she wanted, not what the other woman exacted of him. It was natural enough, in view of his abrupt decision to leave the next day, that he should have arrangements to make, business matters to wind up; it was not even necessary to suppose that his mysterious trip was a visit to the writer of the letters. He might simply have gone to see a client who lived out of town. Of course they would not tell Charlotte at the office; the secretary had hesitated before imparting even such meager information as the fact of Mr. Ashby's absence. Meanwhile she would go on with her joyful preparations, content to learn later in the day to what particular island of the blest she was to be carried.

The hours wore on, or rather were swept forward on a rush of eager preparations. At last the entrance of the maid who came to draw the curtains roused Charlotte from her labors, and she saw to her surprise that the clock marked five. And she did not yet know where they were going the next day! She rang up her husband's office and was told that Mr. Ashby had not been there since the early morning. She asked for his partner, but the partner could add nothing to her information, for he himself, his suburban train having been behind time, had reached the office after Ashby had come and gone. Charlotte stood perplexed; then she decided to telephone to her mother-in-law. Of course Kenneth, on the eve of a month's absence, must have gone to see his mother. The mere fact that the children — in spite of his vague objections — would certainly have to be left with old Mrs. Ashby, made it obvious that he would have all sorts of matters to decide with her. At another time Charlotte might have felt a little hurt at being excluded from their conference, but nothing mattered now that she had won the day, that her husband was still hers and not another woman's. Gaily she called up Mrs. Ashby, heard her friendly voice, and began: "Well, did Kenneth's news surprise you? What do you think of our elopement?"

Almost instantly, before Mrs. Ashby could answer, Charlotte knew what her reply would be. Mrs. Ashby had not seen her son, she had had no word from him and did not know what her daughter-in-law meant. Charlotte stood silent in the intensity of her surprise. "But then, where *has* he been?" she thought. Then, recovering herself, she explained their sudden decision to Mrs. Ashby, and in doing so, gradually regained her own self-confidence, her conviction that nothing could ever again come between Kenneth and herself. Mrs. Ashby took the news calmly and approvingly. She too, had thought that Kenneth looked worried and overtired, and she agreed with her daughter-in-law that in such cases change was the surest remedy. "I'm always so glad when he gets away. Elsie hated traveling; she was always finding pretexts to prevent his going anywhere. With you, thank goodness, it's different." Nor was Mrs. Ashby surprised at his not having had time to let her know of his departure. He must have been in a rush from the moment the decision was taken; but no doubt he'd drop in before dinner. Five minutes' talk was really all they needed. "I hope you'll gradually cure Kenneth of his mania for going over and over a question that could be settled in a dozen words. He never used to be like that, and if he carried the habit into his professional work he'd soon lose all his clients... Yes, do come in for a minute, dear, if you have time; no doubt he'll turn up while you're here." The tonic ring of Mrs. Ashby's voice echoed on reassuringly in the silent room while Charlotte continued her preparations.

Toward seven the telephone rang, and she darted to it. Now she would know! But it was only from the conscientious secretary, to say that Mr. Ashby hadn't been back, or sent any word, and before the office closed she thought she ought to let Mrs. Ashby know. "Oh, that's all right. Thanks a lot!" Charlotte called out cheerfully, and hung up the receiver with a trembling hand. But perhaps by this time, she reflected, he was at his mother's. She shut her drawers and cupboards, put on her hat and coat and called up to the nursery that she was going out for a minute to see the children's grandmother.

Mrs. Ashby lived nearby, and during her brief walk through the cold spring dusk Charlotte imagined that every advancing figure was her husband's. But she did not meet him on the way, and when she entered the house she found her mother-in-law alone. Kenneth had neither telephoned nor come. Old Mrs. Ashby sat by her bright fire, her knitting needles flashing steadily through her active old hands, and her mere bodily presence gave reassurance to Charlotte. Yes, it was certainly odd that Kenneth had gone off for the whole day without letting any of them know; but, after all, it was to be expected. A busy lawyer held so many threads in his hands that any sudden change of plan would oblige him to make all sorts of unforeseen arrangements and adjustments. He might have gone to see some client in the suburbs and been detained there; his mother remembered his telling her that he had charge of the legal business of a queer old recluse somewhere in New Jersey, who was immensely rich but too mean to have a telephone. Very likely Kenneth had been stranded there.

But Charlotte felt her nervousness gaining on her. When Mrs. Ashby asked her at what hour they were sailing the next day and she had to say she didn't know — that Kenneth had simply sent her word he was going to take their passages — the uttering of the words again brought home to her the strangeness of the situation. Even Mrs. Ashby conceded that it was odd; but she immediately added that it only showed what a rush he was in.

"But, mother, it's nearly eight o'clock! He must realize that I've got to know when we're starting tomorrow."

"Oh, the boat probably doesn't sail till evening. Sometimes they have to wait till midnight for the tide. Kenneth's probably counting on that. After all, he has a level head."

Charlotte stood up. "It's not that. Something has happened to him."

73

Mrs. Ashby took off her spectacles and rolled up her knitting. "If you begin to let yourself imagine things — "

"Aren't you in the least anxious?"

"I never am till I have to be. I wish you'd ring for dinner, my dear. You'll stay and dine? He's sure to drop in here on his way home."

Charlotte called up her own house. No, the maid said, Mr. Ashby hadn't come in and hadn't telephoned. She would tell him as soon as he came that Mrs. Ashby was dining at his mother's. Charlotte followed her mother-in-law into the dining-room and sat with parched throat before her empty plate, while Mrs. Ashby dealt calmly and efficiently with a short but carefully prepared repast. "You'd better eat something, child, or you'll be as bad as Kenneth... Yes, a little more asparagus, please, Jane."

She insisted on Charlotte's drinking a glass of sherry and nibbling a bit of toast; then they returned to the drawing-room, where the fire had been made up, and the cushions in Mrs. Ashby's armchair shaken out and smoothed. How safe and familiar it all looked; and out there, somewhere in the uncertainty and mystery of the night, lurked the answer to the two women's conjectures, like an indistinguishable figure prowling on the threshold.

At last Charlotte got up and said: "I'd better go back. At this hour Kenneth will certainly go straight home."

Mrs. Ashby smiled indulgently. "It's not very late, my dear. It doesn't take two sparrows long to dine."

"It's after nine." Charlotte bent down to kiss her. "The fact is, I can't keep still."

Mrs. Ashby pushed aside her work and rested her two hands on the arms of her chair. "I'm going with you," she said, helping herself up.

Charlotte protested that it was too late, that it was not necessary, that she would call up as soon as Kenneth came in, but Mrs. Ashby had already rung for her maid. She was slightly lame, and stood resting on her stick while her wraps were brought. "If Mr. Kenneth turns up, tell him he'll find me at his own house," she instructed the maid as the two women got into the taxi which had been summoned. During the short drive Charlotte gave thanks that she was not returning home alone. There was something warm and substantial in the mere fact of Mrs. Ashby's nearness, something that corresponded with the clearness of her eyes and the texture of her fresh firm complexion. As the taxi drew up she laid her hand encouragingly on Charlotte's. "You'll see; there'll be a message."

The door opened at Charlotte's ring and the two entered. Charlotte's heart beat excitedly; the stimulus of her mother-in-law's confidence was beginning to flow through her veins.

"You'll see — you'll see," Mrs. Ashby repeated.

The maid who opened the door said no, Mr. Ashby had not come in, and there had been no message from him.

"You're sure the telephone's not out of order?" his mother suggested; and the maid said, well, it certainly wasn't half an hour ago; but she'd just go and ring up to make sure. She disappeared, and Charlotte turned to take off her hat and cloak. As she did so her eyes lit on the hall table, and there lay a gray envelope, her husband's name faintly traced on it. "Oh!" she cried out, suddenly aware that for the first time in months she had entered her house without wondering if one of the gray letters would be there.

"What is it, my dear?" Mrs. Ashby asked with a glance of surprise.

Charlotte did not answer. She took up the envelope and stood staring at it as if she could force her gaze to penetrate to what was within. Then an idea occurred to her. She turned and held out the envelope to her mother-in-law.

"Do you know that writing?" she asked.

Mrs. Ashby took the letter. She had to feel with her other hand for her eyeglasses, and when she had adjusted them she lifted the envelope to the light. "Why!" she exclaimed; and then stopped. Charlotte noticed that the letter shook in her usually firm hand. "But this is addressed to Kenneth," Mrs. Ashby said at length, in a low voice. Her tone seemed to imply that she felt her daughter-in-law's question to be slightly indiscreet.

"Yes, but no matter," Charlotte spoke with sudden decision. "I want to know — do you know the writing?"

Mrs. Ashby handed back the letter. "No," she said distinctly.

The two women had turned into the library. Charlotte switched on the electric light and shut the door. She still held the envelope in her hand.

"I'm going to open it," she announced.

She caught her mother-in-law's startled glance. "But, dearest — a letter not addressed to you? My dear, you can't!"

"As if I cared about that — now!" She continued to look intently at Mrs. Ashby. "This letter may tell me where Kenneth is."

Mrs. Ashby's glossy bloom was effaced by a quick pallor; her firm cheeks seemed to shrink and wither. "Why should it? What makes you believe — It can't possibly —"

Charlotte held her eyes steadily on that altered face. "Ah, then you *do* know the writing?" she flashed back.

"Know the writing? How should I? With all my son's correspondents... What I do know is — " Mrs. Ashby broke off and looked at her daughter-in-law entreatingly, almost timidly.

Charlotte caught her by the wrist. "Mother! What do you know? Tell me! You must!"

"That I don't believe any good ever came of a woman's opening her husband's letters behind his back."

The words sounded to Charlotte's irritated ears as flat as a phrase culled from a book of moral axioms. She laughed impatiently and dropped her mother-in-law's wrist. "Is that all? No good can come of this letter, opened or unopened. I know that well enough. But whatever ill comes, I mean to find out what's in it." Her hands had been trembling as they held the envelope, but now they grew firm, and her voice also. She still gazed intently at Mrs. Ashby. "This is the ninth letter addressed in the same hand that has come for Kenneth since we've been married. Always these same gray envelopes. I've kept count of them because after each one he has been like a man who has had some dreadful shock. It takes him hours to shake off their effect. I've told him so. I've told him I must know from whom they come, because I can see they're killing him. He won't answer my questions; he says he can't tell me anything about the letters; but last night he promised to go away with me — to get away from them."

Mrs. Ashby, with shaking steps, had gone to one of the armchairs and sat down in it, her head drooping forward on her breast. "Ah," she murmured.

"So now you understand—"

"Did he tell you it was to get away from them?"

"He said, to get away — to get away. He was sobbing so that he could hardly speak. But I told him I knew that was why."

"And what did he say?"

"He took me in his arms and said he'd go wherever I wanted."

"Ah, thank God!" said Mrs. Ashby. There was a silence, during which she continued to sit with bowed head, and eyes averted from her daughter-in-law. At last she looked up and spoke. "Are you sure there have been as many as nine?"

"Perfectly. This is the ninth. I've kept count."

"And he has absolutely refused to explain?"

"Absolutely."

Mrs. Ashby spoke through pale contracted lips. "When did they begin to come? Do you remember?"

Charlotte laughed again. "Remember? The first one came the night we got back from our honeymoon."

"All that time?" Mrs. Ashby lifted her head and spoke with sudden energy. "Then — yes, open it."

The words were so unexpected that Charlotte felt the blood in her temples, and her hands began to tremble again. She tried to slip her finger under the flap of the envelope, but it was so tightly stuck that she had to hunt on her husband's writing table for his ivory letter opener. As she pushed about the familiar objects his own hands had so lately touched, they sent through her the icy chill emanating from the little personal effects of someone newly dead. In the deep silence of the room the tearing of the paper as she slit the envelope sounded like a human cry. She drew out the sheet and carried it to the lamp.

"Well?" Mrs. Ashby asked below her breath.

Charlotte did not move or answer. She was bending over the page with wrinkled brows, holding it nearer and nearer to the light. Her sight must be blurred, or else dazzled by the reflection of the lamplight on the smooth surface of the paper, for, strain her eyes as she would, she could discern only a few faint strokes, so faint and faltering as to be nearly undecipherable.

"I can't make it out," she said.

"What do you mean, dear?"

"The writing's too indistinct. . . Wait."

She went back to the table and, sitting down close to Kenneth's reading lamp, slipped the letter under a magnifying glass. All this time she was aware that her mother-in-law was watching her intently.

"Well?" Mrs. Ashby breathed.

"Well, it's no clearer. I can't read it."

"You mean the paper is an absolute blank?"

"No, not quite. There is writing on it. I can make out something like 'mine' — oh, and 'come'. It might be 'come'."

Mrs. Ashby stood up abruptly. Her face was even paler than before. She advanced to the table and, resting her two hands on it, drew a deep breath. "Let me see," she said, as if forcing herself to a hateful effort.

Charlotte felt the contagion of her whiteness. "She knows," she thought. She pushed the letter across the table. Her mother-in-law lowered her head over it in silence, but without touching it with her pale wrinkled hands.

Charlotte stood watching her as she herself, when she had tried to read the letter, had been watched by Mrs. Ashby. The latter fumbled for her glasses, held them to her eyes, and bent still closer to the outspread page, in order, as it seemed, to avoid touching it. The light of the lamp fell directly on her old face, and

Charlotte reflected what depths of the unknown may lurk under the clearest and most candid lineaments. She had never seen her mother-in-law's features express any but simple and sound emotions — cordiality, amusement, a kindly sympathy; now and again a flash of wholesome anger. Now they seemed to wear a look of fear and hatred, of incredulous dismay and almost cringing defiance. It was as if the spirits warring within her had distorted her face to their own likeness. At length she raised her head. "I can't — I can't," she said in a voice of childish distress.

"You can't make it out either?"

She shook her head, and Charlotte saw two tears roll down her cheeks.

"Familiar as the writing is to you?" Charlotte insisted with twitching lips.

Mrs. Ashby did not take up the challenge. "I can make out nothing — nothing."

"But you do know the writing?"

Mrs. Ashby lifted her head timidly; her anxious eyes stole with a glance of apprehension around the quiet familiar room. "How can I tell? I was startled at first..."

"Startled by the resemblance?"

"Well, I thought — "

"You'd better say it out, mother! You knew at once it was her writing?"

"Oh, wait, my dear — wait."

"Wait for what?"

Mrs. Ashby looked up; her eyes, traveling slowly past Charlotte, were lifted to the blank wall behind her son's writing table.

Charlotte, following the glance, burst into a shrill laugh of accusation. "I needn't wait any longer! You've answered me now! You're looking straight at the wall where her picture used to hang."

Mrs. Ashby lifted her hand with a murmur of warning. "Sh-h."

"Oh, you needn't imagine that anything can ever frighten me again!" Charlotte cried.

Her mother-in-law still leaned against the table. Her lips moved plaintively. "But we're going mad — we're both going mad. We both know such things are impossible."

Her daughter-in-law looked at her with a pitying stare. "I've known for a long time now that everything was possible."

"Even this?"

"Yes, exactly this."

"But this letter — after all, there's nothing in this letter — "

"Perhaps there would be to him. How can I tell? I remember his saying to me once that if you were used to a handwriting the faintest stroke of it became legible. Now I see what he meant. He *was* used to it."

"But the few strokes that I can make out are so pale. No one could possibly read that letter."

Charlotte laughed again. "I suppose everything's pale about a ghost," she said stridently.

"Oh, my child — my child — don't say it!"

"Why shouldn't I say it, when even the bare walls cry it out? What difference does it make if her letters are illegible to you and me? If even you can see her face on that blank wall, why shouldn't he read her writing on this blank paper? Don't you see that she's everywhere in this house, and the closer to him because to everyone else she's become invisible?" Charlotte dropped into a chair and covered her face with her hands. A turmoil of sobbing shook her from head to foot. At length a touch on her shoulder made her look up, and she saw her mother-in-law bending over her. Mrs. Ashby's face seemed to have grown still smaller and more wasted, but it had resumed its usual quiet look. Through all her tossing anguish, Charlotte felt the impact of that resolute spirit.

"Tomorrow — tomorrow. You'll see. There'll be some explanation tomorrow."

Charlotte cut her short. "An explanation? Who's going to give it, I wonder?"

Mrs. Ashby drew back and straightened herself heroically. "Kenneth himself will," she cried out in a strong voice. Charlotte said nothing, and the old woman went on: "But meanwhile we must act; we must notify the police. Now, without a moment's delay. We must do everything — everything."

Charlotte stood up slowly and stiffly; her joints felt as cramped as an old woman's. "Exactly as if we thought it could do any good to do anything?"

Resolutely Mrs. Ashby cried: "Yes!" and Charlotte went up to the telephone and unhooked the receiver.

ELIZABETH BOWEN

The Demon Lover

Readers and critics of "The Demon Lover" (1941) have debated the exact nature of the presence that stalks Mrs. Kathleen Drover as she visits her bomb-damaged house in World War II London. Is this a story of the dead returning to haunt the living, or is the sinister lost fiancé (missing in action and presumed dead since the previous war) alive but dangerously deranged? — or has Mrs. Drover herself fallen prey to hysteria and delusion? As with most masterpieces of the uncanny, to characterize this story as either a supernatural tale, a suspense thriller, or a narrative of encroaching madness is to impoverish it. It is, in fact, all three.

"The Demon Lover" is the title story in the collection of short fiction which Elizabeth Bowen composed during the second World War, and which explores the singular emotional effects of the war upon London's besieged inhabitants. As the author observed in her preface to the American edition (Ivy Gripped the Steps), *these stories form "a rising tide of hallucination," expressive of a cruelly disorienting time in which "we all lived in a state of lucid abnormality."*[10] *For Bowen's protagonist, as for millions of Londoners during the blitz, home — ordinarily the place of greatest security — has become unsafe. In the still air of her once bustling house, the line between life and death grows tenuous. The years of marriage and family life that had sheltered Kathleen from her girlhood trauma in a time of chaos and destruction are now powerless to protect her.*

The Demon Lover

The story's title recalls the Scottish ballad about a woman whose former lover returns from the spirit world to lure her away from her husband and children. The demon lover's "passion" is dark, obsessive, and primal, wholly foreign to the structure of civil and domestic life. It is with this force of violence and disorder that Mrs. Drover will have to struggle, as around her the curtain of nightmare begins to fall. 〰〰

TOWARDS THE END of her day in London Mrs. Drover went round to her shut-up house to look for several things she wanted to take away. Some belonged to herself, some to her family, who were by now used to their country life. It was late August; it had been a steamy, showery day: at the moment the trees down the pavement glittered in an escape of humid yellow afternoon sun. Against the next batch of clouds, already piling up ink-dark, broken chimneys and parapets stood out. In her once familiar street, as in any unused channel, an unfamiliar queerness had silted up; a cat wove itself in and out of railings, but no human eye watched Mrs. Drover's return. Shifting some parcels under her arm, she slowly forced round her latchkey in an unwilling lock, then gave the door, which had warped, a push with her knee. Dead air came out to meet her as she went in.

The staircase window having been boarded up, no light came down into the hall. But one door, she could just see, stood ajar, so she went quickly through into the room and unshuttered the big window in there. Now the prosaic woman, looking about her, was more perplexed than she knew by everything that she saw, by traces of her long former habit of life — the yellow smoke-stain up the white marble mantelpiece; the ring left by a vase on the top of the escritoire; the bruise in the wallpaper where, on the door being thrown open widely, the china handle had always hit the wall. The piano, having gone away to be stored, had left what looked like claw-marks on its part of the parquet. Though not much dust had seeped in, each object wore a film of another kind; and, the only ventilation being the chimney, the whole

83

drawing-room smelled of the cold hearth. Mrs. Drover put down her parcels on the escritoire and left the room to proceed upstairs; the things she wanted were in a bedroom chest.

She had been anxious to see how the house was — the part-time caretaker she shared with some neighbours was away this week on his holiday, known to be not yet back. At the best of times he did not look in often, and she was never sure that she trusted him. There were some cracks in the structure, left by the last bombing, on which she was anxious to keep an eye. Not that one could do anything —

A shaft of refracted daylight now lay across the hall. She stopped dead and stared at the hall table — on this lay a letter addressed to her.

She thought first — then the caretaker *must* be back. All the same, who, seeing the house shuttered, would have dropped a letter in at the box? It was not a circular, it was not a bill. And the post office redirected, to the address in the country, every-thing for her that came through the post. The caretaker (even if he *were* back) did not know she was due in London today — her call here had been planned to be a surprise — so his negligence in the manner of this letter, leaving it to wait in the dusk and the dust, annoyed her. Annoyed, she picked up the letter, which bore no stamp. But it cannot be important, or they would know . . . She took the letter rapidly upstairs with her, without a stop to look at the writing till she reached what had been her bedroom, where she let in light. The room looked over the garden and other gardens: the sun had gone in; as the clouds sharpened and lowered, the trees and rank lawns seemed already to smoke with dark. Her reluctance to look again at the letter came from the fact that she felt intruded upon — and by someone contemptu-ous of her ways. However, in the tenseness preceding the fall of rain she read it: it was a few lines.

Dear Kathleen: You will not have forgotten that today is our anniversary, and the day we said. The years have gone

The Demon Lover

by at once slowly and fast. In view of the fact that nothing
has changed, I shall rely upon you to keep your promise. I
was sorry to see you leave London, but was satisfied that
you would be back in time. You may expect me, therefore,
at the hour arranged. Until then . . .   K.

Mrs. Drover looked for the date: it was today's. She dropped the
letter on to the bed-springs, then picked it up to see the writing
again — her lips, beneath the remains of lipstick, beginning to go
white. She felt so much the change in her own face that she went
to the mirror, polished a clear patch in it and looked at once
urgently and stealthily in. She was confronted by a woman of
forty-four, with eyes starting out under a hat-brim that had been
rather carelessly pulled down. She had not put on any more powder since she left the shop where she ate her solitary tea. The
pearls her husband had given her on their marriage hung loose
round her now rather thinner throat, slipping in the V of the pink
wool jumper her sister knitted last autumn as they sat round the
fire. Mrs. Drover's most normal expression was one of controlled
worry, but of assent. Since the birth of the third of her little boys,
attended by a quite serious illness, she had had an intermittent
muscular flicker to the left of her mouth, but in spite of this she
could always sustain a manner that was at once energetic and
calm.

Turning from her own face as precipitately as she had gone to
meet it, she went to the chest where the things were, unlocked it,
threw up the lid and knelt to search. But as rain began to come
crashing down she could not keep from looking over her shoulder
at the stripped bed on which the letter lay. Behind the blanket of
rain the clock of the church that still stood struck six — with rapidly heightening apprehension she counted each of the slow
strokes. "The hour arranged . . . My God," she said, "*what* hour?
How should I . . . ? After twenty-five years . . ."

★ ★ ★

85

The young girl talking to the soldier in the garden had not ever completely seen his face. It was dark; they were saying goodbye under a tree. Now and then — for it felt, from not seeing him at this intense moment, as though she had never seen him at all — she verified his presence for these few moments longer by putting out a hand, which he each time pressed, without very much kindness, and painfully, on to one of the breast buttons of his uniform. That cut of the button on the palm of her hand was, principally, what she was to carry away. This was so near the end of a leave from France that she could only wish him already gone. It was August 1916. Being not kissed, being drawn away from and looked at intimidated Kathleen till she imagined spectral glitters in the place of his eyes. Turning away and looking back up the lawn she saw, through branches of trees, the drawing-room window alight: she caught a breath for the moment when she could go running back there into the safe arms of her mother and sister, and cry: "What shall I do, what shall I do? He has gone."

Hearing her catch her breath, her fiancé said, without feeling: "Cold?"

"You're going away such a long way."

"Not so far as you think."

"I don't understand?"

"You don't have to," he said. "You will. You know what we said."

"But that was — suppose you — I mean, suppose."

"I shall be with you," he said, "sooner or later. You won't forget that. You need do nothing but wait."

Only a little more than a minute later she was free to run up the silent lawn. Looking in through the window at her mother and sister, who did not for the moment perceive her, she already felt that unnatural promise drive down between her and the rest of all human kind. No other way of having given herself could have made her feel so apart, lost and foresworn. She could not have plighted a more sinister troth.

Kathleen behaved well when, some months later, her fiancé

was reported missing, presumed killed. Her family not only supported her but were able to praise her courage without stint because they could not regret, as a husband for her, the man they knew almost nothing about. They hoped she would, in a year or two, console herself — and had it been only a question of consolation things might have gone much straighter ahead. But her trouble, behind just a little grief, was a complete dislocation from everything. She did not reject other lovers, for these failed to appear: for years she failed to attract men — and with the approach of her 'thirties she became natural enough to share her family's anxiousness on this score. She began to put herself out, to wonder; and at thirty-two she was very greatly relieved to find herself being courted by William Drover. She married him, and the two of them settled down in this quiet, arboreal part of Kensington: in this house the years piled up, her children were born and they all lived till they were driven out by the bombs of the next war. Her movements as Mrs. Drover were circumscribed, and she dismissed any idea that they were still watched.

As things were — dead or living the letter-writer sent her only a threat. Unable, for some minutes, to go on kneeling with her back exposed to the empty room, Mrs. Drover rose from the chest to sit on an upright chair whose back was firmly against the wall. The desuetude of her former bedroom, her married London home's whole air of being a cracked cup from which memory, with its reassuring power, had either evaporated or leaked away, made a crisis — and at just this crisis the letter-writer had, knowledgeably, struck. The hollowness of the house this evening cancelled years on years of voices, habits and steps. Through the shut windows she only heard rain fall on the roofs around. To rally herself, she said she was in a mood — and for two or three seconds shutting her eyes, told herself that she had imagined the letter. But she opened them — there it lay on the bed.

On the supernatural side of the letter's entrance she was not permitting her mind to dwell. Who, in London, knew she meant to call at the house today? Evidently, however, this had been

87

known. The caretaker, *had* he come back, had had no cause to expect her: he would have taken the letter in his pocket, to forward it, at his own time, through the post. There was no other sign that the caretaker had been in — but, if not? Letters dropped in at doors of deserted houses do not fly or walk to tables in halls. They do not sit on the dust of empty tables with the air of certainty that they will be found. There is needed some human hand — but nobody but the caretaker had a key. Under circumstances she did not care to consider, a house can be entered without a key. It was possible that she was not alone now. She might be being waited for, downstairs. Waited for — until when? Until "the hour arranged." At least that was not six o'clock: six has struck.

She rose from the chair and went over and locked the door.

The thing was, to get out. To fly? No, not that: she had to catch her train. As a woman whose utter dependability was the keystone of her family life, she was not willing to return to the country, to her husband, her little boys and her sister, without the objects she had come up to fetch. Resuming work at the chest she set about making up a number of parcels in a rapid, fumbling-decisive way. These, with her shopping parcels, would be too much to carry; these meant a taxi — at the thought of the taxi her heart went up and her normal breathing resumed. I will ring up the taxi now; the taxi cannot come too soon: I shall hear the taxi out there running its engine, till I walk calmly down to it through the hall. I'll ring up — But no: the telephone is cut off . . . She tugged at a knot she had tied wrong.

The idea of flight . . . He was never kind to me, not really. I don't remember him kind at all. Mother said he never considered me. He was set on me, that was what it was — not love. Not love, not meaning a person well. What did he do, to make me promise like that? I can't remember — But she found that she could.

She remembered with such dreadful acuteness that the twenty-five years since then dissolved like smoke and she instinctively looked for the weal left by the button on the palm of her hand.

She remembered not only all that he said and did but the complete suspension of *her* existence during that August week. I was not myself — they all told me so at the time. She remembered — but with one white burning blank as where acid has dropped on a photograph: *under no conditions* could she remember his face.

So, wherever he may be waiting, I shall not know him. You have no time to run from a face you do not expect.

The thing was to get to the taxi before any clock struck what could be the hour. She would slip down the street and round the side of the square to where the square gave on the main road. She would return in the taxi, safe, to her own door, and bring the solid driver into the house with her to pick up the parcels from room to room. The idea of the taxi driver made her decisive, bold: she unlocked her door, went to the top of the staircase and listened down.

She heard nothing — but while she was hearing nothing the *passé* air of the staircase was disturbed by a draught that travelled up to her face. It emanated from the basement: down there a door or window was being opened by someone who chose this moment to leave the house.

The rain had stopped; the pavements steamily shone as Mrs. Drover let herself out by inches from her own front door into the empty street. The unoccupied houses opposite continued to meet her look with their damaged stare. Making towards the thoroughfare and the taxi, she tried not to keep looking behind. Indeed, the silence was so intense — one of those creeks of London silence exaggerated this summer by the damage of war — that no tread could have gained on hers unheard. Where her street debouched on the square where people went on living, she grew conscious of, and checked, her unnatural pace. Across the open end of the square two buses impassively passed each other: women, a perambulator, cyclists, a man wheeling a barrow signalized, once again, the ordinary flow of life. At the square's most populous corner should be — and was — the short taxi rank. This evening, only one taxi — but this, although it presented its blank rump, appeared already to be alertly waiting for her. Indeed, without looking round the driver started his engine as she panted up from behind and put her hand on the door. As she did so, the clock struck seven. The taxi faced the main road: to make the trip back to her house it would have to turn — she had settled back on the seat and the taxi *had* turned before she, surprised by its knowing movement, recollected that she had not "said where." She leaned forward to scratch at the glass panel that divided the driver's head from her own.

The driver braked to what was almost a stop, turned round and slid the glass panel back: the jolt of this flung Mrs. Drover forward till her face was almost into the glass. Through the aperture driver and passenger, not six inches between them, remained for an eternity eye to eye. Mrs. Drover's mouth hung open for some seconds before she could issue her first scream. After that she continued to scream freely and to beat with her gloved hands on the glass all round as the taxi, accelerating without mercy, made off with her into the hinterland of deserted streets.

JOHN COLLIER

Midnight Blue

Most of John Collier's best stories were written after he moved from England to the United States in the mid-thirties to become a scriptwriter. His work in Hollywood contributed to the economy and dramatic pacing of his fiction, and to his use of dialogue as a propeller of the action. The stories collected in Fancies and Goodnights combine elements of the darkly macabre with the writer's characteristic lightness and wit.

"Midnight Blue" (1943) is a short, gripping tale that has the structure of a thriller. Like much of Collier's fiction, it zeroes in on the violence and horror hidden beneath the surface of mundane, bourgeois existence. It has been said that in Collier's imaginative world, evil appears "with the unexpectedness of a traffic accident."[11] The story's opening is deceptively matter-of-fact: a prosperous accountant returns late one night to his sleeping family after a long day at the office. The plot veers quickly, however, toward the sinister, and we are soon inclined to read a darker meaning into many of the details initially related by the narrator. The conversation at the family breakfast table is a tour de force: Collier's deft touches of humor only heighten the effect of the horrible thought that is ripening, with each sentence, in the reader's incredulous brain. ✎❀

91

Mr. Spiers came in extremely late. He shut the door very quietly, switched on the electric light, and stood for quite a long time on the door-mat.

Mr. Spiers was a prosperous accountant with a long, lean face, naturally pale; a cold eye, and a close mouth. Just behind his jaw-bones a tiny movement was perceptible, like the movement of gills in a fish.

He now took off his bowler hat, looked at it inside and out, and hung it upon the usual peg. He pulled off his muffler, which was a dark one, dotted with polka dots of a seemly size, and he scrutinized this muffler very carefully and hung it on another peg. His overcoat, examined even more scrupulously, was next hung up, and Mr. Spiers went quickly upstairs.

In the bathroom he spent a very long time at the mirror. He turned his face this way and that, tilted it sideways to expose his jaw and neck. He noted the set of his collar, saw that his tiepin was straight, looked at his cuff links, his buttons, and finally proceeded to undress. Again he examined each garment very closely; it was as well Mrs. Spiers did not see him at this moment, or she might have thought he was looking for a long hair, or traces of powder. However, Mrs. Spiers had been asleep for a couple of hours. After her husband had examined every stitch of his clothing, he crept to his dressing room for a clothes-brush, which he used even upon his shoes. Finally he looked at his hands and his nails, and scrubbed them both very thoroughly.

He then sat down on the edge of the bath, put his elbows on his knees and his chin on his hands, and gave himself up to a very profound train of thought. Now and then he marked the checking-off of some point or other by lifting a finger and bringing it back again onto his cheek, or even onto the spot behind his jawbone where there was that little movement, so like the movement of the gills of a fish.

At last Mr. Spiers seemed satisfied, and he turned out the light and repaired to the conjugal bedroom, which was decorated in cream, rose, and old gold.

In the morning, Mr. Spiers arose at his usual hour and descended, with his usual expression, to the breakfast room.

His wife, who was his opposite in all respects, as some say a wife should be, was already busy behind the coffee service. She was as plump, as blonde, as good-humored, and as scatterbrained as any woman should be at a breakfast table, perhaps even more so. The two younger children were there; the two older ones were late.

"So here you are!" said Mrs. Spiers to her husband, in a sprightly tone. "You were late home last night."

"About one," said he, taking up the newspaper.

"It must have been later than that," said she. "I heard one o'clock strike."

"It might have been half past," said he.

"Did Mr. Benskin give you a lift?"

"No."

"All right, my dear, I only asked."

"Give me my coffee," said he.

"A dinner's all right," said she. "A man ought to have an evening with his friends. But you ought to get your rest, Harry. Not that I had much rest last night. Oh, I had such a terrible dream! I dreamed that — "

"If there's one thing," said her husband, "that I hate more than a slop in my saucer — Do you see this mess?"

"Really, dear," said she, "you asked so brusquely for your coffee — "

"Father spilled the coffee," piped up little Patrick. "His hand jerked — like that."

Mr. Spiers turned his eye upon his younger son, and his younger son was silent.

"I was saying," said Mr. Spiers, "that if I detest anything more than a filthy mess in my saucer, it is the sort of fool who blathers out a dream at the breakfast table."

"Oh, my dream!" said Mrs. Spiers with the utmost good humor. "All right, my dear, if you don't want to hear it. It was about you, that's all." With that, she resumed her breakfast.

"Either tell your dream, or don't tell it," said Mr. Spiers.

"You said you didn't want to hear it," replied Mrs. Spiers, not unreasonably.

"There is no more disgusting or offensive sort of idiot," said Mr. Spiers, "than the woman who hatches up a mystery, and then — "

"There is no mystery," said Mrs. Spiers. "You said you didn't want — "

"Will you," said Mr. Spiers, "kindly put an end to this, and tell me, very briefly, whatever nonsense it was that you dreamed, and let us have done with it? Imagine you are dictating a telegram."

"Mr. T. Spiers, Normandene, Radclyffe Avenue, Wrexton Garden Suburb," said his wife. "I dreamed that you were hung."

"*Hanged*, Mother," said little Daphne.

"Hullo, Mums," said her big sister, entering at that moment. "Hullo, Dads. Sorry I'm late. Good morning, children. What's the matter, Daddy? You look as if you'd heard from the Income Tax."

"Because of a murder," continued Mrs. Spiers, "in the middle of the night. It was so vivid, my dear! I was quite glad when you said you were back by half-past one."

"Half-past one, nothing," said the elder daughter.

"Mildred," said her mother, "that's film talk."

"Daddy's an old rip," said Mildred, tapping her egg. "Freddy and I got back from the dance at half-past two, and his hat and coat wasn't there then."

"*Weren't* there," said little Daphne.

"If that child corrects her elder sister, or you, in front of my face once again — " said Mr. Spiers.

"Be quiet, Daphne," said her mother. "Well, that was it, my dear. I dreamed you committed a murder, and you were hanged."

"Daddy hanged?" cried Mildred in the highest glee. "Oh, Mummy, who did he murder? Tell us all the grisly details."

"Well, it really was grisly," said her mother. "I woke up feeling quite depressed. It was poor Mr. Benskin."

"What?" said her husband.

"Yes, you murdered poor Mr. Benskin," said Mrs. Spiers. "Though why you should murder your own partner, I don't know."

"Because he insisted on looking at the books," said Mildred. "They always do, and get murdered. I knew it would be one or the other for Daddy — murdered or hung."

"*Hanged*," said little Daphne. "And *whom* did he murder."

"*Be quiet!*" said her father. "These children will drive me mad."

"Well, my dear," said his wife, "there you were, with Mr. Benskin, late at night, and he was running you home in his car, and you were chatting about business — you know how people can dream the most difficult talk, about things they don't know anything about, and it sounds all right, and of course it's all nonsense. It's the same with jokes. You dream you made the best joke you ever heard, and when you wake up — "

"Go on," said Mr. Spiers firmly.

"Well, my dear, you were chatting, and you drove right into his garage, and it was so narrow that the doors of the car would only open on one side, and so you got out first, and you said to him, "Wait a minute," and you tilted up the front seat of that little Chevrolet of his, and you got in at the back where your coats and hats were. Did I say you were driving along without your overcoats on, because it was one of these mild nights we're having?"

"Go on," said Mr. Spiers.

"Well, there were your coats and hats on the back seat, and Mr. Benskin still sat at the wheel, and there was that dark overcoat he always wears, and your light cheviot you wore yesterday, and your silk mufflers, and your hats and everything, and you picked up one of the mufflers — they both had white polka dots on them — I think he was wearing one like yours last time he came to lunch on Sunday. Only his was dark blue. Well, you picked up the muffler, and you were talking to him, and you tied a knot in it, and all of a sudden you put it round his neck and strangled him."

"Because he'd asked to look at the books," said Mildred.

"Really it's — it's too much," said Mr. Spiers.

"It was nearly too much for me," said his spouse. "I was so upset, in my dream. You got a piece of rope, and tied it to the end of the scarf, and then to the bar across the top of the garage, so it looked as if he'd hanged himself."

"Good heavens!" said Mr. Spiers.

"It was so vivid, I can't tell you," said his wife. "And then it all got mixed up, as dreams do, and I kept on seeing you with that muffler on, and it kept on twisting about your neck. And then you were being tried, and they brought in — the muffler. Only, seeing it by daylight, it was Mr. Benskin's, because it was dark blue. Only by the artificial light it looked black."

Mr. Spiers crumbled his bread. "Very extraordinary," he said.

"It's silly, of course," said his wife. "Only you *would* have me tell you."

"I wonder if it *is* so silly," said her husband. "As a matter of fact, I *did* ride home with Benskin last night. We had a very serious talk. Not to go into details, it happened I'd hit on something very odd at the office. Well, I had it out with him. We sat talking a long time. Maybe it *was* later than I thought when I got home. When I left him, do you know, I had the most horrible premonition. I thought, "That fellow's going to make away with himself." That's what I thought. I very nearly turned back. I felt like a — well, I felt responsible. It's a serious business. I spoke to him very forcefully."

"You don't say Mr. Benskin's a fraud?" cried Mrs. Spiers. "We're not ruined, Harry?"

"Not ruined," said her husband. "But there's been some pretty deep dipping."

"Are you sure it's him?" said Mrs. Spiers. "He — he seems so honest."

"Him or me," said her husband. "And it wasn't me."

"But you don't think he's — he's hanged himself," said Mrs. Spiers.

"Heaven forbid!" said her husband. "But considering that feeling I had — well, perhaps the dream came just from the feeling."

"It's true Rose Waterhouse dreamed of water when her brother was away sailing," said Mrs. Spiers, "but he wasn't drowned."

"There are thousands of such cases," said her husband. "They're generally wrong on all the details."

"I hope so, indeed!" cried Mrs. Spiers.

"For example," said her husband, "it happens we both kept our coats on, and our mufflers too, all the time last night. The atmosphere was hardly intimate."

"I should say not," said Mrs. Spiers. "Who would have thought it of Mr. Benskin?"

"His wife, poor woman, would not have thought it," said Mr. Spiers gravely. "I have resolved to spare her. So, Mildred, children, whatever has happened or has not happened, not a word, not one word, is to be said about this to anyone. Do you hear? To anyone! You know nothing. A single word might lead to disgrace for the whole wretched family."

"You are quite right, my dear," said his wife. "I will see to the children."

"Morning, Mum," cried Fred, bursting into the room. "Morning, Guv'nor. No time for breakfast. I'll just get the train by the skin of my teeth, if I'm lucky. Whose muffler's this, by the way? It's not yours, is it, Dad? This is dark blue. Can I bag it? Why — what's the matter? What on earth's the matter?"

"Come in, Fred," said Mrs. Spiers. "Come in here and shut the door. Don't worry about your train."

Miriam

The writer who would win international fame in the nineteen-sixties with In Cold Blood first captured the attention of the literary public at the age of twenty, with the publication in Mademoiselle of his short story, "Miriam" (1945). Capote grew up in the deep South, and his early stories are often characterized as "southern gothic." "Miriam" displays some of the typical features of this mode of fiction: a lonely, alienated main character, controlled by obsessions and fears, an inter-weaving of reality and dream-like fantasy, and a blending of psycholog-ical suspense with the eerie and the macabre.

Like Elizabeth Bowen's heroine in the earlier story, Capote's pro-tagonist finds herself pursued, closed in upon, by one who has violated the security of her home. Yet here the haunter is not a predatory male, but rather a precocious and willful little girl with large, hazel eyes. Mrs. Miller's feeling of exhilaration upon first meeting Miriam is trans-formed, as the story progresses, into anxiety, apprehension, alarm, and finally terror.

Some critics have interpreted this story as a study of emerging schizo-phrenia. Such a crudely clinical reading takes little account of the mys-tery and dark poetry of the tale. Yet it is true that one of the story's underlying themes is that of the divided psyche; there is a sense in which Mrs. Miller is frightened by the imperatives of her own long-suppressed *self, from which it has become increasingly impossible to hide. She has no one, moreover, to understand or support her in her crisis; faced with the uncanny Other who threatens her in a way she can scarcely articulate even to herself, she is profoundly, utterly, alone.* ⌐⌐⌐⌐⌐

FOR SEVERAL YEARS, Mrs. H. T. Miller had lived alone in a pleasant apartment (two rooms with kitchenette) in a remodeled brownstone near the East River. She was a widow: Mr. H. T. Miller had left a reasonable amount of insurance. Her interests were narrow, she had no friends to speak of, and she rarely journeyed farther than the corner grocery. The other people in the house never seemed to notice her: her clothes were matter-of-fact, her hair iron-gray, clipped and casually waved; she did not use cosmetics, her features were plain and inconspicuous, and on her last birthday she was sixty-one. Her activities were seldom spontaneous: she kept the two rooms immaculate, smoked an occasional cigarette, prepared her own meals and tended a canary.

Then she met Miriam. It was snowing that night. Mrs. Miller had finished drying the supper dishes and was thumbing through an afternoon paper when she saw an advertisement of a picture playing at a neighborhood theater. The title sounded good, so she struggled into her beaver coat, laced her galoshes and left the apartment, leaving one light burning in the foyer: she found nothing more disturbing than a sensation of darkness.

The snow was fine, falling gently, not yet making an impression on the pavement. The wind from the river cut only at street crossings. Mrs. Miller hurried, her head bowed, oblivious as a mole burrowing a blind path. She stopped at a drugstore and bought a package of peppermints.

A long line stretched in front of the box office; she took her place at the end. There would be (a tired voice groaned) a short wait for all seats. Mrs. Miller rummaged in her leather handbag till she collected exactly the correct change for admission. The line seemed to be taking its own time and, looking around for some distraction, she suddenly became conscious of a little girl standing under the edge of the marquee.

Her hair was the longest and strangest Mrs. Miller had ever seen: absolutely silver-white, like an albino's. It flowed waist-length in smooth, loose lines. She was thin and fragilely constructed. There was a simple, special elegance in the way she stood with her thumbs in the pockets of a tailored plum-velvet coat.

Mrs. Miller felt oddly excited, and when the little girl glanced toward her, she smiled warmly. The little girl walked over and said, "Would you care to do me a favor?"

"I'd be glad to, if I can," said Mrs. Miller.

"Oh, it's quite easy. I merely want you to buy a ticket for me; they won't let me in otherwise. Here, I have the money." And gracefully she handed Mrs. Miller two dimes and a nickel.

They went into the theater together. An usherette directed them to a lounge; in twenty minutes the picture would be over.

"I feel just like a genuine criminal," said Mrs. Miller gaily, as she sat down. "I mean that sort of thing's against the law, isn't it? I do hope I haven't done the wrong thing. Your mother knows where you are, dear? I mean she does, doesn't she?"

The little girl said nothing. She unbuttoned her coat and folded it across her lap. Her dress underneath was prim and dark blue. A gold chain dangled about her neck, and her fingers, sensitive and musical-looking, toyed with it. Examining her more attentively, Mrs. Miller decided the truly distinctive feature was not her hair, but her eyes; they were hazel, steady, lacking any childlike quality whatsoever and, because of their size, seemed to consume her small face.

Mrs. Miller offered a peppermint. "What's your name, dear?"

"Miriam," she said, as though, in some curious way, it were information already familiar.

"Why, isn't that funny — my name's Miriam, too. And it's not a terribly common name either. Now, don't tell me your last name's Miller!"

"Just Miriam."

"But isn't that funny?"

"Moderately," said Miriam, and rolled the peppermint on her tongue.

Mrs. Miller flushed and shifted uncomfortably. "You have such a large vocabulary for such a little girl."

"Do I?"

"Well, yes," said Mrs. Miller, hastily changing the topic to: "Do you like the movies?"

"I really wouldn't know," said Miriam. "I've never been before."

Women began filling the lounge; the rumble of the newsreel bombs exploded in the distance. Mrs. Miller rose, tucking her purse under her arm. "I guess I'd better be running now if I want to get a seat," she said. "It was nice to have met you."

Miriam nodded ever so slightly.

It snowed all week. Wheels and footsteps moved soundlessly on the street, as if the business of living continued secretly behind a pale but impenetrable curtain. In the falling quiet there was no sky or earth, only snow lifting in the wind, frosting the window glass, chilling the rooms, deadening and hushing the city. At all hours it was necessary to keep a lamp lighted, and Mrs. Miller lost track of the days: Friday was no different from Saturday and on Sunday she went to the grocery: closed, of course.

That evening she scrambled eggs and fixed a bowl of tomato soup. Then, after putting on a flannel robe and cold-creaming her face, she propped herself up in bed with a hot-water bottle under her feet. She was reading the *Times* when the doorbell rang. At first she thought it must be a mistake and whoever it was would go away. But it rang and rang and settled to a persistent buzz. She looked at the clock: a little after eleven; it did not seem possible, she was always asleep by ten.

Climbing out of bed, she trotted barefoot across the living room. "I'm coming, please be patient." The latch was caught; she turned it this way and that way and the bell never paused an instant. "Stop it," she cried. The bolt gave way and she opened the door an inch. "What in heaven's name?"

"Hello," said Miriam.

"Oh . . . why, hello," said Mrs. Miller, stepping hesitantly into the hall. "You're that little girl."

"I thought you'd never answer, but I kept my finger on the button; I knew you were home. Aren't you glad to see me?"

Mrs. Miller did not know what to say. Miriam, she saw, wore the same plum-velvet coat and now she had also a beret to match; her white hair was braided in two shining plaits and looped at the ends with enormous white ribbons.

"Since I've waited so long, you could at least let me in," she said.

"It's awfully late. . . ."

Miriam regarded her blankly. "What difference does that make? Let me in. It's cold out here and I have on a silk dress." Then, with a gentle gesture, she urged Mrs. Miller aside and passed into the apartment.

She dropped her coat and beret on a chair. She was indeed wearing a silk dress. White silk. White silk in February. The skirt was beautifully pleated and the sleeves long; it made a faint rustle as she strolled about the room. "I like your place," she said. "I like the rug, blue's my favorite color." She touched a paper rose in a vase on the coffee table. "Imitation," she commented wanly. "How sad. Aren't imitations sad?" She seated herself on the sofa, daintily spreading her skirt.

"What do you want?" asked Mrs. Miller.

"Sit down," said Miriam. "It makes me nervous to see people stand."

Mrs. Miller sank to a hassock. "What do you want?" she repeated.

"You know, I don't think you're glad I came."

For a second time Mrs. Miller was without an answer; her hand motioned vaguely. Miriam giggled and pressed back on a mound of chintz pillows. Mrs. Miller observed that the girl was less pale than she remembered; her cheeks were flushed.

"How did you know where I lived?"

Miriam frowned. "That's no question at all. What's your name? What's mine?"

"But I'm not listed in the phone book."

"Oh, let's talk about something else."

Mrs. Miller said, "Your mother must be insane to let a child like you wander around at all hours of the night — and in such ridiculous clothes. She must be out of her mind."

Miriam got up and moved to a corner where a covered bird cage hung from a ceiling chain. She peeked beneath the cover. "It's a canary," she said. "Would you mind if I woke him? I'd like to hear him sing."

"Leave Tommy alone," said Mrs. Miller, anxiously. "Don't you dare wake him."

"Certainly," said Miriam. "But I don't see why I can't hear him sing." And then, "Have you anything to eat? I'm starving! Even milk and a jam sandwich would be fine."

"Look," said Mrs. Miller, arising from the hassock, "look — if I make some nice sandwiches will you be a good child and run along home? It's past midnight, I'm sure."

"It's snowing," reproached Miriam. "And cold and dark."

"Well, you shouldn't have come here to begin with," said Mrs. Miller, struggling to control her voice. "I can't help the weather. If you want anything to eat you'll have to promise to leave."

Miriam brushed a braid against her cheek. Her eyes were thoughtful, as if weighing the proposition. She turned toward the bird cage. "Very well," she said, "I promise."

How old is she? Ten? Eleven? Mrs. Miller, in the kitchen, unsealed a jar of strawberry preserves and cut four slices of bread. She poured a glass of milk and paused to light a cigarette. *And why has she come?* Her hand shook as she held the match, fascinated, till it burned her finger. The canary was singing; singing as he did in the morning and at no other time. "Miriam," she called, "Miriam, I told you not to disturb Tommy." There was no answer. She called again; all she heard was the canary. She inhaled the cigarette and discovered she had lighted the cork-tip end and — oh, really, she mustn't lose her temper.

She carried the food in on a tray and set it on the coffee table. She saw first that the bird cage still wore its night cover. And Tommy was singing. It gave her a queer sensation. And no one was in the room. Mrs. Miller went through an alcove leading to her bedroom; at the door she caught her breath.

"What are you doing?" she asked.

Miriam glanced up and in her eyes there was a look that was not ordinary. She was standing by the bureau, a jewel case opened before her. For a minute she studied Mrs. Miller, forcing their eyes to meet, and she smiled. "There's nothing good here," she said. "But I like this." Her hand held a cameo brooch. "It's charming."

"Suppose — perhaps you'd better put it back," said Mrs. Miller, feeling suddenly the need of some support. She leaned against the door frame; her head was unbearably heavy; a pressure weighted the rhythm of her heartbeat. The light seemed to flutter defectively. "Please, child — a gift from my husband . . ."

"But it's beautiful and I want it," said Miriam. "*Give it to me.*"

As she stood, striving to shape a sentence which would somehow save the brooch, it came to Mrs. Miller there was no one to whom she might turn; she was alone, a fact that had not been among her thoughts for a long time. Its sheer emphasis was stunning. But here in her own room in the hushed snow-city were evidences she could not ignore or, she knew with startling clarity, resist.

Miriam ate ravenously, and when the sandwiches and milk were gone, her fingers made cobweb movements over the plate, gathering crumbs. The cameo gleamed on her blouse, the blonde profile like a trick reflection of its wearer. "That was very nice," she sighed, "though now an almond cake or a cherry would be ideal. Sweets are lovely, don't you think?"

Mrs. Miller was perched precariously on the hassock, smoking a cigarette. Her hair net had slipped lopsided and loose strands straggled down her face. Her eyes were stupidly concentrated on nothing and her cheeks were mottled in red patches, as though a fierce slap had left permanent marks.

"Is there a candy — a cake?"

Mrs. Miller tapped ash on the rug. Her head swayed slightly as she tried to focus her eyes. "You promised to leave if I made the sandwiches," she said.

"Dear me, did I?"

"It was a promise and I'm tired and I don't feel well at all."

"Mustn't fret," said Miriam. "I'm only teasing."

She picked up her coat, slung it over her arm, and arranged her beret in front of a mirror. Presently she bent close to Mrs. Miller and whispered, "Kiss me good night."

"Please — I'd rather not," said Mrs. Miller.

Miriam lifted a shoulder, arched an eyebrow. "As you like," she said, and went directly to the coffee table, seized the vase containing the paper roses, carried it to where the hard surface of the floor lay bare, and hurled it downward. Glass sprayed in all directions and she stamped her foot on the bouquet.

Then slowly she walked to the door, but before closing it she looked back at Mrs. Miller with a slyly innocent curiosity.

Mrs. Miller spent the next day in bed, rising once to feed the canary and drink a cup of tea; she took her temperature and had none, yet her dreams were feverishly agitated; their unbalanced mood lingered even as she lay staring wide-eyed at the ceiling. One dream threaded through the others like an elusively mysterious theme in a complicated symphony, and the scenes it depicted were sharply outlined, as though sketched by a hand of gifted intensity: a small girl, wearing a bridal gown and a wreath of leaves, led a gray procession down a mountain path, and among them there was unusual silence till a woman at the rear asked, "Where is she taking us?" "No one knows," said an old man marching in front. "But isn't she pretty?" volunteered a third voice. "Isn't she like a frost flower . . . so shining and white?"

Tuesday morning she woke up feeling better; harsh slats of

sunlight, slanting through Venetian blinds, shed a disrupting light on her unwholesome fancies. She opened the window to discover a thawed, mild-as-spring day; a sweep of clean new clouds crumpled against a vastly blue, out-of-season sky; and across the low line of rooftops she could see the river and smoke curving from tugboat stacks in a warm wind. A great silver truck plowed the snow-banked street, its machine sound humming on the air.

After straightening the apartment, she went to the grocer's, cashed a check and continued to Schrafft's, where she ate breakfast and chatted happily with the waitress. Oh, it was a wonderful day — more like a holiday — and it would be so foolish to go home.

She boarded a Lexington Avenue bus and rode up to Eighty-sixth Street; it was here that she had decided to do a little shopping.

She had no idea what she wanted or needed, but she idled along, intent only upon the passers-by, brisk and preoccupied, who gave her a disturbing sense of separateness.

It was while waiting at the corner of Third Avenue that she saw the man: an old man, bowlegged and stooped under an armload of bulging packages; he wore a shabby brown coat and a checkered cap. Suddenly she realized they were exchanging a smile: there was nothing friendly about this smile, it was merely two cold flickers of recognition. But she was certain she had never seen him before.

He was standing next to an El pillar, and as she crossed the street he turned and followed. He kept quite close; from the corner of her eye she watched his reflection wavering on the shop-windows.

Then in the middle of the block she stopped and faced him. He stopped also and cocked his head, grinning. But what could she say? Do? Here, in broad daylight, on Eighty-sixth Street? It was useless and, despising her own helplessness, she quickened her steps.

Now Second Avenue is a dismal street, made from scraps and ends; part cobblestone, part asphalt, part cement; and its atmosphere of desertion is permanent. Mrs. Miller walked five blocks without meeting anyone, and all the while the steady crunch of his footfalls in the snow stayed near. And when she came to a florist's shop, the sound was still with her. She hurried inside and watched through the glass door as the old man passed; he kept his eyes straight ahead and didn't slow his pace, but he did one strange, telling thing: he tipped his cap.

"Six white ones, did you say?" asked the florist. "Yes," she told him, "white roses." From there she went to a glassware store and selected a vase, presumably a replacement for the one Miriam had broken, though the price was intolerable and the vase itself (she thought) grotesquely vulgar. But a series of unaccountable purchases had begun, as if by prearranged plan: a plan of which she had not the least knowledge or control.

She bought a bag of glazed cherries, and at a place called the Knickerbocker Bakery she paid forty cents for six almond cakes.

Within the last hour the weather had turned cold again; like blurred lenses, winter clouds cast a shade over the sun, and the skeleton of an early dusk colored the sky; a damp mist mixed with the wind and the voices of a few children who romped high on mountains of gutter snow seemed lonely and cheerless. Soon the first flake fell, and when Mrs. Miller reached the brownstone house, snow was falling in a swift screen and foot tracks vanished as they were printed.

The white roses were arranged decoratively in the vase. The glazed cherries shone on a ceramic plate. The almond cakes, dusted with sugar, awaited a hand. The canary fluttered on its swing and picked at a bar of seed.

At precisely five the doorbell rang. Mrs. Miller *knew* who it was. The hem of her housecoat trailed as she crossed the floor. "Is that you?" she called.

"Naturally," said Miriam, the word resounding shrilly from the hall. "Open this door."

"Go away," said Mrs. Miller.

"Please hurry . . . I have a heavy package."

"Go away," said Mrs. Miller. She returned to the living room, lighted a cigarette, sat down and calmly listened to the buzzer; on and on and on. "You might as well leave. I have no intention of letting you in."

Shortly the bell stopped. For possibly ten minutes Mrs. Miller did not move. Then, hearing no sound, she concluded Miriam had gone. She tiptoed to the door and opened it a sliver; Miriam was half-reclining atop a cardboard box with a beautiful French doll cradled in her arms.

"Really, I thought you were never coming," she said peevishly. "Here, help me get this in, it's awfully heavy."

It was not spell-like compulsion that Mrs. Miller felt, but rather a curious passivity; she brought in the box, Miriam the doll. Miriam curled up on the sofa, not troubling to remove her coat or beret, and watched disinterestedly as Mrs. Miller dropped the box and stood trembling, trying to catch her breath.

"Thank you," she said. In the daylight she looked pinched and drawn, her hair less luminous. The French doll she was loving wore an exquisite powdered wig and its idiot glass eyes sought solace in Miriam's. "I have a surprise," she continued. "Look into my box."

Kneeling, Mrs. Miller parted the flaps and lifted out another doll; then a blue dress which she recalled as the one Miriam had worn that first night at the theater; and of the remainder she said, "It's all clothes. Why?"

"Because I've come to live with you," said Miriam, twisting a cherry stem. "Wasn't it nice of you to buy me the cherries. . .?"

"But you can't! For God's sake go away — go away and leave me alone!"

". . . and the roses and the almond cakes? How really wonderfully generous. You know, these cherries are delicious. The last place I lived was with an old man; he was terribly poor and we never had good things to eat. But I think I'll be happy here." She paused to snuggle her doll closer. "Now, if you'll just show me where to put my things . . ."

Mrs. Miller's face dissolved into a mask of ugly red lines; she began to cry, and it was an unnatural, tearless sort of weeping, as though, not having wept for a long time, she had forgotten how. Carefully she edged backward till she touched the door.

She fumbled through the hall and down the stairs to a landing below. She pounded frantically on the door of the first apartment she came to; a short, redheaded man answered and she pushed past him. "Say, what the hell is this?" he said. "Anything wrong, lover?" asked a young woman who appeared from the kitchen, drying her hands. And it was to her that Mrs. Miller turned.

"Listen," she cried, "I'm ashamed behaving this way but — well, I'm Mrs. H. T. Miller and I live upstairs and ..." She pressed her hands over her face. "It sounds so absurd...."

The woman guided her to a chair, while the man excitedly rattled pocket change. "Yeah?"

"I live upstairs and there's a little girl visiting me, and I suppose that I'm afraid of her. She won't leave and I can't make her and — she's going to do something terrible. She's already stolen my cameo, but she's about to do something worse — something terrible!"

The man asked, "Is she a relative, huh?"

Mrs. Miller shook her head. "I don't know who she is. Her name's Miriam, but I don't know for certain who she is."

"You gotta calm down, honey," said the woman, stroking Mrs. Miller's arm. "Harry here'll tend to this kid. Go on, lover." And Mrs. Miller said, "The door's open — 5A."

After the man left, the woman brought a towel and bathed Mrs. Miller's face. "You're very kind," Mrs. Miller said. "I'm sorry to act like such a fool, only this wicked child..."

"Sure, honey," consoled the woman. "Now, you better take it easy."

Mrs. Miller rested her head in the crook of her arm; she was quiet enough to be asleep. The woman turned a radio dial; a piano and a husky voice filled the silence and the woman, tapping her foot, kept excellent time. "Maybe we oughta go up too," she said.

"I don't want to see her again. I don't want to be anywhere near her."

"Uh huh, but what you shoulda done, you shoulda called a cop."

Presently they heard the man on the stairs. He strode into the room frowning and scratching the back of his neck. "Nobody there," he said, honestly embarrassed. "She musta beat it."

"Harry, you're a jerk," announced the woman. "We been sitting here the whole time and we woulda seen. . ." she stopped abruptly, for the man's glance was sharp.

"I looked all over," he said, "and there just ain't nobody there. Nobody, understand?"

"Tell me," said Mrs. Miller, rising, "tell me, did you see a large box? Or a doll?"

"No, ma'am, I didn't."

And the woman, as if delivering a verdict, said, "Well, for cryinoutloud. . . ."

Mrs. Miller entered her apartment softly; she walked to the center of the room and stood quite still. No, in a sense it had not changed: the roses, the cakes, and the cherries were in place. But this was an empty room, emptier than if the furnishings and familiars were not present, lifeless and petrified as a funeral parlor. The sofa loomed before her with a new strangeness: its vacancy had a meaning that would have been less penetrating and terrible had Miriam been curled on it. She gazed fixedly at the space where she remembered setting the box and, for a moment, the hassock spun desperately. And she looked through the window; surely the river was real, surely snow was falling — but then, one could not be certain witness to anything: Miriam, so vividly *there* — and yet, where was she? Where, where?

As though moving in a dream, she sank to a chair. The room was losing shape; it was dark and getting darker and there was nothing to be done about it; she could not lift her hand to light a lamp.

Suddenly, closing her eyes, she felt an upward surge, like a diver emerging from some deeper, greener depth. In times of terror or immense distress, there are moments when the mind waits, as though for a revelation, while a skein of calm is woven over thought; it is like a sleep, or a supernatural trance; and during this lull one is aware of a force of quiet reasoning: well, what if she had never really known a girl named Miriam? that she had been foolishly frightened on the street? In the end, like everything else, it was of no importance. For the only thing she had lost to Miriam was her identity, but now she knew she had found again the person who lived in this room, who cooked her own meals, who owned a canary, who was someone she could trust and believe in: Mrs. H. T. Miller.

Listening in contentment, she became aware of a double sound: a bureau drawer opening and closing; she seemed to hear it long after completion — opening and closing. Then gradually, the harshness of it was replaced by the murmur of a silk dress and this, delicately faint, was moving nearer and swelling in intensity till the walls trembled with the vibration and the room was caving under a wave of whispers. Mrs. Miller stiffened and opened her eyes to a dull, direct stare.

"Hello," said Miriam.

The Daemon Lover

Shirley Jackson's genius for storytelling was such that she composed an impressive quantity of highly crafted fiction while managing a household and raising four children in North Bennington, Vermont. Many of her short stories, as well as novels such as The Haunting of Hill House, are masterpieces of psychological horror, in which the supernatural and the shadowy recesses of the psyche are inextricably intertwined.

Shirley Jackson was well acquainted with the convolutions of the mind, having been subject to depression most of her adult life. Many of her characters are women whose grounding in the real world is increasingly threatened by the encroachment of fantasy. The thirty-four-year-old protagonist of "The Daemon Lover" (1949) seems ordinary enough, though somewhat anxious and neurotic, as she awakens on the morning of her wedding day. When her fiancé fails to appear, the reader at first assumes some natural explanation; it is difficult to determine the exact moment at which the heroine's reality begins its inexorable slide into nightmare.

Shirley Jackson admired the British writer Elizabeth Bowen, whose "Demon Lover" was published only several years prior to her own, yet the two stories are remarkably dissimilar in plot, structure, and tone. What they do have in common with each other, and with the ballad from which they take their name, is the uncanny force (in the form of a *shadowy, unpredictable male) which preys upon a woman's vulnerability, ultimately shattering all that is reliable in her existence.*

Jackson's husband, the critic Stanley Edgar Hyman, observed after her death that "if she used the resources of supernatural terror, it was to provide metaphors for the all-too-real terrors of the natural."[12] *This is an apt observation of the writer for whom storytelling was a kind of magic, a means of exorcizing the psychic demons that haunted so much of her life.*

SHE HAD NOT SLEPT WELL; from one-thirty, when Jamie left and she went lingeringly to bed, until seven, when she at last allowed herself to get up and make coffee, she had slept fitfully, stirring awake to open her eyes and look into the half-darkness, remembering over and over, slipping again into a feverish dream. She spent almost an hour over her coffee — they were to have a real breakfast on the way — and then, unless she wanted to dress early, had nothing to do. She washed her coffee cup and made the bed, looking carefully over the clothes she planned to wear, worried unnecessarily, at the window, over whether it would be a fine day. She sat down to read, thought that she might write a letter to her sister instead, and began, in her finest handwriting, "Dearest Anne, by the time you get this I will be married. Doesn't it sound funny? I can hardly believe it myself, but when I tell you how it happened, you'll see it's even stranger than that...."

Sitting, pen in hand, she hesitated over what to say next, read the lines already written, and tore up the letter. She went to the window and saw that it was undeniably a fine day. It occurred to her that perhaps she ought not to wear the blue silk dress; it was too plain, almost severe, and she wanted to be soft, feminine. Anxiously she pulled through the dresses in the closet, and hesitated over a print she had worn the summer before; it was too young for her, and it had a ruffled neck, and it was very early in the year for a print dress, but still....

She hung the two dresses side by side on the outside of the closet door and opened the glass doors carefully closed upon the small closet that was her kitchenette. She turned on the burner under the coffeepot, and went to the window; it was sunny. When the coffeepot began to crackle she came back and poured herself coffee, into a clean cup. I'll have a headache if I don't get some solid food soon, she thought, all this coffee, smoking too much, no real breakfast. A headache on her wedding day; she went and got the tin box of aspirin from the bathroom closet and slipped it into her blue pocketbook. She'd have to change to a brown pocketbook if she wore the print dress, and the only brown pocketbook she had was shabby. Helplessly, she stood looking from the blue pocketbook to the print dress, and then put the pocketbook down and went and got her coffee and sat down near the window, drinking her coffee, and looking carefully around the one-room apartment. They planned to come back here tonight and everything must be correct. With sudden horror she realized that she had forgotten to put clean sheets on the bed; the laundry was freshly back and she took clean sheets and pillow cases from the top shelf of the closet and stripped the bed, working quickly to avoid thinking consciously of why she was changing the sheets. The bed was a studio bed, with a cover to make it look like a couch, and when it was finished no one would have known she had just put clean sheets on it. She took the old sheets and pillow cases into the bathroom and stuffed them down into the hamper, and put the bathroom towels in the hamper too, and clean towels on the bathroom racks. Her coffee was cold when she came back to it, but she drank it anyway.

When she looked at the clock, finally, and saw that it was after nine, she began at last to hurry. She took a bath, and used one of the clean towels, which she put into the hamper and replaced with a clean one. She dressed carefully, all her underwear fresh and most of it new; she put everything she had worn the day before, including her nightgown, into the hamper. When she was ready for her dress, she hesitated before the closet door. The blue dress was certainly decent, and clean, and fairly becoming, but she had worn it several times with Jamie, and there was nothing about it which made it special for a wedding day. The print dress was overly pretty, and new to Jamie, and yet wearing such a print this early in the year was certainly rushing the season. Finally she thought, This is my wedding day, I can dress as I please, and she took the print dress down from the hanger. When she slipped it on over her head it felt fresh and light, but when she looked at herself in the mirror she remembered that the ruffles around the neck did not show her throat to any great advantage, and the wide swinging skirt looked irresistibly made for a girl, for someone who would run freely, dance, swing it with her hips when she walked. Looking at herself in the mirror she thought with revulsion, It's as though I was trying to make myself look prettier than I am, just for him; he'll think I want to look younger because he's marrying me; and she tore the print dress off so quickly that a seam under the arm ripped. In the old blue dress she felt comfortable and familiar, but unexciting. It isn't what you're wearing that matters, she told herself firmly, and turned in dismay to the closet to see if there might be anything else. There was nothing even remotely suitable for her marrying Jamie, and for a minute she thought of going out quickly to some little shop nearby, to get a dress. Then she saw that it was close on ten, and she had no time for more than her hair and her make-up. Her hair was easy, pulled back into a knot at the nape of her neck, but her make-up was another delicate balance between looking as well as possible, and deceiving as little. She could not try to disguise the sallowness of her skin, or the lines around her eyes, today, when it might look as though she were only doing it for her wedding, and yet she could not bear the thought of Jamie's bringing to marriage anyone who looked haggard and lined. You're thirty-four years old after *all*, she told herself cruelly in the bathroom mirror. Thirty, it said on the license.

It was two minutes after ten; she was not satisfied with her clothes, her face, her apartment. She heated the coffee again and sat down in the chair by the window. Can't do anything more now, she thought, no sense trying to improve anything the last minute.

Reconciled, settled, she tried to think of Jamie and could not see his face clearly, or hear his voice. It's always that way with someone you love, she thought, and let her mind slip past today and tomorrow, into the farther future, when Jamie was established with his writing and she had given up her job, the golden house-in-the-country future they had been preparing for the last week. "I used to be a wonderful cook," she had promised Jamie, "with a little time and practice I could remember how to make angel-food cake. And fried chicken," she said, knowing how the words would stay in Jamie's mind, half-tenderly. "And Hollandaise sauce."

Ten-thirty. She stood up and went purposefully to the phone. She dialed, and waited, and the girl's metallic voice said, ". . . the time will be exactly ten-twenty-nine." Half-consciously she set her clock back a minute; she was remembering her own voice saying last night, in the doorway: "Ten o'clock then. I'll be ready. Is it really *true?*"

And Jamie laughing down the hallway.

By eleven o'clock she had sewed up the ripped seam in the print dress and put her sewing-box away carefully in the closet. With the print dress on, she was sitting by the window drinking another cup of coffee. I could have taken more time over my dressing after all, she thought; but by now it was so late he might come any minute, and she did not dare try to repair anything without starting all over. There was nothing to eat in the apartment except the food she had carefully stocked up for their life beginning together: the unopened package of bacon, the dozen eggs in their box, the unopened bread and the unopened butter; they were for breakfast tomorrow. She thought of running downstairs to the drugstore for something to eat, leaving a note on the door. Then she decided to wait a little longer.

By eleven-thirty she was so dizzy and weak that she had to go downstairs. If Jamie had had a phone she would have called him then. Instead, she opened her desk and wrote a note: "Jamie, have gone downstairs to the drugstore. Back in five minutes." Her pen leaked onto her fingers and she went into the bathroom and washed, using a clean towel which she replaced. She tacked the note on the door, surveyed the apartment once more to make sure that everything was perfect, and closed the door without locking it, in case he should come.

In the drugstore she found that there was nothing she wanted to eat except more coffee, and she left it half-finished because she suddenly realized that Jamie was probably upstairs waiting and impatient, anxious to get started.

But upstairs everything was prepared and quiet, as she had left it, her note unread on the door, the air in the apartment a little stale from too many cigarettes. She opened the window and sat down next to it until she realized that she had been asleep and it was twenty minutes to one.

Now, suddenly, she was frightened. Waking without preparation into the room of waiting and readiness, everything clean and untouched since ten o'clock, she was frightened, and felt an urgent need to hurry. She got up from the chair and almost ran across the room to the bathroom, dashed cold water on her face, and used a clean towel; this time she put the towel carelessly back on the rack without changing it; time enough for that later. Hatless, still in the print dress with a coat thrown on over it, the wrong blue pocketbook with the aspirin inside in her hand, she locked the apartment door behind her, no note this time, and ran down the stairs. She caught a taxi on the corner and gave the driver Jamie's address.

It was no distance at all; she could have walked it if she had not been so weak, but in the taxi she suddenly realized how imprudent it would be to drive brazenly up to Jamie's door, demanding him. She asked the driver, therefore, to let her off at a corner near Jamie's address and, after paying him, waited till he drove away before she started to walk down the block. She had never been here before; the building was pleasant and old, and Jamie's name was not on any of the mailboxes in the vestibule, nor on the doorbells. She checked the address; it was right, and finally she rang the bell marked "Superintendent." After a minute or two the door buzzer rang and she opened the door and went into the dark hall where she hesitated until a door at the end opened and someone said, "Yes?"

She knew at the same moment that she had no idea what to ask, so she moved forward toward the figure waiting against the light of the open doorway. When she was very near, the figure said, "Yes?" again and she saw that it was a man in his shirtsleeves, unable to see her any more clearly than she could see him.

With sudden courage she said, "I'm trying to get in touch with someone who lives in this building and I can't find the name outside."

"What's the name you wanted?" the man asked, and she realized that she would have to answer.

"James Harris," she said. "Harris."

The man was silent for a minute and then he said, "Harris." He turned around to the room inside the lighted doorway and said, "Margie, come here a minute."

"What now?" a voice said from inside, and after a wait long enough for someone to get out of a comfortable chair a woman joined him in the doorway, regarding the dark hall. "Lady here," the man said. "Lady looking for a guy name of Harris, lives here. Anyone in the building?"

"No," the woman said. Her voice sounded amused. "No men named Harris here."

"Sorry," the man said. He started to close the door. "You got the wrong house, lady," he said, and added in a lower voice, "or the wrong guy," and he and the woman laughed.

When the door was almost shut and she was alone in the dark hall she said to the thin lighted crack still showing, "But he *does* live here; I know it."

"Look," the woman said, opening the door again a little, "it happens all the time."

"Please don't make any mistake," she said, and her voice was very dignified, with thirty-four years of accumulated pride. "I'm afraid you don't understand."

"What did he look like?" the woman said wearily, the door

still only part open.

"He's rather tall, and fair. He wears a blue suit very often. He's a writer."

"No," the woman said, and then, "Could he have lived on the third floor?"

"I'm not sure."

"There was a fellow," the woman said reflectively. "He wore a blue suit a lot, lived on the third floor for a while. The Roysters lent him their apartment while they were visiting her folks upstate."

"That might be it; I thought, though. . . ."

"This one wore a blue suit mostly, but I don't know how tall he was," the woman said. "He stayed there about a month."

"A month ago is when —"

"You ask the Roysters," the woman said. "They come back this morning. Apartment 3 B."

The door closed, definitely. The hall was very dark and the stairs looked darker.

On the second floor there was a little light from a skylight far above. The apartment doors lined up, four on the floor, uncommunicative and silent. There was a bottle of milk outside 2 C.

On the third floor, she waited for a minute. There was the sound of music beyond the door of 3 B, and she could hear voices. Finally she knocked, and knocked again. The door was opened and the music swept out at her, an early afternoon symphony broadcast. "How do you do," she said politely to this woman in the doorway. "Mrs. Royster?"

"That's right." The woman was wearing a housecoat and last night's make-up.

"I wonder if I might talk to you for a minute?"

"Sure," Mrs. Royster said, not moving.

"About Mr. Harris."

"*What* Mr. Harris?" Mrs. Royster said flatly.

"Mr. James Harris. The gentleman who borrowed your apartment."

"O Lord," Mrs. Royster said. She seemed to open her eyes for the first time. "What'd he do?"

"Nothing. I'm just trying to get in touch with him."

"O Lord," Mrs. Royster said again. Then she opened the door wider and said, "Come in," and then, "Ralph!"

Inside, the apartment was still full of music, and there were suitcases half-unpacked on the couch, on the chairs, on the floor. A table in the corner was spread with the remains of a meal, and the young man sitting there, for a minute resembling Jamie, got up and came across the room.

"What about it?" he said.

"Mr. Royster," she said. It was difficult to talk against the music. "The superintendent downstairs told me that this was where Mr. James Harris has been living."

"Sure," he said. "If that was his name."

"I thought you lent him the apartment," she said, surprised.

"*I* don't know anything about him," Mr. Royster said. "He's one of Dottie's friends."

"Not *my* friends," Mrs. Royster said. "No friend of mine." She had gone over to the table and was spreading peanut butter on a piece of bread. She took a bite and said thickly, waving the bread and peanut butter at her husband, "Not *my* friend."

"You picked him up at one of those damn meetings," Mr. Royster said. He shoved a suitcase off the chair next to the radio and sat down, picking up a magazine from the floor next to him. "I never said more'n ten words to him."

"You said it was okay to lend him the place," Mrs. Royster said before she took another bite. "You never said a word against him, after *all*."

"*I* don't say anything about *your* friends," Mr. Royster said.

"If he'd of been a friend of mine you would have said *plenty*, believe me," Mrs. Royster said darkly. She took another bite and said, "Believe me, he would have said *plenty*."

"That's all I want to hear," Mr. Royster said, over the top of the magazine. "No more, now."

"You see." Mrs. Royster pointed the bread and peanut butter

at her husband. "That's the way it is, day and night."

There was silence except for the music bellowing out of the radio next to Mr. Royster, and then she said, in a voice she hardly trusted to be heard over the radio noise, "Has he gone, then?"

"Who?" Mrs. Royster demanded, looking up from the peanut butter jar.

"Mr. James Harris."

"Him? He must've left this morning, before we got back. No sign of him anywhere."

"Gone?"

"Everything was fine, though, perfectly fine. I told you," she said to Mr. Royster, "I told you he'd take care of everything fine. I can always tell."

"You were lucky," Mr. Royster said.

"Not a thing out of place," Mrs. Royster said. She waved her bread and peanut butter inclusively. "Everything just the way we left it," she said.

"Do you know where he is now?"

"Not the slightest idea," Mrs. Royster said cheerfully. "But, like I said, he left everything fine. Why?" she asked suddenly. "You looking for *him?*"

"It's very important."

"I'm sorry he's not here," Mrs. Royster said. She stepped forward politely when she saw her visitor turn toward the door.

"Maybe the super saw him," Mr. Royster said into the magazine.

When the door was closed behind her the hall was dark again, but the sound of the radio was deadened. She was halfway down the first flight of stairs when the door was opened and Mrs. Royster shouted down the stairwell, "If I see him I'll tell him you were looking for him."

What can I do? she thought, out on the street again. It was impossible to go home, not with Jamie somewhere between here and there. She stood on the sidewalk so long that a woman, leaning out of a window across the way, turned and called to someone inside to come and see. Finally, on an impulse, she went into the small delicatessen next door to the apartment house, on the side that led to her own apartment. There was a small man reading a newspaper, leaning against the counter; when she came in he looked up and came down inside the counter to meet her.

Over the glass case of cold meats and cheese she said, timidly, "I'm trying to get in touch with a man who lived in the apartment house next door, and I just wondered if you know him."

"Whyn't you ask the people there?" the man said, his eyes narrow, inspecting her.

It's because I'm not buying anything, she thought, and she said, "I'm sorry. I asked them, but they don't know anything about him. They think he left this morning."

"I don't know what you want *me* to do," he said, moving a little back toward his newspaper. "I'm not here to keep track of guys going in and out next door."

She said quickly, "I thought you might have noticed, that's all. He would have been coming past here, a little before ten o'clock. He was rather tall, and he usually wore a blue suit."

"Now how many men in blue suits go past here every day, lady?" the man demanded. "You think I got nothing to do but —"

"I'm sorry," she said. She heard him say, "For God's sake," as she went out the door.

As she walked toward the corner, she thought, he must have come this way, it's the way he'd go to get to my house, it's the only way for him to walk. She tried to think of Jamie: where would he have crossed the street? What sort of person was he actually — would he cross in front of his own apartment house, at random in the middle of the block, at the corner?

On the corner was a newsstand; they might have seen him there. She hurried on and waited while a man bought a paper and a woman asked directions. When the newsstand man looked at her she said, "Can you possibly tell me if a rather tall young man in a blue suit went past here this morning around ten o'clock?"

When the man only looked at her, his eyes wide and his mouth a little open, she thought, he thinks it's a joke, or a trick, and she said urgently, "It's very important, please believe me. I'm not teasing you."

"*Look*, lady," the man began, and she said eagerly, "He's a writer. He might have bought magazines here."

"What you want him for?" the man asked. He looked at her, smiling, and she realized that there was another man waiting in back of her and the newsdealer's smile included him. "Never mind," she said, but the newsdealer said, "Listen, maybe he did come by here." His smile was knowing and his eyes shifted over her shoulder to the man in back of her. She was suddenly horribly aware of her over-young print dress, and pulled her coat around her quickly. The newsdealer said, with vast thoughtfulness, "Now I don't know for sure, mind you, but there might have been someone like your gentleman friend coming by this morning."

"About ten?"

"About ten," the newsdealer agreed. "Tall fellow, blue suit. I wouldn't be at all surprised."

"Which way did he go?" she said eagerly. "Uptown?"

"Uptown," the newsdealer said, nodding. "He went uptown. That's just exactly it. What can I do for you, sir?"

She stepped back, holding her coat around her. The man who had been standing behind her looked at her over his shoulder and then he and the newsdealer looked at one another. She wondered for a minute whether or not to tip the newsdealer but when both men began to laugh she moved hurriedly on across the street.

Uptown, she thought, that's right, and she started up the avenue, thinking: He wouldn't have to cross the avenue, just go up six blocks and turn down my street, so long as he started uptown. About a block farther on she passed a florist's shop; there was a wedding display in the window and she thought, This is my wedding day after all, he might have gotten flowers to bring me, and she went inside. The florist came out of the back of the shop, smiling and sleek, and she said, before he could speak, so that he wouldn't have a chance to think she was buying anything: "It's *terribly* important that I get in touch with a gentleman who may have stopped in here to buy flowers this morning. *Terribly* important."

She stopped for breath, and the florist said, "Yes, what sort of flowers were they?"

"I don't know," she said, surprised. "He never —" She stopped and said, "He was a rather tall young man, in a blue suit. It was about ten o'clock."

"I see," the florist said. "Well, *really*, I'm afraid. . . ."

"But it's *so* important," she said. "He may have been in a hurry," she added helpfully.

"Well," the florist said. He smiled genially, showing all his small teeth. "For a *lady*," he said. He went to a stand and opened a large book. "Where were they to be sent?" he asked.

"Why," she said, "I don't think he'd have sent them. You see, he was coming — that is, he'd *bring* them."

"Madam," the florist said; he was offended. His smile became deprecatory, and he went on, "Really, you must realize that unless I have *something* to go on. . . ."

"*Please* try to remember," she begged. "He was tall, and had a blue suit, and it was about ten this morning."

The florist closed his eyes, one finger to his mouth, and thought deeply. Then he shook his head. "I simply *can't*," he said.

"Thank you," she said despondently, and started for the door, when the florist said, in a shrill, excited voice, "Wait! Wait just a moment, madam." She turned and the florist, thinking again, said finally, "Chrysanthemums?" He looked at her inquiringly.

"Oh, *no*," she said; her voice shook a little and she waited for a minute before she went on. "Not for an occasion like this, I'm sure."

The florist tightened his lips and looked away coldly. "Well, of *course* I don't know the *occasion*," he said, "but I'm almost certain that the gentleman you were inquiring for came in this morning and purchased one dozen chrysanthemums. No delivery."

"You're *sure?*" she asked.

"Positive," the florist said emphatically. "That was absolutely the man." He smiled brilliantly, and she smiled back and said, "Well, thank you very much."

He escorted her to the door. "Nice corsage?" he said, as they went through the shop. "Red roses? Gardenias?"

"It was very kind of you to help me," she said at the door.

"Ladies always look their best in flowers," he said, bending his head toward her. "Orchids, perhaps?"

"No, thank you," she said, and he said, "I hope you find your young man," and gave it a nasty sound.

Going on up the street she thought, Everyone thinks it's so *funny*: and she pulled her coat tighter around her, so that only the ruffle around the bottom of the print dress was showing.

There was a policeman on the corner, and she thought, Why don't I go to the police — you go to the police for a missing person. And then thought, What a fool I'd look like. She had a quick picture of herself standing in a police station, saying, "Yes, we were going to be married today, but he didn't come," and the policemen, three or four of them standing around listening, looking at her, at the print dress, at her too-bright make-up, smiling at one another. She couldn't tell them any more than that, could not say, "Yes, it looks silly, doesn't it, me all dressed up and trying to find the young man who promised to marry me, but what about all of it you don't know? I have more than this, more than you can see: talent, perhaps, and humor of a sort, and I'm a lady and I have pride and affection and delicacy and a certain clear view of life that might make a man satisfied and productive and happy; there's more than you think when you look at me."

The police were obviously impossible, leaving out Jamie and what he might think when he heard she'd set the police after him. "No, no," she said aloud, hurrying her steps, and someone passing stopped and looked after her.

On the coming corner — she was three blocks from her own

street — was a shoeshine stand, an old man sitting almost asleep in one of the chairs. She stopped in front of him and waited, and after a minute he opened his eyes and smiled at her.

"Look," she said, the words coming before she thought of them, "I'm sorry to bother you, but I'm looking for a young man who came up this way about ten this morning, did you see him?" And she began her description, "Tall, blue suit, carrying a bunch of flowers?"

The old man began to nod before she was finished. "I saw him," he said. "Friend of yours?"

"Yes," she said, and smiled back involuntarily.

The old man blinked his eyes and said, "I remember I thought, You're going to see your girl, young fellow. They all go to see their girls," he said, and shook his head tolerantly.

"Which way did he go? Straight on up the avenue?"

"That's right," the old man said. "Got a shine, had his flowers, all dressed up, in an awful hurry. You got a girl, I thought."

"Thank you," she said, fumbling in her pocket for her loose change.

"She sure must of been glad to see him, the way he looked," the old man said.

"Thank you," she said again, and brought her hand empty from her pocket.

For the first time she was really sure he would be waiting for her, and she hurried up the three blocks, the skirt of the print dress swinging under her coat, and turned into her own block. From the corner she could not see her own windows, could not see Jamie looking out, waiting for her, and going down the block she was almost running to get to him. Her key trembled in her fingers at the downstairs door, and as she glanced into the drugstore she thought of her panic, drinking coffee there this morning, and almost laughed. At her own door she could wait no longer, but began to say, "Jamie, I'm here, I was so worried," even before the door was open.

Her own apartment was waiting for her, silent, barren, after-

126

noon shadows lengthening from the window. For a minute she saw only the empty coffee cup, thought, He has been here waiting, before she recognized it as her own, left from the morning. She looked all over the room, into the closet, into the bathroom.

"I never saw him," the clerk in the drugstore said. "I know because I would of noticed the flowers. No one like that's been in."

The old man at the shoeshine stand woke up again to see her standing in front of him. "Hello again," he said, and smiled.

"Are you *sure?*" she demanded. "Did he go on up the avenue?"

"I watched him," the old man said, dignified against her tone. "I thought, There's a young man's got a girl, and I watched him right into the house."

"What house?" she said remotely.

"Right there," the old man said. He leaned forward to point. "The next block. With his flowers and his shine and going to see his girl. Right into her house."

"Which one?" she said.

"About the middle of the block," the old man said. He looked at her with suspicion, and said, "What you trying to do, anyway?"

She almost ran, without stopping to say "Thank you." Up on the next block she walked quickly, searching the houses from the outside to see if Jamie looked from a window, listening to hear his laughter somewhere inside.

A woman was sitting in front of one of the houses, pushing a baby carriage monotonously back and forth the length of her arm. The baby inside slept, moving back and forth.

The question was fluent, by now. "I'm sorry, but did you see a young man go into one of these houses about ten this morning? He was tall, wearing a blue suit, carrying a bunch of flowers."

A boy about twelve stopped to listen, turning intently from one to the other, occasionally glancing at the baby.

"Listen," the woman said tiredly, "the kid has his bath at ten. Would I see strange men walking around? I ask you."

"Big bunch of flowers?" the boy asked, pulling at her coat. "Big bunch of flowers? I seen him, missus."

She looked down and the boy grinned insolently at her.

"Which house did he go in?" she asked wearily.

"You gonna divorce him?" the boy asked insistently.

"That's not nice to ask the lady," the woman rocking the carriage said.

"Listen," the boy said, "I seen him. He went in there." He pointed to the house next door. "I followed him," the boy said. "He give me a quarter." The boy dropped his voice to a growl, and said, "'This is a big day for me, kid,' he says. Give me a quarter."

She gave him a dollar bill. "Where?" she said.

"Top floor," the boy said. "I followed him till he give me the quarter. Way to the top." He backed up the sidewalk, out of reach, with the dollar bill. "You gonna divorce him?" he asked again.

"Was he carrying flowers?"

"Yeah," the boy said. He began to screech. "You gonna divorce him, missus? You got something on him?" He went careening down the street, howling, "She's got something on the poor guy," and the woman rocking the baby laughed.

The street door of the apartment house was unlocked; there were no bells in the outer vestibule, and no lists of names. The stairs were narrow and dirty; there were two doors on the top floor. The front one was the right one; there was a crumpled florist's paper on the floor outside the door, and a knotted paper ribbon, like a clue, like the final clue in the paper-chase.

She knocked, and thought she heard voices inside, and she thought, suddenly, with terror, What shall I say if Jamie is there, if he comes to the door? The voices seemed suddenly still. She knocked again and there was silence, except for something that might have been laughter far away. He could have seen me from the window, she thought, it's the front apartment and that little boy made a dreadful noise. She waited, and knocked again, but there was silence.

Finally she went to the other door on the floor, and knocked. The door swung open beneath her hand and she saw the empty attic room, bare lath on the walls, floorboards unpainted. She stepped just inside, looking around; the room was filled with bags of plaster, piles of old newspapers, a broken trunk. There was a noise which she suddenly realized was a rat, and then she saw it, sitting very close to her, near the wall, its evil face alert, bright eyes watching her. She stumbled in her haste to be out with the door closed, and the skirt of the print dress caught and tore.

She knew there was someone inside the other apartment, because she was sure she could hear low voices and sometimes laughter. She came back many times, every day for the first week. She came on her way to work, in the mornings; in the evenings, on her way to dinner alone, but no matter how often or how firmly she knocked, no one ever came to the door.

Heartburn

Hortense Calisher published her first story when she was in her late thirties, and since then has never ceased to write. New York City, where she grew up, is the setting for most of her novels and short stories, which explore the difficulties of communication, the loneliness of human relationships, the stresses of intimacy and family life. "Heartburn" (1951) may be Calisher's only work of fiction that ventures into the realm of the preternatural. It is bracingly out of the ordinary, not only within her own body of writing but, one might add, within the uncanny genre as a whole. Once read, it is unforgettable.

"Heartburn" could be described as a modern tale of possession, but with a difference: the psychic vampirism occurs not by one person draining another's vital force, but by his transferring to his victim something monstrous from within himself. There is a powerful resonance to this psychological dynamic; one thinks, for example, of those who seek to free themselves from the weight of a dark secret by foisting it upon an unwitting other. Yet however rich in symbolic implications this story may be, it is the concrete ghastliness of the narrative that glues us to our seat, and the sedate matter-of-factness of the telling that gives it its power to chill.

THE LIGHT, GRITTY wind of a spring morning blew in on the doctor's shining, cleared desk, and on the tall buttonhook of a man who leaned agitatedly toward him.

"I have some kind of small animal lodged in my chest," said the man. He coughed, a slight, hollow apologia to his ailment, and sank back in his chair.

"Animal?" said the doctor, after a pause which had the unfortunate quality of comment. His voice, however, was practiced, deft, colored only with the careful suspension of judgment.

"Probably a form of newt or toad," answered the man, speaking with clipped distaste, as if he would disassociate himself from the idea as far as possible. His face quirked with sad foreknowledge. "Of course, you don't believe me."

The doctor looked at him noncommittally. Paraphrased, an old refrain of the poker table leapt erratically in his mind. "Nits" — no — "newts and gnats and one-eyed jacks," he thought. But already the anecdote was shaping itself, trim and perfect, for display at the clinic luncheon table. "Go on," he said.

"Why won't any of you come right out and say what you think!" the man said angrily. Then he flushed, not hectically, the doctor noted, but with the well-bred embarrassment of the normally reserved. "Sorry. I didn't mean to be rude."

"You've already had an examination?" The doctor was a neurologist, and most of his patients were referrals.

"My family doctor. I live up in Boston."

"Did you tell him — er. . . ?" The doctor sought gingerly for a phrase.

One corner of the man's mouth lifted, as if he had watched others in the same dilemma. "I went through the routine first. Fluoroscope, metabolism, cardiograph. Even gastroscopy." He spoke, the doctor noted, with the regrettable glibness of the patient who has shopped around.

"And — the findings?" said the doctor, already sure of the answer.

The man leaned forward, holding the doctor's glance with his own. A faint smile riffled his mouth. "Positive."

"Positive!"

"Well," said the man, "machines have to be interpreted after all, don't they?" He attempted a shrug, but the quick eye of the doctor saw that the movement masked a slight contortion within his tweed suit, as if the man writhed away from himself but concealed it quickly, as one masks a hiccup with a cough. "A curious flutter in the cardiograph, a strange variation in the metabolism, an alien shadow under the fluoroscope." He coughed again and put a genteel hand over his mouth, but this time the doctor saw it clearly — the slight, cringing motion.

"You see," added the man, his eyes helpless and apologetic above the polite covering hand. "It's alive. It *travels.*"

"Yes. Yes, of course," said the doctor, soothingly now. In his mind hung the word, ovoid and perfect as a drop of water about to fall. Obsession. A beautiful case. He thought again of the luncheon table.

"What did your doctor recommend?" he said.

"A place with more resources, like the Mayo Clinic. It was then that I told him I knew what it was, as I've told you. And how I acquired it." The visitor paused. "Then, of course, he was forced to pretend he believed me."

"Forced?" said the doctor.

"Well," said the visitor, "actually, I think he did believe me. People tend to believe anything these days. All this mass media information gives them the habit. It takes a strong individual to disbelieve evidence."

The doctor was confused and annoyed. Well, "What then?" he said peremptorily, ready to rise from his desk in dismissal.

Again came the fleeting bodily grimace and the quick cough. "He — er . . . he gave me a prescription."

The doctor raised his eyebrows, in a gesture he was swift to retract as unprofessional.

"For heartburn, I think it was," added his visitor demurely.

Tipping back in his chair, the doctor tapped a pencil on the edge of the desk. "Did he suggest you seek help — on another level?"

"Many have suggested it," said the man.

"But I'm not a psychiatrist!" said the doctor irritably.

"Oh, I know that. You see, I came to you because I had the luck to hear one of your lectures at the Academy. The one on 'Overemphasis on the Non-somatic Causes of Nervous Disorder.' It takes a strong man to go against the tide like that. A disbeliever. And that's what I sorely need." The visitor shuddered, this time letting the *frisson* pass uncontrolled. "You see," he added, thrusting his clasped hands forward on the desk, and looking ruefully at the doctor, as if he would cushion him against his next remark, "you see — I am a psychiatrist."

The doctor sat still in his chair.

"Ah, I can't help knowing what you are thinking," said the man. "I would think the same. A streamlined version of the Napoleonic delusion." He reached into his breast pocket, drew out a wallet, and fanned papers from it on the desk.

"Never mind. I believe you!" said the doctor hastily.

"Already?" said the man sadly.

Reddening, the doctor hastily looked over the collection of letters, cards of membership in professional societies, licenses, and so on — very much the same sort of thing he himself would have had to amass, had he been under the same necessity of proving his identity. Sanity, of course, was another matter. The documents were all issued to Dr. Curtis Retz at a Boston address. Stolen, possibly, but something in the man's manner, in fact everything in it except his unfortunate hallucination, made the doctor think otherwise. Poor guy, he thought. Occupational fatigue, perhaps. But what a form! The Boston variant, possibly. "Suppose you start from the beginning," he said benevolently.

"If you can spare the time . . ."

"I have no more appointments until lunch." And what a lunch that'll be, the doctor thought, already cherishing the pop-eyed scene — Travis the clinic's director (that plethoric Nestor), and young Gruenberg (all of whose cases were unique), his hairy nostrils dilated for once in a *mise-en-scène* which he did not dominate.

Holding his hands pressed formally against his chest, almost in the attitude of one of the minor placatory figures in a *Pietà*, the visitor went on. "I have the usual private practice," he said, "and clinic affiliations. As a favor to an old friend of mine, headmaster of a boys' school nearby, I've acted as guidance consultant there for some years. The school caters to boys of above average intelligence and is run along progressive lines. Nothing's ever cropped up except run-of-the-mill adolescent problems, colored a little, perhaps, by the type of parents who tend to send their children to a school like that — people who are — well — one might say, almost tediously aware of their commitments as parents."

The doctor grunted. He was that kind of parent himself.

"Shortly after the second term began, the head asked me to come down. He was worried over a sharp drop of morale which seemed to extend over the whole school — general inattention in classes, excited note-passing, nightly disturbances in the dorms — all pointing, he had thought at first, to the existence of some fancier than usual form of hazing, or to one of those secret societies, sometimes laughable, sometimes with overtones of the corrupt, with which all schools are familiar. Except for one thing. One after the other, a long list of boys had been sent to the infirmary by the various teachers who presided in the dining room. Each of the boys had shown a marked debility, and what the resident doctor called 'All the stigmata of pure fright. Complete unwillingness to confide.' Each of the boys pleaded stubbornly for his own release, and a few broke out of their own accord. The interesting thing was that each child did recover shortly after his own release, and it was only after this that another boy was seen to fall ill. No two were afflicted at the same time."

"Check the food?" said the doctor.

"All done before I got there. According to my friend, all the trouble seemed to have started with the advent of one boy, John Hallowell, a kid of about fifteen, who had come to the school late in the term with a history of having run away from four other schools. Records at these classed him as very bright, but made oblique references to 'personality difficulties' which were not defined. My friend's school, ordinarily pretty independent, had taken the boy at the insistence of old Simon Hallowell, the boy's uncle, who is a trustee. His brother, the boy's father, is well known for his marital exploits which have nourished the tabloids for years. The mother lives mostly in France and South America. One of these perennial dryads, apparently, with a youthfulness maintained by money and a yearly immersion in the fountains of American plastic surgery. Only time she sees the boy . . . Well, you can imagine. What the feature articles call a Broken Home."

The doctor shifted in his chair and lit a cigarette.

"I won't keep you much longer," said the visitor. "I saw the boy." A violent fit of coughing interrupted him. This time his curious writhing motion went frankly unconcealed. He got up from his chair and stood at the window, gripping the sill and breathing heavily until he had regained control, and went on, one hand pulling unconsciously at his collar. "Or, at least, I think I saw him. On my way to visit him in his room I bumped into a tall red-headed boy in a football sweater, hurrying down the hall with a windbreaker and a poncho slung over his shoulder. I asked for Hallowell's room; he jerked a thumb over his shoulder at the door just behind him, and continued past me. It never occurred to me . . . I was expecting some adenoidal gangler with acne . . . or one of these sinister little angel faces, full of neurotic sensibility.

"The room was empty. Except for its finicky neatness, and a rather large amount of livestock, there was nothing unusual about it. The school, according to the current trend, is run like a farm, with the boys doing the chores, and pets are encouraged. There was a tank with a couple of turtles near the window, beside it another, full of newts, and in one corner a large cage of well-tended, brisk white mice. Glass cases, with carefully mounted series of lepidoptera and hymenoptera, showing the metamorphic stages, hung on the walls, and on a drawing board there was a daintily executed study of Branchippus, the 'fairy shrimp.'

"While I paced the room, trying to look as if I wasn't prying, a greenish little wretch, holding himself together as if he had an imaginary shawl draped around him, slunk into the half-dark

room and squeaked 'Hallowell?' When he saw me he started to
duck, but I detained him and found that he had had an appoint-
ment with Hallowell too. When it was clear, from his description,
that Hallowell must have been the redhead I'd seen leaving, the
poor urchin burst into tears.

"'I'll never get rid of it now!' he wailed. From then on it
wasn't hard to get the whole maudlin story. It seems that shortly
after Hallowell's arrival at school he acquired a reputation for
unusual proficiency with animals and for out-of-the-way lore
which would impress the ingenuous. He circulated the rumor
that he could swallow small animals and regurgitate them at will.
No one actually saw him swallow anything, but it seems that in
some mumbo-jumbo with another boy who had shown cynicism
about the whole thing, it was claimed that Hallowell had, well,
divested himself of something, and passed it on to the other boy,
with the statement that the latter would only be able to get rid
of his cargo when he in turn found a boy who would disbelieve
him."

The visitor paused, calmer now, and leaving the window sat
down again in the chair opposite the doctor, regarding him with
such fixity that the doctor shifted uneasily, with the apprehension of one who is about to be asked for a loan.

"My mind turned to the elementary sort of thing we've all
done at times. You know, circle of kids in the dark, piece of
cooked cauliflower passed from hand to hand with the statement
that the stuff is the fresh brains of some neophyte who hadn't
taken his initiation seriously. My young informer, Moulton his
name was, swore however that this hysteria (for of course, that's
what I thought it) was passed on singly, from boy to boy, without any such séances. He'd been home to visit his family, who are
missionaries on leave, and had been infected by his roommate on
his return to school, unaware that by this time the whole school
had protectively turned believers, en masse. His own terror
came, not only from his conviction that he was possessed, but
from his inability to find anybody who would take his dare. And
so he'd finally come to Hallowell. . . .

"By this time the room was getting really dark and I snapped on the light to get a better look at Moulton. Except for an occasional shudder, like a bodily tic, which I took to be the aftereffects of hard crying, he looked like a healthy enough boy who'd been scared out of his wits. I remember that a neat little monograph was already forming itself in my mind, a group study on mass psychosis, perhaps, with effective anthropological references to certain savage tribes whose dances include a rite known as 'eating evil.'

"The kid was looking at me. 'Do you believe me?' he said suddenly. 'Sir?' he added, with a naive cunning which tickled me.

"'Of course,' I said, patting his shoulder absently. 'In a way.'

"His shoulder slumped under my hand. I felt its tremor, direct misery palpitating between my fingers.

"'I thought ... maybe for a man ... it wouldn't be ...' His voice trailed off.

"'Be the same? ... I don't know,' I said slowly, for of course, I was answering, not his actual question, but the overtone of some cockcrow of meaning that evaded me.

"He raised his head and petitioned me silently with his eyes. Was it guile, or simplicity, in his look, and was it for conviction, or the lack of it, that he arraigned me? I don't know. I've gone back over what I did then, again and again, using all my own knowledge of the mechanics of decision, and I know that it wasn't just sympathy, or a pragmatic reversal of therapy, but something intimately important for me, that made me shout with all my strength — 'Of course I don't believe you!'

"Moulton, his face contorted, fell forward on me so suddenly that I stumbled backwards, sending the tank of newts crashing to the floor. Supporting him with my arms, I hung on to him while he heaved, face downwards. At the same time I felt a tickling, sliding sensation in my own ear, and an inordinate desire to follow it with my finger, but both my hands were busy. It wasn't a minute 'til I'd gotten him onto the couch, where he drooped, a little white about the mouth, but with that chastened, purified look of the physically relieved, although he hadn't actually upchucked.

"Still watching him, I stooped to clear up the debris, but he bounded from the couch with amazing resilience.

"'I'll do it,' he said.

"'Feel better?'

"He nodded, clearly abashed, and we gathered up the remains of the tank in a sort of mutual embarrassment. I can't remember that either of us said a word, and neither of us made more than a halfhearted attempt to search for the scattered pests which had apparently sought crannies in the room. At the door we parted, muttering as formal a goodnight as was possible between a grown man and a small boy. It wasn't until I reached my own room and sat down that I realized, not only my own extraordinary behavior, but that Moulton, standing, as I suddenly recalled, for the first time quite straight, had sent after me a look of pity and speculation.

"Out of habit, I reached into my breast pocket for my pencil, in order to take notes as fresh as possible. And then I felt it ... a skittering, sidling motion, almost beneath my hand. I opened my jacket and shook myself, thinking that I'd picked up something in the other room ... but nothing. I sat quite still, gripping the pencil, and after an interval it came again — an inchoate creeping, a twitter of movement almost *lackadaisical*, as of something inching itself lazily along — but this time on my other side. In a frenzy, I peeled off my clothes, inspected myself wildly, and enumerating to myself a reassuring abracadabra of explanation — skipped heartbeat, intercostal pressure of gas — I sat there naked, waiting. And after a moment, it came again, that wandering, aquatic motion, as if something had flipped itself over just enough to make me aware, and then settled itself, this time under the sternum, with a nudge like that of some inconceivable foetus. I jumped up and shook myself again, and as I did so I caught a glimpse of myself in the mirror in the closet door. My face, my own face, was ajar with fright, and I was standing there, hooked over, as if I were wearing an imaginary shawl."

In the silence after his visitor's voice stopped, the doctor sat there in the painful embarrassment of the listener who has played confessor, and whose expected comment is a responsibility he wishes he had evaded. The breeze from the open window fluttered the papers on the desk. Glancing out at the clean, regular façade of the hospital wing opposite, at whose evenly shaded windows the white shapes of orderlies and nurses flickered in consoling routine, the doctor wished petulantly that he had fended off the man and all his papers in the beginning. What right had the man to arraign *him*? Surprised at his own inner vehemence, he pulled himself together. "How long ago?" he said at last.

"Four months."

"And since?"

"It's never stopped." The visitor now seemed brimming with a tentative excitement, like a colleague discussing a mutually puzzling case. "Everything's been tried. Sedatives do obtain some sleep, but that's all. Purgatives. Even emetics." He laughed slightly, almost with pride. "Nothing like that works," he continued, shaking his head with the doting fondness of a patient for some symptom which has confounded the best of them. "It's too cagey for that."

With his use of the word "it," the doctor was propelled back into that shapely sense of reality which had gone admittedly askew during the man's recital. To admit the category of "it," to dip even a slightly cooperative finger in another's fantasy, was to risk one's own equilibrium. Better not to become involved in argument with the possessed, lest one's own apertures of belief be found to have been left ajar.

"I am afraid," the doctor said blandly, "that your case is outside my field."

"As a doctor?" said his visitor. "Or as a man?"

"Let's not discuss me, if you please."

The visitor leaned intently across the desk. "Then you admit that to a certain extent, we *have* been — ?"

"I admit nothing!" said the doctor, stiffening.

"Well," said the man disparagingly, "of course, that too is a kind of stand. The commonest, I've found." He sighed, pressing one hand against his collarbone. "I suppose you have a prescription too, or a recommendation. Most of them do."

The doctor did not enjoy being judged. "Why don't you hunt up young Hallowell?" he said, with malice.

"Disappeared. Don't you think I tried?" said his vis-à-vis ruefully. Something furtive, hope, perhaps, spread its guileful corruption over his face. "That means you do give a certain credence — "

"Nothing of the sort!"

"Well then," said his interrogator, turning his palms upward.

The doctor leaned forward, measuring his words with exasperation. "Do you mean you *want* me to tell you you're crazy!"

"In my spot," answered his visitor meekly, "which would you prefer?"

Badgered to the point of commitment, the doctor stared back at his inconvenient Diogenes. Swollen with irritation, he was only half conscious of an uneasy, vestigial twitching of his ear muscles, which contracted now as they sometimes did when he listened to atonal music.

"O.K., O.K...!" he shouted suddenly, slapping his hand down on the desk and thrusting his chin forward. "Have it your way then! I don't believe you!"

Rigid, the man looked back at him cataleptically, seeming, for a moment, all eye. Then, his mouth stretching in that medieval grimace, risorial and equivocal, whose mask appears sometimes on one side of the stage, sometimes on the other, he fell forward on the desk, with a long, mewing sigh.

Before the doctor could reach him, he had raised himself on his arms and their foreheads touched. They recoiled, staring downward. Between them on the desk, as if one of its mahogany shadows had become animate, something seemed to move — small, seal-colored, and ambiguous. For a moment it filmed back and forth, arching in a crude, primordial inquiry; then, homing straight for the doctor, whose jaw hung down in a rictus of shock, it disappeared from view.

Sputtering, the doctor beat the air and his own person wildly with his hands, and staggered upward from his chair. The breeze blew hypnotically, and the stranger gazed back at him with such perverse calm that already he felt an assailing doubt of the lightning, untoward event. He fumbled back over his sensations of the minute before, but already piecemeal and chimerical, they eluded him now, as they might forever.

"It's unbelievable," he said weakly.

His visitor put up a warding hand, shaking it fastidiously. *"Au contraire!"* he replied daintily, as though by the use of another language he would remove himself still further from commitment. Reaching forward, he gathered up his papers into a sheaf, and stood up, stretching himself straight with an all-over bodily yawn of physical ease that was like an affront. He looked down at the doctor, one hand fingering his wallet. "No," he said reflectively, "guess not." He tucked the papers away. "Shall we leave it on the basis of — er — professional courtesy?" he inquired delicately.

Choking on the sludge of his rage, the doctor looked back at him, inarticulate.

Moving toward the door, the visitor paused. "After all," he said, "with your connections . . . try to think of it as a temporary inconvenience." Regretfully, happily, he closed the door behind him.

The doctor sat at his desk, humped forward. His hands crept to his chest and crossed. He swallowed, experimentally. He hoped it was rage. He sat there, waiting. He was thinking of the luncheon table.

The Screaming Woman

Ray Bradbury's contributions to the genre of supernatural horror came at the start of his career, before he had found his voice as a science fiction writer. Many of these early stories were first published in the pulp magazine Weird Tales, *and later collected in Bradbury's* Dark Carnival *and* The October Country. *It is surprising that "The Screaming Woman" (1951) does not appear in either of these collections, for it is arguably one of the author's most effective pieces.*

With its crisp, lean sentences, pointedly condensed paragraphs, and conversational rhythms (much of the story is told directly through dialogue), "The Screaming Woman" easily carries the reader along with ten-year-old Margaret Leary as she recounts the uncanny events of a hot July afternoon. Paradoxically, although the narrative lends itself to a rapid reading, Bradbury succeeds in making the reader share Margaret's poignant, dream-like sense of time's slowing to a crawl, as she finds herself powerless to convince the adults around her of the truth of the horror she has stumbled upon.

Like most of Bradbury's supernatural fiction, the story is centered on the idea of death: Margaret's frustration and terror grow out of her discovery of a gruesome reality that those around her seem to prefer to deny. While the tale is serious in its implications, Bradbury's light, deft touch makes reading this story a strangely beguiling experience. Many readers

will wish that its author had not entirely abandoned the supernatural
genre as his imagination turned in a quite different direction. ~~~

MY NAME IS Margaret Leary and I'm ten years old and in the
fifth grade at Central School. I haven't any brothers or sisters,
but I've got a nice father and mother except they don't pay much
attention to me. And anyway, we never thought we'd have anything to do with a murdered woman. Or almost, anyway.

When you're just living on a street like we live on, you don't
think awful things are going to happen, like shooting or stabbing
or burying people under the ground, practically in your back
yard. And when it does happen you don't believe it. You just go
on buttering your toast or baking a cake.

I got to tell you how it happened. It was a noon in the middle
of July. It was hot and Mama said to me, "Margaret, you go to the
store and buy some ice cream. It's Saturday, Dad's home for
lunch, so we'll have a treat."

I ran out across the empty lot behind our house. It was a big
lot, where kids had played baseball, and broken glass and stuff.
And on my way back from the store with the ice cream I was just
walking along, minding my own business, when all of a sudden it
happened.

I heard the Screaming Woman.

I stopped and listened.

It was coming up out of the ground.

A woman was buried under the rocks and dirt and glass, and
she was screaming, all wild and horrible, for someone to dig her
out.

I just stood there, afraid. She kept screaming, muffled.

Then I started to run. I fell down, got up, and ran some more.
I got in the screen door of my house and there was Mama, calm
as you please, not knowing what I knew, that there was a real
live woman buried out in back of our house, just a hundred yards
away, screaming bloody murder.

"Mama," I said.

"Don't stand there with the ice cream," said Mama.

"But, Mama," I said.

"Put it in the icebox," she said.

"Listen, Mama, there's a Screaming Woman in the empty lot."

"And wash your hands," said Mama.

"She was screaming and screaming . . ."

"Let's see, now, salt and pepper," said Mama, far away.

"Listen to me," I said, loud. "We got to dig her out. She's buried under tons and tons of dirt and if we don't dig her out, she'll choke up and die."

"I'm certain she can wait until after lunch," said Mama.

"Mama, don't you believe me?"

"Of course, dear. Now wash your hands and take this plate of meat in to your father."

"I don't even know who she is or how she got there," I said. "But we got to help her before it's too late."

"Good gosh," said Mama. "Look at this ice cream. What did you do, just stand in the sun and let it melt?"

"Well, the empty lot . . ."

"Go on, now, scoot."

I went into the dining room.

"Hi, Dad, there's a Screaming Woman in the empty lot."

"I never knew a woman who didn't," said Dad.

"I'm serious," I said.

"You look very grave," said Father.

"We've got to get picks and shovels and excavate, like for an Egyptian mummy," I said.

"I don't feel like an archaeologist, Margaret," said Father. "Now, some nice cool October day, I'll take you up on that."

"But we can't wait that long," I almost screamed. My heart was bursting in me. I was excited and scared and afraid and here was Dad, putting meat on his plate, cutting and chewing and paying me no attention.

"Dad?" I said.

"Mmmm?" he said, chewing.

"Dad, you just gotta come out after lunch and help me," I said. "Dad, Dad, I'll give you all the money in my piggy bank!"

"Well," said Dad. "So it's a business proposition, is it? It must be important for you to offer your perfectly good money. How much money will you pay, by the hour?"

"I got five whole dollars it took me a year to save, and it's all yours."

Dad touched my arm. "I'm touched. I'm really touched. You want me to play with you and you're willing to pay for my time. Honest, Margaret, you make your old Dad feel like a piker. I don't give you enough time. Tell you what, after lunch, I'll come out and listen to your Screaming Woman, free of charge."

"Will you, oh, will you, really?"

"Yes, ma'am, that's what I'll do," said Dad. "But you must promise me one thing?"

"What?"

"If I come out, you must eat all of your lunch first."

"I promise," I said.

"Okay."

Mother came in and sat down and we started to eat.

"Not so fast," said Mama.

I slowed down. Then I started eating fast again.

"You heard your mother," said Dad.

"The Screaming Woman," I said. "We got to hurry."

"I," said Father, "intend sitting here quietly and judiciously giving my attention first to my steak, then to my potatoes, and my salad, of course, and then to my ice cream, and after that to a long drink of iced coffee, if you don't mind. I may be a good hour at it. And another thing, young lady, if you mention her name, this Screaming Whatsis, once more at this table during lunch, I won't go out with you to hear her recital."

"Yes, sir."

"Is that understood?"

"Yes, sir," I said.

Lunch was a million years long. Everybody moved in slow motion, like those films you see at the movies. Mama got up slow and got down slow and forks and knives and spoons moved slow. Even the flies in the room were slow. And Dad's cheek muscles moved slow. It was so slow. I wanted to scream, "Hurry! Oh, please, rush, get up, run around, come on out, run!"

But no, I had to sit, and all the while we sat there slowly, slowly eating our lunch, out there in the empty lot (I could hear her screaming in my mind. *Scream!*) was the Screaming Woman, all alone, while the world ate its lunch and the sun was hot and the lot was empty as the sky.

"There we are," said Dad, finished at last.

"Now will you come out to see the Screaming Woman?" I said.

"First a little more iced coffee," said Dad.

"Speaking of Screaming Women," said Mother, "Charlie Nesbitt and his wife Helen had another fight last night."

"That's nothing new," said Father. "They're always fighting."

"If you ask me, Charlie's no good," said Mother. "Or her, either."

"Oh, I don't know," said Dad. "I think she's pretty nice."

"You're prejudiced. After all, you almost married her."

"You going to bring that up again?" he said. "After all, I was only engaged to her six weeks."

"You showed some sense when you broke it off."

"Oh, you know Helen. Always stagestruck. Wanted to travel in a trunk. I just couldn't see it. That broke it up. She was sweet, though. Sweet and kind."

"What did it get her? A terrible brute of a husband like Charlie."

"Dad," I said.

"I'll give you that. Charlie has got a terrible temper," said Dad. "Remember when Helen had the lead in our high school graduation play? Pretty as a picture. She wrote some songs for it herself. That was the summer she wrote that song for me."

"Ha," said Mother.

"Don't laugh. It was a good song."

"You never told me about that song."

"It was between Helen and me. Let's see, how *did* it go?"

"Dad," I said.

"You'd better take your daughter out in the back lot," said Mother, "before she collapses. You can sing me that wonderful song later."

"Okay, come on, you," said Dad, and I ran him out of the house.

The empty lot was still empty and hot and the glass sparkled green and white and brown all around where the bottles lay.

"Now, where's this Screaming Woman?" laughed Dad.

"We forgot the shovels," I cried.

"We'll get them later, after we hear the soloist," said Dad.

I took him over to the spot. "Listen," I said.

We listened.

"I don't hear anything," said Dad, at last.

"Shh," I said. "Wait."

We listened some more. "Hey, there, Screaming Woman!" I cried.

We heard the sun in the sky. We heard the wind in the trees, real quiet. We heard a bus, far away, running along. We heard a car pass.

That was all.

"Margaret," said Father. "I suggest you go lie down and put a damp cloth on your forehead."

"But she was here," I shouted. "I heard her, screaming and screaming and screaming. See, here's where the ground's been dug up." I called frantically at the earth. "Hey there, you down there!"

"Margaret," said Father. "This is the place where Mr. Kelly dug yesterday, a big hole, to bury his trash and garbage in."

"But during the night," I said, "someone else used Mr. Kelly's burying place to bury a woman. And covered it all over again."

"Well, I'm going back in and take a cool shower," said Dad.
"You won't help me dig?"
"Better not stay out here too long," said Dad. "It's hot."
Dad walked off. I heard the back door slam.
I stamped on the ground. "Darn," I said.
The screaming started again.
She screamed and screamed. Maybe she had been tired and was resting and now she began it all over, just for me.
I stood in the empty lot in the hot sun and I felt like crying. I ran back to the house and banged the door.
"Dad, she's screaming again!"
"Sure, sure," said Dad. "Come on." And he led me to my upstairs bedroom. "Here," he said. He made me lie down and put a cold rag on my head. "Just take it easy."
I began to cry. "Oh, Dad, we can't let her die. She's all buried, like that person in that story by Edgar Allan Poe, and think how awful it is to be screaming and no one paying any attention."
"I forbid you to leave the house," said Dad, worried. "You just lie there the rest of the afternoon." He went out and locked the door. I heard him and Mother talking in the front room. After a while I stopped crying. I got up and tiptoed to the window. My room was upstairs. It seemed high.
I took a sheet off the bed and tied it to the bedpost and let it out the window. Then I climbed out the window and shinnied down until I touched the ground. Then I ran to the garage, quiet, and I got a couple of shovels and I ran to the empty lot. It was hotter than ever. And I started to dig, and all the while I dug, the Screaming Woman screamed. . . .
It was hard work. Shoving in the shovel and lifting the rocks and glass. And I knew I'd be doing it all afternoon and maybe I wouldn't finish in time. What could I do? Run tell other people? But they'd be like Mom and Dad, pay no attention. I just kept digging, all by myself.
About ten minutes later, Dippy Smith came along the path through the empty lot. He's my age and goes to my school.

"Hi, Margaret," he said.

"Hi, Dippy," I gasped.

"What you doing?" he asked.

"Digging."

"For what?"

"I got a Screaming Lady in the ground and I'm digging for her," I said.

"I don't hear no screaming," said Dippy.

"You sit down and wait awhile and you'll hear her scream yet. Or better still, help me dig."

"I don't dig unless I hear a scream," he said.

We waited.

"Listen!" I cried. "Did you *hear* it?"

"Hey," said Dippy, with slow appreciation, his eyes gleaming. "That's okay. Do it again."

"Do what again?"

"The scream."

"We got to wait," I said, puzzled.

"Do it again," he insisted, shaking my arm. "Go on." He dug in his pocket for a brown aggie. "Here." He shoved it at me. "I'll give you this marble if you do it again."

A scream came out of the ground.

"Hot dog!" said Dippy. "Teach *me* to do it!" He danced around as if I was a miracle.

"I don't . . ." I started to say.

"Did you get the *Throw-Your-Voice* book for a dime from that Magic Company in Dallas, Texas?" cried Dippy. "You got one of those tin ventriloquist contraptions in your mouth?"

"Y-yes," I lied, for I wanted him to help. "If you'll help dig, I'll tell you about it later."

"Swell," he said. "Give me a shovel."

We both dug together, and from time to time the woman screamed.

"Boy," said Dippy. "You'd think she was right under foot. You're wonderful, Maggie." Then he said, "What's her name?"

"Who?"

"The Screaming Woman. You must have a name for her."

"Oh, sure." I thought a moment. "Her name's Wilma Schweiger and she's a rich old woman, ninety-six years old, and she was buried by a man named Spike, who counterfeited ten-dollar bills."

"Yes, *sir*," said Dippy.

"And there's hidden treasure buried with her, and I, I'm a grave robber come to dig her out and get it," I gasped, digging excitedly.

Dippy made his eyes Oriental and mysterious. "Can I be a grave robber, too?" He had a better idea. "Let's pretend it's the Princess Ommanatra, an Egyptian queen, covered with diamonds!"

We kept digging and I thought, Oh, we will rescue her, we *will*. If only we keep on!

"Hey, I just got an idea," said Dippy. And he ran off and got a piece of cardboard. He scribbled on it with crayon.

"Keep digging!" I said. "We can't stop!"

"I'm making a sign. See? SLUMBERLAND CEMETERY! We can bury some birds and beetles here, in matchboxes and stuff. I'll go find some butterflies."

"No, Dippy!"

"It's more fun that way. I'll get me a dead cat, too, maybe. . . ."

"Dippy, use your shovel! Please!"

"Aw," said Dippy. "I'm tired. I think I'll go home and take a nap."

"You can't do that."

"Who says so?"

"Dippy, there's something I want to tell you."

"What?"

He gave the shovel a kick.

I whispered in his ear. "There's really a woman buried here."

"Why sure there is," he said. "You said it, Maggie."

"You don't believe me, either."

"Tell me how you throw your voice and I'll keep on digging."

"But I can't tell you, because I'm not doing it," I said. "Look, Dippy. I'll stand way over here and you listen there."

The Screaming Woman screamed again.

"Hey!" said Dippy. "There really *is* a woman here!"

"That's what I tried to say."

"Let's dig!" said Dippy.

We dug for twenty minutes.

"I wonder who she is?"

"I don't know."

"I wonder if it's Mrs. Nelson or Mrs. Turner or Mrs. Bradley. I wonder if she's pretty. Wonder what color her hair is? Wonder if she's thirty or ninety or sixty?"

"Dig!" I said.

The mound grew high.

"Wonder if she'll reward us for digging her up."

"Sure."

"A quarter, do you think?"

"More than that. I bet it's a dollar."

Dippy remembered as he dug, "I read a book once of magic. There was a Hindu with no clothes on who crept down in a grave and slept there sixty days, not eating anything, no malts, no chewing gum or candy, no air, for sixty days." His face fell. "Say, wouldn't it be awful if it was only a radio buried here and us working so hard?"

"A radio's nice, it'd be all ours."

Just then a shadow fell across us.

"Hey, you kids, what you think you're doing?"

We turned. It was Mr. Kelly, the man who owned the empty lot. "Oh, hello, Mr. Kelly," we said.

"Tell you what I want you to do," said Mr. Kelly. "I want you to take those shovels and take that soil and shovel it right back in that hole you been digging. That's what I want you to do."

My heart started beating fast again. I wanted to scream myself.

"But Mr. Kelly, there's a Screaming Woman and . . ."

"I'm not interested. I don't hear a thing."

"Listen!" I cried.

The scream.

Mr. Kelly listened and shook his head. "Don't hear nothing. Go on now, fill it up and get home with you before I give you my foot!"

We filled the hole all back in again. And all the while we filled it in, Mr. Kelly stood there, arms folded, and the woman screamed, but Mr. Kelly pretended not to hear it.

When we were finished, Mr. Kelly stomped off, saying, "Go on home now. And if I catch you here again . . ."

I turned to Dippy. "He's the one," I whispered.

"Huh?" said Dippy.

"He *murdered* Mrs. Kelly. He buried her here, after he strangled her, in a box, but she came to. Why, he stood right here and she screamed and he wouldn't pay any attention."

"Hey," said Dippy. "That's right. He stood right here and lied to us."

"There's only one thing to do," I said. "Call the police and have them come arrest Mr. Kelly."

We ran for the corner store telephone.

The police knocked on Mr. Kelly's door five minutes later. Dippy and I were hiding in the bushes, listening.

"Mr. Kelly?" said the police officer.

"Yes, sir, what can I do for you?"

"Is Mrs. Kelly at home?"

"Yes, sir."

"May we see her, sir?"

"Of course. Hey, Anna!"

Mrs. Kelly came to the door and looked out. "Yes, sir?"

"I beg your pardon," apologized the officer. "We had a report that you were buried out in an empty lot, Mrs. Kelly. It sounded like a child made the call, but we had to be certain. Sorry to have troubled you."

"It's those blasted kids," cried Mr. Kelly, angrily. "If I ever catch them, I'll rip them limb from limb!"

"Cheezit!" said Dippy, and we both ran.

"What'll we do now?" I said.

"I got to go home," said Dippy. "Boy, we're really in trouble. We'll get a licking for this."

"But what about the Screaming Woman?"

"To heck with her," said Dippy. "We don't dare go near that empty lot again. Old man Kelly'll be waiting around with his razor strap and lambast heck out'n us. And I just happened to remember, Maggie. Ain't old man Kelly sort of deaf, hard-of-hearing?"

"Oh, my gosh," I said. "No *wonder* he didn't hear the screams."

"So long," said Dippy. "We sure got in trouble over your darn old ventriloquist voice. I'll be seeing you."

I was left all alone in the world, no one to help me, no one to believe me at all. I just wanted to crawl down in that box with the Screaming Woman and die. The police were after me now, for lying to them, only I didn't know it was a lie, and my father was probably looking for me, too, or would be once he found my bed empty. There was only one last thing to do, and I did it.

I went from house to house, all down the street, near the empty lot. And I rang every bell and when the door opened I said: "I beg your pardon, Mrs. Griswold, but is anyone missing from your house?" or "Hello, Mrs. Pikes, you're looking fine today. Glad to see you *home*." And once I saw that the lady of the house was home I just chatted awhile to be polite, and went on down the street.

The hours were rolling along. It was getting late. I kept thinking, oh, there's only so much air in that box with that woman under the earth, and if I don't hurry, she'll suffocate, and I got to rush! So I rang bells and knocked on doors, and it got later, and I was just about to give up and go home, when I knocked on the *last* door, which was the door of Mr. Charlie Nesbitt, who lives next to us. I kept knocking and knocking.

Instead of Mrs. Nesbitt, or Helen as my father calls her, coming to the door, why it was Mr. Nesbitt, Charlie, *himself*.

"Oh," he said. "It's you, Margaret."

"Yes," I said. "Good afternoon."

"What can I do for you, kid?" he said.

"Well, I thought I'd like to see your wife, Mrs. Nesbitt," I said.

"Oh," he said.

"May I?"

"Well, she's gone out to the store," he said.

"I'll wait," I said, and slipped in past him.

"Hey," he said.

I sat down in a chair. "My, it's a hot day," I said, trying to be
calm, thinking about the empty lot and air going out of the box,
and the screams getting weaker and weaker.

"Say, listen, kid," said Charlie, coming over to me, "I don't
think you better wait."

"Oh, sure," I said. "Why not?"

"Well, my wife won't be back," he said.

"Oh?"

"Not today, that is. She's gone to the store, like I said, but,
but, she's going on from there to visit her mother. Yeah. She's
going to visit her mother, in Schenectady. She'll be back, two or
three days, maybe a week."

"That's a shame," I said.

"Why?"

"I wanted to tell her something."

"What?"

"I just wanted to tell her there's a woman buried over in the
empty lot, screaming under tons and tons of dirt."

Mr. Nesbitt dropped his cigarette.

"You dropped your cigarette, Mr. Nesbitt," I pointed out,
with my shoe.

"Oh, did I? Sure. So I did," he mumbled. "Well, I'll tell Helen
when she comes home, your story. She'll be glad to hear it."

"Thanks. It's a real woman."

"How do you know it is?"

"I heard her."

"How, how you know it isn't, well, a *mandrake* root?"

"What's that?"

"You know. A mandrake. It's a kind of a plant, kid. They scream. I know, I read it once. How you know it ain't a mandrake?"

"I never thought of that."

"You better start thinking," he said, lighting another cigarette. He tried to be casual. "Say, kid, you, eh, you *say* anything about this to anyone?"

"Sure, I told lots of people."

Mr. Nesbitt burned his hand on his match.

"Anybody doing anything about it?" he asked.

"No," I said. "They won't believe me."

He smiled. "Of course. Naturally. You're nothing but a kid. Why should they listen to you?"

"I'm going back now and dig her out with a spade," I said.

"Wait."

"I got to go," I said.

"Stick around," he insisted.

"Thanks, but no," I said, frantically.

He took my arm. "Know how to play cards, kid? Black jack?"

"Yes, sir."

He took out a deck of cards from a desk. "We'll have a game."

"I got to go dig."

"Plenty of time for that," he said, quiet. "Anyway, maybe my wife'll be home. Sure. That's it. You wait for her. Wait awhile."

"You think she will be?"

"Sure, kid. Say, about that voice; is it very strong?"

"It gets weaker all the time."

Mr. Nesbitt sighed and smiled. "You and your kid games. Here now, let's play that game of black jack, it's more fun than Screaming Women."

"I got to go. It's late."

"Stick around, you got nothing to do."

I knew what he was trying to do. He was trying to keep me in his house until the screaming died down and was gone. He was trying to keep me from helping her. "My wife'll be home in ten minutes," he said. "Sure. Ten minutes. You wait. You sit right there."

We played cards. The clock ticked. The sun went down the sky. It was getting late. The screaming got fainter and fainter in my mind. "I got to go," I said.

"Another game," said Mr. Nesbitt. "Wait another hour, kid. My wife'll come yet. Wait."

In another hour he looked at his watch. "Well, kid, I guess you can go now." And I knew what his plan was. He'd sneak down in the middle of the night and dig up his wife, still alive, and take her somewhere else and bury her, good. "So long, kid. So long." He let me go, because he thought that by now the air must all be gone from the box.

The door shut in my face.

I went back near the empty lot and hid in some bushes. What could I do? Tell my folks? But they hadn't believed me. Call the police on Mr. Charlie Nesbitt? But he said his wife was away visiting. Nobody would believe me!

I watched Mr. Kelly's house. He wasn't in sight. I ran over to the place where the screaming had been and just stood there.

The screaming had stopped. It was so quiet I thought I would never hear a scream again. It was all over. I was too late, I thought.

I bent down and put my ear against the ground.

And then I heard it, way down, way deep, and so faint I could hardly hear it.

The woman wasn't screaming any more. She was singing.

Something about, "I loved you fair, I loved you well."

It was sort of a sad song. Very faint. And sort of broken. All of those hours down under the ground in that box must have sort of made her crazy. All she needed was some air and food and she'd be all right. But she just kept singing, not wanting to scream any more, not caring, just singing.

I listened to the song.

And then I turned and walked straight across the lot and up the steps to my house and I opened the front door.

"Father," I said.

"So there you are!" he cried.

"Father," I said.

"You're going to get a licking," he said.

"She's not screaming any more."

"Don't talk about her!"

"She's singing now," I cried.

"You're not telling the truth!"

"Dad," I said. "She's out there and she'll be dead soon if you don't listen to me. She's out there, singing, and this is what she's singing." I hummed the tune. I sang a few of the words. "I loved you fair, I loved you well . . ."

Dad's face grew pale. He came and took my arm.

"What did you say?" he said.

I sang it again: "I loved you fair, I loved you well."

"Where did you *hear* that song?" he shouted.

"Out in the empty lot, just now."

"But that's *Helen's* song, the one she wrote, years ago, for *me!*" cried Father. "You *can't* know it. *Nobody* knew it, except Helen and me. I never sang it to anyone, not you or anyone."

"Sure," I said.

"Oh, my God!" cried Father, and ran out the door to get a shovel. The last I saw of him he was in the empty lot, digging, and lots of other people with him, digging.

I felt so happy I wanted to cry.

I dialed a number on the phone and when Dippy answered I said, "Hi, Dippy. Everything's fine. Everything's worked out keen. The Screaming Woman isn't screaming any more."

"Swell," said Dippy.

"I'll meet you in the empty lot with a shovel in two minutes," I said.

"Last one there's a monkey! So long!" cried Dippy.

"So long, Dippy!" I said, and ran.

L. P. HARTLEY

W. S.

Like the novelist in his story *"W. S."* (*1952*), L. P. Hartley lived a life devoted to books and writing. He once declared, *"I have been more actively frightened by a book than by anything that has happened to me in my own life."*[13] If that were entirely true, however, one suspects that Hartley would not have been the powerful writer that he was. Indeed, he later affirmed that the brutality of the first World War, in which he briefly served, radically transformed his vision of humanity. Throughout his literary career, he would eloquently explore the darkness and disorder at the core of existence. The social realism of his novels is invariably balanced by an evocation of mysterious forces pulsating beneath the surface of societal relations. In Hartley's several collections of short stories, these forces assume center stage.

The uncanny enters the life of the protagonist of *"W. S."* as a succession of ominous postcards, signed only with initials and postmarked from locations ever nearer his own. Like much of Hartley's work, this story takes as its subject the cavernous depths of the subconscious psyche. Yet here the focus is on the imaginative artist, the professional storyteller. The very nature of the author's craft, Hartley suggests, renders him peculiarly vulnerable to those mysterious processes by which hidden parts of the mind, projected outwards, can return to haunt one.

Hartley once remarked that the short story of the supernatural is

W. S.

"the most exacting form of literary art, and perhaps the only one in which there is almost no intermediate step between success and failure."[14] *The following tale can be counted as one of the genre's successes.* ⟡

THE FIRST POSTCARD came from Forfar. "I thought you might like a picture of Forfar," it said. "You have always been so interested in Scotland, and that is one reason why I am interested in you. I have enjoyed all your books, but do you really get to grips with people? I doubt it. Try to think of this as a handshake from your devoted admirer, W. S."

Like other novelists, Walter Streeter was used to getting communications from strangers. Usually they were friendly but sometimes they were critical. In either case he always answered them, for he was conscientious. But answering them took up the time and energy he needed for his writing, so that he was rather relieved that W. S. had given no address. The photograph of Forfar was uninteresting and he tore it up. His anonymous correspondent's criticism, however, lingered in his mind. Did he really fail to come to grips with his characters? Perhaps he did. He was aware that in most cases they were either projections of his own personality or, in different forms, the antithesis of it. The Me and the Not Me. Perhaps W. S. had spotted this. Not for the first time Walter made a vow to be more objective.

About ten days later arrived another postcard, this time from Berwick-on-Tweed. "What do you think of Berwick-on-Tweed?" it said. "Like you, it's on the Border. I hope this doesn't sound rude. I don't mean that you are a border-line case! You know how much I admire your stories. Some people call them other-worldly. I think you should plump for one world or the other. Another firm handshake from W. S."

Walter Streeter pondered over this and began to wonder about the sender. Was his correspondent a man or a woman? It looked like a man's handwriting — commercial, unself-conscious — and the criticism was like a man's. On the other hand, it was like a woman to probe — to want to make him feel at the same time flattered and unsure of himself. He felt the faint stirrings of curiosity but soon dismissed them; he was not a man to experiment with acquaintances. Still it was odd to think of this unknown person speculating about him, sizing him up. Other-worldly, indeed! He re-read the last two chapters he had written. Perhaps they didn't have their feet firm on the ground. Perhaps he was too ready to escape, as other novelists were nowadays, into an ambiguous world, a world where the conscious mind did not have things too much its own way. But did that matter? He threw the picture of Berwick-on-Tweed into his November fire and tried to write; but the words came haltingly, as though contending with an extra-strong barrier of self-criticism. And as the days passed he became uncomfortably aware of self-division, as though someone had taken hold of his personality and was pulling it apart. His work was no longer homogeneous, there were two strains in it, unreconciled and opposing, and it went much slower as he tried to resolve the discord. Never mind, he thought: perhaps I was getting into a groove. These difficulties may be growing pains, I may have tapped a new source of supply. If only I could correlate the two and make their conflict fruitful, as many artists have!

The third postcard showed a picture of York Minster. "I know you are interested in cathedrals," it said. "I'm sure this isn't a sign of megalomania in your case, but smaller churches are sometimes more rewarding. I'm seeing a good many churches on my way south. Are you busy writing or are you looking round for ideas? Another hearty handshake from your friend W. S."

It was true that Walter Streeter was interested in cathedrals. Lincoln Cathedral had been the subject of one of his youthful fantasies and he had written about it in a travel book. And it was also true that he admired mere size and was inclined to undervalue parish churches. But how could W. S. have known that? And was it really a sign of megalomania? And who was W. S. anyhow?

For the first time it struck him that the initials were his own.

No, not for the first time. He had noticed it before, but they were such commonplace initials; they were Gilbert's, they were Maugham's, they were Shakespeare's — a common possession. Anyone might have them. Yet now it seemed to him an odd coincidence; and the idea came into his mind — suppose I have been writing postcards to myself? People did such things, especially people with split personalities. Not that he was one, of course. And yet there were these unexplained developments — the cleavage in his writing, which had now extended from his thought to his style, making one paragraph languorous with semi-colons and subordinate clauses, and another sharp and incisive with main verbs and full-stops.

He looked at the handwriting again. It had seemed the perfection of ordinariness — anybody's hand — so ordinary as perhaps to be disguised. Now he fancied he saw in it resemblances to his own. He was just going to pitch the postcard in the fire when suddenly he decided not to. I'll show it to somebody, he thought.

His friend said, "My dear fellow, it's all quite plain. The woman's a lunatic. I'm sure it's a woman. She has probably fallen in love with you and wants to make you interested in her. I should pay no attention whatsoever. People whose names are mentioned in the papers are always getting letters from lunatics. If they worry you, destroy them without reading them. That sort of person is often a little psychic, and if she senses that she's getting a rise out of you she'll go on."

For a moment Walter Streeter felt reassured. A woman, a little mouse-like creature, who had somehow taken a fancy to him! What was there to feel uneasy about in that? It was really rather sweet and touching, and he began to think of her and wonder what she looked like. What did it matter if she was a little mad? Then his subconscious mind, searching for something to torment him with, and assuming the authority of logic, said: Supposing those postcards are a lunatic's, and you are writing them to yourself, doesn't it follow that you must be a lunatic too?

He tried to put the thought away from him; he tried to destroy the postcard as he had the others. But something in him wanted to preserve it. It had become a piece of him, he felt. Yielding to an irresistible compulsion, which he dreaded, he found himself putting it behind the clock on the chimney-piece. He couldn't see it but he knew that it was there.

He now had to admit to himself that the postcard business had become a leading factor in his life. It had created a new area of thoughts and feelings and they were most unhelpful. His being was strung up in expectation of the next postcard.

Yet when it came it took him, as the others had, completely by surprise. He could not bring himself to look at the picture. "I hope you are well and would like a postcard from Coventry," he read. "Have you ever been sent to Coventry? I have — in fact you sent me there. It isn't a pleasant experience, I can tell you. I am getting nearer. Perhaps we shall come to grips after all. I advised you to come to grips with your characters, didn't I? Have I given you any new ideas? If I have you ought to thank me, for they are what novelists want, I understand. I have been re-reading your novels, living in them, I might say. Another hard handshake. As always, W. S."

A wave of panic surged up in Walter Streeter. How was it that he had never noticed, all this time, the most significant fact about the postcards — that each one came from a place geographically closer to him than the last? "I am coming nearer." Had his mind, unconsciously self-protective, worn blinkers? If it had, he wished he could put them back. He took an atlas and idly traced out W. S.'s itinerary. An interval of eighty miles or so seemed to separate the stopping-places. Walter lived in a large West Country town about ninety miles from Coventry.

Should he show the postcards to an alienist? But what could an alienist tell him? He would not know, what Walter wanted to know, whether he had anything to fear from W. S.

Better go to the police. The police were used to dealing with poison-pens. If they laughed at him, so much the better.

They did not laugh, however. They said they thought the postcards were a hoax and that W. S. would never show up in the flesh. Then they asked if there was anyone who had a grudge against him. "No one that I know of," Walter said. They, too, took the view that the writer was probably a woman. They told him not to worry but to let them know if further postcards came.

A little comforted, Walter went home. The talk with the police had done him good. He thought it over. It was quite true what he had told them — that he had no enemies. He was not a man of strong personal feelings: such feelings as he had went into his books. In his books he had drawn some pretty nasty characters. Not of recent years, however. Of recent years he had felt a reluctance to draw a very bad man or woman: he thought it morally irresponsible and artistically unconvincing, too. There was good in everyone: Iagos were a myth. Latterly — but he had to admit that it was several weeks since he laid pen to paper, so much had this ridiculous business of the postcards weighed upon his mind — if he had to draw a really wicked person he represented him as a Communist or a Nazi — someone who had deliberately put off his human characteristics. But in the past, when he was younger and more inclined to see things as black or white, he had let himself go once or twice. He did not remember his old books very well but there was a character in one, "The Outcast," into whom he had really got his knife. He had written about him with extreme vindictiveness, just as if he was a real person whom he was trying to show up. He had experienced a curious pleasure in attributing every kind of wickedness to this man. He never gave him the benefit of the doubt. He had never felt a twinge of pity for him, even when he paid the penalty for his misdeeds on the gallows. He had so worked himself up that the idea of this dark creature, creeping about brimful of malevolence, had almost frightened him.

Odd that he couldn't remember the man's name.

He took the book down from the shelf and turned the pages — even now they affected him uncomfortably. Yes, here it was, William ... William ... he would have to look back to find the surname. William Stainsforth.

His own initials.

Walter did not think the coincidence meant anything but it coloured his mind and weakened its resistance to his obsession. So uneasy was he that when the next postcard came it came as a relief.

"I am quite close now," he read, and involuntarily he turned the postcard over. The glorious central tower of Gloucester Cathedral met his eye. He stared at it as if it could tell him something, then with an effort went on reading. "My movements, as you may have guessed, are not quite under my control, but all being well I look forward to seeing you some time this week-end. Then we can really come to grips. I wonder if you'll recognize me! It won't be the first time you have given me hospitality. My hand feels a bit cold to-night, but my handshake will be just as hearty. As always, W. S."

"P. S. Does Gloucester remind you of anything? Gloucester gaol?"

Walter took the postcard straight to the police station, and asked if he could have police protection over the week-end. The officer in charge smiled at him and said he was quite sure it was a hoax; but he would tell someone to keep an eye on the premises.

"You still have no idea who it could be?" he asked.

Walter shook his head.

It was Tuesday; Walter Streeter had plenty of time to think about the week-end. At first he felt he would not be able to live through the interval, but strange to say his confidence increased instead of waning. He set himself to work as though he *could* work, and presently he found he could — differently from before, and, he thought, better. It was as though the nervous strain he had been living under had, like an acid, dissolved a layer of non-conductive thought that came between him and his subject: he was nearer to it now, and his characters, instead of obeying woodenly his stage directions, responded wholeheartedly and with all their beings to the tests he put them to. So passed the days, and the dawn of Friday seemed like any other day until something jerked him out of his self-induced trance and suddenly he asked himself, "When does a week-end begin?"

A long week-end begins on Friday. At that his panic returned. He went to the street door and looked out. It was a suburban, unfrequented street of detached Regency houses like his own. They had tall square gate-posts, some crowned with semicircular iron brackets holding lanterns. Most of these were out of repair: only two or three were ever lit. A car went slowly down the street; some people crossed it: everything was normal.

Several times that day he went to look and saw nothing unusual, and when Saturday came, bringing no postcard, his panic had almost subsided. He nearly rang up the police station to tell them not to bother to send anyone after all.

They were as good as their word: they did send someone. Between tea and dinner, the time when week-end guests most commonly arrive, Walter went to the door and there, between two unlit gate-posts, he saw a policeman standing — the first policeman he had ever seen in Charlotte Street. At the sight, and at the relief it brought him, he realized how anxious he had been. Now he felt safer than he had ever felt in his life, and also a little ashamed at having given extra trouble to a hardworked body of men. Should he go and speak to his unknown guardian, offer him a cup of tea or a drink? It would be nice to hear him laugh at Walter's fancies. But no — somehow he felt his security the greater when its source was impersonal and anonymous. "P. C. Smith" was somehow less impressive than "police protection."

Several times from an upper window (he didn't like to open the door and stare) he made sure that his guardian was still there; and once, for added proof, he asked his housekeeper to verify the strange phenomenon. Disappointingly, she came back saying she had seen no policeman; but she was not very good at seeing things, and when Walter went a few minutes later he saw him plain enough. The man must walk about, of course, perhaps he had been taking a stroll when Mrs. Kendal looked.

It was contrary to his routine to work after dinner but tonight he did, he felt so much in the vein. Indeed, a sort of exaltation possessed him; the words ran off his pen; it would be foolish to check the creative impulse for the sake of a little extra sleep.

On, on. They were right who said the small hours were the time to work. When his housekeeper came in to say good night he scarcely raised his eyes.

In the warm, snug little room the silence purred around him like a kettle. He did not even hear the door bell till it had been ringing for some time.

A visitor at this hour?

His knees trembling, he went to the door, scarcely knowing what he expected to find; so what was his relief on opening it, to see the doorway filled by the tall figure of a policeman. Without waiting for the man to speak —

"Come in, come in, my dear fellow," he exclaimed. He held his hand out, but the policeman did not take it. "You must have been very cold standing out there. I didn't know that it was snowing, though," he added, seeing the snowflakes on the policeman's cape and helmet. "Come in and warm yourself."

"Thanks," said the policeman. "I don't mind if I do."

Walter knew enough of the phrases used by men of the policeman's stamp not to take this for a grudging acceptance. "This way," he prattled on. "I was writing in my study. By Jove, it *is* cold, I'll turn the gas on more. Now won't you take your traps off, and make yourself at home?"

"I can't stay long," the policeman said, "I've got a job to do, as *you* know."

"Oh yes," said Walter, "such a silly job, a sinecure." He stopped, wondering if the policeman would know what a sinecure was. "I suppose you know what it's about — the postcards?"

The policeman nodded.

"But nothing can happen to me as long as you are here," said Walter. "I shall be as safe . . . as safe as houses. Stay as long as you can, and have a drink."

"I never drink on duty," said the policeman. Still in his cape and helmet, he looked round. "So this is where you work," he said.

"Yes, I was writing when you rang."

"Some poor devil's for it, I expect," the policeman said.

"Oh, why?" Walter was hurt by his unfriendly tone, and noticed how hard his gooseberry eyes were.

"I'll tell you in a minute," said the policeman, and then the telephone bell rang. Walter excused himself and hurried from the room.

"This is the police station," said a voice. "Is that Mr. Streeter?"

Walter said it was.

"Well, Mr. Streeter, how is everything at your place? All right, I hope? I'll tell you why I ask. I'm sorry to say we quite forgot about that little job we were going to do for you. Bad co-ordination, I'm afraid."

"But," said Walter, "you did send someone."

"No, Mr. Streeter, I'm afraid we didn't."

"But there's a policeman here, here in this very house."

There was a pause, then his interlocutor said, in a less casual voice:

"He can't be one of our chaps. Did you see his number by any chance?"

"No."

A longer pause and then the voice said:

"Would you like us to send somebody now?"

"Yes, p . . . please."

"All right then, we'll be with you in a jiffy."

Walter put back the receiver. What now? he asked himself. Should he barricade the door? Should he run out into the street? Should he try to rouse his housekeeper? A policeman of any sort was a formidable proposition, but a rogue policeman! How long would it take the real police to come? A jiffy, they had said. What was a jiffy in terms of minutes? While he was debating the door opened and his guest came in.

"No room's private when the street door's once passed," he said. "Had you forgotten I was a policeman?"

"Was?" said Walter, edging away from him. "You *are* a policeman."

"I have been other things as well," the policeman said. "Thief, pimp, blackmailer, not to mention murderer. *You* should know."

The policeman, if such he was, seemed to be moving towards him and Walter suddenly became alive to the importance of small distances — the distance from the sideboard to the table, the distance from one chair to another.

"I don't know what you mean," he said. "Why do you speak like that? I've never done you any harm. I've never set eyes on you before."

"Oh, haven't you?" the man said. "But you've thought about me and" — his voice rose — "and you've written about me. You got some fun out of me, didn't you? Now I'm going to get some fun out of you. You made me just as nasty as you could. Wasn't that doing me harm? You didn't think what it would feel like to be me, did you? You didn't put yourself in my place, did you? You hadn't any pity for me, had you? Well, I'm not going to have any pity for you."

"But I tell you," cried Walter, clutching the table's edge, "I don't know you!"

"And now you say you don't know me! You did all that to me and then forgot me!" His voice became a whine, charged with self-pity. "You forgot William Stainsforth."

"William Stainsforth!"

"Yes. I was your scapegoat, wasn't I? You unloaded all your self-dislike on me. You felt pretty good while you were writing about me. You thought, what a noble, upright fellow you were, writing about this rotter. Now, as one W. S. to another, what shall I do, if I behave in character?"

"I . . . I don't know," muttered Walter.

"You don't know?" Stainsforth sneered. "You ought to know, you fathered me. What would William Stainsforth do if he met his old dad in a quiet place, his kind old dad who made him swing?"

Walter could only stare at him.

"You know what he'd do as well as I," said Stainsforth. Then his face changed and he said abruptly, "No, you don't, because you never really understood me. I'm not so black as you painted me." He paused, and a flicker of hope started in Walter's breast. "You never gave me a chance, did you? Well, I'm going to give you one. That shows you never understood me, doesn't it?"

Walter nodded.

"And there's another thing you have forgotten."

"What is that?"

"I was a kid once," the ex-policeman said.

Walter said nothing.

"You admit that?" said William Stainsforth grimly. "Well, if you can tell me of one virtue you ever credited me with — just one kind thought — just one redeeming feature—"

"Yes?" said Walter, trembling.

"Well, then I'll let you off."

"And if I can't?" whispered Walter.

"Well, then, that's just too bad. We'll have to come to grips and you know what that means. You took off one of my arms but I've still got the other. 'Stainsforth of the iron hand' you called me."

Walter began to pant.

"I'll give you two minutes to remember," Stainsforth said. They both looked at the clock. At first the stealthy movement of the hand paralysed Walter's thought. He stared at William Stainsforth's face, his cruel, crafty face, which seemed to be always in shadow, as if it was something the light could not touch. Desperately he searched his memory for the one fact that would save him; but his memory, clenched like a fist, would give up nothing. "I must invent something," he thought, and suddenly his mind relaxed and he saw, printed on it like a photograph, the last page of the book. Then, with the speed and magic of a dream, each page appeared before him in perfect clarity until the first was reached, and he realized with overwhelming force that what he looked for was not there. In all that evil there was not one hint of good. And he felt, compulsively and with a kind of exaltation, that unless he testified to this the cause of goodness everywhere would be betrayed.

"There's nothing to be said for you!" he shouted. "And you know it! Of all your dirty tricks this is the dirtiest! You want me to whitewash you, do you? The very snowflakes on you are turning black! How dare you ask me for a character? I've given you one already! God forbid that I should ever say a good word for you! I'd rather die!"

Stainsforth's one arm shot out. "Then die!" he said.

The police found Walter Streeter slumped across the dining-table. His body was still warm, but he was dead. It was easy to tell how he died; for it was not his hand that his visitor had shaken, but his throat. Walter Streeter had been strangled. Of his assailant there was no trace. On the table and on his clothes were flakes of melting snow. But how it came there remained a mystery, for no snow was reported from any district on the day he died.

ROBERT AICKMAN

The Inner Room

The name of Robert Aickman, already held in high esteem by connoisseurs of the literary uncanny, deserves to be far more widely known. To read his stories for the first time is to discover a fictional world as subtle and bewitching as poetry. For Aickman, as for Freud, the preternatural is a gateway into the labyrinth of the unconscious, but Aickman was also a staunch believer in the truth of Sacheverell Sitwell's maxim, "In the end it is the mystery that lasts and not the explanation."[15]

Aickman was the sensitive only child of parents who, as long as he could remember, scorned and despised one another. Early on, he was forced to confront in those he most loved a splitting of the personality that, as he later observed in his autobiography, superimposes upon the kind, idealistic part of the self a shadowy, pernicious twin.

The dolls' house in "The Inner Room" (1968), like so many houses in literary tradition, offers a symbolic analogy with the many-chambered human psyche. Yet in his elaboration of this motif, Aickman is mesmerizingly original. As we follow the protagonist, Lena, from her initial acquisition of the oversized, intricately decorated toy, with its eight woolly-haired female inhabitants, to her unsettling encounter years later with a life-sized version of both house and occupants deep in the English countryside, the reader suspects that Lena's family relationships and unacknowledged emotions may hold the key to this enigmatic story.

Like most of Aickman's "strange tales," "The Inner Room" can be

171

read again and again without exhausting its mysteries or diminishing its power to haunt. "The Inner Room" may even move some readers to concur with the author's lifelong conviction that "the supernatural, Freud's Unheimliche, can give one . . . a sensation of knowing oneself and the world that otherwise can be found (equally rarely) only through poetry, music, travel, and love."[16]

It was never less than half an hour after the engine stopped running that my father deigned to signal for succour. If in the process of breaking down, we had climbed, or descended, a bank, then first we must all exhaust ourselves pushing. If we had collided, there was, of course, a row. If, as had happened that day, it was simply that, while we coasted along, the machinery had ceased to churn and rattle, then my father tried his hand as a mechanic. That was the worst contingency of all; at least, it was the worst one connected with motoring.

I had learned by experience that neither rain nor snow made much difference, and certainly not fog; but that afternoon it was hotter than any day I could remember. I realized later that it was the famous Long Summer of 1921, when the water at the bottom of cottage wells turned salt, and when eels were found baked and edible in their mud. But to know this at the time, I should have had to read the papers, and though, through my mother's devotion, I had the trick of reading before my third birthday, I mostly left the practice to my younger brother, Constantin. He was reading now from a pudgy volume, as thick as it was broad, and resembling his own head in size and proportion. As always, he had resumed his studies immediately the bumping of our almost springless car permitted, and even before motion had ceased. My mother sat in the front seat inevitably correcting pupils' exercises. By teaching her native German in five schools at once, three of them distant, one of them fashionable, she surprisingly managed to maintain the four of us, and even our car. The front offside door of the car leaned dangerously open into the seething highway.

"I say," cried my father.

The young man in the big yellow racer shook his head as he tore by. My father had addressed the least appropriate car on the road.

"I say."

I cannot recall what the next car looked like, but it did not stop.

My father was facing the direction from which we had come, and sawing the air with his left arm, like a very inexperienced policeman. Perhaps no one stopped because all thought him eccentric. Then a car going in the opposite direction came to a standstill behind my father's back. My father perceived nothing. The motorist sounded his horn. In those days, horns squealed, and I covered my ears with my hands. Between my hands and my head my long fair hair was like brittle flax in the sun.

My father darted through the traffic. I think it was the Portsmouth Road. The man in the other car got out and came to us. I noticed his companion, much younger and in a cherry-coloured cloche, begin to deal with her nails.

"Broken down?" asked the man. To me it seemed obvious, as the road was strewn with bits of the engine and oozy blobs of oil. Moreover, surely my father had explained?

"I can't quite locate the seat of the trouble," said my father.

The man took off one of his driving gauntlets, big and dirty.

"Catch hold for a moment." My father caught hold.

The man put his hand into the engine and made a casual movement. Something snapped loudly.

"Done right in. If you ask me, I'm not sure she'll ever go again."

"Then I don't think I'll ask you," said my father affably. "Hot, isn't it?" My father began to mop his tall corrugated brow, and front-to-back ridges of grey hair.

"Want a tow?"

"Just to the nearest garage." My father always spoke the word in perfect French.

"Where to?"

"To the nearest car repair workshop. If it would not be troubling you too much."

"Can't help myself now, can I?"

173

From under the back seat in the other car, the owner got out a thick, frayed rope, black and greasy as the hangman's. The owner's friend simply said, "Pleased to meet you," and began to replace her scalpels and enamels in their cabinet. We jolted towards the town we had traversed an hour or two before; and were then untied outside a garage on the outskirts.

"Surely it is closed for the holiday?" said my mother. Hers is a voice I can always recall upon an instant: guttural, of course, but beautiful, truly golden.

"'Spect he'll be back," said our benefactor, drawing in his rope like a fisherman. "Give him a bang." He kicked three times very loudly upon the dropped iron shutter. Then without another word he drove away.

It was my birthday, I had been promised the sea, and I began to weep. Constantin, with a fretful little wriggle, closed further into himself and his book; but my mother leaned over the front seat of the car and opened her arms to me. I went to her and sobbed on the shoulder of her bright red dress.

"Kleine Lene, wir stecken schön in der Tinte."

My father, who could pronounce six languages perfectly but speak only one of them, never liked my mother to use her native tongue within the family. He rapped more sharply on the shutter. My mother knew his ways, but, where our welfare was at stake, ignored them.

"Edgar," said my mother, "let us give the children presents. Especially my little Lene." My tears, though childish, and less viscous than those shed in later life, had turned the scarlet shoulder of her dress to purple. She squinted smilingly sideways at the damage.

My father was delighted to defer the decision about what next to do with the car. But, as pillage was possible, my mother took with her the exercises, and Constantin his fat little book.

We straggled along the main road, torrid, raucous, adequate only for a gentler period of history. The grit and dust stung my face and arms and knees, like granulated glass. My mother and I went first, she holding my hand. My father struggled to walk at her other side, but for most of the way, the path was too narrow. Constantin mused along in the rear, abstracted as usual.

"It is true what the papers say," exclaimed my father. "British roads were never built for motor traffic. Beyond the odd car, of course."

My mother nodded and slightly smiled. Even in the lineless hopsacks of the twenties, she could not ever but look magnificent, with her rolling, turbulent, honey hair, and Hellenic proportions. Ultimately we reached the High Street. The very first shop had one of its windows stuffed with toys; the other being stacked with groceries and draperies and coal-hods, all dingy. The name "Popular Bazaar," in wooden relief as if glued on in building blocks, stretched across the whole front, not quite centre.

It was not merely an out-of-fashion shop, but a shop that at the best sold too much of what no one wanted. My father comprehended the contents of the Toy Department window with a single, anxious glance, and said, "Choose whatever you like. Both of you. But look very carefully first. Don't hurry." Then he turned away and began to hum a fragment from "The Lady of the Rose."

But Constantin spoke at once. "I choose those telegraph wires." They ranged beside a line of tin railway that stretched right across the window, long undusted and tending to buckle. There were seven or eight posts, with six wires on each side of the post. Though I could not think why Constantin wanted them, and though in the event he did not get them, the appearance of them, and of the rusty track beneath them, is all that remains clear in my memory of that window.

"I doubt whether they're for sale," said my father. "Look again. There's a good boy. No hurry."

"They're all I want," said Constantin, and turned his back on the uninspiring display.

"Well, we'll see," said my father. "I'll make a special point of it with the man . . ." He turned to me. "And what about you? Very few dolls, I'm afraid."

"I don't like dolls any more." As a matter of fact, I had never owned a proper one, although I suffered from this fact only when competing with other girls, which meant very seldom, for our friends were few and occasional. The dolls in the window were flyblown and detestable.

"I think we could find a better shop from which to give Lene a birthday present," said my mother, in her correct, dignified English.

"We must not be unjust," said my father, "when we have not even looked inside."

The inferiority of the goods implied cheapness, which unfortunately always mattered; although, as it happened, none of the articles seemed actually to be priced.

"I do not like this shop," said my mother. "It is a shop that has died."

Her regal manner when she said such things was, I think, too Germanic for my father's Englishness. That, and the prospect of unexpected economy, perhaps led him to be firm.

"We have Constantin's present to consider as well as Lene's. Let us go in."

By contrast with the blazing highway, the main impression of the interior was darkness. After a few moments, I also became aware of a smell. Everything in the shop smelt of that smell, and, one felt, always would do so; the mixed odour of any General Store, but at once enhanced and passé. I can smell it now.

"We do not necessarily want to buy anything," said my father, "but, if we may, should like to look round?"

Since the days of Mr. Selfridge the proposition is supposed to be taken for granted, but at that time the message had yet to spread. The bazaar keeper seemed hardly to welcome it. He was younger than I had expected (an unusual thing for a child, but I had probably been awaiting a white-bearded gnome); though pale, nearly bald, and perceptibly grimy. He wore an untidy grey suit and bedroom slippers.

"Look about you, children," said my father. "Take your time. We can't buy presents every day."

I noticed that my mother still stood in the doorway.

"I want those wires," said Constantin.

"Make quite sure by looking at the other things first."

Constantin turned aside bored, his book held behind his back. He began to scrape his feet. It was up to me to uphold my father's position. Rather timidly, I began to peer about, not going far from him. The bazaar keeper silently watched me with eyes colourless in the twilight.

"Those toy telegraph poles in your window," said my father after a pause, fraught for me with anxiety and responsibility. "How much would you take for them?"

"They are not for sale," said the bazaar keeper, and said no more.

"Then why do you display them in the window?"

"They are a kind of decoration, I suppose." Did he not know? I wondered.

"Even if they're not normally for sale, perhaps you'll sell them to me," said my vagabond father, smiling like Rothschild. "My son, you see, has taken a special fancy to them."

"Sorry," said the man in the shop.

"Are you the principal here?"

"I am."

"Then surely as a reasonable man," said my father, switching from superiority to ingratiation —

"They are to dress the window," said the bazaar man. "They are not for sale."

This dialogue entered through the back of my head as, diligently and unobtrusively, I conned the musty stock. At the back of the shop was a window, curtained all over in grey lace: to judge by the weak light it offered, it gave on to the living quarters. Through this much filtered illumination glimmered the façade of an enormous dolls' house. I wanted it at once. Dolls had never been central to my happiness, but this abode of theirs was the most grown-up thing in the shop.

It had battlements, and long straight walls, and a variety of pointed windows. A gothic revival house, no doubt; or even mansion. It was painted the colour of stone; a grey stone darker than the grey light, which flickered round it. There was a two-leaved front door, with a small classical portico. It was impossible to see the whole house at once, as it stood grimed and neglected on the corner of the wide trestle-shelf. Very slowly I walked along two of the sides; the other two being dark against the walls of the shop. From a first floor window in the side not immediately visible as one approached, leaned a doll, droopy and unkempt. It was unlike any real house I had seen, and, as for dolls' houses, they were always after the style of the villa near Gerrard's Cross belonging to my father's successful brother. My uncle's house itself looked much more like a toy than this austere structure before me.

"Wake up," said my mother's voice. She was standing just behind me.

"What about some light on the subject?" enquired my father.

A switch clicked.

The house really was magnificent. Obviously, beyond all financial reach.

"Looks like a model for Pentonville Gaol," observed my father.

"It is beautiful," I said. "It's what I want."

"It's the most depressing looking plaything I ever saw."

"I want to pretend I live in it," I said, "and give masked balls." My social history was eager but indiscriminate.

"How much is it?" asked my mother. The bazaar keeper stood resentfully in the background, sliding each hand between the thumb and fingers of the other.

"It's only second-hand," he said. "Tenth-hand, more like. A lady brought it in and said she needed to get rid of it. I don't want to sell you something you don't want."

"But suppose we *do* want it?" said my father truculently. "Is nothing in this shop for sale?"

"You can take it away for a quid," said the bazaar keeper. "And glad to have the space."

"There's someone looking out," said Constantin. He seemed to be assessing the house, like a surveyor or valuer.

"It's full of dolls," said the bazaar keeper. "They're thrown in. Sure you can transport it?"

"Not at the moment," said my father, "but I'll send someone down." This, I knew, would be Moon the seedman, who owned a large canvas-topped lorry, and with whom my father used to fraternize on the putting green.

"Are you quite sure?" my mother asked me.

"Will it take up too much room?"

My mother shook her head. Indeed, our home, though out of date and out at elbows, was considerably too large for us.

"Then, please."

Poor Constantin got nothing.

Mercifully, all our rooms had wide doors; so that Moon's driver, assisted by the youth out of the shop, lent specially for the purpose, could ease my birthday present to its new resting place without tilting it or inflicting a wound upon my mother's new and self-applied paint. I noticed that the doll at the first floor side window had prudently withdrawn.

For my house, my parents had allotted me the principal spare room, because in the centre of it stood a very large dinner table, once to be found in the servants' hall of my father's childhood home in Lincolnshire, but now the sole furniture our principal spare room contained. (The two lesser spare rooms were filled with cardboard boxes, which every now and then toppled in heart-arresting avalanches on still summer nights.) On the big table the driver and the shop boy set my house. It reached almost to the sides, so that those passing along the narrow walks would be in peril of tumbling into a gulf; but, the table being much longer than it was wide, the house was provided at front and back with splendid parterres of deal, embrocated with caustic until they glinted like fluorspar.

When I had settled upon the exact site for the house, so that the garden front would receive the sun from the two windows, and a longer parterre stretched at the front than at the back, where the columned entry faced the door of the room, I withdrew to a distant corner while the two males eased the edifice into exact alignment.

"Snug as a bug in a rug," said Moon's driver when the perilous walks at the sides of the house had been made straight and equal.

"Snugger," said Moon's boy.

I waited for their boots, nailed with crescent slivers of steel, to reach the bottom of our creaking, coconut-matted stair, then I tiptoed to the landing, looked, and listened. The sun had gone in just before the lorry arrived, and down the passage the motes had ceased to dance. It was three o'clock, my mother was still at one of her schools, my father was at the rifle range. I heard the men shut the back door. The principal spare room had never before been occupied, so that the key was outside. In a second, I transferred it to the inside, and shut and locked myself in.

As before in the shop, I walked slowly round my house, but this time round all four sides of it. Then, with the knuckles of my thin white forefinger, I tapped gently at the front door. It seemed not to have been secured, because it opened, both leaves of it, as I touched it. I pried in, first with one eye, then with the other. The lights from various of the pointed windows blotched the walls and floor of the miniature Entrance Hall. None of the dolls was visible.

It was not one of those dolls' houses of commerce from which sides can be lifted in their entirety. To learn about my house, it would be necessary, albeit impolite, to stare through the windows, one at a time. I decided first to take the ground floor. I started in a clockwise direction from the front portico. The front door was still open, but I could not see how to shut it from the outside.

There was a room to the right of the hall, leading into two other rooms along the right side of the house, of which, again, one led into the other. All the rooms were decorated and furnished in a Mrs. Fitzherbert-ish style; with handsomely striped wallpapers, botanical carpets, and chairs with legs like sticks of brittle golden sweetmeat. There were a number of pictures. I knew just what they were: family portraits. I named the room next the Hall, the Occasional Room, and the room beyond it, the Morning Room. The third room was very small: striking out confidently, I named it the Canton Cabinet, although it contained neither porcelain nor fans. I knew what the rooms in a great house should be called, because my mother used to show me the pictures in large, once fashionable volumes on the subject which my father had bought for their bulk at junk shops.

Then came the Long Drawing Room, which stretched across the entire garden front of the house, and contained the principal concourse of dolls. It had four pointed French windows, all made to open, though now sealed with dust and rust; above which were bulbous triangles of coloured glass, in tiny snowflake panes. The apartment itself played at being a cloister in a Horace Walpole convent; lierne vaulting ramified across the arched ceiling, and the spidery gothic pilasters were tricked out in mediaeval patchwork, as in a Puseyite church. On the stout golden wallpaper were decent Swiss pastels of indeterminate subjects. There was a grand piano, very black, scrolly, and, no doubt, resounding; four shapely chandeliers; a baronial fireplace with a mythical blazon above the mantel; and eight dolls, all of them female, dotted about on chairs and ottomans with their backs to me. I hardly dared to breathe as I regarded their woolly heads, and noted the colours of their hair: two black, two nondescript, one grey, one a discoloured silver beneath the dust, one blonde, and one a dyed-looking red. They wore woolen Victorian clothes, of a period later, I should say, than that when the house was built, and certainly too warm for the present season; in varied colours, all of them dull. Happy people, I felt even then, would not wear these variants of rust, indigo, and greenwood.

I crept onwards; to the Dining Room. It occupied half its side of the house, and was dark and oppressive. Perhaps it might look more inviting when the chandelier blazed, and the table candles, each with a tiny purple shade, were lighted. There was no cloth on the table, and no food or drink. Over the fireplace was a big portrait of a furious old man: his white hair was a spiky aureole round his distorted face, beetroot-red with rage; the mouth was open, and even the heavy lips were drawn back to show the savage, strong teeth; he was brandishing a very thick walking stick which seemed to leap from the picture and stun the beholder. He was dressed neutrally, and the painter had not provided him with a background: there was only the aggressive figure menacing the room. I was frightened.

Two rooms on the ground floor remained before I once more reached the front door. In the first of them a lady was writing with her back to the light and therefore to me. She frightened me also; because her grey hair was disordered and of uneven length, and descended in matted plaits, like snakes escaping from a basket, to the shoulders of her coarse grey dress. Of course, being a doll, she did not move, but the back of her head looked mad. Her presence prevented me from regarding at all closely the furnishings of the Writing Room.

Back at the North Front, as I resolved to call it, perhaps superseding the compass rather than leading it, there was a cold-looking room, with a carpetless stone floor and white walls, upon which were the mounted heads and horns of many animals. They were all the room contained, but they covered the walls from floor to ceiling. I felt sure that the ferocious old man in the Dining Room had killed all these creatures, and I hated him for it. But I knew what the room would be called: it would be the Trophy Room.

Then I realized that there was no kitchen. It could hardly be upstairs. I had never heard of such a thing. But I looked.

It wasn't there. All the rooms on the first floor were bedrooms. There were six of them, and they so resembled one another, all with dark ochreous wallpaper and narrow brass bedsteads corroded with neglect, that I found it impracticable to distinguish them other than by numbers, at least for the present. Ultimately I might know the house better. Bedrooms 2, 3 and 6 contained two beds each. I recalled that at least nine people lived in the house. In one room the dark walls, the dark floor, the bed linen, and even the glass in the window were splashed, smeared, and further darkened with ink: it seemed apparent who slept there.

I sat on an orange box and looked. My house needed painting and dusting and scrubbing and polishing and renewing; but on the whole I was relieved that things were not worse. I had felt that the house had stood in the dark corner of the shop for no one knew how long, but this, I now saw, could hardly have been true. I wondered about the lady who had needed to get rid of it. Despite that need, she must have kept things up pretty thoroughly. How did she do it? How did she get in? I resolved to ask my mother's advice. I determined to be a good landlord, although, like most who so resolve, my resources were nil. We simply lacked the money to regild my Long Drawing Room in proper gold leaf. But I would bring life to the nine dolls now drooping with boredom and neglect . . .

Then I recalled something. What had become of the doll who had been sagging from the window? I thought she must have been jolted out, and felt myself a murderess. But none of the windows was open. The sash might easily have descended with the shaking; but more probably the poor doll lay inside on the floor of her room. I again went round from room to room, this time on tiptoe, but it was impossible to see the areas of floor just below the dark windows . . . It was not merely sunless outside, but heavily overcast. I unlocked the door of our principal spare room and descended pensively to await my mother's return and tea.

Wormwood Grange, my father called my house, with penological associations still on his mind. (After he was run over, I realized for the first time that there might be a reason for this, and for his inability to find work worthy of him.) My mother had made the most careful inspection on my behalf, but had been unable to suggest any way of making an entry, or at least of passing beyond the Hall, to which the front doors still lay open. There seemed no question of whole walls lifting off, of the roof being removable, or even of a window being opened, including, mysteriously, on the first floor.

"I don't think it's meant for children, Liebchen," said my Mother, smiling her lovely smile. "We shall have to consult the Victoria and Albert Museum."

"Of course it's not meant for children," I replied. "That's why I wanted it. I'm going to receive, like La Belle Otero."

Next morning, after my mother had gone to work, my father came up, and wrenched and prodded with his unskillful hands.

"I'll get a chisel," he said. "We'll prise it open at each corner, and when we've got the fronts off, I'll go over to Woolworths and buy some hinges and screws. I expect they'll have some."

At that I struck my father in the chest with my fist. He seized my wrists, and I screamed that he was not to lay a finger on my beautiful house, that he would be sure to spoil it, that force never got anyone anywhere. I knew my father: when he took an idea for using tools into his head, the only hope for one's property lay in a scene, and in the implication of tears without end in the future, if the idea were not dropped.

While I was screaming and raving, Constantin appeared from the room below, where he worked at his books.

"Give us a chance, Sis," he said. "How can I keep it all in my head about the Thirty Years War when you haven't learnt to control your tantrums?"

Although two years younger than I, Constantin should have known that I was past the age for screaming except of set purpose.

"You wait until he tries to rebind all your books, you silly sneak," I yelled at him.

My father released my wrists.

"Wormwood Grange can keep," he said. "I'll think of something else to go over to Woolworths for." He sauntered off.

Constantin nodded gravely. "I understand," he said. "I understand what you mean. I'll go back to my work. Here, try this." He gave me a small, chipped nail file.

I spent most of the morning fiddling very cautiously with the imperfect jemmy, and trying to make up my mind about the doll at the window.

I failed to get into my house, and I refused to let my parents give me any effective aid. Perhaps by now I did not really want to get in, although the dirt and disrepair, and the apathy of the dolls, who so badly needed plumping up and dispersing, continued to cause me distress. Certainly I spent as long trying to shut the front door as trying to open a window or find a concealed spring (that idea was Constantin's). In the end I wedged the two halves of the front door with two halves of match; but I felt that the arrangement was makeshift and undignified. I refused everyone access to the principal spare room until something more appropriate could be evolved. My plans for routs and orgies had to be deferred: one could hardly riot among dust and cobwebs.

Then I began to have dreams about my house, and about its occupants.

One of the oddest dreams was the first. It was three or four days after I entered into possession. During that time it had remained cloudy and oppressive, so that my father took to leaving off his knitted waistcoat; then suddenly it thundered. It was long, slow, distant, intermittent thunder; and it continued all the evening, until, when it was quite dark, my bedtime and Constantin's could no longer be deferred.

"Your ears will get accustomed to the noise," said my father. "Just try to take no notice of it."

Constantin looked dubious; but I was tired of the slow, rumbling hours, and ready for the different dimension of dreams.

I slept almost immediately, although the thunder was rolling round my big, rather empty bedroom, round the four walls, across the floor, and under the ceiling, weighting the black air as with a smoky vapour. Occasionally, the lightning glinted, pink and green. It was still the long-drawn-out preliminary to a storm; the tedious, imperfect dispersal of the accumulated energy of the summer. The rollings and rumblings entered my dreams, which flickered, changed, were gone as soon as come, failed, like the lightning, to concentrate or strike home, were as difficult to profit by as the events of an average day.

After exhausting hours of phantasmagoria, anticipating so many later nights in my life, I found myself in a black wood, with huge, dense trees. I was following a path, but reeled from tree to tree, bruising and cutting myself on their hardness and roughness. There seemed no end to the wood or to the night; but suddenly, in the thick of both, I came upon my house. It stood solid, immense, hemmed in, with a single light, little more, it seemed, than a night-light, burning in every upstairs window (as often in dreams, I could see all four sides of the house at once), and illuminating two wooden wedges, jagged and swollen, which held tight the front doors. The vast trees dipped and swayed their elephantine boughs over the roof; the wind peeked and creaked through the black battlements. Then there was a blaze of whitest lightning, proclaiming the storm itself. In the second it endured, I saw my two wedges fly through the air, and the double front door burst open.

For the hundredth time, the scene changed, and now I was back in my room, though still asleep or half-asleep, still dragged from vision to vision. Now the thunder was coming in immense, calculated bombardments; the lightning ceaseless and searing the face of the earth. From being a weariness the storm had become an ecstasy. It seemed as if the whole world would be in dissolution before the thunder had spent its impersonal, unregarding strength. But, as I say, I must still have been at least half asleep, because between the fortissimi and the lustre I still from time to time saw scenes, meaningless or nightmarish, which could not be found in the wakeful world; still, between and through the volleys, heard impossible sounds.

I do not know whether I was asleep or awake when the storm rippled into tranquillity. I certainly did not feel that the air had been cleared; but this may have been because, surprisingly, I heard a quick soft step passing along the passage outside my room, a passage uncarpeted through our poverty. I well knew all the footsteps in the house, and this was none of them.

Always one to meet trouble half-way, I dashed in my night-gown to open the door. I looked out. The dawn was seeping, without effort or momentum, through every cranny, and showed shadowy the back of a retreating figure, the size of my mother but with woolly red hair and long rust-coloured dress. The padding feet seemed actually to start soft echoes amid all that naked woodwork. I had no need to consider who she was or whither she was bound. I burst into the purposeless tears I so despised.

In the morning, and before deciding upon what to impart, I took Constantin with me to look at the house. I more than half expected big changes; but none was to be seen. The sections of match-stick were still in position, and the dolls as inactive and diminutive as ever, sitting with their backs to me on chairs and sofas in the Long Drawing Room; their hair dusty, possibly even mothy. Constantin looked at me curiously, but I imparted nothing.

Other dreams followed; though at considerable intervals. Many children have recurring nightmares of oppressive realism and terrifying content; and I realized from past experience that I must outgrow the habit or lose my house — my house at least. It is true that my house now frightened me, but I felt that I must not be foolish and should strive to take a grown-up view of painted woodwork and nine understuffed dolls. Still it was bad when I began to hear them in the darkness; some tapping, some stumping, some creeping, and therefore not one, but many, or all; and worse when I began not to sleep for fear of the mad doll (as I was sure she was) doing something mad, although I refused to think what. I never dared again to look; but when something happened, which, as I say, was only at intervals (and to me, being young, they seemed long intervals), I lay taut and straining among the forgotten sheets. Moreover, the steps themselves were never quite constant, certainly too inconstant to report to others; and I am not sure that I should have heard anything significant if

I had not once seen. But now I locked the door of our principal spare room on the outside, and altogether ceased to visit my beautiful, impregnable mansion.

I noticed that my mother made no comment. But one day my father complained of my ingratitude in never playing with my handsome birthday present. I said I was occupied with my holiday task: *Moby-Dick*. This was an approved answer, and even, as far as it went, a true one, though I found the book pointless in the extreme, and horribly cruel.

"I told you the Grange was the wrong thing to buy," said my father. "Morbid sort of object for a toy."

"None of us can learn except by experience," said my mother.

My father said "Not at all," and bristled.

All this, naturally, was in the holidays. I was going at the time to one of my mother's schools, where I should stay until I could begin to train as a dancer, upon which I was conventionally but entirely resolved. Constantin went to another, a highly cerebral co-educational place, where he would remain until, inevitably, he won a scholarship to a University, perhaps a foreign one. Despite our years, we went our different ways dangerously on small dingy bicycles. We reached home at assorted hours, mine being the longer journey.

One day I returned to find our dining-room table littered with peculiarly uninteresting printed drawings. I could make nothing of them whatever (they did not seem even to belong to the kind of geometry I was — regretfully — used to); and they curled up on themselves when one tried to examine them, and bit one's finger. My father had a week or two before taken one of his infrequent jobs; night work of some kind a long way off, to which he had now departed in our car. Obviously the drawings were connected with Constantin, but he was not there.

I went upstairs, and saw that the principal spare room door was open. Constantin was inside. There had, of course, been no question of the key to the room being removed. It was only necessary to turn it.

"Hallo, Lene," Constantin said in his matter-of-fact way. "We've been doing axonometric projection, and I'm projecting your house." He was making one of the drawings; on a sheet of thick white paper. "It's for home-work. It'll knock out all the others. They've got to do their real houses."

It must not be supposed that I did not like Constantin, although often he annoyed me with his placidity and precision. It was weeks since I had seen my house, and it looked unexpectedly interesting. A curious thing happened: nor was it the last time in my life that I experienced it. Temporarily I became a different person; confident, practical, simple. The clear evening sun of autumn may have contributed.

"I'll help," I said. "Tell me what to do."

"It's a bore I can't get in to take measurements. Although we haven't *got* to. In fact, the Clot told us not. Just a general impression, he said. It's to give us the *concept* of axonometry. But, golly, it would be simpler with feet and inches."

To judge by the amount of white paper he had covered in what could only have been a short time, Constantin seemed to me to be doing very well, but he was one never to be content with less than perfection.

"Tell me," I said, "what to do, and I'll do it."

"Thanks," he replied, sharpening his pencil with a special instrument. "But it's a one-man job this. In the nature of the case. Later I'll show you how to do it, and you can do some other building if you like."

I remained, looking at my house and fingering it, until Constantin made it clearer that I was a distraction. I went away, changed my shoes, and put on the kettle against my mother's arrival, and our High Tea.

When Constantin came down (my mother had called for him three times, but that was not unusual), he said, "I say, Sis, here's a rum thing."

My mother said, "Don't use slang, and don't call your sister Sis."

He said, as he always did when reproved by her, "I'm sorry,

Mother." Then he thrust the drawing paper at me. "Look, there's a bit missing. See what I mean?" He was showing me with his stub of emerald pencil, pocked with toothmarks.

Of course, I didn't see. I didn't understand a thing about it.

"After Tea," said my mother. She gave to such familiar words not a maternal but an imperial decisiveness.

"But Mum —" pleaded Constantin.

"Mother," said my mother.

Constantin started dipping for sauerkraut.

Silently we ate ourselves into tranquillity; or, for me, into the appearance of it. My alternative personality, though it had survived Constantin's refusal of my assistance, was now beginning to ebb.

"What is all this that you are doing?" enquired my mother in the end. "It resembles the Stone of Rosetta."

"I'm taking an axonometric cast of Lene's birthday house."

"And so?"

But Constantin was not now going to expound immediately. He put in his mouth a finger of rye bread smeared with home-made cheese. Then he said quietly: "I got down a rough idea of the house, but the rooms don't fit. At least, they don't on the bottom floor. It's all right, I think, on the top floor. In fact that's the rummest thing of all. Sorry, Mother." He had been speaking with his mouth full, and now filled it fuller.

"What nonsense is this?" To me it seemed that my mother was glaring at him in a way most unlike her.

"It's not nonsense, Mother. Of course, I haven't measured the place, because you can't. But I haven't done axonometry for nothing. There's a part of the bottom floor I can't get at. A secret room or something."

"Show me."

"Very well, Mother." Constantin put down his remnant of bread and cheese. He rose, looking a little pale. He took the drawing round the table to my mother.

"Not that thing. I can't understand it, and I don't believe you can understand it either." Only sometimes to my father did my mother speak like that. "Show me in the house."

I rose too.

"You stay here, Lene. Put some more water in the kettle and boil it."

"But it's my house. I have a right to know."

My mother's expression changed to one more familiar. "Yes, Lene," she said, "you have a right. But please not now. I ask you."

I smiled at her and picked up the kettle.

"Come, Constantin."

I lingered by the kettle in the kitchen, not wishing to give an impression of eavesdropping or even undue eagerness, which I knew would distress my mother. I never wished to learn things that my mother wished to keep from me; and I never questioned her implication of "All in good time."

But they were not gone long, for well before the kettle had begun even to grunt, my mother's beautiful voice was summoning me back.

"Constantin is quite right," she said, when I had presented myself at the dining room table, "and it was wrong of me to doubt it. The house is built in a funny sort of way. But what does it matter?"

Constantin was not eating.

"I am glad that you are studying well, and learning such useful things," said my mother.

She wished the subject to be dropped, and we dropped it.

Indeed, it was difficult to think what more could be said. But I waited for a moment in which I was alone with Constantin. My father's unhabitual absence made this difficult, and it was completely dark before the moment came.

And when, as was only to be expected, Constantin had nothing to add, I felt, most unreasonably, that he was joined with my mother in keeping something from me.

"But what *happened?*" I pressed him. "What happened when you were in the room with her?"

"What do you think happened?" replied Constantin, wishing, I thought, that my mother would re-enter. "Mother realized that I was right. Nothing more. What does it matter anyway?"

That final query confirmed my doubts.

"Constantin," I said. "Is there anything I ought to do?"

"Better hack the place open," he answered, almost irritably.

But a most unexpected thing happened, that, had I even considered adopting Constantin's idea, would have saved me the trouble. When next day I returned from school, my house was gone.

Constantin was sitting in his usual corner, this time absorbing Greek paradigms. Without speaking to him (nothing unusual in that when he was working), I went straight to the principal spare room. The vast deal table, less scrubbed than once, was bare. The place where my house had stood was very visible, as if indeed a palace had been swept off by a djinn. But I could see no other sign of its passing: no scratched woodwork, or marks of boots, or disjoined fragments.

Constantin seemed genuinely astonished at the news. But I doubted him.

"You knew," I said.

"Of course I didn't know."

Still, he understood what I was thinking.

He said again: "I didn't know."

Unlike me on occasion, he always spoke the truth.

I gathered myself together and blurted out, "Have they done it themselves?" Inevitably I was frightened, but in a way I was also relieved.

"Who do you mean?"

"They."

I was inviting ridicule, but Constantin was kind.

He said: "I know who I think has done it, but you mustn't let on. I think Mother's done it."

I did not again enquire uselessly into how much more he knew than I. I said: "But *how?*"

Constantin shrugged. It was a habit he had assimilated with so much else.

"Mother left the house with us this morning and she isn't back yet."

"She must have put Father up to it."

"But there are no marks."

"Father might have got help." There was a pause. Then Constantin said, "Are you sorry?"

"In a way," I replied. Constantin with precocious wisdom left it at that.

When my mother returned, she simply said that my father had already lost his new job, so that we had had to sell things.

"I hope you will forgive your father and me," she said. "We've had to sell one of my watches also. Father will soon be back to Tea."

She too was one I had never known to lie; but now I began to perceive how relative and instrumental truth could be.

I need not say: not in those terms. Such clear concepts, with all they offer of gain and loss, come later, if they come at all. In fact, I need not say that the whole of what goes before is so heavily filtered through later experience as to be of little evidential value. But I am scarcely putting forward evidence. There is so little. All I can do is to tell something of what happened, as it now seems to me to have been.

I remember sulking at my mother's news, and her explaining to me that really I no longer liked the house and that something better would be bought for me in replacement when our funds permitted.

I did ask my father when he returned to our evening meal, whistling and falsely jaunty about the lost job, how much he had been paid for my house.

"A trifle more than I gave for it. That's only business."

"Where is it now?"

"Never you mind."

"Tell her," said Constantin. "She wants to know."

"Eat your herring," said my father very sharply. "And mind your own business."

And, thus, before long my house was forgotten, my occasional nightmares returned to earlier themes.

It was, as I say, for two or three months in 1921 that I owned the house and from time to time dreamed that creatures I supposed to be its occupants had somehow invaded my home. The next thirty years, more or less, can be disposed of quickly: it was the period when I tried conclusions with the outer world.

I really became a dancer; and, although the upper reaches alike of the art and of the profession notably eluded me, yet I managed to maintain myself for several years, no small achievement. I retired, as they say, upon marriage. My husband aroused physical passion in me for the first time, but diminished and deadened much else. He was reported missing in the late misguided war. Certainly he did not return to me. I at least still miss him, though often I despise myself for doing so.

My father died in a street accident when I was fifteen: it happened on the day I received a special commendation from the sallow Frenchwoman who taught me to dance. After his death my beloved mother always wanted to return to Germany. Before long I was spiritually self-sufficient enough, or said I was, to make that possible. Unfailingly, she wrote to me twice a week, although to find words in which to reply was often difficult for me. Sometimes I visited her, while the conditions in her country became more and more uncongenial to me. She had a fair position teaching English Language and Literature at a small university; and she seemed increasingly to be infected by the new notions and emotions raging around her. I must acknowledge that sometimes their tumult and intoxication unsteadied my own mental gait, although I was a foreigner and by no means of sanguine temperament. It is a mistake to think that all professional dancers are gay.

Despite what appeared to be increasing sympathies with the new régime, my mother disappeared. She was the first of the two people who mattered to me in such very different ways, and who so unreasonably vanished. For a time I was ill, and of course I love her still more than anybody. If she had remained with me, I am sure I should never have married. Without involving myself in psychology, which I detest, I shall simply say that the thought and recollection of my mother lay, I believe, behind the self-absorption my husband complained of so bitterly and so justly. It was not really myself in which I was absorbed but the memory of perfection. It is the plain truth that such beauty, and goodness, and depth, and capacity for love were my mother's alone.

Constantin abandoned all his versatile reading and became a priest, in fact a member of the Society of Jesus. He seems exalted (possibly too much so for his colleagues and superiors), but I can no longer speak to him or bear his presence. He frightens me. Poor Constantin!

On the other hand, I, always dubious, have become a complete unbeliever. I cannot see that Constantin is doing anything but listening to his own inner voice (which has changed its tone since we were children); and mine speaks a different language. In the long run, I doubt whether there is much to be desired but death; or whether there is endurance in anything but suffering. I no longer see myself feasting crowned heads on quails.

So much for biographical intermission. I proceed to the circumstances of my second and recent experience of landlordism.

In the first place, I did something thoroughly stupid. Instead of following the road marked on the map, I took a short cut. It is true that the short cut was shown on the map also, but the region was much too unfrequented for a wandering footpath to be in any way dependable, especially in this generation which has ceased to walk beyond the garage or the bus stop. It was one of the least populated districts in the whole country, and, moreover, the slow autumn dusk was already perceptible when I pushed at the first, dilapidated gate.

To begin with, the path trickled and flickered across a sequence of small damp meadows, bearing neither cattle nor crop. When it came to the third or fourth of these meadows, the way had all but vanished in the increasing sogginess, and could be continued only by looking for the stile or gate in the unkempt hedge ahead. This was not especially difficult as long as the fields remained small; but after a time I reached a depressing expanse which could hardly be termed a field at all, but was rather a large marsh. It was at this point that I should have returned and set about tramping the winding road.

But a path of some kind again continued before me, and I perceived that the escapade had already consumed twenty minutes. So I risked it, although soon I was striding laboriously from tussock to brown tussock in order not to sink above my shoes into the surrounding quagmire. It is quite extraordinary how far one can stray from a straight or determined course when thus preoccupied with elementary comfort. The hedge on the far side of the marsh was still a long way ahead, and the tussocks themselves were becoming both less frequent and less dense, so that too often I was sinking through them into the mire. I realized that the marsh sloped slightly downwards in the direction I was following, so that before I reached the hedge, I might have to cross a river. In the event, it was not so much a river, as an indeterminately bounded augmentation of the softness, and moistness, and ooziness: I struggled across, jerking from false foothold to palpable pitfall, and before long despairing even of the attempt to step securely. Both my feet were now soaked to well above the ankles, and the visibility had become less than was entirely convenient.

When I reached what I had taken for a hedge, it proved to be the boundary of an extensive thicket. Autumn had infected much of the greenery with blotched and dropping senility; so that bare brown briars arched and tousled, and purple thorns tilted at all possible angles for blood. To go further would demand an axe. Either I must retraverse the dreary bog in the perceptibly waning light, or I must skirt the edge and seek an opening in the thicket. Undecided, I looked back. I realized that I had lost the gate through which I had entered upon the marsh on the other side. There was nothing to do but creep as best I could upon the still treacherous ground along the barrier of dead dogroses, mildewed blackberries, and rampant nettles.

But it was not long before I reached a considerable gap, from which through the tangled vegetation seemed to lead a substantial track, although by no means a straight one. The track wound on unimpeded for a considerable distance, even becoming firmer underfoot; until I realized that the thicket had become an entirely indisputable wood. The brambles clutching maliciously from the sides had become watching branches above my head. I could not recall that the map had showed a wood. If, indeed, it had done so, I should not have entered upon the footpath, because the only previous occasion in my life when I had been truly lost, in the sense of being unable to find the way back as well as being unable to go on, had been when my father had once so effectively lost us in a wood that I have never again felt the same about woods. The fear I had felt for perhaps an hour and a half on that occasion, though told to no one, and swiftly evaporating from consciousness upon our emergence, had been the veritable fear of death. Now I drew the map from where it lay against my thigh in the big pocket of my dress. It was not until I tried to read it that I realized how near I was to night. Until it came to print, the problems of the route had given me cat's eyes.

I peered, and there was no wood, no green patch on the map, but only the wavering line of dots advancing across contoured whiteness to the neck of yellow road where the short cut ended. But I did not reach any foolish conclusion. I simply guessed that I had strayed very badly: the map was spattered with green marks in places where I had no wish to be; and the only question was in which of those many thickets I now was. I could think of no way to find out. I was nearly lost, and this time I could not blame my father.

The track I had been following still stretched ahead, as yet not too indistinct; and I continued to follow it. As the trees around me became yet bigger and thicker, fear came upon me; though not the death fear of that previous occasion, I felt now that I knew what was going to happen next; or, rather, I felt I knew one thing that was going to happen next, a thing which was but a small and far from central part of an obscure, inapprehensible totality. As one does on such occasions, I felt more than half outside my body. If I continued much further, I might change into somebody else.

But what happened was not what I expected. Suddenly I saw a flicker of light. It seemed to emerge from the left, to weave momentarily among the trees, and to disappear to the right. It was not what I expected, but it was scarcely reassuring. I wondered if it could be a will-o'-the-wisp, a thing I had never seen, but which I understood to be connected with marshes. Next a still more prosaic possibility occurred to me, one positively hopeful: the headlights of a motor car turning a corner. It seemed the likely answer, but my uneasiness did not perceptibly diminish.

I struggled on, and the light came again: a little stronger, and twisting through the trees around me. Of course another car at the same corner of the road was not an impossibility, even though it was an unpeopled area. Then, after a period of soft but not comforting dusk, it came a third time; and, soon, a fourth. There was no sound of an engine: and it seemed to me that the transit of the light was too swift and fleeting for any car.

And then what I had been awaiting, happened. I came suddenly upon a huge square house. I had known it was coming, but still it struck at my heart.

It is not every day that one finds a dream come true; and, scared though I was, I noticed details: for example, that there did not seem to be those single lights burning in every upstairs window. Doubtless dreams, like poems, demand a certain licence; and, for the matter of that, I could not see all four sides of the house at once, as I had dreamed I had. But that perhaps was the worst of it: I was plainly not dreaming now.

A sudden greeny-pink radiance illuminated around me a morass of weed and neglect; and then seemed to hide itself among the trees on my right. The explanation of the darting lights was that a storm approached. But it was unlike other lightning I had encountered: being slower, more silent, more regular.

There seemed nothing to do but run away, though even then it seemed sensible not to run back into the wood. In the last memories of daylight, I began to wade through the dead knee-high grass of the lost lawn. It was still possible to see that the wood continued, opaque as ever, in a long line to my left; I felt my way along it, in order to keep as far as possible from the house. I noticed, as I passed, the great portico, facing the direction from which I had emerged. Then, keeping my distance, I crept along the grey east front with its two tiers of pointed windows, all shut and one or two broken; and reached the southern parterre, visibly vaster, even in the storm-charged gloom, than the northern, but no less ravaged. Ahead, and at the side of the parterre far off to my right, ranged the encircling woodland. If no path manifested, my state would be hazardous indeed; and there seemed little reason for a path, as the approach to the house was provided by that along which I had come from the marsh.

As I struggled onwards, the whole scene was transformed: in a moment the sky became charged with roaring thunder, the earth with tumultuous rain. I tried to shelter in the adjacent wood, but instantly found myself enmeshed in bines and suckers, lacerated by invisible spears. In a minute I should be drenched. I plunged through the wet weeds towards the spreading portico.

Before the big doors I waited for several minutes, watching the lightning, and listening. The rain leapt up where it fell, as if the earth hurt it. A rising chill made the old grass shiver. It seemed unlikely that anyone could live in a house so dark; but suddenly I heard one of the doors behind me scrape open. I turned. A dark head protruded between the portals, like Punch from the side of his booth.

"Oh." The shrill voice was of course surprised to see me.

I turned. "May I please wait until the rain stops?"

"You can't come inside."

I drew back; so far back that a heavy drip fell on the back of my neck from the edge of the portico. With absurd melodrama, there was a loud roll of thunder.

"I shouldn't think of it," I said. "I must be on my way the moment the rain lets me." I could still see only the round head sticking out between the leaves of the door.

"In the old days we often had visitors." This statement was made in the tone of a Cheltenham lady remarking that when a child she often spoke to gypsies. "I only peeped out to see the thunder."

Now, within the house, I heard another, lower voice, although I could not hear what it said. Through the long crack between the doors, a light slid out across the flagstones of the porch and down the darkening steps.

"She's waiting for the rain to stop," said the shrill voice.

"Tell her to come in," said the deep voice. "Really, Emerald, you forget your manners after all this time."

"I *have* told her," said Emerald very petulantly, and withdrawing her head. "She won't do it."

"Nonsense," said the other. "You're just telling lies." I got the idea that thus she always spoke to Emerald.

Then the doors opened, and I could see the two of them silhouetted in the light of a lamp which stood on a table behind them; one much the taller, but both with round heads, and both wearing long, unshapely garments. I wanted very much to escape, and failed to do so only because there seemed nowhere to go.

"Please come in at once," said the taller figure, "and let us take off your wet clothes."

"Yes, yes," squeaked Emerald, unreasonably jubilant.

"Thank you. But my clothes are not at all wet."

"None the less, please come in. We shall take it as a discourtesy if you refuse."

Another roar of thunder emphasized the impracticability of

continuing to refuse much longer. If this was a dream, doubtless, and to judge by experience, I should awake.

And a dream it must be, because there at the front door were two big wooden wedges; and there to the right of the Hall, shadowed in the lamplight, was the Trophy Room; although now the animal heads on the walls were shoddy, fungoid ruins, their sawdust spilled and clotted on the cracked and uneven flagstones of the floor.

"You must forgive us," said my tall hostess. "Our landlord neglects us sadly, and we are far gone in wrack and ruin. In fact, I do not know what we should do were it not for our own resources." At this Emerald cackled. Then she came up to me, and began fingering my clothes.

The tall one shut the door.

"Don't touch," she shouted at Emerald, in her deep, rather grinding voice. "Keep your fingers off."

She picked up the large oil lamp. Her hair was a discoloured white in its beams.

"I apologize for my sister," she said. "We have all been so neglected that some of us have quite forgotten how to behave. Come, Emerald."

Pushing Emerald before her, she led the way.

In the Occasional Room and the Morning Room, the gilt had flaked from the gingerbread furniture, the family portraits started from their heavy frames, and the striped wallpaper drooped in the lamplight like an assembly of sodden, half-inflated balloons.

At the door of the Canton Cabinet, my hostess turned. "I am taking you to meet my sisters," she said.

"I look forward to doing so," I replied, regardless of truth, as in childhood.

She nodded slightly, and proceeded. "Take care," she said. "The floor has weak places."

In the little Canton Cabinet, the floor had, in fact, largely given way, and been plainly converted into a hospice for rats.

And then, there they all were, the remaining six of them,

thinly illumined by what must surely be rushlights in the four shapely chandeliers. But now, of course, I could see their faces.

"We are all named after our birthstones," said my hostess. "Emerald you know. I am Opal. Here are Diamond and Garnet, Cornelian and Chrysolite. The one with the grey hair is Sardonyx, and the beautiful one is Turquoise."

They all stood up. During the ceremony of introduction, they made odd little noises.

"Emerald and I are the eldest, and Turquoise of course is the youngest."

Emerald stood in the corner before me, rolling her dyed-red head. The Long Drawing Room was raddled with decay. The cobwebs gleamed like steel filigree in the beam of the lamp, and the sisters seemed to have been seated in cocoons of them, like cushions of gossamer.

"There is one other sister, Topaz. But she is busy writing."

"Writing all our diaries," said Emerald.

"Keeping the record," said my hostess.

A silence followed.

"Let us sit down," said my hostess. "Let us make our visitor welcome."

The six of them gently creaked and subsided into their former places. Emerald and my hostess remained standing.

"Sit down, Emerald. Our visitor shall have *my* chair as it is the best." I realized that inevitably there was no extra seat.

"Of course not," I said. "I can only stay for a minute. I am waiting for the rain to stop," I explained feebly to the rest of them.

"I insist," said my hostess.

I looked at the chair to which she was pointing. The padding was burst and rotten, the woodwork bleached and crumbling to collapse. All of them were watching me with round, vague eyes in their flat faces.

"Really," I said, "no, thank you. It's kind of you, but I must go." All the same, the surrounding wood and the dark marsh beyond it loomed scarcely less appalling than the house itself and its inmates.

"We should have more to offer, more and better in every way, were it not for our landlord." She spoke with bitterness, and it seemed to me that on all the faces the expression changed. Emerald came towards me out of her corner, and again began to finger my clothes. But this time her sister did not correct her; and when I stepped away, she stepped after me and went on as before.

"She has failed in the barest duty of sustentation."

I could not prevent myself starting at the pronoun. At once, Emerald caught hold of my dress, and held it tightly.

"But there is one place she cannot spoil for us. One place where we can entertain in our own way."

"Please," I cried. "Nothing more. I am going now."

Emerald's pygmy grip tautened.

"It is the room where we eat."

All the watching eyes lighted up, and became something they had not been before.

"I may almost say where we feast."

The six of them began again to rise from their spidery bowers.

"Because *she* cannot go there."

The sisters clapped their hands, like a rustle of leaves.

"There we can be what we really are."

The eight of them were now grouped round me. I noticed that the one pointed out as the youngest was passing her dry, pointed tongue over her lower lip.

"Nothing unladylike, of course."

"Of course not," I agreed.

"But firm," broke in Emerald, dragging at my dress as she spoke. "Father said that must always come first."

"Our father was a man of measureless wrath against a slight," said my hostess. "It is his continuing presence about the house which largely upholds us."

"Shall I show her?" asked Emerald.

"Since you wish to," said her sister disdainfully.

From somewhere in her musty garments Emerald produced a scrap of card, which she held out to me.

"Take it in your hand. I'll allow you to hold it."

It was a photograph, obscurely damaged.

"Hold up the lamp," squealed Emerald. With an aloof gesture her sister raised it.

It was a photograph of myself when a child, bobbed and waist-less. And through my heart was a tiny brown needle.

"We've all got things like it," said Emerald jubilantly. "Wouldn't you think her heart would have rusted away by now?"

"She never had a heart," said the elder sister scornfully, putting down the light.

"She might not have been able to help what she did," I cried. I could hear the sisters catch their fragile breath.

"It's what you do that counts," said my hostess, regarding the discoloured floor, "not what you feel about it afterwards. Our father always insisted on that. It's obvious."

"Give it back to me," said Emerald, staring into my eyes. For a moment I hesitated.

"Give it back to her," said my hostess in her contemptuous way. "It makes no difference now. Everyone but Emerald can see that the work is done."

I returned the card, and Emerald let go of me as she stuffed it away.

"And now will you join us?" asked my hostess. "In the inner room?" As far as was possible, her manner was almost casual.

"I am sure the rain has stopped," I replied. "I must be on my way."

"Our father would never have let you go so easily, but I think we have done what we can with you."

I inclined my head.

"Do not trouble with adieux," she said. "My sisters no longer expect them." She picked up the lamp. "Follow me. And take care. The floor has weak places."

"Goodbye," squealed Emerald.

"Take no notice, unless you wish," said my hostess.

I followed her through the mouldering rooms and across the rotten floors in silence. She opened both the outer doors and stood waiting for me to pass through. Beyond, the moon was shining, and she stood dark and shapeless in the silver flood.

On the threshold, or somewhere on the far side of it, I spoke. "I did nothing," I said. "Nothing."

So far from replying, she dissolved into the darkness and silently shut the door.

I took up my painful, lost, and forgotten way through the wood, across the dreary marsh, and back to the little yellow road.

Mrs. Acland's Ghosts

*William Trevor was born in Ireland, but moved to England when he
was in his twenties. He started writing fiction after having achieved
early success as a sculptor. Dozens of novels and short stories later, he
is now acclaimed as one of the master storytellers of our century. The
American writer Mary Gordon has called Trevor "the modern English-
speaking world's Chekhov."*[17]

    *"Mrs. Acland's Ghosts" (1975) is unique among Trevor's stories in
that it utilizes and embroiders upon the conventions of the supernatural.
Yet the uncanny in this tale only furthers the expression of Trevor's per-
vasive themes: loneliness, isolation, obsession, and the deep but often frus-
trated urge to communicate. The thirty-nine year old Mrs. Acland, like
many of Trevor's protagonists, is an outsider, marginalized by main-
stream society. Her exclusion has come about as a result of her purported
encounter with family ghosts. Yet the poignancy and drama of the tale,
as it unfolds, lies not so much in the apparitions themselves as in the compelling revelation of their connection with the circumstances of Mrs.
Acland's traumatic childhood.*

    *Trevor is masterly in the way he shifts the perspective from inside to
outside his character's mind, heightening the reader's awareness of the
truth — or truths — of Mrs. Acland's experience. "Mrs. Acland's
Ghosts" confirms the observation of one critic that "[Trevor] manages*

to stuff a short story with as much emotional incident as most people cram into a novel, without ever straining the tale's skin."[18] *From its very first pages to its unexpected ending, this is a story that will surprise and even shock us, while deepening our sense of the mystery of the human heart.* ⬎

MR. MOCKLER was a tailor. He carried on his business in a house that after twenty-five years of mortgage arrangements had finally become his: 22 Juniper Street, S.W. 17. He had never married and since he was now sixty-three it seemed likely that he never would. In an old public house, the Charles the First, he had a drink every evening with his friends Mr. Uprichard and Mr. Tile, who were tailors also. He lived in his house in Juniper Street with his cat Sam, and did his own cooking and washing and cleaning: he was not unhappy.

On the morning of October 19th, 1972, Mr. Mockler received a letter that astonished him. It was neatly written in a pleasantly rounded script that wasn't difficult to decipher. It did not address him as "Dear Mr. Mockler," nor was it signed, nor conventionally concluded. But his name was used repeatedly, and from its contents it seemed to Mr. Mockler that the author of the letter was a Mrs. Acland. He read the letter in amazement and then read it again and then, more slowly, a third time.

Dr. Scott-Rowe is dead, Mr. Mockler. I know he is dead because a new man is here, a smaller, younger man, called Dr. Friend-man. He looks at us, smiling, with his unblinking eyes. Miss Acheson says you can tell at a glance that he has practised hypnosis.

They're so sure of themselves, Mr. Mockler: beyond the limits of their white-coated world they can accept nothing. I am a woman imprisoned because I once saw ghosts. I am paid for by the man who was my husband, who writes out monthly cheques for the peaches they bring to my room, and the beef olives and the *marrons glacés*. "She must above all things be happy," I can imagine the stout man who was my husband saying, walking with Dr. Scott-Rowe over the sunny lawns and among the rose-beds. In this house there are twenty disturbed people in private rooms, cosseted by luxury because other people feel guilty. And when we walk ourselves on the lawns and among the rosebeds we murmur at the folly of those who have so expensively committed us, and at the greater folly of the medical profession: you can be disturbed without being mad. Is this the letter of a lunatic, Mr. Mockler?

I said this afternoon to Miss Acheson that Dr. Scott-Rowe was dead. She said she knew. All of us would have Dr. Friendman now, she said, with his smile and his tape recorders. "May Dr. Scott-Rowe rest in peace," said Miss Acheson: it was better to be dead than to be like Dr. Friendman. Miss Acheson is a very old lady, twice my age exactly: I am thirty-nine and she is seventy-eight. She was committed when she was eighteen, in 1913, a year before the First World War. Miss Acheson was disturbed by visions of St. Olaf of Norway and she still is. Such visions were an embarrassment to Miss Acheson's family in 1913 and so they quietly slipped her away. No one comes to see her now, no one has since 1927.

"You must write it all down," Miss Acheson said to me when I told her, years ago, that I'd been committed because I'd seen ghosts and that I could prove the ghosts were real because the Rachels had seen them too. The Rachels are living some normal existence somewhere, yet they were terrified half out of their wits at the time and I wasn't frightened at all. The trouble nowadays, Miss Acheson says and I quite agree, is that if you like having ghosts near you people think you're round the bend.

I was talking to Miss Acheson about all this yesterday and she said why didn't I do what Sarah Crookham used to do? There's nothing the matter with Sarah Crookham, any more than there is with Miss Acheson or myself: all that Sarah Crookham suffers from is a broken heart. "You must write it all down," Miss Acheson said to her when she first came here, weeping, poor thing, every minute of the day. So she wrote it down and posted it to A. J. Rawson, a person she found in the telephone directory. But Mr. Rawson never came, nor another person Sarah Crookham wrote to. I have looked you up in the telephone directory, Mr. Mockler. It is nice to have a visitor.

"You must begin at the beginning," Miss Acheson says, and so I am doing that. The beginning is back a bit, in January 1949, when I was fifteen. We lived in Richmond then, my parents and one brother, George, and my sisters Alice and Isabel. On Sundays, after lunch, we used to walk all together in Richmond Park with our dog, a Dalmatian called Salmon. I was the oldest and Alice was next, two years younger, and George was eleven and Isabel eight. It was lovely walking together in Richmond Park and then going home to Sunday tea. I remember the autumns and winters best, the cosiness of the coal fire, hot sponge cake and special Sunday sandwiches, and little buns that Alice and I always helped to make on Sunday mornings. We played Monopoly by the fire, and George would always have the ship and Anna the hat and Isabel the racing-car and Mummy the dog. Daddy and I would share the old boot. I really loved it.

I loved the house: 17 Lorelei Avenue, an ordinary suburban house built some time in the early nineteen-twenties, when Miss Acheson was still quite young. There were bits of stained glass on either side of the hall-door and a single stained glass pane, Moses in the bulrushes, in one of the landing windows. At Christmas especially it was lovely: we'd have the Christmas tree in the hall and always on Christmas Eve, as long as I can remember, there'd be a party. I can remember the parties quite vividly. There'd be people standing round drinking punch and all the children would play hide-and-seek upstairs, and nobody could ever find George. It's George, Mr. Mockler, that all this is about. And Alice, of course, and Isabel.

When I first described them to Dr. Scott-Rowe he said they

sounded marvellous, and I said I thought they probably were, but I suppose a person can be prejudiced in family matters of that kind. Because they were, after all, my brother and my two sisters and because, of course, they're dead now. I mean, they were probably ordinary children, just like any children. Well, you can see what you think, Mr. Mockler.

George was small for his age, very wiry, dark-haired, a darting kind of boy who was always laughing, who had often to be reprimanded by my father because his teachers said he was the most mischievous boy in his class. Alice, being two years older, was just the opposite: demure and silent, but happy in her quiet way, and beautiful, far more beautiful than I was. Isabel wasn't beautiful at all. She was all freckles, with long pale plaits and long legs that sometimes could run as fast as George's. She and George were as close as two persons can get, but in a way we were all close: there was a lot of love in 17 Lorelei Avenue.

I had a cold the day it happened, a Saturday it was. I was cross because they all kept worrying about leaving me in the house on my own. They'd bring me back Black Magic chocolates, they said, and my mother said she'd buy a bunch of daffodils if she saw any. I heard the car crunching over the gravel outside the garage, and then their voices telling Salmon not to put his paws on the upholstery. My father blew the horn, saying goodbye to me, and after that the silence began. I must have known even then, long before it happened, that nothing would be the same again.

When I was twenty-two, Mr. Mockler, I married a man called Acland, who helped me to get over the tragedy. George would have been eighteen, and Alice twenty and Isabel fifteen. They would have liked my husband because he was a good-humoured and generous man. He was very plump, many years older than I was, with a fondness for all food. "You're like a child," I used to say to him and we'd laugh together. Cheese in particular he liked, and ham and all kinds of root vegetables, parsnips, turnips, celeriac, carrots, leeks, potatoes. He used to come back to the house and take four or five pounds of gammon from the car, and chops, and blocks of ice-cream, and biscuits, and two or even three McVitie's fruitcakes. He was very partial to McVitie's fruitcakes. At night, at nine or ten o'clock, he'd make cocoa for both of us and we'd have it while we were watching the television, with a slice or two of fruitcake. He was such a kind man in those days. I got quite fat myself, which might surprise you, Mr. Mockler, because I'm on the thin side now.

My husband was, and still is, both clever and rich. One led to the other: he made a fortune designing metal fasteners for the aeroplane industry. Once, in May 1960, he drove me to a house in Worcestershire. "I wanted it to be a surprise," he said, stopping his mustard-coloured Alfa-Romeo in front of this quite extensive Victorian façade. "There," he said, embracing me, reminding me that it was my birthday. Two months later we went to live there.

We had no children. In the large Victorian house I made my life with the man I'd married and once again, as in 17 Lorelei Avenue, I was happy. The house was near a village but otherwise remote. My husband went away from it by day, to the place where his aeroplane fasteners were manufactured and tested. There were — and still are — aeroplanes in the air which would have fallen to pieces if they hadn't been securely fastened by the genius of my husband.

The house had many rooms. There was a large square drawing-room with a metal ceiling — beaten tin, I believe it was. It had patterns like wedding-cake icing on it. It was painted white and blue and gave, as well as the impression of a wedding-cake, a Wedgwood effect. People remarked on this ceiling and my husband used to explain that metal ceilings had once been very popular, especially in the large houses of Australia. Well-to-do Australians, apparently, would have them shipped from Birmingham in colonial imitation of an English fashion. My husband and I, arm in arm, would lead people about the house, pointing out the ceiling or the green wallpaper in our bedroom or the portraits that hung on the stairs.

The lighting was bad in the house. The long first-floor landing was a gloomy place by day and lit by a single wall-light at night. At the end of this landing another flight of stairs, less grand than the stairs that led from the hall, wound upwards to the small rooms that had once upon a time been servants' quarters, and another flight continued above them to attics and store-rooms. The bathroom was on the first floor, tiled in green Victorian tiles, and there was a lavatory next door to it, encased in mahogany.

In the small rooms that had once been the servants' quarters lived Mr. and Mrs. Rachels. My husband had had a kitchen and a bathroom put in for them so that their rooms were quite self-contained. Mr. Rachels worked in the garden and his wife cleaned the house. It wasn't really necessary to have them at all: I could have cleaned the house myself and even done the gardening, but my husband insisted in his generous way. At night I could hear the Rachels moving about above me. I didn't like this and my husband asked them to move more quietly.

In 1962 my husband was asked to go to Germany, to explain his aeroplane fasteners to the German aircraft industry. It was to be a prolonged trip, three months at least, and I was naturally unhappy when he told me. He was unhappy himself, but on March 4th he flew to Hamburg, leaving me with the Rachels.

They were a pleasant enough couple, somewhere in their fifties I would think, he rather silent, she inclined to talk. The only thing that worried me about them was the way they used to move about at night above my head. After my husband had gone to Germany I gave Mrs. Rachels money to buy slippers, but I don't think she ever did because the sounds continued just as before. I naturally didn't make a fuss about it.

On the night of March 7th I was awakened by a band playing in the house. The tune was an old tune of the fifties called, I believe, "Looking for Henry Lee." The noise was very loud in my bedroom and I lay there frightened, not knowing why this noise should be coming to me like this, Victor Silvester in strict dance tempo. Then a voice spoke, a long babble of French, and I realised that I was listening to a radio programme. The wireless was across the room, on a table by the windows. I put on my bed-side light and got up and switched it off. I drank some orange juice and went back to sleep. It didn't even occur to me to won-der who had turned the wireless on.

The next day I told Mrs. Rachels about it, and it was she, in fact, who made me think that it was all rather stranger than it seemed. I definitely remembered turning the wireless off myself before going to bed, and in any case I was not in the habit of lis-tening to French stations, so that even if the wireless had some-how come on of its own accord it should not have been tuned in to a French station.

Two days later I found the bath half-filled with water and the towels all rumpled and damp, thrown about on the floor. The water in the bath was tepid and dirty: someone, an hour or so ago, had had a bath.

I climbed the stairs to the Rachels' flat and knocked on their door. "Is your bathroom out of order?" I said when Mr. Rachels came to the door, not wearing the slippers I'd given them money for. I said I didn't at all mind their using mine, only I'd be grate-ful if they'd remember to let the water out and to bring down their own towels. Mr. Rachels looked at me in the way people have sometimes, as though you're insane. He called his wife and all three of us went down to look at my bathroom. They denied emphatically that either of them had had a bath.

When I came downstairs the next morning, having slept badly, I found the kitchen table had been laid for four. There was a table-cloth on the table, which was something I never bothered about, and a kettle was boiling on the Aga. Beside it, a large brown teapot, not the one I normally used, was heating. I made some tea and sat down, thinking about the Rachels. Why should they behave like this? Why should they creep into my bedroom in the middle of the night and turn the wireless on? Why should they have a bath in my bathroom and deny it? Why should they lay the breakfast table as though we had overnight guests? I left the table just as it was. Butter had been rolled into pats. Marmalade had been placed in two china dishes. A silver toast-rack that an aunt of my husband had given us as a wedding present was waiting for toast.

"Thank you for laying the table," I said to Mrs. Rachels when she entered the kitchen an hour later.

She shook her head. She began to say that she hadn't laid the table but then she changed her mind. I could see from her face that she and her husband had been discussing the matter of the bath the night before. She could hardly wait to tell him about the breakfast table. I smiled at her.

"A funny thing happened the other night," I said. "I woke up to find Victor Silvester playing a tune called 'Looking for Henry Lee.'"

"Henry Lee?" Mrs. Rachels said, turning around from the sink. Her face, usually blotched with pink, like the skin of an apple, was white.

"It's an old song of the fifties."

It was while saying that that I realised what was happening in the house. I naturally didn't say anything to Mrs. Rachels, and I at once began to regret that I'd said anything in the first place. It had frightened me, finding the bathroom like that, and clearly it must have frightened the Rachels. I didn't want them to be frightened because naturally there was nothing to be frightened about. George and Alice and Isabel wouldn't hurt anyone, not unless death had changed them enormously. But even so I knew I couldn't ever explain that to the Rachels.

"Well, I suppose I'm just getting absentminded," I said. "People do, so they say, when they live alone." I laughed to show I wasn't worried or frightened, to make it all seem ordinary.

"You mean, you laid the table yourself?" Mrs. Rachels said. "And had a bath?"

"And didn't turn the wireless off properly. Funny," I said, "how these things go in threes. Funny, how there's always an explanation." I laughed again and Mrs. Rachels had to laugh too.

After that it was lovely, just like being back in 17 Lorelei

Avenue. I bought Black Magic chocolates and bars of Fry's and Cadbury's Milk, all the things we'd liked. I often found bathwater left in and the towels crumpled, and now and again I came down in the morning to find the breakfast table laid. On the first-floor landing, on the evening of March 11th, I caught a glimpse of George, and in the garden, three days later, I saw Isabel and Alice.

On March 15th the Rachels left. I hadn't said a word to them about finding the bathroom used again or the breakfast laid or actually seeing the children. I'd been cheerful and smiling whenever I met them. I'd talked about how Brasso wasn't as good as it used to be to Mrs. Rachels, and had asked her husband about the best kinds of soil for bulbs.

"We can't stay a minute more," Mrs. Rachels said, her face all white and tight in the hall, and then to my astonishment they attempted to persuade me to go also.

"The house isn't fit to live in," Mr. Rachels said.

"Oh now, that's nonsense," I began to say, but they both shook their heads.

"There's children here," Mrs. Rachels said. "There's three children appearing all over the place."

"Come right up to you," Mr. Rachels said. "Laugh at you sometimes."

They were trembling, both of them. They were so terrified I thought they might die, that their hearts would give out there in the hall and they'd just drop down. But they didn't. They walked out of the hall-door with their three suitcases, down the drive to catch a bus. I never saw them again.

I suppose, Mr. Mockler, you have to be frightened of ghosts: I suppose that's their way of communicating. I mean, it's no good being like me, delighting in it all, being happy because I wasn't lonely in that house any more. You have to be like the Rachels, terrified half out of your wits. I think I knew that as I watched the Rachels go: I think I knew that George and Isabel and Alice would go with them, that I was only a kind of go-between, that the Rachels were what George and Isabel and Alice could really have fun with. I almost ran after the Rachels, but I knew it would be no good.

Without the Rachels and my brother and my two sisters, I was frightened myself in that big house. I moved everything into the kitchen: the television set and the plants I kept in the drawing-room, and a camp-bed to sleep on. I was there, asleep in the camp-bed, when my husband returned from Germany; he had changed completely. He raved at me, not listening to a word I said. There were cups of tea all over the house, he said, and bits of bread and biscuits and cake and chocolates. There were notes in envelopes, and messages scrawled in my handwriting on the wallpaper in various rooms. Everywhere was dusty. Where, he wanted to know, were the Rachels?

He stood there with a canvas bag in his left hand, an airline bag that had the word *Lufthansa* on it. He'd put on at least a stone, I remember thinking, and his hair was shorter than before.

"Listen," I said, "I would like to tell you." And I tried to tell him, as I've told you, Mr. Mockler, about George and Isabel and Alice in 17 Lorelei Avenue and how we all went together for a walk with our dog, every Sunday afternoon in Richmond Park, and how on Christmas Eve my mother always gave a party. I told him about the stained-glass pane in the window, Moses in the bul-rushes, and the hide-and-seek we played, and how my father and I always shared the old boot in Monopoly. I told him about the day of the accident, how the tyre on the lorry suddenly exploded and how the lorry went whizzing around on the road and then just tumbled over on top of them. I'd put out cups of tea, I said, and bis-cuits and cake and the little messages, just in case they came back again — not for them to eat or to read particularly, but just as a sign. They'd given me a sign first, I explained: George had turned on my wireless in the middle of the night and Isabel had had baths and Alice had laid the breakfast table. But then they'd gone because they'd been more interested in annoying the Rachels than in comforting me. I began to weep, telling him how lonely I'd been without them, how lonely I'd been ever since the day of the accident, how the silence had been everywhere. I couldn't control myself: tears came out of my eyes as though they'd never stop. I felt sickness all over my body, paining me in my head and my chest, sour in my stomach. I wanted to die because the loneliness was too much. Loneliness was the worst thing in the world, I said, gasping out words, with spit and tears going cold on my face. People were only shadows, I tried to explain, when you had loneliness and silence like that, like a shroud around you. You couldn't reach out of the shroud sometimes, you couldn't connect because shadows are hard to connect with and it's frightening when you try because everyone is looking at you. But it was lovely, I whispered, when the children came back to annoy the Rachels. My husband replied by telling me I was insane.

The letter finished there, and Mr. Mockler was more astonished each time he read it. He had never in his life received such a document before, nor did he in fact very often receive letters of any kind, apart from bills and, if he was fortunate, cheques in settlement. He shook his head over the letter and placed it in the inside pocket of his jacket.

That day, as he stitched and measured, he imagined the place Mrs. Acland wrote of, the secluded house with twenty female inmates, and the lawn and the rosebeds. He imagined the other house, 17 Lorelei Avenue in Richmond, and the third house, the Victorian residence in the Worcestershire countryside. He imagined Mrs. Acland's obese husband with his short hair and his aeroplane fasteners, and the children who had been killed in a motor-car accident, and Mr. and Mrs. Rachels whom they had haunted. All day long the faces of these people flitted through Mr. Mockler's mind, with old Miss Acheson and Sarah Crookham and Dr. Scott-Rowe and Dr. Friendman. In the evening, when he met his friends Mr. Tile and Mr. Uprichard in the Charles the First, he showed them the letter before even ordering them drinks.

"Well, I'm beggared," remarked Mr. Uprichard, a man known locally for his gentle nature. "That poor creature."

Mr. Tile, who was not given to expressing himself, shook his head.

Mr. Mockler asked Mr. Uprichard if he should visit this Mrs. Acland. "Poor creature," Mr. Uprichard said again, and added that without a doubt Mrs. Acland had written to a stranger because of the loneliness she mentioned, the loneliness like a shroud around her.

Some weeks later Mr. Mockler, having given the matter further thought and continuing to be affected by the contents of the letter, took a Green Line bus out of London to the address that Mrs. Acland had given him. He made enquiries, feeling quite adventurous, and was told that the house was three-quarters of a mile from where the bus had dropped him, down a side road. He found it without further difficulty. It was a house surrounded by a high brick wall in which large, black wrought-iron gates were backed with sheets of tin so that no one could look through the ornamental scrollwork. The gates were locked. Mr. Mockler rang a bell in the wall.

"Yes?" a man said, opening the gate that was on Mr. Mockler's left.

"Well," said Mr. Mockler and found it difficult to proceed.

"Yes?" the man said.

"Well, I've had a letter. Asking me to come, I think. My name's Mockler."

The man opened the gate a little more and Mr. Mockler stepped through.

The man walked ahead of him and Mr. Mockler saw the lawns that had been described, and the rosebeds. The house he considered most attractive: a high Georgian building with beautiful windows. An old woman was walking slowly by herself with the assistance of a stick: Miss Acheson, Mr. Mockler guessed. In the distance he saw other women, walking slowly on leaf-strewn paths.

Autumn was Mr. Mockler's favourite season and he was glad to be in the country on this pleasantly autumnal day. He thought of remarking on this to the man who led him towards the house, but since the man did not incline towards conversation he did not do so.

In the yellow waiting-room there were no magazines and no pictures on the walls and no flowers. It was not a room in which Mr. Mockler would have cared to wait for long, and in fact he did not have to. A woman dressed as a nurse except that she wore a green cardigan came in. She smiled briskly at him and said that Dr. Friendman would see him. She asked Mr. Mockler to follow her.

"How very good of you to come," Dr. Friendman said, smiling at Mr. Mockler in the way that Mrs. Acland had described in her letter. "How very humane," said Dr. Friendman.

"I had a letter, from a Mrs. Acland."

"Quite so, Mr. Mockler. Mr. Mockler, could I press you towards a glass of sherry?"

Mr. Mockler, surprised at this line of talk, accepted the sherry, saying it was good of Dr. Friendman. He drank the sherry while Dr. Friendman read the letter. When he'd finished, Dr. Friendman crossed to the window of the room and pulled aside a curtain and asked Mr. Mockler if he'd mind looking out.

There was a courtyard, small and cobbled, in which a gardener was sweeping leaves into a pile. At the far end of it, sitting on a tapestry-backed dining-chair in the autumn sunshine, was a woman in a blue dress. "Try these," said Dr. Friendman and handed Mr. Mockler a pair of binoculars.

It was a beautiful face, thin and seeming fragile, with large blue eyes and lips that were now slightly parted, smiling in the sunshine. Hair the colour of corn was simply arranged, hanging on either side of the face and curling in around it. The hair shone in the sunlight, as though it was for ever being brushed.

"I find them useful," Dr. Friendman said, taking the binoculars from Mr. Mockler's hands. "You have to keep an eye, you know."

"That's Mrs. Acland?" Mr. Mockler asked.

"That's the lady who wrote to you: the letter's a bit inaccurate, Mr. Mockler. It wasn't quite like that in 17 Lorelei Avenue."

"Not quite like it?"

"She cannot forget Lorelei Avenue. I'm afraid she never will. That beautiful woman, Mr. Mockler, was a beautiful girl, yet she married the first man who asked her, a widower thirty years older than her, a fat designer of aircraft fasteners. He pays her bills just as she says in her letter, and even when he's dead they'll go on being paid. He used to visit her at first, but he found it too painful. He stood in this very room one day, Mr. Mockler, and said to Dr. Scott-Rowe that no man had ever been appreciated by a woman as much as he had by her. And all because he'd been kind to her in the most ordinary ways."

Mr. Mockler said he was afraid that he didn't know what Dr. Friendman was talking about. As though he hadn't heard this quiet protest, Dr. Friendman smiled and said:

"But it was, unfortunately, too late for kindness. 17 Lorelei Avenue had done its damage, like a cancer in her mind: she could not forget her childhood."

"Yes, she says in her letter. George and Alice and Isabel — "

"All her childhood, Mr. Mockler, her parents did not speak to one another. They didn't quarrel, they didn't address each other in any way whatsoever. When she was five they'd come to an agreement: that they should both remain in 17 Lorelei Avenue because neither would ever have agreed to give up an inch of the child they'd between them caused to be born. In the house there was nothing, Mr. Mockler, for all her childhood years: nothing except silence."

"But there was George and Alice and Isabel — "

"No, Mr. Mockler. There was no George and no Alice and no Isabel. No hide-and-seek or parties on Christmas Eve, no Monopoly on Sundays by the fire. Can you imagine 17 Lorelei Avenue, Mr. Mockler, as she is now incapable of imagining it? Two people so cruel to one another that they knew that either of them could be parted from the child in some divorce court. A woman bitterly hating the man whom once she'd loved, and he returning each evening, hurrying back from an office in case his wife and the child were having a conversation. She would sit, Mr. Mockler, in a room with them, with the silence heavy in the air, and their hatred for one another. All three of them would sit down to a meal and no one would speak. No other children came to that house, no other people. She used to hide on the way back from school: she'd go down the area steps of other houses and crouch beside dustbins."

"Dustbins?" repeated Mr. Mockler, more astonished than ever. "*Dustbins?*"

"Other children didn't take to her. She couldn't talk to them. She'd never learned to talk to anyone. He was a patient man, Mr. Acland, when he came along, a good and patient man."

Mr. Mockler said that the child's parents must have been monsters, but Dr. Friendman shook his head. No one was a monster, Dr. Friendman said in a professional manner, and in the circumstances Mr. Mockler didn't feel he could argue with him. But the people called Rachels were real, he did point out, as real as the fat designer of aircraft fasteners. Had they left the house, he asked, as it said in the letter? And if they had, what had they been frightened of?

Dr. Friendman smiled again. "I don't believe in ghosts," he said, and he explained at great length to Mr. Mockler that it was Mrs. Acland herself who had frightened the Rachels, turning on a wireless in the middle of the night and running baths and laying tables for people who weren't there. Mr. Mockler listened and was interested to note that Dr. Friendman used words that were not easy to understand, and quoted from experts who were in Dr. Friendman's line of business but whose names meant nothing to Mr. Mockler.

Mr. Mockler, listening to all of it, nodded but was not convinced. The Rachels had left the house, just as the letter said: he knew that, he felt it in his bones and it felt like the truth. The Rachels had been frightened of Mrs. Acland's ghosts even though they'd been artificial ghosts. They'd been real to her, and they'd been real to the Rachels because she'd made them so. Shadows had stepped out of her mind because in her loneliness she'd wished them to. They'd laughed and played, and frightened the Rachels half out of their wits.

"There's always an explanation," said Dr. Friendman.

Mr. Mockler nodded, profoundly disagreeing.

"She'll think you're Mr. Rachels," said Dr. Friendman, "come to say he saw the ghosts. If you wouldn't mind saying you did, it keeps her happy."

"But it's the truth," Mr. Mockler cried with passion in his voice. "Of course it's the truth: there can be ghosts like that, just as there can be in any other way."

"Oh, come now," murmured Dr. Friendman with his sad, humane smile.

Mr. Mockler followed Dr. Friendman from the room. They crossed a landing and descended a back staircase, passing near a kitchen in which a chef with a tall chef's hat was beating pieces of meat. "Ah, Wiener Schnitzel," said Dr. Friendman.

In the cobbled courtyard the gardener had finished sweeping up the leaves and was wheeling them away in a wheelbarrow. The woman was still sitting on the tapestry-backed chair, still smiling in the autumn sunshine.

"Look," said Dr. Friendman, "a visitor."

A woman rose and went close to Mr. Mockler. "They didn't mean to frighten you," she said, "even though it's the only way ghosts can communicate. They were only having fun, Mr. Rachels."

"I think Mr. Rachels realises that now," Dr. Friendman said.

"Yes, of course," said Mr. Mockler.

"No one ever believed me, and I kept on saying, 'When the Rachels come back, they'll tell the truth about poor George and Alice and Isabel.' You saw them, didn't you, Mr. Rachels?"

"Yes," Mr. Mockler said. "We saw them."

She turned and walked away, leaving the tapestry-backed chair behind her.

"You're a humane person," Dr. Friendman said, holding out

his right hand, which Mr. Mockler shook. The same man led him back through the lawns and the rosebeds, to the gates.

It was an experience that Mr. Mockler found impossible to forget. He measured and stitched, and talked to his friends Mr. Uprichard and Mr. Tile in the Charles the First; he went for a walk morning and evening, and no day passed during which he did not think of the woman whom people looked at through binoculars. Somewhere in England, or at least somewhere in the world, the Rachels were probably still alive, and had Mr. Mockler been a younger man he might even have set about looking for them. He would have liked to bring them to the secluded house where the woman now lived, to have been there himself when they told the truth to Dr. Friendman. It seemed a sadness, as he once remarked to Mr. Uprichard, that on top of everything else a woman's artificial ghosts should not be honoured, since she had brought them into being and given them life, as other women give other children life.

The Chimney

Since the early seventies, the British writer Ramsey Campbell has enjoyed a growing preeminence in the realm of supernatural horror fiction. His work has been described as "urban Gothic," since much of it unfolds in the chaotic, slightly surreal setting of middle- and lower-class Liverpool, where the author grew up. In Campbell's chilling stories, the uncanny adapts itself effortlessly to the realities of the contemporary world without any of the sacrifices in style, texture, or psychological complexity that characterize much present-day horror writing.

"The Chimney" (1977), one of Campbell's most unnerving tales, takes place almost entirely within one suburban household, seen through the eyes of a twelve-year-old only child. In this story, Campbell brilliantly recreates the shadowy, nightmare world of childhood fear. The reader can not help but be mesmerized as the morbidly sensitive young protagonist spins, cocoon-like, his obsessive dreads and paranoiac distortions out of the vague notions that he has acquired about Father Christmas. Campbell evokes with both starkness and nuance the deep psychological roots of the uncanny: the suppressed hostility and aggression within the family triangle of mother, father, and son erupt into supernatural form, driving the story inexorably towards its shocking conclusion.

The Chimney

MAYBE MOST OF IT was only fear. But not the last thing, not that. To blame my fear for that would be worst of all.

I was twelve years old and beginning to conquer my fears. I even went upstairs to do my homework, and managed to ignore the chimney. I had to be brave, because of my parents — because of my mother.

She had always been afraid for me. The very first day I had gone to school I'd seen her watching. Her expression had reminded me of the face of a girl I'd glimpsed on television, watching men lock her husband behind bars; I was frightened all that first day. And when children had hysterics or began to bully me, or the teacher lost her temper, these things only confirmed my fears — and my mother's, when I told her what had happened each day.

Now I was at grammar school. I had been there for much of a year. I'd felt awkward in my new uniform and old shoes; the building seemed enormous, crowded with too many strange children and teachers. I'd felt I was an outsider; friendly approaches made me nervous and sullen, when people laughed and I didn't know why I was sure they were laughing at me. After a while the other boys treated me as I seemed to want to be treated: the lads from the poorer districts mocked my suburban accent, the suburban boys sneered at my old shoes.

Often I'd sat praying that the teacher wouldn't ask me a question I couldn't answer, sat paralyzed by my dread of having to stand up in the waiting watchful silence. If a teacher shouted at someone my heart jumped painfully; once I'd felt the stain of my shock creeping insidiously down my thigh. Yet I did well in the end-of-term examinations, because I was terrified of failing; for nights afterward they were another reason why I couldn't sleep.

My mother read the signs of all this on my face. More and more, once I'd told her what was wrong, I had to persuade her there was nothing worse that I'd kept back. Some mornings as I lay in bed, trying to hold back half-past seven, I'd be sick; I would grope miserably downstairs, white-faced, and my mother would keep me home. Once or twice, when my fear wasn't quite enough, I made myself sick. "Look at him. You can't expect him to go like that" — but my father would only shake his head and grunt, dismissing us both.

I knew my father found me embarrassing. This year he'd had less time for me than usual; his shop — The Anything Shop, nearby in the suburbanized village — was failing to compete with the new supermarket. But before that trouble I'd often seen him staring up at my mother and me: both of us taller than him, his eyes said, yet both scared of our own shadows. At those times I glimpsed his despair.

So my parents weren't reassuring. Yet at night I tried to stay with them as long as I could — for my worst fears were upstairs, in my room.

It was a large room, two rooms knocked into one by the previous owner. It overlooked the small back gardens. The smaller of the fireplaces had been bricked up; in winter, the larger held a fire, which my mother always feared would set fire to the room — but she let it alone, for I'd screamed when I thought she was going to take that light away: even though the firelight only added to the terrors of the room.

The shadows moved things. The mesh of the fireguard fluttered enlarged on the wall; sometimes, at the edge of sleep, it became a swaying web, and its spinner came sidling down from a corner of the ceiling. Everything was unstable; walls shifted, my clothes crawled on the back of the chair. Once, when I'd left my jacket slumped over the chair, the collar's dark upturned lack of a face began to nod forward stealthily; the holes at the ends of the sleeves worked like mouths, and I didn't dare get up to hang the jacket properly. The room grew in the dark: sounds outside, footsteps and laughter, dogs encouraging each other to bark, only emphasized the size of my trap of darkness, how distant everything else was. And there was a dimmer room, in the mirror of the wardrobe beyond the foot of the bed. There was a bed in that room, and beside it a dim nightlight in a plastic lantern. Once I'd awakened to see a face staring dimly at me from the mirror; a figure had sat up when I had, and I'd almost cried out. Often I'd stared at the dim staring face, until I'd had to hide beneath the sheets.

Of course this couldn't go on for the rest of my life. On my twelfth birthday I set about the conquest of my room.

I was happy amid my presents. I had a jigsaw, a box of colored pencils, a book of space stories. They had come from my father's shop, but they were mine now. Because I was relaxed, no doubt because she wished I could always be so, my mother said, "Would you be happier if you went to another school?"

It was Saturday; I wanted to forget Monday. Besides, I imagined all schools were as frightening. "No, I'm all right," I said.

"Are you happy at school now?" she said incredulously.

"Yes, it's all right."

"Are you sure?"

"Yes, really, it's all right. I mean, I'm happy now."

The snap of the letter slot saved me from further lying. Three birthday cards: two from neighbors who talked to me when I served them in the shop — an old lady who always carried a poodle, our next-door neighbor Dr. Flynn — and a card from my parents. I'd seen all three cards in the shop, which spoiled them somehow.

As I stood in the hall I heard my father. "You've got to control yourself," he was saying. "You only upset the child. If you didn't go on at him he wouldn't be half so bad."

It infuriated me to be called a child. "But I worry so," my mother said brokenly. "He can't look after himself."

"You don't let him try. You'll have him afraid to go up to bed next."

But I already was. Was that my mother's fault? I remembered her putting the nightlight by my bed when I was very young, checking the flex and the bulb each night — I'd taken to lying awake, dreading that one or the other would fail. Standing in the hall, I saw dimly that my mother and I encouraged each other's fears. One of us had to stop. I had to stop. Even when I was frightened, I mustn't let her see. It wouldn't be the first time I'd hidden my feelings from her. In the living room I said, "I'm going upstairs to play."

Sometimes in summer I didn't mind playing there — but this was March, and a dark day. Still, I could switch the light on. And my room contained the only table I could have to myself and my jigsaw.

I spilled the jigsaw onto the table. The chair sat with its back to the dark yawn of the fireplace; I moved it hastily to the foot of the bed, facing the door. I spread the jigsaw. There was a piece of the edge, another. By lunchtime I'd assembled the edge. "You look pleased with yourself," my father said.

I didn't notice the approach of night. I was fitting together my own blue sky, above fragmented cottages. After dinner I hurried to put in the pieces I'd placed mentally while eating. I hesitated outside my room. I should have to reach into the dark for the light switch. When I did, the wallpaper filled with bright multiplied airplanes and engines. I wished we could afford to redecorate my room, it seemed childish now.

The fireplace gaped. I retrieved the fireguard from the cupboard under the stairs, where my father had stored it now the nights were a little warmer. It covered the soot-encrusted yawn. The room felt comfortable now. I'd never seen before how much space it gave me for play.

I even felt safe in bed. I switched out the nightlight — but that was too much; I grabbed the light. I didn't mind its glow on its own, without the jagged lurid jig of the shadows. And the fireguard was comforting. It made me feel that nothing could emerge from the chimney.

On Monday I took my space stories to school. People asked to look at them; eventually they lent me books. In the following weeks some of my fears began to fade. Questions darting from desk to desk still made me uneasy, but if I had to stand up without the answer at least I knew the other boys weren't sneering at me, not all of them; I was beginning to have friends. I started to sympathize with their own ignorant silences. In the July examinations I was more relaxed, and scored more marks. I was even sorry to leave my friends for the summer; I invited some of them home.

I felt triumphant. I'd calmed my mother and my room all by myself, just by realizing what had to be done. I suppose that sense of triumph helped me. It must have given me a little strength with which to face the real terror.

It was early August, the week before our holiday. My mother was worrying over the luggage, my father was trying to calculate his accounts; they were beginning to chafe against each other. I went to my room, to stay out of their way.

I was halfway through a jigsaw, which one of my friends had swapped for mine. People sat in back gardens, letting the evening settle on them; between the houses the sky was pale yellow. I inserted pieces easily, relaxed by the nearness of our holiday. I listened to the slowing of the city, a radio fluttering along a street, something moving behind the fireguard, in the chimney.

No. It was my mother in the next room, moving luggage. It was someone dragging, dragging something, anything, outside. But I couldn't deceive my ears. In the chimney something large had moved.

It might have been a bird, stunned or dying, struggling feebly — except that a bird would have sounded wilder. It could have been a mouse, even a rat, if such things are found in chimneys. But it sounded like a large body, groping stealthily in the dark: something large that didn't want me to hear it. It sounded like the worst terror of my infancy.

I'd almost forgotten that. When I was three years old my mother had let me watch television; it was bad for my eyes, but just this once, near Christmas — I'd seen two children asleep in bed, an enormous crimson man emerging from the fireplace, creeping toward them. They weren't going to wake up! "Burglar! Burglar!" I'd screamed, beginning to cry. "No, dear, it's Father

Christmas," my mother said, hastily switching off the television. "He always comes out of the chimney."

Perhaps if she'd said "down" rather than "out of"... For months after that, and in the weeks before several Christmases, I lay awake listening fearfully for movement in the chimney: I was sure a fat grinning figure would creep upon me if I slept. My mother had told me the presents that appeared at the end of my bed were left by Father Christmas, but now the mysterious visitor had a face and a huge body, squeezed into the dark chimney among the soot. When I heard the wind breathing in the chimney I had to trap my screams between my lips.

Of course at last I began to suspect there was no Father Christmas: how did he manage to steal into my father's shop for my presents? He was a childish idea, I was almost sure — but I was too embarrassed to ask my parents or my friends. But I wanted not to believe in him, that silent lurker in the chimney; and now I didn't, not really. Except that something large was moving softly behind the fireguard.

It had stopped. I stared at the wire mesh, half-expecting a fat pale face to stare out of the grate. There was nothing but the fenced dark. Cats were moaning in a garden, an ice-cream van wandered brightly. After a while I forced myself to pull the fireguard away.

I was taller than the fireplace now. But I had to stoop to peer up the dark, soot-ridged throat, and then it loomed over me, darkness full of menace, of the threat of a huge figure bursting out at me, its red mouth crammed with sparkling teeth. As I peered up, trembling a little, and tried to persuade myself that what I'd heard had flown away or scurried back into its hole, soot came trickling down from the dark — and I heard the sound of a huge body squeezed into the sooty passage, settling itself carefully, more comfortably in its burrow.

I slammed the guard into place, and fled. I had to gulp to breathe. I ran onto the landing, trying to catch my breath so as to cry for help. Downstairs my mother was nervously asking whether she should pack another of my father's shirts. "Yes, if you like," he said irritably.

No, I mustn't cry out. I'd vowed not to upset her. But how could I go back into my room? Suddenly I had a thought that seemed to help. At school we'd learned how sweeps had used to send small boys up chimneys. There had hardly been room for the boys to climb. How could a large man fit in there?

He couldn't. Gradually I managed to persuade myself. At last I opened the door of my room. The chimney was silent; there was no wind. I tried not to think that he was holding himself still, waiting to squeeze out stealthily, waiting for the dark. Later, lying in the steady glow from my plastic lantern, I tried to hold onto the silence, tried to believe there was nothing near me to shatter it. There was nothing except, eventually, sleep.

Perhaps if I'd cried out on the landing I would have been saved from my fear. But I was happy with my rationality. Only once, nearly asleep, I wished the fire were lit, because it would burn anything that might be hiding in the chimney; that had never occurred to me before. But it didn't matter, for the next day we went on holiday.

My parents liked to sleep in the sunlight, beneath newspaper masks; in the evenings they liked to stroll along the wide sandy streets. I didn't, and befriended Nigel, the son of another family who were staying in the boardinghouse. My mother encouraged the friendship: such a nice boy, two years older than me; he'd look after me. He had money, and the hope of a moustache shadowing his pimply upper lip. One evening he took me to the fairground, where we met two girls; he and the older girl went to buy ice creams while her young friend and I stared at each other timidly. I couldn't believe the young girl didn't like jigsaws. Later, while I was contradicting her, Nigel and his companion disappeared behind the Ghost Train — but Nigel reappeared almost at once, red-faced, his left cheek redder. "Where's Rose?" I asked, bewildered.

"She had to go." He seemed furious that I'd asked.

RAMSEY CAMPBELL

"Isn't she coming back?"

"No." He was glancing irritably about for a change of subject.
"What a super bike," he said, pointing as it glided between the
stalls. "Have you got a bike?"

"No," I said. "I keep asking Father Christmas, but —" I
wished that hadn't got past me, for he was staring at me, winking at the young girl.

"Do you still believe in him?" he demanded scornfully.

"No, of course I don't. I was only kidding." Did he believe me?
He was edging toward the young girl now, putting his arm
around her; soon she excused herself, and didn't come back — I
never knew her name. I was annoyed he'd made her run away.
"Where did Rose go?" I said persistently.

He didn't tell me. But perhaps he resented my insistence, for
as the family left the boardinghouse I heard him say loudly to his
mother: "He still believes in Father Christmas." My mother
heard that too, and glanced anxiously at me.

Well, I didn't. There was nobody in the chimney, waiting for
me to come home. I didn't care that we were going home the next
day. That night I pulled away the fireguard and saw a fat pale face
hanging down into the fireplace, like an underbelly, upside down
and smiling. But I managed to wake, and eventually the sea lulled
me back to sleep.

As soon as we reached home I ran upstairs. I uncovered the
fireplace and stood staring, to discover what I felt. Gradually I
filled with the scorn Nigel would have felt, had he known of my
fear. How could I have been so childish? The chimney was only a
passage for smoke, a hole into which the wind wandered sometimes. That night, exhausted by the journey home, I slept at
once.

The nights darkened into October; the darkness behind the
mesh grew thicker. I'd used to feel, as summer waned, that the
chimney was insinuating its darkness into my room. Now the
sight only reminded me I'd have a fire soon. The fire would be
comforting.

It was October when my father's Christmas cards arrived, on

a Saturday; I was working in the shop. It annoyed him to have to anticipate Christmas so much, to compete with the supermarket. I hardly noticed the cards: my head felt muffled, my body cold — perhaps it was the weather's sudden hint of winter.

My mother came to the shop that afternoon. I watched her pretend not to have seen the cards. When I looked away she began to pick them up timidly, as if they were unfaithful letters, glancing anxiously at me. I didn't know what was in her mind. My head was throbbing. I wasn't going home sick; I earned pocket money in the shop. Besides, I didn't want my father to think I was still weak.

Nor did I want my mother to worry. That night I lay slumped in a chair, pretending to read. Words trickled down the page; I felt like dirty clothes someone had thrown on the chair. My father was at the shop taking stock. My mother sat gazing at me. I pretended harder; the words waltzed slowly. At last she said, "Are you listening?"

I was now, though I didn't look up. "Yes," I said hoarsely, unplugging my throat with a roar.

"Do you remember when you were a baby? There was a film you saw, of Father Christmas coming out of the chimney." Her voice sounded bravely careless, falsely light, as if she were determined to make some awful revelation. I couldn't look up. "Yes," I said.

Her silence made me glance up. She looked as she had on my first day at school: full of loss, of despair. Perhaps she was realizing I had to grow up, but to my throbbing head her look suggested only terror — as if she were about to deliver me up as a sacrifice. "I couldn't tell you the truth then," she said. "You were too young."

The truth was terror; her expression promised that. "Father Christmas isn't really like that," she said.

My illness must have shown by then. She gazed at me; her lips trembled. "I can't," she said, turning her face away. "Your father must tell you."

But that left me poised on the edge of terror. I felt unnerved, rustily tense. I wanted very much to lie down. "I'm going to my room," I said. I stumbled upstairs, hardly aware of doing so. As much as anything I was fleeing her unease. The stairs swayed a little, they felt unnaturally soft underfoot. I hurried dully into my room. I slapped the light switch and missed. I was walking uncontrollably forward into blinding dark. A figure came to meet me, soft and huge in the dark of my room.

I cried out. I managed to stagger back onto the landing, grabbing the light switch as I went. The lighted room was empty. My mother came running upstairs, almost falling. "What is it, what is it?" she cried.

I mustn't say. "I'm ill. I feel sick." I did, and a minute later I was. She patted my back as I knelt by the toilet. When she'd put me to bed she made to go next door, for the doctor. "Don't leave me," I pleaded. The walls of the room swayed as if tugged by firelight; the fireplace was huge and very dark. As soon as my father opened the front door she ran downstairs, crying, "He's ill, he's ill! Go for the doctor!"

The doctor came and prescribed for my fever. My mother sat up beside me. Eventually my father came to suggest it was time she went to bed. They were going to leave me alone in my room. "Make a fire," I pleaded.

My mother touched my forehead. "But you're burning," she said.

"No, I'm cold! I want a fire! Please!" So she made one, tired as she was. I saw my father's disgust as he watched me use her worry against her to get what I wanted, his disgust with her for letting herself be used.

I didn't care. My mother's halting words had overgrown my mind. What had she been unable to tell me? Had it to do with the sounds I'd heard in the chimney? The room lolled around me; nothing was sure. But the fire would make sure for me. Nothing in the chimney could survive it.

I made my mother stay until the fire was blazing. Suppose a huge shape burst forth from the hearth, dripping fire? When at last I let her go I lay lapped by the firelight and meshy shadows, which seemed lulling now, in my warm room.

I felt feverish, but not unpleasantly. I was content to voyage on my rocking bed; the ceiling swayed past above me. While I slept the fire went out. My fever kept me warm; I slid out of bed and, pulling away the fireguard, reached up the chimney. At the length of my arms I touched something heavy, hanging down in the dark; it yielded, then soft fat fingers groped down and closed on my wrist. My mother was holding my wrist as she washed my hands. "You mustn't get out of bed," she said when she realized I was awake.

I stared stupidly at her. "You'd got out of bed. You were sleepwalking," she explained. "You had your hands right up the chimney." I saw now that she was washing caked soot from my hands; tracks of ash led toward the bed.

It had been only a dream. One moment the fat hand had been gripping my wrist, the next it was my mother's cool slim fingers. My mother played word games and timid chess with me while I stayed in bed, that day and the next.

The third night I felt better. The fire fluttered gently; I felt comfortably warm. Tomorrow I'd get up. I should have to go back to school soon, but I didn't mind that unduly. I lay and listened to the breathing of the wind in the chimney.

When I awoke the fire had gone out. The room was full of darkness. The wind still breathed, but it seemed somehow closer. It was above me. Someone was standing over me. It couldn't be either of my parents, not in the sightless darkness.

I lay rigid. Most of all I wished that I hadn't let Nigel's imagined contempt persuade me to do without a nightlight. The breathing was slow, irregular; it sounded clogged and feeble. As I tried to inch silently toward the far side of the bed, the source of the breathing stooped toward me. I felt its breath waver on my face, and the breath sprinkled me with something like dry rain.

When I had lain paralyzed for what felt like blind hours, the breathing went away. It was in the chimney, dislodging soot; it might be the wind. But I knew it had come out to let me know that whatever the fire had done to it, it hadn't been killed. It had emerged to tell me it would come for me on Christmas Eve. I began to scream.

I wouldn't tell my mother why. She washed my face, which was freckled with soot. "You've been sleepwalking again," she tried to reassure me, but I wouldn't let her leave me until daylight. When she'd gone I saw the ashy tracks leading from the chimney to the bed.

Perhaps I had been sleepwalking and dreaming. I searched vainly for my nightlight. I would have been ashamed to ask for a new one, and that helped me to feel I could do without. At dinner I felt secure enough to say I didn't know why I had screamed.

"But you must remember. You sounded so frightened. You upset me."

My father was folding the evening paper into a thick wad the size of a pocketbook, which he could read beside his plate. "Leave the boy alone," he said. "You imagine all sorts of things when you're feverish. I did when I was his age."

It was the first time he'd admitted anything like weakness to me. If he'd managed to survive his nightmares, why should mine disturb me more? Tired out by the demands of my fever, I slept soundly that night. The chimney was silent except for the flapping of flames.

But my father didn't help me again. One November afternoon I was standing behind the counter, hoping for customers. My father pottered, grumpily fingering packets of nylons, tins of pet food, Dinky toys, baby's rattles, cards, searching for signs of theft. Suddenly he snatched a Christmas card and strode to the counter. "Sit down," he said grimly.

He was waving the card at me, like evidence. I sat down on a shelf, but then a lady came into the shop; the bell thumped. I stood up to sell her nylons. When she'd gone I gazed at my father, anxious to hear the worst. "Just sit down," he said.

He couldn't stand my being taller than he was. His size

embarrassed him, but he wouldn't let me see that; he pretended I had to sit down out of respect. "Your mother says she tried to tell you about Father Christmas," he said.

She must have told him that weeks earlier. He'd put off talking to me — because we'd never been close, and now we were growing farther apart. "I don't know why she couldn't tell you," he said.

But he wasn't telling me either. He was looking at me as if I were a stranger he had to chat to. I felt uneasy, unsure now that I wanted to hear what he had to say. A man was approaching the shop. I stood up, hoping he'd interrupt.

He did, and I served him. Then, to delay my father's revelation, I adjusted stacks of tins. My father stared at me in disgust. "If you don't watch out you'll be as bad as your mother."

I found the idea of being like my mother strange, indefinably disturbing. But he wouldn't let me be like him, wouldn't let me near. All right, I'd be brave, I'd listen to what he had to say. But he said, "Oh, it's not worth me trying to tell you. You'll find out."

He meant I must find out for myself that Father Christmas was a childish fantasy. He didn't mean he wanted the thing from the chimney to come for me, the disgust in his eyes didn't mean that, it didn't. He meant that I had to behave like a man.

And I could. I'd show him. The chimney was silent. I needn't worry until Christmas Eve. Nor then. There was nothing to come out.

One evening as I walked home I saw Dr. Flynn in his front room. He was standing before a mirror, gazing at his red fur-trimmed hooded suit; he stooped to pick up his beard. My mother told me that he was going to act Father Christmas at the children's hospital. She seemed on the whole glad that I'd seen. So was I: it proved the pretense was only for children.

Except that the glimpse reminded me how near Christmas was. As the nights closed on the days, and the days rushed by — the end-of-term party, the turkey, decorations in the house — I grew tense, trying to prepare myself. For what? For nothing, nothing at all. Well, I would know soon — for suddenly it was Christmas Eve.

I was busy all day. I washed up as my mother prepared Christmas dinner. I brought her ingredients, and hurried to buy some she'd used up. I stuck the day's cards to tapes above the mantelpiece. I carried home a tinsel tree which nobody had bought. But being busy only made the day move faster. Before I knew it the windows were full of night.

Christmas Eve. Well, it didn't worry me. I was too old for that sort of thing. The tinsel tree rustled when anyone passed it, light rolled in tinsel globes, streamers flinched back when doors opened. Swinging restlessly on tapes above the mantelpiece were half a dozen red-cheeked, smiling bearded faces.

The night piled against the windows. I chattered to my mother about her shouting father, her elder sisters, the time her sisters had locked her in a cellar. My father grunted occasionally — even when I'd run out of subjects to discuss with my mother, and tried to talk to him about the shop. At least he hadn't noticed how late I was staying up. But he had. "It's about time everyone was in bed," he said with a kind of suppressed fury.

"Can I have some more coal?" My mother would never let me have a coal scuttle in the bedroom — she didn't want me going near the fire. "To put on now," I said. Surely she must say yes. "It'll be cold in the morning," I said.

"Yes, you take some. You don't want to be cold when you're looking at what Father — at your presents."

I hurried upstairs with the scuttle. Over its clatter I heard my father say, "Are you still at that? Can't you let him grow up?"

I almost emptied the scuttle into the fire, which rose roaring and crackling. My father's voice was an angry mumble, seeping through the floor. When I carried the scuttle down my mother's eyes were red, my father looked furiously determined. I'd always found their arguments frightening; I was glad to hurry to my room.

It seemed welcoming. The fire was bright within the mesh.

I heard my mother come upstairs. That was comforting too: she was nearer now. I heard my father go next door — to wish the doctor Happy Christmas, I supposed. I didn't mind the reminder. There was nothing of Christmas Eve in my room, except the pillowcase waiting to be filled with presents on the floor at the foot of the bed. I pushed it aside with one foot, the better to ignore it.

I slid into bed. My father came upstairs; I heard further mumblings of argument through the bedroom wall. At last they stopped, and I tried to relax. I lay, glad of the silence.

A wind was rushing the house. It puffed down the chimney; smoke trickled through the fireguard. Now the wind was breathing brokenly. It was only the wind. It didn't bother me.

Perhaps I'd put too much coal on the fire. The room was hot; I was sweating. I felt almost feverish. The huge mesh flicked over the wall repeatedly, nervously, like a rapid net. Within the mirror the dimmer room danced.

Suddenly I was a little afraid. Not that something would come out of the chimney, that was stupid: afraid that my feeling of fever would make me delirious again. It seemed years since I'd been disturbed by the sight of the room in the mirror, but I was disturbed now. There was something wrong with that dim jerking room.

The wind breathed. Only the wind, I couldn't hear it changing. A fat billow of smoke squeezed through the mesh. The room seemed more oppressive now, and smelled of smoke. It didn't smell entirely like coal smoke, but I couldn't tell what else was burning. I didn't want to get up to find out.

I must lie still. Otherwise I'd be writhing about trying to clutch at sleep, as I had the second night of my fever, and sometimes in summer. I must sleep before the room grew too hot. I must keep my eyes shut. I mustn't be distracted by the faint trickling of soot, nor the panting of the wind, nor the shadows and orange light that snatched at my eyes through my eyelids.

I woke in darkness. The fire had gone out. No, it was still there when I opened my eyes: subdued orange crawled on embers, a few weak flames leaped repetitively. The room was moving more slowly now. The dim room in the mirror, the face peering out at me, jerked faintly, as if almost dead.

I couldn't look at that. I slid farther down the bed, dragging the pillow into my nest. I was too hot, but at least beneath the sheets I felt safe. I began to relax. Then I realized what I'd seen. The light had been dim, but I was almost sure the fireguard was standing away from the hearth.

I must have mistaken that, in the dim light. I wasn't feverish, I couldn't have sleepwalked again. There was no need for me to look, I was comfortable. But I was beginning to admit that I had better look when I heard the slithering in the chimney.

Something large was coming down. A fall of soot: I could hear the scattering pats of soot in the grate, thrown down by the harsh halting wind. But the wind was emerging from the fire-place, into the room. It was above me, panting through its obstructed throat.

I lay staring up at the mask of my sheets. I trembled from holding myself immobile. My held breath filled me painfully as lumps of rock. I had only to lie there until whatever was above me went away. It couldn't touch me.

The clogged breath bent nearer; I could hear its dry rattling. Then something began to fumble at the sheets over my face. It plucked feebly at them, trying to grasp them, as if it had hardly anything to grasp with. My own hands clutched at the sheets from within, but couldn't hold them down entirely. The sheets were being tugged from me, a fraction at a time. Soon I would be face to face with my visitor.

I was lying there with my eyes squeezed tight when it let go of the sheets and went away. My throbbing lungs had forced me to take shallow breaths; now I breathed silently open-mouthed, though that filled my mouth with fluff. The tolling of my ears subsided, and I realized the thing had not returned to the chimney. It was still in the room.

I couldn't hear its breathing; it couldn't be near me. Only that thought allowed me to look — that, and the desperate hope that I might escape, since it moved so slowly. I peeled the sheets down from my face slowly, stealthily, until my eyes were bare. My heartbeats shook me. In the sluggishly shifting light I saw a figure at the foot of the bed.

Its red costume was thickly furred with soot. It had its back to me; its breathing was muffled by the hood. What shocked me most was its size. It occurred to me, somewhere amid my engulfing terror, that burning shrivels things. The figure stood in the mirror as well, in the dim twitching room. A face peered out of the hood in the mirror, like a charred turnip carved with a rigid grin.

The stunted figure was still moving painfully. It edged round the foot of the bed and stooped to my pillowcase. I saw it draw the pillowcase up over itself and sink down. As it sank its hood fell back, and I saw the charred turnip roll about in the hood, as if there were almost nothing left to support it.

I should have had to pass the pillowcase to reach the door. I couldn't move. The room seemed enormous, and was growing darker; my parents were far away. At last I managed to drag the sheets over my face, and pulled the pillow, like muffs, around my ears.

I had lain sleeplessly for hours when I heard movement at the foot of the bed. The thing had got out of its sack again. It was coming toward me. It was tugging at the sheets, more strongly now. Before I could catch hold of the sheets I glimpsed a red fur-trimmed sleeve, and was screaming.

"Let go, will you," my father said irritably. "Good God, it's only me."

He was wearing Dr. Flynn's disguise, which flapped about him — the jacket, at least; his pajama cuffs peeked beneath it. I stopped screaming and began to giggle hysterically. I think he would have struck me, but my mother ran in. "It's all right. All right," she reassured me, and explained to him, "It's the shock."

He was making angrily for the door when she said, "Oh, don't go yet, Albert. Stay while he opens his presents," and, lifting the bulging pillowcase from the floor, dumped it beside me.

I couldn't push it away, I couldn't let her see my terror. I made myself pull out my presents into the daylight, books, sweets, ballpoints; as I groped deeper I wondered whether the charred face would crumble when I touched it. Sweat pricked my hands; they shook with horror — they could, because my mother couldn't see them.

The pillowcase contained nothing but presents and a pinch of soot. When I was sure it was empty I slumped against the headboard, panting. "He's tired," my mother said, in defense of my ingratitude. "He was up very late last night."

Later I managed an accident, dropping the pillowcase on the fire downstairs. I managed to eat Christmas dinner, and to go to bed that night. I lay awake, even though I was sure nothing would come out of the chimney now. Later I realized why my father had come to my room in the morning dressed like that; he'd intended me to catch him, to cure me of the pretense. But it was many years before I enjoyed Christmas very much.

When I left school I went to work in libraries. Ten years later I married. My wife and I crossed town weekly to visit my parents. My mother chattered, my father was taciturn. I don't think he ever quite forgave me for laughing at him.

One winter night our telephone rang. I answered it, hoping it wasn't the police. My library was then suffering from robberies. All I wanted was to sit before the fire and imagine the glittering cold outside. But it was Dr. Flynn.

"Your parents' house is on fire," he told me. "Your father's trapped in there. Your mother needs you."

They'd had a friend to stay. My mother had lit the fire in the guest room, my old bedroom. A spark had eluded the fireguard; the carpet had caught fire. Impatient for the fire engine, my father had run back into the house to put the fire out, but had been overcome. All this I learned later. Now I drove coldly across town, toward the glow in the sky.

The glow was doused by the time I arrived. Smoke scrolled over the roof. But my mother had found a coal sack and was struggling still to run into the house, to beat out the fire; her friend and Dr. Flynn held her back. She dropped the sack and ran to me. "Oh, it's your father. It's Albert," she repeated through her weeping.

The firemen withdrew their hose. The ambulance stood winking. I saw the front door open, and a stretcher carried out. The path was wet and frosty. One stretcher-bearer slipped, and the contents of the stretcher spilled over the path.

I saw Dr. Flynn glance at my mother. Only the fear that she might turn caused him to act. He grabbed the sack and, running to the path, scooped up what lay scattered there. I saw the charred head roll on the lip of the sack before it dropped within. I had seen that already, years ago.

My mother came to live with us, but we could see she was pining; my parents must have loved each other, in their way. She died a year later. Perhaps I killed them both. I know that what emerged from the chimney was in some sense my father. But surely that was a premonition. Surely my fear could never have reached out to make him die that way.

The Double Poet

The Pulitzer Prize-winning novelist Alison Lurie has given us an unexpected treat with her first foray into the supernatural, Women and Ghosts (1994). In this volume of short stories, in which Lurie's prose style is as deft and luminescent as ever, an engaging assortment of female protagonists find their lives disrupted and illuminated by the uncanny.

The heroine of "The Double Poet," a successful writer on the poetry reading circuit, may seem on the surface an unlikely candidate for preternatural persecution or paranoiac delusion. Yet as the plot unfolds through the wittily perceptive entries in her journal, everything seems to point to the existence of a perfidious double — or to some ill-intentioned stranger who is waging a subtle campaign of impersonation.

Just about a century earlier, the French writer Guy de Maupassant chose the journal form for his fantastic tale "The Horla," which chronicled its narrator's descent into madness as the real or imagined victim of psychic vampirism. The ordeal of Lurie's heroine, like that of Maupassant's troubled diary writer, is symptomatic of a crisis of identity, a psyche somehow divided against itself. Lurie's masterful story invites reflection, too, on the uneasy relationship between the private self and the public self which, when one least expects it, can take on a dangerous life of its own. ⟳

The Double Poet

AFTER OVER TWO WEEKS, I'm still unsettled, uneasy here. I agreed to be this year's Visiting Poet largely because the photographs in the college catalogue showed a landscape as lovely and transcendent as my enchanted Cape Cod pond. They lied: I'm awash in shopping malls and Lego-brick dormitories, boxed into a cardboard box apartment complex. I believe I *have* an apartment complex — have had one since I arrived. Claustrophobia: three cramped lowering rooms. Paranoia: the kitchenette sink's chronic water-torture drip. Hallucinations: ugly voices and uglier music seeping from adjoining apartments as a nearly visible sludge. No wonder I'm finding it difficult to write.

Yet the countryside is handsome: it lacks delicacy and subtlety but has a sweep, a fecundity — Rounded fields like sleeping beasts, covered with a blonde pelt of ripening hay and corn. One can almost imagine them breathing.

I've met my classes, undifferentiated masses as yet, but perhaps among them will be interesting if unformed beings. And I know how grateful they'll be for a teacher who celebrates poetry instead of picking it apart till a seamless, shimmering garment is reduced to shreds and tatters. Am also looking forward to knowing the other writers who teach here, perhaps finding a community. And beginning to regret the seven readings in six cities I let my new lecture agent, Bryan Wood, persuade me to do this year. Will they strain my slow-forming bond with this place, be physically, emotionally wearying?

Yet no matter how weary I am, there's always the thrilling gathering, surge, and flood of energy that comes when I hear "Please welcome Karo McKay" and the soft clatter of applause rises, then falls into a hush and I glide forward in my long dress and they're all out there, dim rapt flower faces turned to the light — waiting, wanting, needing what I bring them.

Because somehow I validate their private experience — especially their experience of the sensual world. My words, my voice somehow allow them to see, hear, touch, smell, feel; to, as one used to put it, Be Here Now — not shut themselves off from life with sad self-conscious hesitation.

As even I once used to. How long ago they seem now, my first awkward, fearful readings before tiny audiences — back when I was still only Carrie Martin. When I knew nothing, expected no reward, hardly dared dream of what was to come. In dusty black beatnik outfit of leotard and dance skirt, I stumbled through a shaking sheaf of papers. I didn't even know enough to memorize my poems, didn't know how to project them, project my voice, project myself.

I didn't yet realize that a poet is, must be, both creator and performer. Those whose work, however deeply felt or original, is essentially addressed only to the printed page are only half-poets. They won't or can't let themselves be truly, vividly *heard*, they read flatly, badly, rarely, sometimes not at all. Their poems are half-poems.

Bryan W has been most helpful, not only in asking for higher fees, which one can't gracefully do oneself, but in arranging all the details. Assuring that I shall never be roused till nine, will always have an hour alone to rest and recharge after I arrive, and iced Perrier on the podium instead of tap water. I anticipated difficulty over these requests, but Bryan assures me that in fact his clients like to think that writers have special needs, are more sensitive to their environment. Which I suppose we are.

I believe I'll wear the midnight-blue cape again — it has such a fine sweep and flow — and alternate the white lace dress and the new sea-green silk that the interviewer in Washington said made me look like a classical sibyl. Must get shoes to go with it — a darker green silk perhaps? Renew the little V prescription, I've used so many during this wretched move. And redo my tape: the ocean sounds should fade more gradually at the end, and I need something to go with "Distant Pleasures" — more Satie? Bird song?

Four weeks now. Heavy, hot weather, and I am tiring of the heavy, hot inland landscape. Even out in the countryside I feel confined by the stale weight of the air, the ponderous laden trees and dense shrubbery; by the sense of being a hundred miles from my shining, ever-changing sea.

Janey phoned tonight; she wanted to apologize for her short-time companion Tom who, she said, was in Oakland for a meeting last week and saw me in his hotel but didn't have time to come over and speak. He hoped I wasn't "peeved." (Ugly, inappropriate word — I may be displeased or angry, I'm surely never "peeved.") I told Janey that was quite all right, since it hadn't been me.

"You didn't see Tom in Oakland last week, Mom?"

"No. As a matter of fact, darling, I don't think I've ever been in Oakland."

"Really? Tom was positive it was you. He said you looked right at him and smiled."

"Someone may have looked right at him, but it wasn't me."

"I guess you must have a double, Mom," said Janey, laughing. "They say everyone does, somewhere in the world."

I didn't laugh. Instead I felt a sort of shiver; why? Something unpleasant about the idea that everyone has a double, if it's true — which I doubt in my case, though one does often meet people who seem to be cut from a standard Simplicity or Butterick pattern.

Or did the chill come from the realization that my lovely Janey is living with one of those muddleheaded mortals who can't see the world clearly? They literally can't tell an oak from an elm, or a goose from a swan, so any woman in her forties with thick flowing dark hair, wide-set hazel eyes, and a longish pale striking face might register as "Karo McKay/Janey's mother."

The idea of doubling. In poetry it can be beautifully satisfying: the refrain, the villanelle — most of all when on each reappearance the line has a subtly altered meaning. In life? Twins, mirror images — I would hate to be a twin, though Janey as a child once wished she were. It would be company, she said.

Body doubles in the films, for modest actresses or those whose bodies aren't ideal. Or stand-ins, sparing the performer boredom and annoyance before the cameras turn. That could be convenient — To have a stand-in who would take my place for all the tedious chores that go with giving a reading but aren't mentioned in the contract: someone who would be polite and charming to the nervous students who meet the flight, make conversation at long receptions, sign books, give interviews to local newspapers and radio stations — Yes, that's what I'd wish for, if wishes were horses — Pegasus?

OCTOBER

Back from Ohio, a half-satisfactory trip. Reasonably intelligent and appreciative audience, unreasonable weather. Drenching thunderstorms, the entire campus vibrating and flashing and sloshing about like a sinking liner. I stepped from some thoughtless professor's car into half a foot of foul water, and had to come onstage trailing yards of sodden white lace and with my new satin slippers soaked and muddied.

Yet worse, they'd put me in an immense hall. I spoke to a hundred bodies and perhaps three times that many empty seats. Though I knew the storm had kept people away, I continuously had to repel the thought that my sponsors had expected Karo McKay to draw a larger crowd and were disappointed. In me. So much better when the auditorium is somewhat too small, standing room only, and everyone has the sense of being at an important event; how the energy builds then!

Not really glad to be back here. The weather's improved, but not my apartment, and I haven't finished a poem since August. Near-strangers keep asking (don't they know how impolite this is, how hurtful?), "What are you writing now?"

"Oh, I'm working on something," I lie.

Also, I'm discouraged by the local literary scene. The fiction people are overrun with small children, and haven't been especially forthcoming. There are also three poets in the department: but the best one's out of town and the others seem to look upon me mainly as a professional resource (recommendations, advice on grants and fellowships and writers' colonies). They aren't in the least interested in me, want to talk about their careers, their reviews, their students, their publications (slim limp small-press volumes).

Why did I come here, why didn't I stay in my enchanted cottage on the silver pond? Because I thought I couldn't afford to. I believed that if I wanted to exist above subsistence level I couldn't, daren't turn down a job. Not that I need much; I care nothing for the latest car or kitchen appliance. But if I'm to work well I must have a warm, quiet room flowing with soft music; the scent and color of fresh flowers; simple but perfect meals with good wine; the look and feel of almond silk and lace and taffeta against my skin.

But this is the last time. With the lecture fees Bryan Wood can — so easily, it seems! — arrange, I need never again be a Visiting Poet (that anomalous role, something like a Visiting Nurse, something like a Visiting Diplomat). I need never again live among repellent shapes and sounds and odors, among people whose voices and faces sandpaper my nerves.

One example: an unsettling incident today in the department office. As I was collecting my mail one of the secretaries came over and noisily thanked me for signing a copy of *Moon Thunder* for her mother.

"Your mother? —" I tried to search my memory bank, but I must have signed twenty or thirty books in Ohio.

"Maybe Moms didn't mention my being here; she was probably too excited. But she was really thrilled with what you wrote. She's a poet herself — well, you know that."

How did I know that, I wondered. "Oh? What did I write?"

"You said: 'With best wishes to a budding poetess.'"

"Really?" I frowned; was I losing my mind? "This was in Columbus, Ohio, last week?"

"No no, in Denver. Moms lives in Denver."

"There must be some mistake," I said pleasantly. "I didn't give a reading in Denver last week; I was in Ohio."

"Oh, it wasn't at a reading. It was in a bookstore. There's this very fine bookstore in Denver, you know, and Moms saw you there. She recognized you from your picture. Anyhow, I just wanted to thank you —"

"You're welcome, but —" I began. Then the girl's phone started ringing, and I departed to puzzle the thing out.

I thought at first that it was simply a mistake: "Moms" must have met a poet with a similar name (Carolyn Kizer? Carolyn Forche?). Then another possibility occurred to me: that some woman in Denver had been taken for me and decided to play along. I suppose it's the sort of thing a certain sort of person might do on impulse, to have the temporary sensation of being a well-known writer.

A dreadful idea. To be imitated like that — and what's worse, falsified — for whoever sees that phony inscription will think I, Karo McKay, used a vulgar cliché like "budding poetess." I detest the word "poetess" and "budding" is a wholly dead image — or if live, a hideous one: Daphne covered with acne lumps of half-formed leaf. And surely neither Carolyn F. nor Carolyn K. would write such a phrase.

Also, neither they nor I would ever write that some complete stranger was a poet, budding or otherwise. Noncommittal blandness, that's the only policy. Though there have been times when I've had the impulse to scribble something insulting. When someone's been really obnoxious, holding up the line, wanting to argue stupidly and lengthily —

Or even worse, when book dealers appear with six or eight first editions wrapped in clammy transparent plastic. Sometimes they don't even trouble to attend the reading, merely skulk about outside and then, when I appear, rush in ahead of everyone else. They heave their stack of volumes onto the table and push the title pages at me one after the other, always asking that I include the place and date as well as my name, which apparently increases their markup. "With worst wishes" or even "Your enemy" are phrases that have passed through my mind at these moments.

Meanwhile I suppose I must return to the department office

and tell the secretary that her mother was deceived, my book defaced. Dismally embarrassing, painful for everyone. And is it even possible? Not only don't I know her name, I'm not absolutely sure which of the three young women there she is. They look rather alike really, and I was distressed at the time —

So I'll have to let the matter rest. And after all, who will see that phony inscription? At the most, only a few obscure souls somewhere in Colorado.

Then why do I feel harm has been done? I think because the ceremony of book-signing isn't just a formality. It sometimes seems that way: all my fans do is thank me for the reading and hold out a volume of poems (and usually a scratchy Bic, which is why I always bring my italic pen). They're far more innocent than the dealers, of course. They don't intend to sell the book; might even be shocked at the idea. For them it's a sort of ritual. The volume a poet has touched and signed develops an instant invisible aura, becomes a minor sort of holy icon in the religion of poetry.

A religion, yes, or at least a cult, with its own temples and altars, its dead saints, its living hierarchy of priests and priest-esses; its deacons, vergers, and sextons (the critics), and its sta-tistically small but devout congregations. Yes, and the rare-book dealers are like those shoddy sellers of religious goods whose shops you see near European cathedrals — not true believers, merely peddlers with a sharp eye to profits.

And I am a part of it all — a member of the Poetrian clergy: priestess, prophetess. Hence the sense of sacrilege I feel at the idea of some dishonest laywoman (or perhaps even an infidel) donning invisible false vestments, pretending to consecrate *Moon Thunder* with my name.

NOVEMBER

Away for three hectic days in the Midwest. Two successful read-ings, one less so. The trouble began at the pre-reading dinner, where there was a really irritating faculty wife: a self-satisfied, preening straw-blonde in a floor-dragging tawny mink coat that surely involved the murder of at least twenty innocent animals. Immensely pleased with herself and greedily garrulous; she actually interrupted me twice in mid-sentence.

I forgot her for most of the performance, but when I came to "The Leopard" I remembered and gave her an accusing sibyl's stare. She only smirked and nestled further into her soft silvery fur. Somehow that broke the spell; I went on effectively, but for the first time in years with conscious effort, as if I were acting a part, pretending to be Karo McKay. Only for a minute or two, but it was disagreeable, disorienting.

Perhaps it didn't always work for the sibyls either. Perhaps sometimes, confronting some shallow, self-satisfied person, they suddenly weren't inspired and possessed, but merely tired and strained, breathing with difficulty in the hot odorous smoke, projecting their voices, moving in the motions.

Otherwise all went well. Agreeable hosts, large loving audiences — yes, it is love I feel coming from them as I stand in the spotlight, in some ways as satisfying as any I've known. Compared to that generous anonymous outpouring, other loves appear flawed and greedy. The older I grow, the less romantic physical sex seems to me. It grabs, shoves itself at one like those rare-book dealers (three of them at the last reading). But, worse than them, it wants me to inscribe a name — theirs — on my body, my soul. Then it packs up and takes off.

I'm beginning to realize that for me sensuality has always meant more than sex, been a deeper experience, focusing not only, not even most often, on another person, but on whatever is physically subtle and fine: the perfumed ivory satin of a camellia, a sudden sweet penetration of flute or cello, the taste of a tangerine warmed in the sun, the furred touch of grass, the pure green light after rain, and the sharp, almost sour scent of wet oak leaves. That's how one should be, surely: open to the multitudinous sensual delights of the world.

★ ★ ★

A strange and annoying bill came this afternoon, from a store in Minneapolis: "Sweater ... $39.00." "I still remember our very good talk," said the note stapled to it. "Hope you haven't forgotten this." Well, I did remember accompanying that pleasant woman from the Arts Council into a shop after lunch, but surely I made no purchase. Was I losing my memory?

Or was there a more likely but equally unpleasant explanation: that the woman who impersonated me in Denver and wrote "budding poetess" in a copy of *Moon Thunder* was now in Minneapolis and pretending again to be Karo McKay? It could happen; one reads about things like that.

What might such a woman be like? Lonely, needy, obviously a misfit. No, not obviously, or she couldn't deceive anyone — though perhaps this doesn't apply, because ordinary people expect oddness in artists. Possibly she has fantasized being a famous writer.

Suppose she was intoxicated with the success of her first, impulsive masquerade in the bookshop in Denver. Then this month, in Minneapolis, she saw my poster in a shop window and tried the same act deliberately — Perhaps not so much in order to steal a sweater as to have the intoxicating experience of being Karo McKay again.

What was most dreadful was the idea that someone could pass herself off as me and get away with it. I couldn't think what to do, could barely swallow supper. Finally I phoned Janey. "That woman, you know, the one who pretended to be me in Denver, she's at it again," I said, trying but failing to speak in a calm, even amused tone.

Janey, being rational and unimaginative like her father (I often regret this inheritance, but I suppose it has advantages), treated my story as the joke I half-tried to make it, and suggested that my first explanation might have been correct.

"Maybe you just forgot, you know, Mom, like with the lime tree," she said, recalling that incident years ago when my father was so ill. I went into a flower store to find something to take to the hospital, and then was overcome by a beautiful fragrant living presence. But by the time I'd got home from seeing Dad it had gone totally out of my head.

The lime tree arrived that evening, causing Janey, then four, to announce to a roomful of relatives and guests, "Mommy, there's a man here with a big bush for you." It was an amusing family story, back when we were an amusing family. Later it became first an example of my hopeless absentmindedness, then one of the things my former husband threw up against me. Yes, threw, like a series of stale cream pies in some low farce.

"That might be possible," I told Janey. "Except I haven't got a new sweater."

"Maybe the store is waiting for your check," Janey suggested.

"Well, I'm not going to send one," I said. Because if I write a check I lose either way. Either some garment I don't need will come, proving that my memory is failing; or it won't, proving that I have been impersonated and ripped off.

Hideous weather here now. Cold throbbing rain or half-snow, trees sifted down into sodden heaps, sky lowered like a water-stained canvas circus tent. And I'm stuck in the circus doing my ringmistress act, snapping my whip four times a week at rooms full of performing tigers — No, nothing so interesting: seals. Rewarding them with a bit of fishy praise when they blow some simple tune on their row of brass trumpets. Mainly though it's discords, poetic burps and farts — and the little seals all so proud of their cacophony!

Meanwhile I'm not blowing any tunes myself. (Distressed about this, don't think about this.)

DECEMBER

It's happened again. Today I received a holograph love letter from some man in Chicago called — hard to tell from the signature — Hal or Hull. No other name or return address, only the postmark. "My wonderful dearest," it began, "it's 3 A.M. but I can't sleep, thinking of you, the sheets still warm where you lay looking at me with your great topaz cat's eyes. How lucky I am, how fantastic you were ..." It went on in this vein for over a page, moderately erudite (ending with a line from Byron), romantic, sensual, occasionally edging toward pornographic, and clearly addressed to some woman Hal or Hull had just been intimate with for the first time.

At first, reading this letter, I had a frightening fantasy. I think because of the topaz eyes. I imagined that it was really addressed to me, that I was suffering from pernicious amnesia and that somehow somewhere in the Middle West I had spent a night with an unknown man. I almost persuaded myself that I remembered, that stormy night in Chicago when I was so exhausted and shaky, some large fellow with his arm round me, helping me out of a car into a moonglow whirl of snow — Beyond that, nothing.

I suppose I also imagined this because of occasional encounters in the past — that time in Toronto, the amazing Belgian — or the famous poet in Cambridge, long before I was famous — I don't often think of those moments now; they were impulsive detours, not on my real route. And nowadays I would surely never — For one thing, the chance of distasteful, even disastrous medical results.

Then I knew what had really happened. That psychotic kleptomaniac woman who impersonated me in the store in Minneapolis, and wrote "budding poetess" in somebody's copy of *Moon Thunder* in Denver, had been in Chicago. She'd been pretending to be Karo McKay again, and picked up some man who now believes he made love to me. No doubt it was easy to attract him that way: people adore the idea of being romantically involved with a poet — they imagine verses dedicated to them, their name preserved in anthologies.

Yes, and now Hall/Hull will boast about this pickup — her bold approach, his easy conquest, his hot night with "Karo McKay" — to everyone who will listen. The tale will go round, will be elaborated on, will spread. One day, Hal/Hull will be in my biography.

Janey was wrong: Not-Karo exists. She is out there somewhere in the Midwest, moving through the winter and the darkening light. Maybe in Denver her masquerade was only the casual impulse of a moment. But now she's planning it, enjoying it, getting more skilled, taking ever greater chances, without caring about the effect on my reputation. She deliberately walked off with that sweater, knowing that if I don't pay for it for the rest of my life some shopkeeper in Minnesota will despise (and describe) Karo McKay as a deadbeat.

Or perhaps it's not only opportunism, but actual malice. Not-Karo wants to make me look bad, get me in trouble. Perhaps she's Not-Fan as well. Perhaps she's someone else's fan, or she thinks I was rude to her somewhere, or she took something I wrote or said personally — people do that. If you become famous, you acquire unknown enemies as well as unknown friends.

Perhaps Not-Karo actually hates me, the way so many members of the public, sometimes without even knowing it, envy and hate writers and artists. Because our lives are more interesting and meaningful than theirs, because we're loved and rewarded for what to them looks like mere play. Doing what we like: not holding down a full-time job, not having to please the boss, getting away with things.

And now Not-Karo has experienced firsthand the public rewards of being a writer — strangers in bookshops approaching her with awe and admiration, shopkeepers trusting her with merchandise, interesting men becoming eager and desirous at first sight — She's not going to stop now, why should she? Next time she may use my name to buy something wildly expensive or sleep with someone coarse and vulgar, or do something even more indelicate and awful, so awful I can't even imagine it now.

No, she's not just some sad lost creature. She's deranged, of course, but not obviously so, and full of cunning and spite. Also she vaguely resembles me, and knows enough about my life and work to impersonate me successfully. And she's either financially independent or has a job that makes it possible — even necessary? — for her to travel from one Midwestern city to another. Denver — Minneapolis — Chicago.

What if Not-Karo is also the woman Janey's Tom saw in Oakland? Sitting in some hotel, deliberately got up as Karo McKay — If that's so, she's not limited to the Midwest; she could appear anywhere, anytime. And what's so hopeless, so horrible, there's nothing I can do about it.

JANUARY

Sanctuary at last on Cape Cod. The term's ended, two batches of performing seals disposed of (though two new ones will be waiting for me back at Convers College next week). Tranquil Christmas with Janey and her friend Tom, who seems to have become a household fixture (clothes hook? door latch?). Pale fine winter, the sky and pond and clouds shimmering, subtle shades of silver, ice-green, azure.

The day after Janey arrived I told her about Not-Karo's latest exploit. I'd been dreading that she would suggest I was losing my memory again, but she had a much simpler explanation: the billet-doux had got into the wrong envelope, as I'm afraid my checks (but never hers, of course) sometimes do.

If she's right, My Wonderful Dearest has received a polite business letter from Hal/Hull — inviting me to read at his college, for instance. This harmless missive presumably has my name and address typed out, so Dearest will know what's happened. She'll be embarrassed, angry at Hal/Hull. And disappointed: a man who makes that kind of error after one night's acquaintance isn't a good risk for a long-term relationship, one would imagine. Janey also suggested that probably Dearest, if she has any sense of responsibility, will forward my real letter.

"And I suppose you don't believe in the woman in Oakland either," I said.

"Absolutely not," declared Janey, and she pointed out that whoever smiled at Tom in the hotel couldn't possibly have known of his connection with me. Moreover now Tom had

changed his story. "She didn't look all that much like you anyhow," he told me. "She was heavier, for one thing."

"I've lost weight this fall," I said; but I felt soothed, relieved.
"Very well, darling. If you look at it your way there's a rational
explanation for each incident. But what troubles me is that there
are so many of them, and they seem to make a pattern."

"I know what you mean," agreed Janey. "But really, Mom, I
think it's just coincidence."

Suppose that's so. Things that really don't match, superim-
posed to make a false design. And as Janey also pointed out before
she left, nothing that might fit such a design has happened for
well over a month.

"You've been working too hard and traveling too much, I
think," Janey said; and she's right. I must pace myself, cut out all
those extraneous unpaid activities that have nothing to do with
my real work in life, which is to write and read poetry. Politely
decline to give lectures, be on panels, sign petitions, fill in ques-
tionnaires, judge student writing contests, donate books or manuscripts to be auctioned for some worthy cause, or contribute a
poem to some pale new magazine.

For a start, I must write to say that I can't possibly speak at
the county library benefit or judge the high school Poetry Award.
And ask Bryan Wood to cancel my expenses-only talk to the Vol-
unteers for Literacy in Detroit next month. He'll be cross,
because it's all arranged: the flights, the hotel — Perhaps it
would be better to wait until the last minute, tell him I'm ill;
everyone's sympathetic when you're ill.

I'm alone here now and at peace, watching the cloud shadows
skate on the pond. The gulls wheeling and dipping above, living
grey and white origami kites. What still troubles me though,
comes between me and the page when I sit at my desk, are recurring images of Not-Karo. Even if she doesn't exist, never existed,
she exists in my mind, a grey flapping kite, blocking out the few
words I've scratched on the white page. And if I'm not writing,
I'm as unreal, or as much of an impostor, as she is.

FEBRUARY

The dead dark of winter. Yet another storm outside the apartment complex. Whirling flakes, clots of snow sliding down the black glass as if some monster were spitting on my window.

Also a bad, frightening thing has happened. Yesterday my old college friend Merry Carson sent me a clipping from the Detroit paper, with a terse note complaining that after all these years of declining to visit her I'd been in town without letting her know, speaking at a lunch to promote literacy.

Except of course I wasn't there. Two days before the event I called Bryan to wail that I had the flu and couldn't make it. I even, at his suggestion, phoned the woman in Detroit to say I was desolated and pledge my support.

Truly, I wasn't there. But here was the apparent proof: a women's-page article with an unflattering picture of me and a horrible, unrecognizable quote, nothing like what I'd said on the phone.

'The other speakers have emphasized the practical advantages of literacy,' declared Miss [not "Ms.," not even "Mrs."] McKay, 'but in my personal opinion, what's most meaningful about literacy is that it puts you in real human contact with the world of literature. For example, once you know how to read you can, hopefully, forge a personal relationship with great contemporary American poets like Adrienne Rich and Denise Levertov.'

Besides everything else that's truly awful about this statement — jargon, repetition, defunct metaphor — there's the assertion that Adrienne and Denise are great American poets. *Good*, I could have said, or even *important*. Never *great*, that's for the future to judge.

I called Merry at once and told her the truth, that I'd known for a month that I couldn't manage Detroit but had waited until the last minute to cancel so as not to infuriate Bryan. I suggested that the newspaper had confused the story, attributed someone else's remarks to me. But Merry wasn't soothed, wasn't convinced. I could hear her thinking: Lying to her agent, lying to me. She agreed that the quote didn't sound much like me ("but then, Carrie, I haven't seen you in nearly ten years, have I?" — aggrieved tone here).

Besides, Merry thought the ideas in the quote were exactly like mine. "You know how you were always claiming that art was more important than security and family happiness," she announced, reminding me that even in college she used to maintain the opposite view. I thought then it was just for the sake of argument — but now she has five children and a Tudor castle in Grosse Pointe. And when I think how we used to be Carrie Martin and Merry Carson in Bertram Hall, almost twin-named freshman roommates, soulmates, inseparable!

Next I phoned the Detroit newspaper. The woman I eventually reached was polite at first but unhelpful. She hadn't written that story, hadn't been to the luncheon, didn't know who had. Oh no (less polite), they were always careful to check their facts. No, she couldn't promise that they'd print a retraction — she'd have to consult her boss. What did I say my name was? (huffy, suspicious). At this I became so upset that I raised my voice — actually, I more or less started to scream. Which of course made her sure I was an impostor.

An impostor. All right. Suppose it wasn't just an editorial mix-up. Suppose it was Not-Karo again, suppose she does exist and is still impersonating me all over the country and making me look terrible. Only now she's not content with making me look terrible to one person at a time. She wants to reach a wider audience. The public self has a life of its own, I remember someone saying that. And now Not-Karo is becoming my public self, in order to destroy me.

Near panic, I phoned Bryan Wood and told him nearly the whole story. At first he was very irritating, suggesting that sick and feverish as I had been (I couldn't tell him the truth about this of course), I'd really given that turgid statement. When I denied this, he grudgingly considered the possibility of an impostor, but hadn't any suggestion for dealing with the situation, and (under his professionally solicitous condolences) seemed actually to find it amusing. "It's the price of fame, I suppose," he said, and gave a snuffly giggle, covering it with a cough and the remark (lie? both of us lying about being ill?) that he had a bad cold. When I asked if he thought I should go to the police he said he didn't see much future in that.

"Now let's get this clear," he said (I could hear him trying not to laugh). "You're proposing to complain to the Detroit cops that some woman may have posed as you and told a reporter that Denise and Adrienne" (also his clients, incidentally) "are great poets? Confidentially, Karo, I don't quite see it." (Another giggle, or sneeze.) "I think if I were you I'd try to forget the whole thing. Even if this person exists, she really hasn't done you much damage."

"No, she only made me look like an utter fool and a terrible writer, and stole a sweater in Minneapolis and told some woman in Denver that she was a budding poetess," I said; I was unable to mention the letter from Hal/Hull.

"I thought you'd decided that was a case of mistaken identity."

"I did at first, but — Oh, never mind." I gave up; hung up, took another V. (Must refill my prescription again.) As soon as Janey should have been home from work, I phoned her, but couldn't get through until after eleven. And then she wasn't any help.

"I think it was probably just a mistake, Mom," she said. "The publicity people assumed you'd be there, so they turned in a press release early. They do that in my office sometimes. SIXTY LOBBY FOR ABORTION RIGHTS, somebody sent that out last month, and then there was a blizzard and half of us couldn't get to the statehouse. But it was printed in the *Globe* and they didn't correct it."

Besides, it had to be a mistake, Janey said, because even if Not-Karo existed, and was in Detroit, and knew that you were going to speak there, why would she have wanted to give the newspaper a false statement?

"Because she hates me, because she wants to make me look bad," I said.

There was a silence on the phone, but I could hear what Janey was thinking; I remembered her four-year-old voice saying for the first, but not the last time, "Mommy's silly." And then I heard her twenty-six-year-old voice saying that I mustn't worry, that I must try to put it out of my mind and get some sleep. Which was what she probably wanted herself, so I said I would and good night.

Off balance; mocked or suspected by everyone, that's how I feel. Unsure of myself, of the truth. Which I suppose is what Not-Karo wants me to feel. And the clues keep coming in. For instance, I've never received the respectable letter from Hall/Hull that Janey predicted.

About midnight, unable to sleep, I found an old road map of the United States in a drawer. Oakland — Denver — Minneapolis — Chicago — Detroit. Finally I saw the pattern: I saw that Not-Karo was moving eastward, moving toward me. Coming to get me, for some crazy reason, for the reason that she's crazy.

MARCH

Chill drenching rains, low and confused in spirit. I've had a viscid cold for weeks. Still intermittently feverish, barely meeting my classes. Not-Karo hasn't manifested herself again in any way I can tell anyone of, yet what happened last week in Buffalo has left a fog of fear over my life, especially whenever I appear in public.

It was in the Buffalo airport. As I entered the terminal I saw, fifty feet away behind the barrier, two obvious young academic types, one carrying a white placard — evidently my welcoming committee. Then I saw them approach and greet someone else, a dark-haired woman only visible to me from behind, who after a moment walked on, leaving them to stare about and then wave tentatively at me. A minor case of mistaken identity, they explained as I stood there, nearly unable to speak.

Because a shudder of dread had gone through me: Not-Karo. I was only safe, I thought, because I hadn't seen her face; if I'd seen her face I would have died.

Don't be silly, it couldn't have been Not-Karo, I told myself on the way to town. She might have known I was giving a reading in Buffalo; she couldn't have known what plane I was arriving on. But whoever that woman was, if she had claimed to be Karo McKay they would have accepted her and left me standing in the terminal as if I didn't exist.

At the motel I still felt strained, strange. Took a little V, lay down on the bed but couldn't relax, got up, put on my cream lace dress and French chandelier earrings, brushed out my hair, redid my makeup, sprayed myself with Ma Griffe. In the glass I looked like Karo McKay.

But all through what followed I didn't feel like her. The food at the official dinner tasted strange, and whenever I spoke to anyone I felt as if I was reading from a script, a script I'd read from too often before.

Then when I came onstage it was wrong from the start. I could see the hands clapping in the half-dark, but they sounded like canned TV applause. There was no transforming rush and glow of energy, nothing. I smiled, spoke, started the tape. But as I gestured, as I modulated and projected my voice, every word sounded false, every movement was like time-lapse photography, artificially slowed down or speeded up.

And then, toward the end of the reading, I had this sensation that it wasn't me the audience was staring at, it was someone else, someone standing just behind me and a little to the left. I felt frightened, dizzy, literally dragged myself through the final two poems. As I left the stage I glanced over my shoulder; no one was there. But everything was still wrong; all the praises and thanks afterward, and my replies, seemed coerced and artificial. I can't do this anymore, I thought; I can't go on.

But I must go on. The world demands that I exhibit myself regularly onstage, and at the obligatory accompanying parties, lunches, dinners, receptions. It threatens me with poverty and obscurity if I don't perform, and bribes me with fame and fees — sometimes more for one reading than most of my books earn in years.

And it's not only me. Haven't I seen how many good writers — great writers — have gone on appearing in public far more often and longer than they should, because of these bribes and threats? Haven't I seen them onstage, worn down, slowed down physically and emotionally, stumbling and repeating themselves? Exhausting themselves, so that they haven't the energy or tranquillity to write? It could happen to me. Maybe it's already begun to happen, and that's why I can't — Don't think about it.

Everything I felt in Buffalo can be explained rationally, no doubt: that I was tired, airsick, getting over a cold, had too much to drink, etc. But what I can't explain is the absolute terror of that moment at the airport when I thought I saw the back of Not-Karo, whoever she was. Or what. She resembled a normal woman, but suppose she wasn't.

Suppose she never was real, but was, is, a kind of vampire or specter, moving toward me. Oakland — Denver — Minneapolis — Chicago — Detroit . . . Buffalo. And in an almost straight line. Not a human being at all, but an evil spirit, like those demons in oriental folklore who can't turn corners.

That would explain how she always knows where I am, how she can slide from city to city. Spreading slime wherever she goes like a crawling snail, souring and destroying my life. So that once she's done the public things, I become unable to do them; it's as if they've been slimed and fouled. Already I can't smile at attractive strangers, sign books, or speak to fans in the easy, graceful way I once did. And now even being onstage feels false.

No, no, I mustn't think that way, that's mad. I've been ill, I must give myself time to recover. Call Bryan, cancel those last two readings. Yes, and tell him to hold off for a while on scheduling anything for the summer or fall. Panic: if I can't perform, can't teach, how will I survive?

And I daren't take too much time off. If I don't appear anywhere, gradually I'll cease to exist as far as the literary world is concerned. Lovers of poetry are as restless and fickle as most lovers; if you don't continually remind them of your existence they soon forget you. Especially if you haven't written any new — (Don't think about that.) Sooner than you can imagine you're unknown.

APRIL

It's over, everything's over, my writing my life everything. I made a fatal error: I let Bryan Wood persuade me not to cancel the Albany reading. He was so shocked, so insistent, telling me over and over that it was so near, so important, so well paid.

"I'm thinking of you, Karo darling," he said, "your reputation," but wasn't he really thinking of his own reputation for being able to produce performing poets reliably?

Even on the plane I suspected I'd made a terrible mistake. We began to lurch through cold boiling clouds and I opened the airsick magazine to the map scored with spidery routes and traced that particular strand of the web. Oakland — Denver — Minneapolis — Chicago — Detroit — Buffalo ... Albany. Again I was moving toward Not-Karo, who was moving toward me.

And in Albany, from the first moment, everything was wrong, the air soupy white with spring fog like spoilt vichyssoise, people's faces and voices foggy. I was still queasy, and when I put on my sea-green silk in the motel room it hung round me like some sea nymph's discarded washing — I was still losing weight — and my face in the mirror was bruised and painted. I'm not well, I thought, I shouldn't have come.

Lay down, got up, swallowed another little V, no visible effect. Unlocked the miniature fridge, found a miniature bottle of orange juice and one of vodka, poured them together, became minimally able to function. Then the reception and dinner, with more drinking and talking and canned laughing. I heard myself talking and laughing too, but as if someone else, some ventriloquist, were doing it at a distance while I tried to sit upright and not be sick in my plate.

At the building where I was to read I asked for a washroom. Someone pointed the way, down a bare ill-lit corridor, a long hot stuffy space, rows of beige tiles, beige sinks, beige metal doors, all of them closed as if people with no feet were sitting inside the cubicles. I felt hot, dizzy, nauseous. Tried to vomit, couldn't, turned on the water and splashed myself. It didn't change anything, except that now my reflection in the long mirror was splashed and distorted, with stringy wet hair, the eyes yellow, unfocused.

I can't do it, I thought. I staggered into the corridor, ran in the other direction, turning, a dead end, turned again, into a cavernous curved space. Crowds crowding in. I slid and crowded through them, toward an open door.

Outside it was mercifully cooler. The fog was shredding, lifting, everything damp, dark, shining spring-flecked trees. I stood, swallowing cold clear air. For God's sake, Karo McKay, I thought, what the hell are you doing? You go back in there and read your poems like you promised.

So I stumbled back up the rain-speckled sidewalk. The lobby was almost empty now, and I started through the doors opposite, but a bulky young man on the other side blocked my way, demanded my ticket.

"Oh, I don't need a ticket, I'm the poet." I smiled. He didn't smile, or move.

"Sorry, ma'am. No free admission tonight. The box office is right over there. Better hurry, it's about to start."

I thought, Very well, I'll buy a ticket, they'll pay me back, it'll be a joke — But I had no money with me, only my brocade folder of poems and tape recorder. "You don't understand," I said, dizzy and nauseous again. "I'm the poet who's reading here — I'm Karo McKay."

The usher glanced at the poster on the wall, comparing the

photo (years younger, pounds heavier) with me; it was clear that in his opinion they didn't remotely mesh. "Sorry, ma'am," he repeated in the flat voice one uses for gatecrashers and crazies.

He might have said more, but a gaggle of people was now hastening across the lobby with tickets extended. As he held the door wide for them I heard a woman's voice inside speaking, no, I thought, reading the first verse of "Distant Pleasures." That's my voice, I thought, from the tape I made for the Poetry Library, they're playing it to keep the audience quiet till I come.

I squeezed past the ticket-taker, pretending not to hear his protests, and stumbled down the aisle. But when I looked up at the stage a woman was already standing there, also with a bush of dark hair, a green dress, moving her arms around — I screamed, slipped, grabbed the wooden curve of a seatback, fell. Other people screamed, crowded round — It was over.

Exhaustion, the flu, everyone said afterward politely, sympathetically. I suppose behind my back some of them also said drugs, drink, breakdown, who knows? I don't remember the rest of it very well. At some point I was throwing up into a metal wastebasket, in a sort of seminar room with words in a foreign language chalked on the board. Or perhaps I'd just forgotten how to read, because I couldn't understand most of what people were saying to me either.

Later there was the backseat of a car with gum wrappers on the floor, and then a dowdy little bedroom with pink venetian blinds drawn and a pink candlewick bedspread, cups of lukewarm tea I pushed away.

But I couldn't sleep. I was sweating, running a fever, kept seeing Not-Karo, hearing her voice over and over and over. Horrible, and not just the voice, but the words, my words. It was as if I was hearing "Distant Pleasures" deliberately read wrong, in a false, theatrical manner, so that it sounded phony, inflated, secondrate.

I lay there in the dark, too hot and sick to sleep, hearing other lines of mine in my head, echoing and repeating as if in some infernal auditorium. They sounded out flawed and false, like the false name "Karo McKay," part stolen (from Janey's father) and never returned, part invented. And it seemed to me that every line I'd ever written or read was flawed and false: a pastiche of sentimental and melodramatic words soaked in overdramatic style like Karo syrup, cheap and sweet and sticky and colorless.

For a long time I lay there, sunk into the bed, and the light changed from night to day, and Janey came from Boston. She spoke with the doctor, she arranged everything. She also insisted that the woman in the green dress was only the professor who was supposed to introduce Karo McKay; that her dress wasn't green anyhow, but blue, and her hair was lighter than mine and only shoulder length. I'm not so sure. I think I saw what I saw. What I was supposed to see.

Then Janey came back to the apartment complex with me; later she helped me pack, and she and Tom drove me to Cape Cod. They or somebody must have sorted everything out, got the cottage opened and the heat turned on; somebody must have taught my last two weeks of classes.

I suppose Bryan Wood apologized to the Albany people. I don't know; I haven't wanted to speak to him, and he probably doesn't want to speak to me. I don't care. I prefer to think how I'll never again have to make lively conversation with deadly stupid strangers, jolt up and down on dwarf planes, and lie awake on rock-hard giant beds in airless anonymous motel rooms, listening to the asthmatic rattle of the air conditioner and trucks choking and wheezing out on some dirty unknown highway.

It's true spring here. The pond shimmers with life, is shrill with birds, boisterous every evening with croaking frogs. I walk beside it, or in the thin wet woods among sawdust-covered unfurling spirals of bracken and red-veined skunk cabbage, dangerous with growth. I'm gaining weight, sleeping through the night again.

Haven't heard anything more of Not-Karo. Perhaps in destroying Karo McKay she's also been destroyed, dissolved "into thin
air." No doubt Shakespeare was right: the air that phantoms dis-
solve into has to be especially thin, or they'd clog it like industrial
pollutants.

At other times I think she was only a human impostor after all,
and is still out there, lying to people, going on with Karo McKay's
public life. I expect to come across her picture in the *Times*, read
an interview, hear that someone's met her somewhere or been
to a reading. I don't expect her to publish anything: impostors
and evil spirits can't write poetry. And of course, if she doesn't
publish, after a while everyone will forget her, even assume she
is dead.

But it doesn't matter, because as far as I'm concerned she's
already won. There's nobody here but Carrie Martin, a forty-
eight-year-old divorced woman with a sensible and wonderful
grown daughter. She knows shorthand and bookkeeping but is
currently unemployed. She has a small — an inadequate —
income, so she will have to look for some sort of work soon. She
has pale dry skin and a long mop of dyed black hair growing out
moss-gray, and used to be quite attractive. She wears reading
glasses and has a partial plate. She doesn't accept mail addressed
to Karo McKay. She likes orange-scented soap and white flowers
and ripe avocados with lemon juice and olive oil. She has a vacant
look in her eyes.

Her only problem is that lately she's started to hear phrases,
lines, even whole stanzas of poetry, whispering at her everywhere — from the heaps of dusty potatoes and papery pale-
auburn onions in the grocery, through the wet bluish mist over
the pond. They won't let her alone; they echo, repeat themselves, shaping and reshaping themselves.

Usually she tries not to listen. But once in a while, to silence
them, she scribbles them down and shuts them in a drawer.
They want to get out, but she won't let them. Because as long as
they're safe in the drawer, so am I.

The Doll

In Joyce Carol Oates's twenty-first volume of short stories, Haunted: Tales of the Grotesque (1994), she continues to explore the theme that has dominated her prodigious literary output — the "night-side" of the mind. The darker realm of human experience is the subject both of her naturalistic fiction and works such as this, which venture across the borders of realism into the fantastic and supernatural. Many of her most haunted characters are women who, like Florence Parr in "The Doll," find themselves alarmingly out of control, caught up in an experience that pushes them to their psychological limit.

The uncanny enters Florence Parr's life without any warning one balmy day in late April, on a tree-lined avenue in a city she is visiting for the first time. What she encounters there will soon expose cracks in the surface of her self-sufficient, coolly professional "daytime self," making her vulnerable to incursions from an irrational, blindly instinctual realm to which she had formerly thought herself immune. "The Doll" is one of Oates's most memorable fictional accounts of how a woman's life, once safely contained within fixed parameters, can become twisted, formless, and threateningly strange, the way one's reflection does in the crazy distorting mirrors at an amusement park.

The Doll

MANY YEARS AGO a little girl was given, for her fourth birthday, an antique dolls' house of unusual beauty and complexity, and size: for it seemed large enough, almost, for a child to crawl into.

The dolls' house was said to have been built nearly one hundred years before, by a distant relative of the little girl's mother. It had come down through the family and was still in excellent condition: with a steep gabled roof, many tall, narrow windows fitted with real glass, dark green shutters that closed over, three fireplaces made of stone, mock lightning rods, mock shingleboard siding (white), a veranda that nearly circled the house, stained glass at the front door and at the first floor landing, and even a cupola whose tiny roof lifted miraculously away. In the master bedroom there was a canopied bed with white organdy flounces and ruffles; there were tiny window boxes beneath most of the windows; the furniture — all of it Victorian, of course — was uniformly exquisite, having been made with the most fastidious care and affection. The lampshades were adorned with tiny gold fringes, there was a marvelous old tub with claw feet, and nearly every room had a chandelier. When she first saw the dolls' house on the morning of her fourth birthday the little girl was so astonished she could not speak: for the present was unexpected, and uncannily "real." It was to be the great present, and the great memory, of her childhood.

Florence had several dolls which were too large to fit into the house, since they were average-size dolls, but she brought them close to the house, facing its open side, and played with them there. She fussed over them, and whispered to them, and scolded them, and invented little conversations between them. One day, out of nowhere, came the name *Bartholomew* — the name of the family who owned the dolls' house. Where did you get that name from, her parents asked, and Florence replied that those were the people who lived in the house. Yes, but where did the name come from? they asked.

The child, puzzled and a little irritated, pointed mutely at the dolls.

One was a girl-doll with shiny blond ringlets and blue eyes that were thickly lashed, and almost too round; another was a red-haired freckled boy in denim coveralls and a plaid shirt. It was obvious that they were sister and brother. Another was a woman-doll, perhaps a mother, who had bright red lips and who wore a hat cleverly made of soft gray-and-white feathers. There was even a baby-doll, made of the softest rubber, hairless and expressionless, and oversized in relationship to the other dolls; and a spaniel, about nine inches in length, with big brown eyes and a quizzical upturned tail. Sometimes one doll was Florence's favorite, sometimes another. There were days when she preferred the blond girl, whose eyes rolled in her head, and whose complexion was a lovely pale peach. There were days when the mischievous red-haired boy was obviously her favorite. Sometimes she banished all the human dolls and played with the spaniel, who was small enough to fit into most of the rooms of the dolls' house.

Occasionally Florence undressed the human dolls, and washed them with a tiny sponge. How strange they were, without their clothes...! Their bodies were poreless and smooth and blank, there was nothing secret or nasty about them, no crevices for dirt to hide in, no trouble at all. Their faces were unperturbable, as always. Calm wise fearless staring eyes that no harsh words or slaps could disturb. But Florence loved her dolls very much, and rarely felt the need to punish them.

Her treasure was, of course, the dolls' house with its steep Victorian roof and its gingerbread trim and its many windows and that marvelous veranda, upon which little wooden rocking chairs, each equipped with its own tiny cushion, were set. Visitors — friends of her parents or little girls her own age — were always astonished when they first saw it. They said: Oh, isn't it beautiful! They said: Why, it's almost the size of a real house, isn't it? — though of course it wasn't, it was only a dolls' house, a little less than thirty-six inches high.

★ ★ ★

Nearly four decades later while driving along East Fainlight Avenue in Lancaster, Pennsylvania, a city she had never before visited, and about which she knew nothing, Florence Parr was astonished to see, set back from the avenue, at the top of a stately elm-shaded knoll, her old dolls' house — that is, the replica of it. The house. The house itself.

She was so astonished that for the passage of some seconds she could not think what to do. Her most immediate reaction was to brake her car — for she was a careful, even fastidious driver; at the first sign of confusion or difficulty she always brought her car to a stop.

A broad handsome elm- and plane tree-lined avenue, in a charming city, altogether new to her. Late April: a fragrant, even rather giddy spring, after a bitter and protracted winter. The very air trembled, rich with warmth and color. The estates in this part of the city were as impressive, as stately, as any she had ever seen: the houses were really mansions, boasting of wealth, their sloping, elegant lawns protected from the street by brick walls, or wrought-iron fences, or thick evergreen hedges. Everywhere there were azaleas, that most gorgeous of spring flowers — scarlet and white and yellow and flamey-orange, almost blindingly beautiful. There were newly cultivated beds of tulips, primarily red; and exquisite apple blossoms, and cherry blossoms, and flowering trees Florence recognized but could not identify by name. *Her* house was surrounded by an old-fashioned wrought-iron fence, and in its enormous front yard were red and yellow tulips that had pushed their way through patches of weedy grass.

She found herself on the sidewalk, at the front gate. Like the unwieldy gate that was designed to close over the driveway, this gate was not only open but its bottom spikes had dug into the ground; it had not been closed for some time and could probably not be dislodged. Someone had put up a hand-lettered sign in black, not long ago: 1377 EAST FAINLIGHT. But no name, no family name. Florence stood staring up at the house, her heart beating rapidly. She could not quite believe what she was seeing. Yes, there it was, of course — yet it *could* not be, not in such detail.

The antique dolls' house. *Hers.* After so many years. There was the steep gabled roof, in what appeared to be slate; the old lightning rods; the absurd little cupola that was so charming; the veranda; the white shingleboard siding (which was rather weathered and gray in the bright spring sunshine); most of all, most striking, the eight tall, narrow windows, four to each floor, with their dark shutters. Florence could not determine if the shutters were painted a very dark green, or black. What color had they been on the dolls' house . . . She saw that the gingerbread trim was badly rotted.

The first wave of excitement, almost of vertigo, that had overtaken her in the car had passed; but she felt, still, an unpleasant sense of urgency. Her old doll's house. Here on East Fainlight Avenue in Lancaster, Pennsylvania. Glimpsed so suddenly, on this warm spring morning. And what did it mean. . . ? Obviously there was an explanation. Her distant uncle, who had built the house for his daughter, had simply copied this house, or another just like it; no doubt there were many houses like this one. Florence knew little about Victorian architecture but she supposed that there were many duplications, even in large, costly houses. Unlike contemporary architects, the architects of that era must have been extremely limited, forced to use again and again certain basic structures, and certain basic ornamentation — the cupolas, the gables, the complicated trim. What struck her as so odd, so mysterious, was really nothing but a coincidence. It would make an interesting story, an amusing anecdote, when she returned home; though perhaps it was not even worth mentioning. Her parents might have been intrigued but they were both dead. And she was always careful about dwelling upon herself, her private life, since she halfway imagined that her friends and acquaintances and colleagues would interpret nearly anything she said of a personal nature according to their vision of her as a public person, and she wanted to avoid that.

There was a movement at one of the upstairs windows that caught her eye. It was then transmitted, fluidly, miraculously, to the other windows, flowing from right to left. . . . But no, it was only the reflection of clouds being blown across the sky, up behind her head.

She stood motionless. It was unlike her, it was quite uncharacteristic of her, yet there she stood. She did not want to walk up to the veranda steps, she did not want to ring the doorbell, such a gesture would be ridiculous, and anyway there was no time: she really should be driving on. They would be expecting her soon. Yet she could not turn away. Because it *was* the house. Incredibly, it was her old dolls' house. (Which she had given away, of course, thirty — thirty-five? — years ago. And had rarely thought about since.) It was ridiculous to stand here, so astonished, so slow-witted, so perversely vulnerable ... yet what other attitude was appropriate, what other attitude would not violate the queer sense of the sacred, the otherworldly, that the house had evoked?

She would ring the doorbell. And why not? She was a tall, rather wide-shouldered, confident woman, tastefully dressed in a cream-colored spring suit; she was rarely in the habit of apologizing for herself, or feeling embarrassment. Many years ago, perhaps, as a girl, a shy, silly, self-conscious girl: but no longer. Her wavy graying hair had been brushed back smartly from her wide, strong forehead. She wore no makeup, had stopped bothering with it years ago, and with her naturally high-colored, smooth complexion, she was a handsome woman, especially attractive when she smiled and her dark staring eyes relaxed. She *would* ring the doorbell, and see who came to the door, and say whatever flew into her head. She was looking for a family who lived in the neighborhood, she was canvassing for a school millage vote, she was inquiring whether they had any old clothes, old furniture, for ...

Halfway up the walk she remembered that she had left the keys in the ignition of her car, and the motor running. And her purse on the seat.

She found herself walking unusually slowly. It was unlike her, and the disorienting sense of being unreal, of having stepped into another world, was totally new. A dog began barking somewhere near: the sound seemed to pierce her in the chest and bowels. An attack of panic. An involuntary fluttering of the eyelids. . . . But it was nonsense of course. She would ring the bell, someone would open the door, perhaps a servant, perhaps an elderly woman, they would have a brief conversation, Florence would glance behind her into the foyer to see if the circular staircase looked the same, if the old brass chandelier was still there, if the "marble" floor remained. Do you know the Parr family, Florence would ask, we've lived in Cummington, Massachusetts, for generations, I think it's quite possible that someone from my family visited you in this house, of course it was a very long time ago. I'm sorry to disturb you but I was driving by and I saw your striking house and I couldn't resist stopping for a moment out of curiosity. . . .

There were the panes of stained glass on either side of the oak door! But so large, so boldly colored. In the dolls' house they were hardly visible, just chips of colored glass. But here they were each about a foot square, starkly beautiful: reds, greens, blues. Exactly like the stained glass of a church.

I'm sorry to disturb you, Florence whispered, but I was driving by and . . .

I'm sorry to disturb you but I am looking for a family named Bartholomew, I have reason to think that they live in this neighborhood. . . .

But as she was about to step onto the veranda the sensation of panic deepened. Her breath came shallow and rushed, her thoughts flew wildly in all directions, she was simply terrified and could not move. The dog's barking had become hysterical.

When Florence was angry or distressed or worried she had a habit of murmuring her to herself, Florence Parr, Florence Parr, it was soothing, it was mollifying, Florence Parr, it was often vaguely reproachful, for after all she *was* Florence Parr and that carried with it responsibility as well as authority. She named herself, identified herself. It was usually enough to bring her undisciplined thoughts under control. But she had not experienced an attack of panic for many years. All the strength of her body seemed to have fled, drained away; it terrified her to think that she might faint here. What a fool she would make of herself. . . .

As a young university instructor she had nearly succumbed to panic one day, mid-way through a lecture on the metaphysical poets. Oddly, the attack had come not at the beginning of the semester but well into the second month, when she had come to believe herself a thoroughly competent teacher. The most extraordinary sensation of fear, unfathomable and groundless fear, which she had never been able to comprehend afterward. . . . One moment she had been speaking of Donne's famous image in "The Relic" — a bracelet of "bright hair about the bone" — and the next moment she was so panicked she could hardly catch her breath. She wanted to run out of the classroom, wanted to run out of the building. It was as if a demon had appeared to her. It breathed into her face, shoved her about, tried to pull her under. She would suffocate: she would be destroyed. The sensation was possibly the most unpleasant she had ever experienced in her life though it carried with it no pain and no specific images. Why she was so frightened she could not grasp. Why she wanted nothing more than to run out of the classroom, to escape her students' curious eyes, she was never to understand.

But she did not flee. She forced herself to remain at the podium. Though her voice faltered she did not stop; she continued with the lecture, speaking into a blinding haze. Surely her students must have noticed her trembling. . . ? But she was stubborn, she was really quite tenacious for a young woman of twenty-four, and by forcing herself to imitate herself, to imitate her normal tone and mannerisms, she was able to overcome the attack. As it lifted, gradually, and her eyesight strengthened, her heartbeat slowed, she seemed to know that the attack would never come again in a classroom. And this turned out to be correct.

But now she could not overcome her anxiety. She hadn't a podium to grasp, she hadn't lecture notes to follow, there was no one to imitate, she was in a position to make a terrible fool of herself. And surely someone was watching from the house. . . . It struck her that she had no reason, no excuse, for being here. What on earth could she say if she rang the doorbell? How would she explain herself to a skeptical stranger? I simply must see the inside of your house, she would whisper, I've been led up this walk by a force I can't explain, please excuse me, please humor me, I'm not well, I'm not myself this morning, I only want to see the inside of your house to see if it *is* the house I remember. . . . I had a house like yours. It was yours. But no one lived in my house except dolls; a family of dolls. I loved them but I always sensed that they were blocking the way, standing between me and something else. . . .

The barking dog was answered by another, a neighbor's dog. Florence retreated. Then turned and hurried back to her car, where the keys were indeed in the ignition, and her smart leather purse lay on the seat where she had so imprudently left it.

So she fled the dolls' house, her poor heart thudding. What a fool you are, Florence Parr, she thought brutally, a deep hot blush rising into her face.

The rest of the day — the late afternoon reception, the dinner itself, the after-dinner gathering — passed easily, even routinely, but did not seem to her very real; it was not very convincing. That she was Florence Parr, the president of Champlain College, that she was to be a featured speaker at this conference of administrators of small private liberal arts colleges: it struck her for some reason as an imposture, a counterfeit. The vision of the dolls' house kept rising in her mind's eye. How odd, how very odd the experience had been, yet there was no one to whom she might speak about it, even to minimize it, to transform it into an amusing anecdote. . . . The others did not notice her discomfort. In fact they claimed that she was looking well, they were delighted to see her and to shake her hand. Many were old acquaintances, men and women, but primarily men, with whom she had worked in the past at one college or another; a number were strangers, younger administrators who had heard of her heroic effort at Champlain College, and who wanted to be introduced to her. At the noisy cocktail hour, at dinner, Florence heard her somewhat distracted voice speaking of the usual matters: declining enrollments, building fund campaigns, alumni support, endowments, investments, state and federal aid. Her remarks were met with the same respectful attention as always, as though there were nothing wrong with her.

For dinner she changed into a linen dress of pale blue and dark blue stripes which emphasized her tall, graceful figure, and drew the eye away from her wide shoulders and her stolid thighs; she wore her new shoes with the fashionable three-inch heel, though she detested them. Her haircut was becoming, she had manicured and even polished her nails the evening before, and she supposed she looked attractive enough, especially in this context of middle-aged and older people. But her mind kept drifting away from the others, from the handsome though rather dark colonial dining room, even from the spirited, witty after-dinner speech of a popular administrator and writer, a retired president of Williams College, and formerly — a very long time ago, now — a colleague of Florence's at Swarthmore. She smiled with the others, and laughed with the others, but she could not attend to the courtly, white-haired gentleman's astringent witticisms; her mind kept drifting back to the dolls' house, out there on East Fainlight Avenue. It was well for her that she hadn't rung the doorbell, for what if someone who was attending the conference had answered the door; it was, after all, being hosted by Lancaster College. What an utter fool she would have made of herself. . . .

She went to her room in the fieldstone alumni house shortly after ten, though there were people who clearly wished to talk with her, and she knew a night of insomnia awaited. Once in the room with its antique furniture and its self-consciously quaint wallpaper she regretted having left the ebullient atmosphere downstairs. Though small private colleges were in trouble these days, and though most of the administrators at the conference were having serious difficulties with finances, and faculty morale, there was nevertheless a spirit of camaraderie, of heartiness. Of course it was the natural consequence of people in a social gathering. One simply cannot resist, in such a context, the droll remark, the grateful laugh, the sense of cheerful complicity in even an unfortunate fate. How puzzling the human personality is, Florence thought, preparing for bed, moving uncharacteristically slowly, when with others there is a public self, alone there is a private self, and yet both are real. . . . Both are experienced as real. . . .

She lay sleepless in the unfamiliar bed. There were noises in the distance; she turned on the air conditioner, the fan only, to drown them out. Still she could not sleep. The house on East Fainlight Avenue, the dolls' house of her childhood, she lay with her eyes open, thinking of absurd, disjointed things, wondering now why she had *not* pushed her way through that trivial bout of anxiety to the veranda steps, and to the door, after all she was Florence Parr, she had only to imagine people watching her — the faculty senate, students, her fellow administrators — to know how she should behave, with what alacrity and confidence. It was only when she forgot who she was, and imagined herself utterly alone, that she was crippled by uncertainty and susceptible to fear.

The luminous dials of her watch told her it was only 10:35. Not too late, really, to dress and return to the house and ring the doorbell. Of course she would only ring it if the downstairs was lighted, if someone was clearly up. . . . Perhaps an elderly gentleman lived there, alone, someone who had known her grandfather, someone who had visited the Parrs in Cummington. For there *must* be a connection. It was very well to speak of coincidences, but she knew, she knew with a deep, unshakable conviction, that there was a connection between the dolls' house and the house here in town, and a connection between her childhood and the present house. . . . When she explained herself to whoever opened the door, however, she would have to be casual, conversational. Years of administration had taught her diplomacy; one must not appear to be *too* serious. Gravity in leaders is disconcerting, what is demanded is the light, confident touch, the air of private and even secret knowledge. People do not want equality with their leaders: they want, they desperately need, them to be superior. The superiority must be tacitly communicated, however, or it becomes offensive. . . .

Suddenly she was frightened: it seemed to her quite possible that the panic attack might come upon her the next morning, when she gave her address ("The Future of the Humanities in American Education"). She was scheduled to speak at 9:30, she would be the first speaker of the day, and the first real speaker of the conference. And it was quite possible that that disconcerting weakness would return, that sense of utter, almost infantile helplessness. . . .

She sat up, turned on the light, and looked over her notes. They were handwritten, not typed, she had told her secretary not to bother typing them, the address was one she'd given before in different forms, her approach was to be conversational rather than formal though of course she would quote the necessary statistics. . . . But it had been a mistake, perhaps, not to have the notes typed. There were times when she couldn't decipher her own handwriting.

A drink might help. But she couldn't very well go over to the Lancaster Inn, where the conference was to be held, and where there was a bar; and of course she hadn't anything with her in the room. As a rule she rarely drank. She never drank alone. . . . However, if a drink would help her sleep: would calm her wild racing thoughts.

The dolls' house had been a present for her birthday. Many years ago. She could not recall how many. And there were her dolls, her little family of dolls, which she had not thought of for a lifetime. She felt a pang of loss, of tenderness. . . .

Florence Parr who suffered quite frequently from insomnia. But of course no one knew.

Florence Parr who had had a lump in her right breast removed, a cyst really, harmless, absolutely harmless, shortly after her thirty-eighth birthday. But none of her friends at Champlain knew. Not even her secretary knew. And the ugly little thing turned out to be benign: absolutely harmless. So it was well that no one knew.

Florence Parr of whom it was said that she was distant, even guarded, at times. You can't get close to her, someone claimed. And yet it was often said of her that she was wonderfully warm and open and frank and totally without guile. A popular president. Yet she had the support of her faculty. There might be individual jealousies here and there, particularly among the vice presidents and deans, but in general she had everyone's support and she knew it and was grateful for it and intended to keep it.

It was only that her mind worked, late into the night. Raced. Would not stay still.

Should she surrender to her impulse, and get dressed quickly and return to the house? It would take no more than ten minutes. And quite likely the downstairs lights would *not* be on, the inhabitants would be asleep, she could see from the street that the visit was totally out of the question, she would simply drive on past. And be saved from her audacity.

If I do this, the consequence will be. . . .

If I fail to do this. . . .

She was not, of course, an impulsive person. Nor did she admire impulsive "spontaneous" people: she thought them immature, and frequently exhibitionistic. It was often the case that they were very much aware of their own spontaneity. . . .

She would defend herself against the charge of being calculating. Of being overly cautious. Her nature was simply a very pragmatic one. She took up tasks with extreme interest, and absorbed herself deeply in them, one after another, month after month and year after year, and other considerations simply had to be shunted to the side. For instance, she had never married. The surprise would have been not that Florence Parr had married, but that she had had time to cultivate a relationship that would end in marriage. I am not opposed to marriage for myself, she once said, with unintentional naiveté, but it would take so much

282

time to become acquainted with a man, to go out with him, and talk.... At Champlain where everyone liked her, and shared anecdotes about her, it was said that she'd been even as a younger woman so oblivious to men, even to attentive men, that she had failed to recognize a few years later a young linguist whose carrel at the Widener Library had been next to hers, though the young man claimed to have said hello to her every day, and to have asked her out for coffee occasionally. (She had always refused, she'd been far too busy.) When he turned up at Champlain, married, the author of a well-received book on linguistic theory, an associate professor in the Humanities division, Florence had not only been unable to recognize him but could not remember him at all, though he remembered her vividly, and even amused the gathering by recounting to Florence the various outfits she had worn that winter, even the colors of her knitted socks. She had been deeply embarrassed, of course, and yet flattered, and amused. It was proof, after all, that Florence Parr was always at all times Florence Parr.

Afterward she was somewhat saddened, for the anecdote meant, did it not, that she really *had* no interest in men. She was not a spinster because no one had chosen her, not even because she had been too fastidious in her own choosing, but simply because she had no interest in men, she did not even "see" them when they presented themselves before her. It was sad, it was irrefutable. She was an ascetic not through an act of will but through temperament.

It was at this point that she pushed aside the notes for her talk, her heart beating wildly as a girl's. She had no choice, she *must* satisfy her curiosity about the house, if she wanted to sleep, if she wanted to remain sane.

As the present of the dolls' house was the great event of her childhood, so the visit to the house on East Fainlight Avenue was to be the great event of her adulthood: though Florence Parr was never to allow herself to think of it, afterward.

★ ★ ★

It was a mild, quiet night, fragrant with blossoms, not at all intimidating. Florence drove to the avenue, to the house, and was consoled by the numerous lights burning in the neighborhood: of course it wasn't late, of course there was nothing extraordinary about what she was going to do.

Lights were on downstairs. Whoever lived there was up, in the living room. Waiting for her.

Remarkable, her calmness. After so many foolish hours of indecision.

She ascended the veranda steps, which gave slightly beneath her weight. Rang the doorbell. After a minute or so an outside light went on: she felt exposed: began to smile nervously. One smiled, one soon learned how. There was no retreating.

She saw the old wicker furniture on the porch. Two rocking chairs, a settee. Once painted white but now badly weathered. No cushions.

A dog began barking angrily.

Florence Parr, Florence Parr. She knew who she was, but there was no need to tell *him*. Whoever it was, peering out at her through the dark stained glass, an elderly man, someone's left-behind grandfather. Still, owning this house in this part of town meant money and position: you might sneer at such things but they do have significance. Even to pay the property taxes, the school taxes. . . .

The door opened and a man stood staring out at her, half smiling, quizzical. He was not the man she expected, he was not elderly, but of indeterminate age, perhaps younger than she. "Yes? Hello? What can I do for. . . ?" he said.

She heard her voice, full-throated and calm. The rehearsed question. Questions. An air of apology beneath which her confidence held firm. ". . . driving in the neighborhood earlier today, staying with friends. . . . Simply curious about an old connection between our families. . . . Or at any rate between my family and the people who built this. . . ."

Clearly he was startled by her presence, and did not quite

grasp her questions. She spoke too rapidly, she would have to repeat herself.

He invited her in. Which was courteous. A courtesy that struck her as unconscious, automatic. He was very well mannered. Puzzled but not suspicious. Not unfriendly. Too young for this house, perhaps — for so old and shabbily elegant a house. Her presence on his doorstep, her bold questions, the bright strained smile that stretched her lips must have baffled him but he did not think her *odd*: he respected her, was not judging her. A kindly, simple person. Which was of course a relief. He might even be a little simpleminded. Slow-thinking. He certainly had nothing to do with . . . with whatever she was involved in, in this part of the world. He would tell no one about her.

". . . a stranger to the city? . . . staying with friends?"

"I only want to ask: does the name Parr mean anything to you?"

A dog was barking, now frantically. But kept its distance.

Florence was being shown into the living room, evidently the only lighted room downstairs. She noted the old staircase, graceful as always. But they had done something awkward with the wainscoting, painted it a queer slate blue. And the floor was no longer of marble but a poor imitation, some sort of linoleum tile. . . .

"The chandelier," she said suddenly.

The man turned to her, smiling his amiable quizzical worn smile.

"Yes . . . ?"

"It's very attractive," she said. "It must be an antique."

In the comfortable orangish light of the living room she saw that he had sandy red hair, thinning at the crown. But boyishly frizzy at the sides. He might have been in his late thirties but his face was prematurely lined and he stood with one shoulder slightly higher than the other, as if he were very tired. She began to apologize again for disturbing him. For taking up his time with her impulsive, probably futile curiosity.

"Not at all," he said. "I usually don't go to bed until well past midnight."

Florence found herself sitting at one end of an overstuffed sofa. Her smile was strained but as wide as ever, her face had begun to grow very warm. Perhaps he would not notice her blushing.

". . . insomnia?"

"Yes. Sometimes."

"I too . . . sometimes."

He was wearing a green-and-blue plaid shirt, with thin red stripes. A flannel shirt. The sleeves rolled up to his elbows. And what looked like work-trousers. Denim. A gardener's outfit perhaps. Her mind cast about desperately for something to say and she heard herself asking about his garden, his lawn. So many lovely tulips. Most of them red. And there were plane trees, and several elms. . . .

He faced her, leaning forward with his elbows on his knees. A faintly sunburned face. A redhead's complexion, somewhat freckled.

The chair he sat in did not look familiar. It was an ugly brown, imitation brushed velvet. Florence wondered who had bought it: a silly young wife perhaps.

". . . Parr family?"

"From Lancaster?"

"Oh no. From Cummington, Massachusetts. We've lived there for many generations."

He appeared to be considering the name, frowning at the carpet.

". . . *does* sound familiar. . . ."

"Oh, does it? I had hoped. . . ."

The dog approached them, no longer barking. Its tail wagged and thumped against the side of the sofa, the leg of an old-fashioned table, nearly upsetting a lamp. The man snapped his fingers at the dog and it came no further; it quivered, and made a half growling, half sighing noise, and lay with its snout on its paws and its skinny tail outstretched, a few feet from Florence.

She wanted to placate it, to make friends. But it was such an ugly creature — partly hairless, with scruffy white whiskers, a naked sagging belly.

"If the dog bothers you . . ."

"Oh no, no. Not at all."

"He only means to be friendly."

"I can see that," Florence said, laughing girlishly. ". . . He's very handsome."

"Hear that?" the man said, snapping his fingers again. "The lady says you're very handsome! Can't you at least stop drooling, don't you have any manners at all?"

"I haven't any pets of my own. But I like animals."

She was beginning to feel quite comfortable. The living room was not exactly what she had expected but it was not *too* bad. There was the rather low, overstuffed sofa in which she sat, the cushions made of a silvery-white, silvery-gray material, with a feathery sheen, plump, immense, like bellies or breasts, a monstrous old piece of furniture yet nothing one would want to sell: for certainly it had come down in the family, it must date from the turn of the century. There was the Victorian table with its coy ornate legs, and its tasseled cloth, and its extraordinary oversized lamp: the sort of thing Florence would smile at in an antique shop, but which looked fairly reasonable here. In fact she should comment on it, since she was staring at it so openly.

". . . antique? European?"

"I think so, yes," the man said.

"Is it meant to be fruit, or a tree, or . . ."

Bulbous and flesh-colored, peach-colored. With a tarnished brass stand. A dust-dimmed golden lampshade with embroidered blue trim that must have been very pretty at one time.

They talked of antiques. Of old houses. Families.

A queer odor defined itself. It was not unpleasant, exactly.

"Would you like something to drink?"

"Why yes I —"

"Excuse me just a moment."

Alone she wondered if she might prowl about the room. But it was long and narrow and poorly lighted at one end: in fact, one end dissolved into darkness. A faint suggestion of furniture there, an old spinet piano, a jumble of chairs, a bay window that must look out onto the garden. She wanted very much to examine a portrait above the mantel of the fireplace but perhaps the dog would bark, or grow excited, if she moved.

It had crept closer to her feet, shuddering with pleasure.

The redheaded man, slightly stooped, brought a glass of something dark to her. In one hand was his own drink, in the other hand hers.

"Taste it. Tell me what you think."

"It seems rather strong. . . ."

Chocolate. Black and bitter. And thick.

"It should really be served hot," the man said.

"Is there a liqueur of some kind in it?"

"Is it too strong for you?"

"Oh no. No. Not at all."

Florence had never tasted anything more bitter. She nearly gagged.

But a moment later it was all right: she forced herself to take a second swallow, and a third. And the prickling painful sensation in her mouth faded.

The redheaded man did not return to his chair, but stood before her, smiling. In the other room he had done something hurried with his hair: had tried to brush it back with his hands, perhaps. A slight film of perspiration shone on his high forehead.

"Do you live alone here?"

"The house does seem rather large, doesn't it? — for a person to live in it alone."

"Of course you have your dog. . . ."

"Do *you* live alone now?"

Florence set the glass of chocolate down. Suddenly she remembered what it reminded her of: a business associate of her father's, many years ago, had brought a box of chocolates back from a trip to Russia. The little girl had popped one into her mouth and had been dismayed by their unexpectedly bitter taste.

She had spat the mess out into her hand. While everyone stared.

As if he could read her thoughts the redheaded man twitched, moving his jaw and his right shoulder jerkily. But he continued smiling as before and Florence did not indicate that she was disturbed. In fact she spoke warmly of the living room's furnishings, and repeated her admiration for handsome old houses like this one. The man nodded, as if waiting for her to say more.

"... a family named Bartholomew? Of course it was many years ago."

"Bartholomew? Did they live in this neighborhood?"

"Why yes I think so. That's the real reason I stopped in. I once knew a little girl who — "

"Bartholomew, Bartholomew," the man said slowly, frowning. His face puckered. One corner of his mouth twitched with the effort of his concentration: and again his right shoulder jerked. Florence was afraid he would spill his chocolate drink.

Evidently he had a nervous ailment of some kind. But she could not inquire.

He murmured the name *Bartholomew* to himself, his expression grave, even querulous. Florence wished she had not asked the question because it was a lie, after all. She rarely told lies. Yet it had slipped from her, it had glided smoothly out of her mouth.

She smiled guiltily, ducking her head. She took another swallow of the chocolate drink.

Without her having noticed, the dog had inched forward. His great head now rested on her feet. His wet brown eyes peered up at her, oddly affectionate. A baby's eyes. It was true that he was drooling, in fact he was drooling on her ankles, but of course he could not help it. . . . Then she noted that he had wet on the carpet. Only a few feet away. A dark stain, a small puddle.

Yet she could not shrink away in revulsion. After all, she was a guest and it was not time for her to leave.

". . . Bartholomew. You say they lived in this neighborhood?"

"Oh yes."

"But when?"

"Why I really don't . . . I was only a child at the. . . ."

"But when was this?"

He was staring oddly at her, almost rudely. The twitch at the corner of his mouth had gotten worse. He moved to set his glass down and the movement was jerky, puppet-like. Yet he stared at her all the while. Florence knew people often felt uneasy because of her dark over-large staring eyes: but she could not help it. She did not *feel* the impetuosity, the reproach, her expression suggested. So she tried to soften it by smiling. But sometimes the smile failed, it did not deceive anyone at all.

Now that her host had stopped smiling she could see that he was really quite mocking. His tangled sandy eyebrows lifted ironically.

"You said you were a stranger to this city, and now you're saying you've been here. . . ."

"But it was so long ago, I was only a . . ."

He drew himself up to his full height. He was not a tall man, nor was he solidly built. In fact his waist was slender, for a man's — and he wore odd trousers, or jeans, tight-fitting across his thighs and without zipper or snaps, crotchless. They fit him tightly in the crotch, which was smooth, seamless. His legs were rather short for his torso and arms.

He began smiling at Florence. A sly accusing smile. His head jerked mechanically, indicating something on the floor. He was trying to point with his chin and the gesture was clumsy.

"You did something nasty on the floor there. On the carpet."

Florence gasped. At once she drew herself away from the dog, at once she began to deny it. "I didn't — It wasn't — "

"Right on the carpet there. For everyone to see. To smell."

"I certainly did not," Florence said, blushing angrily. "You know very well it was the — "

"Somebody's going to have to clean it up and it isn't going to be *me*," the man said, grinning.

But his eyes were still angry.

He did not like her at all: she saw that. The visit was a mistake, but how could she leave, how could she escape, the dog had crawled up to her again and was nuzzling and drooling against her ankles, and the redheaded man who had seemed so friendly was now leaning over her, his hands on his slim hips, grinning rudely.

As if to frighten her, as one might frighten an animal or a child, he clapped his hands smartly together. Florence blinked at the sudden sound. And then he leaned forward and clapped his hands together again, right before her face. She cried out for him to leave her alone, her eyes smarted with tears, she was leaning back against the cushions, her head back as far as it would go, and then he clapped his hands once again, hard, bringing them against her burning cheeks, slapping both her cheeks at once, and a sharp thin white-hot sensation ran through her body, from her face and throat to her belly, to the pit of her belly, and from the pit of her belly up into her chest, into her mouth, and even down into her stiffened legs. She screamed for the redheaded man to stop, and twisted convulsively on the sofa to escape him.

"Liar! Bad girl! Dirty girl!" someone shouted.

She wore her new reading glasses, with their attractive plastic frames. And a spring suit, smartly styled, with a silk blouse in a floral pattern. And the tight but fashionable shoes.

Her audience, respectful and attentive, could not see her trembling hands behind the podium, or her slightly quivering knees. They would have been astonished to learn that she hadn't been able to eat breakfast that morning — that she felt depressed and exhausted though she had managed to fall asleep the night before, probably around two, and had evidently slept her usual dreamless sleep.

She cleared her throat several times in succession, a habit she detested in others.

But gradually her strength flowed back into her. The morning was so sunny, so innocent. These people were, after all, her colleagues and friends: they certainly wished her well, and even appeared to be genuinely interested in what she had to say about the future of the humanities. Perhaps Dr. Parr knew something they did not, perhaps she would share her professional secrets with them. . . .

As the minutes passed Florence could hear her voice grow richer and firmer, easing into its accustomed rhythms. She began to relax. She began to breathe more regularly. She was moving into familiar channels, making points she had made countless times before, at similar meetings, with her deans and faculty chairmen at Champlain, with other educators. A number of people applauded heartily when she spoke of the danger of small private colleges competing unwisely with one another; and again when she made a point, an emphatic point, about the need for the small private school in an era of multiversities. Surely these were remarks anyone might have made, there was really nothing original about them, yet her audience seemed extremely pleased to hear them from her. They *did* admire Florence Parr — that was clear.

She removed her reading glasses. Smiled, spoke without needing to glance at her notes. This part of her speech — an amusing summary of the consequences of certain experimental programs at Champlain, initiated since she'd become president — was more specific, more interesting, and of course she knew it by heart.

The previous night had been one of her difficult nights. At least initially. Her mind racing in that way she couldn't control, those flame-like pangs of fear, insomnia. And no help for it. And no way out. She'd fallen asleep while reading through her notes and awakened suddenly, her heart beating erratically, body drenched in perspiration — and there she was, lying twisted back against the headboard, neck stiff and aching and her left leg numb beneath her. She'd been dreaming she'd given in and driven out to see the dolls' house; but of course she had not, she'd been in her hotel room all the time. *She'd never left her hotel room.*

She'd never left her hotel room but she'd fallen asleep and dreamt she had but she refused to summon back her dream, not that dream nor any others; in fact she rather doubted she did dream, she never remembered afterward. Florence Parr was one of those people who, as soon as they awake, are *awake*. And eager to begin the day.

At the conclusion of Florence's speech everyone applauded enthusiastically. She'd given speeches like this many times before and it had been ridiculous of her to worry.

Congratulations, handshakes. Coffee was being served.

Florence was flushed with relief and pleasure, crowded about by well-wishers. This was her world, these people her colleagues, they knew her, admired her. Why does one worry about anything! Florence thought, smiling into these friendly faces, shaking more hands. These were all good people, serious professional people, and she liked them very much.

At a distance a faint fading jeering cry *Liar! Dirty girl!* but Florence was listening to the really quite astute remarks of a youngish man who was a new dean of arts at Vassar. How good the hot, fresh coffee was. And a thinly layered apricot brioche she'd taken from a proffered silver tray.

The insult and discomfort of the night were fading; the vision of the doll's house was fading, dying. She refused to summon it back. She would not give it another thought. Friends — acquaintances — well-wishers were gathering around her, she knew her skin was glowing like a girl's, her eyes were bright and clear and hopeful; at such times, buoyed by the presence of others as by waves of applause, you forget your age, your loneliness — the very perimeters of your soul.

Day is the only reality. She'd always known.

Though the conference was a success, and colleagues at home heard that Florence's contribution had been particularly well received, Florence began to forget it within a few weeks. So many conferences! — so many warmly applauded speeches! Florence was a professional woman who, by nature more than design, pleased both women and men; she did not stir up controversy, she "stimulated discussion." Now she was busily preparing for her first major conference, to be held in London in September: "The Role of the Humanities in the 21st Century." Yes, she was apprehensive, she told friends — "But it's a true challenge."

When a check arrived in the mail for five hundred dollars, an honorarium for her speech in Lancaster, Pennsylvania, Florence was puzzled at first — not recalling the speech, nor the circumstances. How odd! She'd never been there, had she? Then, to a degree, as if summoning forth a dream, she remembered: the beautiful Pennsylvania landscape, ablaze with spring flowers; a small crowd of well-wishers gathered around to shake her hand. Why, Florence wondered, had she ever worried about her speech? — her public self? Like an exquisitely precise clockwork mechanism, a living mannequin, she would always do well: you'll applaud too, when you hear her.

Notes

1. E. F. Bleiler, ed., *Supernatural Fiction Writers: Fantasy and Horror*, 2 vols. (New York: Charles Scribner's Sons, 1985), 2: 960.
2. Julia Briggs, *Night Visitors: The Rise and Fall of the English Ghost Story* (London: Faber & Faber Ltd., 1977), 48.
3. Edith Wharton, *Ghosts* (New York: D. Appleton-Century Company, 1937), vii.
4. Sigmund Freud, "The Uncanny," in *On Creativity and the Unconscious*, ed. Benjamin Nelson (New York: Harper & Row, Publishers, 1958), 158.
5. Sallie Sears, *The Negative Imagination: Form and Perspective in the Novels of Henry James* (Ithaca, NY: Cornell UP, 1968), 126.
6. Edward Wagenknecht, *Seven Masters of Supernatural Fiction* (New York: Greenwood Press, 1991), 27.
7. M. R. James, *Ghosts and Marvels* (Oxford UP, 1928), vi.
8. Peter Haining, ed., *The Ghost-Feeler: Stories of Terror and the Supernatural by Edith Wharton* (London and Chester Springs, Pa.: Peter Owen, 1996), 7.
9. Philip Stevick, ed., *The American Short Story 1900–1945: A Critical History* (Boston, Ma.: Twayne Publishers, 1984), 41.
10. Elizabeth Bowen, *Ivy Gripped the Steps* (New York: Alfred A. Knopf, 1948), ix.
11. Betty Richardson, *John Collier* (Boston: Twayne Publishers, 1983), 90.
12. Judy Oppenheimer, *Private Demons: The Life of Shirley Jackson* (New York: G. P. Putnam's Sons, 1988), 276.
13. Bleiler, ed., 2: 639.
14. Bleiler, ed., 2: 639–640.
15. Epigraph to Robert Aickman's *Cold Hand in Mine: Eight Strange Stories* (London: Victor Gollancz, Ltd., 1975).
16. Robert Aickman, *The Attempted Rescue* (London: Victor Gollancz, Ltd., 1966), 55.
17. Suzanne Morrow Paulson, *William Trevor: A Study of the Short Fiction* (New York: Twayne Publishers, 1993), 164.
18. Stephen Schiff, "The Shadows of William Trevor," *The New Yorker* 28 Dec. 1992 /4 Jan. 1993: 161.

Acknowledgments

M. R. James, "Oh, Whistle, and I'll Come to You, My Lad," from *Ghost Stories of an Antiquary* (Edward Arnold, copyright © 1904). Reprinted by permission of N. R. James, owner and administrator of the Estate of M. R. James.

Robert Graves, "The Shout," from *Complete Short Stories* by Robert Graves, ed. Lucia Graves (Carcanet Press Ltd., 1995). Reprinted by permission of Carcanet Press Ltd. Copyright © 1950 by Robert Graves.

Edith Wharton, "Pomegranate Seed," copyright © 1931 by The Curtis Publishing Co., renewed 1959. Reprinted by permission of the Estate of Edith Wharton and the Watkins/Loomis Agency.

Elizabeth Bowen, "The Demon Lover," from *Collected Stories* by Elizabeth Bowen. Copyright © 1946 and renewed 1974 by Elizabeth Bowen. Reprinted by permission of Alfred A. Knopf, a Division of Random House, Inc.

John Collier, "Midnight Blue," copyright © 1951 by John Collier, renewed 1978. Reprinted by permission of Harold Matson Co., Inc.

Truman Capote, "Miriam," copyright © 1945 by The Truman Capote Literary Trust. Reprinted by permission of Alan U. Schwartz, Trustee.

Shirley Jackson, "The Daemon Lover," from *The Lottery* by Shirley Jackson. Copyright © 1948, 1949 by Shirley Jackson. Copyright renewed 1976, 1977 by Laurence Hyman, Barry Hyman, Mrs. Sarah Webster and Mrs. Joanne Schnurer. Reprinted by permission of Farrar, Straus and Giroux, LLC.

Hortense Calisher, "Heartburn," copyright © 1951 by Hortense Calisher. Reprinted by permission of Donadio & Olson, Inc.

Ray Bradbury, "The Screaming Woman," copyright © 1951 by the Westminster Press, renewed 1979 by Ray Bradbury. Reprinted by permission of Don Congdon Associates, Inc.

L. P. Hartley, "W. S.," copyright © 1954. Reprinted by permission of The Society of Authors as the literary representative of the Estate of L. P. Hartley.

Robert Aickman, "The Inner Room," from *Sub Rosa: Strange Tales*, copyright © 1968. Reprinted by permission of The Pimlico Agency Inc., agents for the Estate of Robert Aickman.

William Trevor, "Mrs. Acland's Ghosts," from *Angels at the Ritz and Other Stories* by William Trevor (Bodley Head, 1975), copyright © 1975 by William Trevor. Reprinted by permission of The Random House Group Ltd. and John Johnson Ltd.

NIGHT SHADOWS

has been set in Van Dijck, a digital version of a face produced in
1937 by the Monotype Corporation as part of the company's pro-
gram to revive historic types for machine composition. Van Dijck
was modeled on types traditionally ascribed to the Dutch punch-
cutter and typefounder Christoffel van Dijck, although there is
some possibility that the types in question were actually cut by
Christoffel's son, Abraham. The types' later history is cloudy at
best, as the original punches and matrices passed through numerous hands during the seventeenth and eighteenth centuries,
finally coming to rest at the printing house of Johannes Enschedé
en Zonen in Haarlem in 1799. The types soon fell into commercial
disfavor, and most of the original punches and matrices were sold
for scrap in the nineteenth century. ⁂ The present types, both
roman and italic, were derived primarily from printed specimens
and from a handful of punches that survived the depredations of
the melting pot. Their development benefitted from the advice of
the noted typographer Jan van Krimpen, who participated in the
project despite his aversion to the resurrection of historical types
for modern use. Nonetheless, Van Dijck — with its strong seven-
teenth-century flavor and decidedly eccentric italic — carries its
heritage admirably, especially when a type of distinct
elegance and delicacy is required.

⁂

Design and composition by
Carl W. Scarbrough